SHE

A dystopian novel

Caroline Cooper

For my children, Scarlett and Logan.

ACKNOWLEDGEMENTS

To Wendy Shell, your advice and guidance on the nature of a virus has been invaluable. Flowers alone don't cut it, you have been amazing.

To Ruth, who read draft after draft, corrected my lazy grammar and encouraged me with flattery and honesty in equal measure.

To my patient friends and family, who listened to my ideas, read my drafts and no doubt know this book as well as I do.

You are all fabulous. Thankyou.

SHE

1985

Am I alive?
Afraid to move, scared that they might come back. Remember
a car driving away, maybe they are gone? Maybe I dreamt it.
Stiff body.
Feel sick.
Move an inch.
Ouch.
Stones digging into my leg and hip.
Horrible taste. So cold I can't feel my toes.
MUMMY.
She will be angry I didn't go straight home from school.
'SIT UP JEAN!' She would say.
I try.
OUCH. I'm dizzy.
Eyes open. Can't see well.
My hair is in the way.
Eye is really sticky.
Hair stuck to it.
Use the other eye.
See the room, lighter now. It's dirty.
I see clothes.
I crawl towards them, wrist really sore.
I am slow.
Shirt here, ripped, buttons gone.
Can't wear it.
Cardigan with my school patch.
Put it on.

Fingers hurt, hands sticky with blood.
Skirt here.
Ripped but ok.
Have to stand up though to pull it up.
Too dizzy, lean on the wall.
NO shoes.
NO pants.
NO socks.
Men took them.
Turn around, go to the door.
Hurts a lot, more tears.
Door swings open when I push it. Good.
I'm outside. Road is empty, quiet.
Trees all around, no lights.
Don't like dark forests.
Scared now.
Don't want to stay here.
Men might come back and find me.
Hide.
NO. FIND MUMMY.
Mummy always turns left on the way to school.
Turn left, walk.
OUCH.
Can't stand up straight, everything hurts.
Walk like a granny.
Sharp stones cutting my feet.
Walk on grass.
Tummy hurts.
Arm hurts.
So sore down there.
Thirsty too.
Sun is coming out.
A turn in the road. It goes left.
Decide, Jean.
Left or straight on?
Need to find help.

Look left and see a light, far away.
Don't cry.
Turn left.
It's a house.
Feet hurt.
Lots of stones on this road.
I make bloody footsteps.
Keep going Jean.
Heart racing.
Men could come back. Walk faster Jean.
Closer.
What if the men live there?
STOP.
Can't go back, must go forward.
Don't knock, just look in the window.
See who lives there first.
An old lady, looks like my nanny-in-heaven.
She looks nice, knock the door.
I hear footsteps. Scared.
HIDE.
I'm behind the hedge. The lady comes out.
'Hello?'
I come out and I try to speak.
'Can you ring my Mummy and tell her I'm sorry I didn't come home".
The lady's mouth opens in a big O.
'Barry, come quickly! There is a little girl at the door.'
NO! Just you.
I cry.

2025

Before the Beginning

That night, before it begins, she gives a radio address. To the women listening, she is almost god-like and they are invigorated by her words, reminding them why her vision is so compelling and stripping away any remaining doubts. They are part of something monumental. Women will read about this triumph for centuries.

With the skill of soldiers, they prepare for what is to come, gathering equipment and going through well-practiced drills. They pack refrigerated vehicles methodically, taking particular care to ensure the barrels of liquid are stowed safely. They carry out final checks and then climb aboard. Engines roar into life, the sound cutting through the stillness of the night. One by one, each van heads out on quiet, though not quite empty roads. Drivers are careful, sticking to the speed limit in perfectly maintained, inconspicuously labelled vehicles, each one heading to a different destination.

Once they arrive, they unload the cargo silently, gaining entry to each facility with ease thanks to the expertise and reach of their group. They move the barrels into position. It is an epic day.

1985

I wake up with a start. My heart races.

WHERE AM I?

WHAT'S THAT NOISE?

IS IT THE BAD MEN?

I'm back in the house. I am in danger.

JEAN.

OPEN YOUR EYES.

NOW.

I don't open them. I don't want to see. But I do start to notice different things. I am not cold. I am warm. I am not on a hard floor. I am lying on a soft bed. I am not naked. But I'm not in my clothes either. I'm dressed in something scratchy.

I open my eyes.

The room I am lying in is light and clean, the bed surrounded by a blue curtain, like a tent. I turn my head. Mummy is here! She is asleep in the chair by the side of my bed. I breathe. I say her name, too quietly. 'Mummy'.

I notice other things. Everything stings but I feel less dirty. I look down and see that my wrist is in a white plaster cast. Mummy has written on it in black pen 'I love you, Jeanie xxx'. She must have done that while I was asleep because I don't remember it. I try to lean over and tap Mummy on the arm and pain shoots from my tummy straight down my leg. I scream and Mummy wakes up with a start, jumps off her chair and leans over me. 'Are you okay, Jeanie?'

My eyes fill with tears before I can stop it 'My tummy hurts.'

She leans forward and hugs me. 'I know, my baby, I know.' She is crying now. She holds my face in her hands. 'You are safe now. I promise.'

I make a scrunched-up face as she is hurting me a bit. She looks at me.

'Does it hurt here, or here?'

I point to where it hurts.

'That's your rib. The doctor says that you have broken it, he can give you some medicine to stop that hurting if you want?' HE.

I look at her, I'm scared. I don't want the bad men to come.

'Is he… I mean, I…'

'He is nice, don't worry. I'm here.'

She presses a button next to the bed and asks 'Do you want me to read to you while we wait for him?'

Before, we were reading a book called 'Flowers in the Attic' but I don't want to read it anymore. I don't know what I want. Everything is wrong. I shake my head. Mummy holds my hand tight and then the curtain moves quickly back with a loud noise. A man is there.

Make myself small.

The man is tall and has dark hair. My heart races. I am going to die.

Don't look at me.

I pull the covers over my head. I say to Mummy in a tiny whisper. 'Make him go away. I don't like him.'

Mummy lifts the covers off my head gently. The man is still there. She leans in and whispers 'Do you trust me, Jeanie?' I nod.

'I will never let anyone hurt you again, I promise. This man isn't going to hurt you. He is a doctor. He wants to help you. Will you let him? I will be here the whole time. Okay?'

I don't want to say yes but Mummy looks worried. I don't want to upset her, so I nod, quickly. 'Thank you, Jeanie.'

I look at the man and he smiles at me and says 'Hello Jean, my name is Doctor Bob, what seems to be the problem here?'

I point at my tummy. Mummy says to the man 'Her rib is hurting.'

'Okay, I can give you a little injection to help with that, do you think you can be brave for me?'

I do not feel brave. I am scared. I want the man to go away. The doctor leans forward and I try to make myself small but he comes closer and closer until his hand touches my arm and then I scream.

'AAAAAAAAAAAAAAAAAAAAAAAAAAAAAh'

The man leaves quickly. Mummy looks at me. She isn't cross. She is sad. A lady nurse comes to give me the injection and although it hurts a bit, I don't even wince because everything else hurts so much more. I am still shaking when the nurse leaves and Mummy has to hug me really tight until I stop.

2025

Day One. Lakeside Shopping centre, January sales.

Hazel joined the back of a short queue in the coffee shop, casting a lazy eye around at the customers in an attempt to convince them that the security uniform was not just for show. As her eye moved from table to table, her gaze fell upon a red-faced, balding man, sat a few feet away. He was sweating and wheezing and though he was a sizable man, the wheezing seemed more laboured than she considered normal for his size. An open bottle of water in his hand sploshed uncontrollably onto the table with each laboured breath. She stepped out of the queue and approached him, her heart sinking as the queue closed behind her, her place in it immediately lost.
'Are you okay Sir?'
The man gaped at her, his breath seemed stuck in his throat and desperation flooded his eyes. As she reached to slap him on the back he coughed violently. Blood sprayed onto the table and across her chest and she recoiled instinctively, stepping back into the table behind her and startling a woman sat there with her small son. The woman took one look at the blood on the table and reached for the child's arm. As Hazel turned back to the man she heard a chair scrape back behind her as the woman made a hasty exit, dragging her reluctant her son behind her.
Hazel heart began to hammer in her chest as she radioed for an ambulance.

* * *

A teenager sat with his two friends towards the rear of the coffee shop, watching the drama unfold. As he picked up his full fat caramel Frappuccino, he nudged his friend. 'Look! Wonder what's wrong with him?' He turned and stared into the bulging eyes of his friend, then frowned. 'Mate, what the fuck is wrong with YOU?'
His friend coughed violently, lurching forwards. The cup in front of him toppled over, splattering cream, caramel and coffee onto the table, the floor and his trainers.

* * *

Outside the café, a man was walking alongside his wife, dragging his feet. His face was ashen and waxy and he slowed for a moment and loosened his collar. His wife walked on, oblivious, then paused to peer into the window of a nearby shop 'Ooh, John. Look at those curtains, they would go really well in the lounge, don't you think?'
She turned, but her husband wasn't where she expected him to be. She turned back and looked behind her. Her husband was on the floor a few feet away, blood staining his cheek and the collar of the fresh white shirt she had ironed that morning. As she ran towards him, shouting 'John?! John!' another man fell over a few feet away, also coughing. A teenaged boy staggered passed them, over to the coffee shop window and leant against it, wheezing, then fell, crashing into the chairs outside the coffee shop and falling to the floor. A woman dropped her shopping and ran for the exit, screaming and a man streaked ahead of her, shouting 'Get everyone out! It's in the air!'

* * *

Hazel shouted into her radio from the door of the coffee shop. 'Evacuate the centre! Get everyone out!'
Her radio crackled. There was no-one on the other end.

1985

Mummy has not left the hospital once, it's been days and she is still in the same clothes. I am in a room on my own now which I like. My head feels fuzzy, like I have slept forever. I want to go home but Mummy says that I can't yet. I have 'internal injuries' which means that there is some bleeding inside me. This doesn't make sense because there is always blood inside me, so where is it going?

Daddy arrives with a bag. When he opens the door my heart races until I see that it is him. Though I relax, Mummy doesn't. She stands up quickly and goes to the door. She turns around and says 'I'll be back in a minute, Jean. I'm just outside, okay?' Then she ushers him out.

I don't like being alone because I remember being on my own on the floor of the other place and it makes me scared. My heart starts to beat really fast and I shout 'MUMMY!'

The door opens with a rush of wind and Mummy runs in. She is holding the bag that Daddy had in his hand. 'Please don't leave me again.'

'I'm sorry, I won't, I promise.'

2025

Jenny Robinson, St Thomas's Hospital, London, 9am

The doors swung closed, narrowly missing Jenny as she ran into A&E behind the paramedics. They raced the gurney across the room and through a second set of doors but when Jenny tried to follow the doors swung back, barring her way. A no entry sign caused Jenny to pause and a receptionist called out, stopping her in her tracks. 'Hello? You can't go in after them I'm afraid. I need to take some details from you. Is that your son?'

Jenny nodded. 'What is his name please?'

'Jasper Robinson.'

'Age?'

'He is fifteen.'

'Date of birth, please?"

'1st July, 2009'

Jenny answered a barrage of questions, her eyes on the door the whole time until eventually the receptionist closed her clipboard.

'All done. Stay in the waiting room. Someone will be out to speak to you soon. There's a pay phone in the hall.'

She waited for the receptionist to turn away and ignoring the 'no mobiles' sign, called Mark's number. After a few rings, the phone diverted to voicemail. Infuriating. She waited for the beep and started to talk, trying to control her shaky voice.

'I'm at St Thomas's hospital, it's Jasper. He unconscious, I couldn't wake him. We came in an ambulance and they have rushed him straight into A&E. I'm in the waiting room. Why aren't you answering your bloody phone? Call me back as soon as you get this.'

She hung up and called her sister, Lisa.

'Hi, it's me.

'Hi Jenny, I can't talk right now, I'm driving. What's up?'

'It's Jasper. He's in St Thomas. I'm in the waiting room, can you come?'

'Jasper? what happened? Did he have an accident?'

'No, he is unconscious, with a high temperature.'

'Okay. I'm actually on my way there now. One of the kids in my class is ill, I'm following the ambulance in my car. I'll see you in five.'

Lisa hung up abruptly and Jenny sat on one of the plastic chairs for a moment to draw breath, looking around at the anxious faces of the other people in the room. Still angry with Mark after a row the night before and now anxious because of Jasper, she could feel herself edging into fury. She took a deep breath and closed her eyes, replaying the morning in her head.

She woke up at 6.45am and reached for Mark but his pillow was empty. Irritated that he'd left without apologising, she got up and gingerly made her way downstairs to get coffee. Her body was stiff and she inwardly cursed the ageing process. She switched on the coffee machine and considered doing half an hour of yoga but a quick look at her watch confirmed that she didn't have time. She had a busy day ahead and needed to get to work early.

Jasper was still fast asleep when she came upstairs with her morning coffee. She poked her head around his door. 'Jasper, it's not like you to sleep in! Up you get, it's nearly time to go.' She watched as he slowly opened his eyes. When he spoke his voice was thick and groggy. 'Mum, I don't feel good. My head hurts.' Jenny approached his bed, wrinkling her nose at the smell.

'Jasper, you really must give your room a clean.' She sat down beside him and put her palm on his forehead. He was hot and even in the dim light she could see that he was pale. She stood up and smiled sympathetically. 'You are hot, love. I'll be back in a second'. She headed out to the medicine cabinet in the bathroom to fetch the thermometer which after a quick check confirmed that Jasper had a fever. She gave him some paracetamol to try and bring his temperature down and called her office. Claire would understand but it wasn't ideal to work at home today. Her office didn't run as smoothly without Jenny there to keep things tight.

She called the doctor next to make an appointment but the earliest one she could get was 6pm, so she pulled out her laptop, intending to quickly check her emails and then go back upstairs. She opened her inbox and became instantly embroiled in work. Special Adviser to the Justice Minister, her job was always busy. Claire had high expectations and Jenny worked long hours trying to meet them. At times, she missed the midweek banter at home, but made the most of each precious weekend to compensate.

Today an outbreak of the flu had struck several prisons and as she scanned her emails she could see that the outbreak had picked up pace overnight. Prisoners were kept in such close proximity that the risk of viral outbreaks was not a new one but this strain sounded particularly vicious, so she emailed all prison governors, asking for briefings and treatment plans by midday.

She heard Jasper coughing and tore herself away from work. He opened his eyes briefly when she sat down on the bed and mumbled. 'Mum, I think there's something really wrong with me' before coughing violently and shutting his eyes once more. Jenny gave him a hug to mask her concern. Usually so full of energy, Jasper was wonderfully child-like for his age with a charm that captivated everyone he met. Lately this had extended to some of the local girls which had gone to his head a little bit. In the mornings, when most teenagers had to be pried out of bed with a crowbar, he was always cheerful, making the mornings they had together as a family full of laughter. She made a decision. 'Jasper, get dressed. I'm taking you to the drop-in clinic.'

He smiled weakly. 'Thanks Mum, love you.'

She turned away to his wardrobe. 'Love you too. I'll get out something comfy and warm. You can snuggle up on the sofa when we get back and watch TV.' She pulled out a jumper and tracksuit bottoms. When she turned back Jasper looked asleep. Exasperated, she shook him gently 'Jasper! Come on love. Wake up.' He didn't stir. She shook his shoulder hard. Still nothing. She felt his forehead. He was much hotter than he was an hour ago and as she stood up she noticed spots of blood on his pillow. She felt a rush of panic and checked he was still breathing- he was, just. She ran downstairs to her phone and called an ambulance, the familiar shadow of mother's guilt looming over her.

In the hospital, she shifted on the uncomfortable plastic chair, tormenting herself with questions. Would it have made a difference if she'd called an ambulance straight away? She looked again at her watch. Where the hell was Mark?

She called him again and left another voicemail. Maybe he was driving? She called his secretary but when her phone went to voicemail as well she hung up, bewildered. Harriet was a bit of a stick-in-the-mud but prided herself on never missing a call. She checked her watch again, 9.30am already. Still no news and the waiting room was filling up.

She felt an urge to call Mia but knew that her voice would betray her. Mia's university was so far away she didn't want to worry her so she sent her a text instead.

'Mia, it's Mum. When you are free can you give me a call? Thanks love, hope you are okay. Xxx'

Sighing, she stood up to find a coffee machine. She felt very alone.

1985

I'm happy to be going home, I hate this hospital, there are too many smells. When we get home, there is a policeman outside the door. Mummy is cross. She tells me to wait in the car and marches up to the him. I hear her say 'I've said it a million times. She is terrified of men, you need to send a female police officer. I'm going to call your supervisor.'

The policeman walks down the path towards the car, with Mummy close behind him. He bends down outside my window and looks at me so I shrink back against the seat. His face is too big and his smile is scary. Mummy is cross again. She shouts at him 'For god sake, didn't you hear me!? You're scaring her.'

The police man straightens up and says to Mummy, 'We need to talk to her. We've caught one of them but the rest of them are still out there. I know this is difficult but I don't want another little girl to get taken.' He leaves and when the car turns the corner Mummy and I go into the house. I go straight upstairs to my bedroom to check it. It looks the same, but I am not.

2025

Lisa Swift, 9.32am

Jenny's sister Lisa rushed in to the waiting room and scanned the crowd until she spotted them, looking anxiously toward the door.

'Hi Mr Edwards, Mrs Edwards. Jonathan has been taken straight to a ward for assessment. The doctors have asked that you wait here. Have you told the receptionist you are here?'

'Yes, they know.'

Mr Edwards stood up to greet her. 'Do they know what it is?'

Lisa shook her head. 'Not yet, he was coughing and then he just passed out at his desk. I'm sorry Mr Edwards, I don't really know any more than that, I drove here behind the ambulance and they took him straight into assessment. I'm sure they will come out with some news soon.'

Mr Edwards sat back into the chair heavily. 'Okay, thanks. Maybe it's a bug, I'm not feeling great myself.'

Lisa was looking around for Jenny but she wasn't in the waiting room. 'It could well be Mr Edwards, there seems to be something going around. I'm going to pop to reception, if that's okay? My nephew is here too. I just want to check what's happening.'

She joined the end of a long, snaking queue at reception just as her phone rang. It was the head teacher. 'Hi Felicity, we have just arrived, Jonathan is in assessment...' Felicity interrupted. 'Stay where you are, there are ten more children on their way to hospital and I'm closing the school. I've notified the parents; can you be the point of contact for the school at the hospital until I can get there? I'll text you a list of the children who have been taken in.'

'Ten?! My god, any idea what on earth it is? Something they caught at school maybe?'
'No idea at this stage.' Felicity said, crossly. 'Please don't speculate to parents. I don't want the school implicated.'
Lisa winced slightly. 'Of course I won't, I...' The phone went dead.
Lisa put her phone back in her bag and turned in time to see Jenny walk across the waiting room, carrying coffee. She caught her eye and Jenny rushed over, spilling a sizable splash of coffee onto the floor in the process.
'Thank god you're here. I'm so worried.'
'I'll be here a while, the head called, ten more kids are on their way in. They are closing the school.'
'What?' Jenny's stomach jolted. 'Do bugs spread that quickly?'
'I don't know. Is Mark here yet?
'Nope, I can't get hold of him.'
'Okay, sit down, I stay in the queue, I need to talk to the receptionist.'
Lisa watched as Jenny looked for a seat. The queue hadn't moved, the desk was now empty and while they had been talking the waiting room had filled up considerably. There were no unoccupied chairs and people were standing in small clusters in the corridor, muttering quietly.
She spotted Jonathan's parents at the back of the room just as Mr Edwards slid off his chair onto the floor. His wife shrieked 'Oh my god, Bob? Someone, help us!'
Lisa pushed through the crowd, followed closely by Jenny and together they pulled Mr Edwards onto his side. He was struggling to breathe, his breath rasping and wheezing from his chest. A porter and a nurse appeared as if out of nowhere with a gurney. The porter lowered it and he and the nurse transferred Mr Edwards onto it and prepared to move him.

They took Mr Edwards away, leaving Mrs Edwards to provide his details to the receptionist while her husband was being assessed.

'That poor woman. As if she hasn't got enough to worry about.' Jenny muttered to Lisa as Mrs Edwards joined the long queue at reception, tears streaming down her face.

Lisa went to comfort Mrs Edwards and Jenny turned to find a place to stand. People were streaming into reception and the room was already so full that it felt suddenly claustrophobic. Jenny found herself catastrophizing. She had been in the A&E a number of times over the years with the children but had never seen so many people in the waiting room. What could it be? This flu going around? A big accident perhaps? She strained to hear people's conversations in an effort to pick up a clue but the room was too noisy. She studied the people waiting, looking for signs. Were they all parents? No, there were elderly people there too. The queue still hadn't moved and she watched Lisa talking to Mrs Edwards and a couple of people in the queue ahead of her. Lisa was listening intently but Jenny couldn't hear the conversation.

She turned to the woman standing next to her left, who was looking down at her phone.

'There are a lot of people here aren't there? Do you know what happened?' The woman was about Jenny's age, she was pale and her voice trembled as she spoke.

'My brother is here but we didn't come with any of these people. Have you been here long?'

Jenny shook her head. 'Not really. Half an hour maybe? It wasn't this busy when I arrived.' The woman nodded and turned back to her phone.

Jenny turned to her right. A young girl was sat holding hands with an older woman. They looked so alike Jenny assumed they were mother and daughter. She caught the woman's eye and smiled sympathetically. The woman turned back to the girl, who had started to cry and pulled the girl into an embrace.

As Jenny looked around something struck her. There were very few men in the room. Odd. She started to count them, her eyes moving quickly over the crowd. One boy, no older than five, one man, another towards the back of the room, one in the queue… maybe nine, certainly no more than a dozen, in a room full of people. It could just be a coincidence? She saw a woman jump out of her seat as someone she recognised pushed through the crowd and strained to hear the conversation. She caught just a few words but enough '…just collapsed…no warning…burning up…'

Her heart sank as she thought of Jasper. What if this was the beginning of a new strain of the flu or some kind of virus? She cursed herself for leaving her work phone at home. If it were anything major she would have received an email. She sighed. Speculation was only making her more anxious.

She looked back towards the front desk. It was hard to see Lisa now, there were so many people packed into the room that the queue was indistinguishable from the rest of the crowd. Jenny stood on her tiptoes and peered over people's heads. She could see a doctor and the receptionist who originally questioned her. A number of people in suits with name badges were also standing behind the desk.

'Can I have your attention please?' The receptionists voice rang loud over the hum of the crowd and Jenny heard her voice shaking. Everyone in the room fell silent.

'Thank you.' The doctor stood on a chair to address the room. 'A number of patients have been brought here this morning exhibiting similar symptoms. When this happens, emergency protocols are triggered which are there to protect patients and the wider public. A temporary quarantine has been imposed which means that, for the time being everyone already in the building must remain here and no-one outside the building will be permitted to enter. The exits have been sealed to prevent contamination.' There were gasps and shrieks from the crowd and the doctor raised her voice to be heard over the noise.

'PLEASE KEEP CALM. There is no cause for concern at this stage. It is simply a precaution, we do not yet know what we are dealing with or whether it is contagious. With your co-operation, we will be able to lift the quarantine much more quickly. My team will shortly be issuing questionnaires to everyone. Please fill in one for yourself and one on behalf of any patients that you have accompanied to the hospital today. The information provided will help us determine patient movements in the last 24 hours and establish any links.'

'We will also be taking blood samples from everyone and will test these samples for markers indicating infection. If the results are clear, you will be released from the hospital. If you have relatives here and chose to remain at that point you do so at your own risk. The staff at reception have no new information at this stage and so I would ask that you wait patiently in this room for further news. My name is Doctor Susan Smith and I will provide you with regular updates over the next few hours. I can't answer any questions about individual patients at this stage but I will be back in 30 minutes to talk to you again. A list of patients exhibiting the symptoms will be posted on the wall next to the front desk.'

The doctor and the hospital trust people left the room and there was a very brief hush as everyone absorbed the information, then, all at once everyone started talking and a surge of people made their way to the front desk. The receptionist held her hand up and shouted;

'QUIET! Please form an orderly queue and check the list for your friend or relative. If they are not on the list, please contact me immediately.'

Jenny began moving towards the front of the room with the throng. You could feel the rising panic as the receptionist started pinning a small pile of papers to the wall

After a few minutes of jostling, Jenny and Lisa reached the front and strained to catch sight of the list. Jenny scanned the pages and mumbled to Lisa 'Look...there are no women on the list. It's all men.' Her eye stopped suddenly there he was.

She turned to Lisa, her lower lip trembling. 'He's on it.' A tear rolled down her face. 'Oh my god, I can't believe this is happening'.

Lisa was still staring at the list. She couldn't process what she was seeing. She turned to Jenny. 'Look again at the list, Jenny.' She pointed to the name below Jasper's. 'Mark's name is there too.'

1985

I am sitting on Mummy's lap and she is holding my hand really tight with one hand and stroking my hair with the other. Daddy is sitting on the other side of Mummy and I can see by his face that he is angry. I think he is angry at me because he can't look at me.

The police lady starts to talk so I look at her instead. She asks me to describe the men who hurt me but every time I try I remember being back in that room with them and I get so scared that I can't talk.

Daddy is cross and snaps at me 'You have to try harder, Jean. These heathens need to be caught.'

Mummy is angry too now. 'For goodness sake Neal, she is terrified. You aren't helping.'

Daddy stands up quickly. His chair clatters back and falls onto the floor. He looks down at Mummy and snaps 'Fine. You deal with it. I'm going back home. You don't need me but then, when do you ever?' His face is very red and he stomps out of the room, slamming the door behind him.

The police lady looks at Mummy. 'It's hard on everyone.' She says. 'Men find this especially difficult.' She looks at me and says 'Jean, do you think you would recognise the men if you saw a picture of them?'

I nod. She opens the envelope in front of her and pulls out some photographs of different men. She lays them out in front of me. Most of them just look a bit scary but a blonde man looks like the man who hurt me the most. I point at him and say to the police lady 'He looks like one of them. He had a funny voice, I don't think he was from here.'

The police lady smiles and says 'You have done really well. If you hear his voice again do you think you will recognise it?' I nod. The police lady says to Mummy

'That's all for now, you can take her home. I'll be in touch.'

Mummy carries me back to her car. She carries me everywhere now and I feel like a baby. I know that I can walk just fine now, though it still hurts a little bit, but I like being carried, it feels safe, so I never ask to be put down. When we get to our car I see that Daddy's car is already gone. I say to her. 'Has Daddy gone back to his new house?' She nods and looks angry again so I don't say anything else. I put my arms around her neck instead and give her a cuddle.

In the car she says brightly 'Do you want to go and get some cake now? I thought we could have a little treat.' I think about it. The café near our house is always really busy and I don't want to go anywhere where the bad men could hide, so I say 'Can we buy ingredients and make a cake at home?' Mummy smiles and says 'What a good idea!'

When we get to the shop, Mummy turns around and says 'Are you okay to come in with me?' I nod, then say 'Will you carry me?' She nods.

In the shop, the man behind the counter smiles and says to Mummy 'Ooh, she's a bit big to be carried, isn't she?' She looks at the man with her cold face and the man stops smiling. We buy flour, sugar, eggs, milk and chocolate powder. Mummy carries me back to the car, with one arm and carries the shopping in the other hand. She is red in the face by the time we get back to the car but she smiles and says 'Well this is good exercise, isn't it? I'll be thin as a rake soon!'

When we get home, Mummy locks the door and pulls the new bolt across. Then she closes all the windows and draws the curtains. She smiles and says, 'Snug as a bug in a rug.'

When the cake is iced, we cut big slices and eat it with some hot tea. Mummy looks at me and says, 'You know that you are safe here with me, don't you?' I nod. She stands up and looks out of the window. When she turns back she has tears all down her face. She says 'I think we need a change of scene. How do you feel about moving to a new house, somewhere far away, just us?'

I've always wanted to live near the sea. I've only seen the sea once, a long time ago, when Daddy still lived with us. I remember wiggling my toes in the sand, feeling it scratch and slide between them. I remember the sound and the smell of the sea. I like the beach. I say to her 'Can we move to the beach?' She nods and says 'I think we should visit soon and find a new house, don't you?' She sits back down and I climb onto her lap for a cuddle. I lay my head on her lap while she strokes my hair, until I fall asleep, still thinking about the sea.

2025

Rt. Hon. Claire Flint MP, Justice Secretary, Ministry of Justice, 10am

Claire Flint sat in her office reading. At forty-five, she was a young Secretary of State but didn't feel it that morning. She'd woken up at 4.45am and arrived in the office at 6.30am. Her chin-length dark hair was tucked behind her ears, her efforts to remove the natural wave abandoned at 5am after several fruitless attempts to tame it. The hem of her expensive purple dress persisted in riding up above her knee despite her best efforts to restrain it and her tights were in danger of heading south towards her ankles. She was uncomfortable, on her fifth cup of coffee and desperately in need of some breakfast. Sighing, she abandoned the briefing and stretched, then rose from her chair.

She stepped out of the office. 'Jenny?' Jenny's desk was empty. Claire turned to the desk next to Jenny's 'Ruby, where is Jenny?'

Ruby, was a new 'fast streamer', short hand for a member of the fast track promotion scheme in the Civil Service. This meant she would be in Claire's team for six months, learning how a Private Office works, before moving on to another department. She was unfamiliar with how Claire worked.

'She called in earlier and said she was working at home, Minister. Her son is sick.'

'Okay. Ruby can you please go and get me some toast from the café? I'm starving.' 'Of course, Minister. I'll be right back.'

Ruby dashed off down the corridor at 100 miles an hour, her long blonde ponytail bouncing up and down behind her. Claire watched her go, smiling. It was good to have young people like Ruby around, her enthusiasm was infectious, even if it didn't quite yet match her skills.

She sat back down at the conference table, and began reading the next submission with a sigh. The pile of papers she had yet to read was still half an inch thick and covered a variety of topics, from things like prison riots, backlogs in the courts, the number of cracked and abandoned trails and plans to cut legal aid. As usual they made grim reading. She sat back in her chair, it was no good. She couldn't concentrate. The departmental budget had been reduced again by the Treasury and she seemed to be the only Minister who didn't believe cuts were a prudent move. Services were creaking at the seams, too many people were in court or prison and there weren't enough staff to process them all. The problems were never-ending and there were no clear answers. Her officials were dedicated, professional and kept their thoughts to themselves but she felt their anger bubbling away under the surface as their teams shrank. She tried to thank them regularly, knowing it was not enough after years of pay freezes and problems with no solutions.

Ruby marched in without knocking, toast in hand. 'Here you are, Minister. Did you want another coffee?'

'No thank you Ruby, another coffee and I'll be climbing the walls. Can you bring me my schedule for tomorrow please?'

'Yes, Minister. Oh, and here is a briefing from No. 10. Seems quite serious.'

Ruby handed her a memo from the Prime Minister. She glanced through it while she ate, frowning. It was a health memo about a potential viral outbreak. There were several clusters of sick patients with similar symptoms who had been quarantined in isolation units across the country. A number of patients were critically ill. The memo was for information only, the story was about to hit the press and the PM wanted ministers to stick to scripted answers if asked for information about it. She put the memo into her briefcase and stacked her papers up on the desk. Her first meeting was due to start and Ruby hadn't brought in any papers for it. She sighed and went to the door, 'Ruby, can you bring my papers for the meeting in five minutes please?'

'Yes Minister, sorry, I was just printing your schedule.'

Claire went back into the office and shut the door. She grabbed her phone from the table and sent her Mum a quick text before the officials arrived.

'Hi Mum, just me. Did Ben get off to school okay?'

Her Mum took Ben every morning before school and picked him up in the evenings when her ex-husband James didn't have him.

'Hi Claire, all fine. Ben was very excited about his school trip today! See you this evening. Don't forget to eat lunch!! Love Mum. X'

Her office door swung open and Ruby raced in, carrying the papers for the meeting. Shuffling in behind her were officials from the Victim and Witness Unit. Claire cursed Ruby inwardly for bringing them in without giving her time to prepare. 'Morning everyone, take a seat, I'll be right with you. Ruby, can I have a quick word before we begin?' She followed Ruby out of the room to ask her what the meeting was about, resigning herself to another frantic day. She missed Jenny.

* * *

As officials filed out of the room after her third meeting, Claire reached into her pocket for her phone. She'd felt it buzz several times and had begun to worry about Ben. 'The curse of a working mother', she thought.

She'd received several notifications, including three news reports about a virus 'sweeping the country', a missed call from her ex-husband, James and a voicemail. She opened the news first and skimmed the report, which described hospitals filling up with male patients. There had been several fatalities and a few hospitals had been closed to new patients, creating a growing sense of panic. As she was reading it, the door opened and Ruby bounded in.

'Ruby, are there any messages for me?'

'Several, Minister. I didn't want to disturb your meeting. The PM's office called, the virus is spreading quickly and a meeting has been called at No. 10. You need to go now so I've cancelled your next meeting. You won't get a chance to stop for lunch, so here is a sandwich.'

Claire smiled. 'Thank you, Ruby, I appreciate that. Is the car ready?' Ruby nodded and Claire grabbed her things and headed towards the lift. Once inside she reached for her phone again, remembering the call from James. She played the voicemail.

'Mrs Flint, this is Leicester Royal Infirmary. We have admitted a James Flint today and you are listed as his next of kin. Can you please contact us urgently on 0300 303 1573.'

Claire got out of the lift in the car park and walked to her car. As the driver pulled away she called the hospital.

'Hello, this is Claire Flint returning your call about my ex-husband, James Flint?'

'Ah, yes. Mr Flint is currently in our infectious diseases unit being assessed.'

'Is anyone with him?'

'A woman brought him to the hospital. A Miss Townsend?'

Claire grimaced. Okay, can you ask her to call me please?'

'Certainly. Would you like the doctor to call you back as well?'

'Yes please.'

Claire ended the call and immediately called her mum.

'Mum, it's Claire. Are you and Ben okay?'

'I'm good. Ben is here, he was sent home from school. They have closed most of the schools in the area because of this virus, do you know anything about it?' Claire sighed and wondered what other news she had missed during her meetings.

Ruby was a nice girl but Jenny would have interrupted the meetings to update her.

'No, I've been in meetings all morning but I'm on my way to a briefing now. Mum, James is in Leicester Royal Infirmary, he has the virus. Keep it from Ben and make sure he doesn't watch the news. I don't want him to worry.'

'Okay Claire. Do you feel okay?'

'Yes, Mum, I'm fine. Are you both okay?'

'We are fine, I've taken Ben's temperature five times already, I think he is getting fed up with me shoving the thermometer in his ear every ten minutes!'

Claire couldn't help but smile at the thought. 'Okay Mum, look after each other.'

As soon as Claire ended the call her mobile rang again. It was Ruby.

'Minister, I have some bad news. Officials have just confirmed that all the male prisons across the estate have reported symptomatic prisoners. I have emailed you details. There are too many patients to consider transfers to hospital and have recommended creating isolation wings and bringing in doctors.'

'It makes me uncomfortable. We have a duty of care to prisoners, security risks or not. How many prisoners are sick?'

'Twenty thousand men, Minister. All showing signs of the virus.'

'Twenty thousand?! That's a quarter of the prison population, are you sure?' 'Yes, Minister. I checked three times.'

'Okay, put in place isolation wings, make sure there are sufficient doctors, equipment and medication to treat them and update me every thirty minutes.' 'Very good, Minister.'

Claire was about to hang up when something occurred to her. She spoke quickly into the phone 'Ruby?

'Yes, Minister?'

'What about the women's prisons?'

'No outbreaks there, Minister.'

'Okay. Thanks, Ruby.'

She ended the call and sat back as the car picked up speed, her eyes wide. What was going on?

1986

Mummy is reading the newspaper at the breakfast table when I come downstairs for breakfast. She is so engrossed that she doesn't hear me come in, so I watch her from the door for a while. She has her cross face on, her fists are clenched and her eyes are full of tears. I wonder what she is reading about, it must be terrible. She slams her fist down on the table, which makes me jump and I squeak before I can stop myself. Her head whips up and she says,

'Ooh you made me jump, you little monkey!'

Her expression changes into her kind-smile, she puts the newspaper away quickly and pats the chair next to her. I sit down and say to her 'what are you reading?' She says 'The news, which made me cross. Do you want some breakfast? How about eggs? I say 'yes please' and sit down at the table.

Mummy says that after we have eaten our eggs we are going to go to the seaside to look for a new house, and stay in a hotel overnight. I'm so excited that I rush my breakfast and run upstairs to get ready. We put on our coats, gloves and scarves and walk to the station. Mummy carries our overnight bag. She buys two tickets to Brighton and we sit on a bench on the platform to wait for the train. Lots of people are here and I wriggle closer to Mummy, who puts her arms tightly around me. When the train comes we get on but Mummy says we need to walk down the train where it is a bit quieter, so we wobble along until we find an empty carriage. She says she has a surprise for me and pulls a new puzzle book out of her bag. I do love a puzzle. After a few puzzles I get tired, so I lean on

Mummy and fall asleep.

When I wake up we have to change trains. We walk through tunnels that go under the ground, until we reach the platform. The tunnel is long and dark. A really dirty train arrives and we get on it. It's so busy that there is nowhere to sit and so we stand up and mummy holds onto the bar. I don't like the dirty train. Everyone stands so close that you can smell all their smells and hear their breath. I start to shake and she grabs my hand and says to me quietly 'You are fine. I am here. Nothing bad is going to happen.' Some people standing near us look at me and she says 'It's rude to stare' with her cross face on.

Finally, we get off the dirty train and come back up from under the ground. The next train is much cleaner. Mummy gives the man our tickets and we climb aboard.

'This is better.' Mummy says. I sit up in my seat to look out of the window, which is really grubby. Mummy warns me not to touch it and hands me an egg sandwich. It is a very grey day but I can still see a long way and by the time we get to the seaside I have seen six cows and ten sheep (I think it is ten but we are going so fast I have to count really quickly so I may have missed some.)

It is very windy at the seaside. I can see the beach already but Mummy says that we have to go straight to see a house, so we walk in the opposite direction, up a hill and zigzag along some streets until we reach a house. The door opens straight onto the road. Mummy knocks and a lady with kind eyes answers. 'Hello there.' she says 'Come on inside.'

We go into the house, which is smaller than the house we live in. The kitchen is tiny but behind it is a nice room with big windows. Mummy and the lady are talking about the rent but all I really want to see is my bedroom. The lady sees me hopping from one foot to the other and asks 'Do you need to go to the toilet?' I shake my head 'no, I need to see my bedroom.' The lady laughs. 'Come along then let's go.'

The bedrooms have flowery wallpaper and thick carpets you can sink your toes into. There are three, one more than our house. Mummy smiles at me and whispers 'For your baby.' She looks at the lady. 'Can we take it please?'

2025

Jenny Robinson, 11am

Jenny waited outside the ward for the nurse. The gown, gloves, mask and shoe covers rustled with every movement, making her slow and cumbersome. The nurse came out and motioned for her to come in. They passed room after room until finally the nurse stopped by a door.

'We have put your son and husband in adjoining rooms. This is your son's room. Let me know when you are ready to see your husband.'

Jasper was dwarfed by the equipment all around him. He looked pale and drawn and almost thinner, even though she had only seen him a couple of hours before.

'He woke for a short time an hour ago.' The nurse checked his pulse as she spoke to Jenny and wrote something on a chart at the bottom of his bed.

'Did he say anything? Was he in pain?'

'No, he didn't speak. We have given him morphine. He was coughing and his breathing is still very laboured. You can sit with him but please, try not to touch him. I know it is difficult but we are trying to restrict contact until we know how the virus is passed from one person to another.'

Jenny sat down, waited for the nurse to leave and then took her sons hand.

'Jasper? Can you hear me love? It's Mum.' Jasper stirred slightly but didn't open his eyes.

'You are in the hospital, they are taking good care of you. All you need to do is rest and focus on getting better. I'll be here the whole time.' She sat quietly holding his hand, a lump in her throat. Tears were streaming down her face under the mask, making her feel clammy and hot. He looked so frail and innocent, like a young child.

'If I get a chance to pop home I'll bring some books and lots of food. When I was in hospital having you, I had to get your Dad to sneak in treats, I hated the food so much!'

She watched his face intently, looking for movement but there was nothing. She had never felt more powerless. As a young mum, she'd struggled with anxiety, grasping the kids hands in the street, hovering when they played, checking all the doors and smoke alarms ten times before bed every night. Eventually she'd sought counselling and learnt techniques to ease the symptoms. None of those techniques were working and she felt the familiar feeling of fear envelope her.

Lisa arrived, bearing books from the hospital gift shop. 'They won't let us bring food in, something to do with contamination, so we will have to go down to the coffee shop to eat.' There was no indication that Jenny had heard her, so Lisa touched her shoulder gently. 'I'll stay, why don't you go and see Mark? You must be so worried.'

Jenny shook her head. 'I'm can't leave Jasper. What if something happens…? He needs his mum.'

'I'll call you if he wakes up or if anything changes. Mark is alone. If he wakes up, he will be worried about you, Jasper and Mia? At least go and tell him what's going on.'

Jenny hadn't stopped to think about who was sitting with Mark and reluctantly stood up, feeling terrible for neglecting him. Leaning forward, she whispered 'Jasper, I won't be long, I'm popping to see Daddy. I love you buddy.'

She paused outside the door to steady herself. She knew Mark was alone, though his secretary Harriet had initially accompanied him to hospital. By the time Lisa and Jenny had found her in the waiting room she was in an awful state, wringing her hands and fretting about neglecting her duties. They had left her sitting there, waiting to be told she could leave. Torn be-tween Jasper and Mark, Jenny stood between the two rooms, tears rolling down her cheek. Eventually she turned away from her son and headed towards Marks room.

1986

Daddy used to see me every other weekend but I haven't seen him for five weekends now. Today he visits our new house and the first thing he does is look at my tummy with disgust. He says to Mummy 'Well you aren't doing a very good job of hiding that.' I pull my t-shirt down quickly. His face is red and angry which makes Mummy angry too, so I turn around and walk into the lounge because I hate it when they fight. I can hear angry whispering through the door so I turn on the radio and turn it up until I can't hear them. The radio is playing 'Manic Monday' by The Bangles. I like that song so I sing along. Halfway through Daddy comes in and turns off the radio. He sits next to me and tells me that he has driven a very long way to talk to me because he has something important to say.

He reaches into his bag and pulls out a package, wrapped in brown paper. He puts it on the chair and tells me to open it later, then he sighs and says 'This is difficult for me, Jean. You and Mummy have moved far away from me and I have been alone a lot. I was sad for a while but I have met a nice lady and when I'm with her I don't feel sad anymore. She wants me to go and live in America with her and I have decided to go. I'll miss you but I will write to you and you can write to me. When you are older, I will send you a ticket so that you can come and visit me.'

When he is talking I am watching his face but his eyes dart all over the room and he doesn't look at me once. When we all lived together he would sometimes cuddle me on the sofa but today he is sitting right on the edge with his back straight and he looks like he is about to jump up and leave. I don't want him to leave because I think if he does I won't see him again, so I try to think of things I could say to make him stay. I remember that he gets angry when I cry so even though I want to cry a lot, I hold it in and then I can't speak because if I speak I will cry so I look at the floor and I don't say anything at all.

After a while he says 'Jean, did you hear me?' I nod. Mummy comes into the room and sits down next to me. She says 'Jean, are you okay?' I look at her and she looks so sad that I can't hold it in anymore and I cry. She pulls me into her lap and gives me a big squeeze. Daddy just sits on the edge of the sofa looking at the floor and I think he must be really angry now because I cried.

Mummy says that we all need a cup of tea, so we go in the kitchen to make one. I stop crying and drink my tea at the kitchen table. Mummy gives me one of the special biscuits that she usually saves for visitors. I dunk it in my tea until it goes soft then take big, soggy bites. Daddy says 'I will miss you Jean.' I give him a hug and Daddy hugs me back which is so nice that I don't want to let go but he pulls away, drains his tea and says that he has a long drive back. He stands up and I look at Mummy, who is staring at Daddy with a cross face. She says 'Really? You have to go now?' and he nods and goes to the door. She takes my hand and we go to see him out. He turns around and says 'Bye Jean. Look after Mummy. I'll see you before I go to America, I promise.' Then he is gone.

Later, Mummy brings me the package that Daddy left and says 'Do you want to open this now?' I nod. I tear away the wrapping and pull out a book. It is an old copy of the bible. I have a copy of the bible already but the writing is so small that I have never read it. Mummy looks cross. She leans over and opens the book. On the inside cover is some writing from Daddy.

'Dear Jean,

This bible was given to me by my father when I was a boy and now I am giving it to you. I hope that this book provides you with some spiritual guidance and that you will read it as often

as I did. Remember that God loves you no matter what you do. He will wash away your sins and make you pure again. Live a good life and trust in God to punish those who do you harm. 'Whoever causes one of these little ones who believe in me to sin, it would be better for him if a great millstone were hung around his neck and he were thrown into the sea.'
Mark 9:42
Your loving father'

Mummy closes the book and takes it from me. She smiles with a sad face and says 'He does love you, he just struggles to show it. His parents were very strict and didn't show him a lot of love.' I nod but I don't understand. If Grandpa and Grandma didn't show Daddy a lot of love then he must have been sad when he was little, like me. I don't know why he would copy them. Mummy kisses me on the forehead.
'Goodnight Jeanie. Sleep tight.'
I lay awake for a long time, thinking about it.

2025

Jenny Robinson, 11.15am

Jenny pushed open the door to Mark's room. A doctor was standing at the foot of the bed reading his chart and a nurse was changing a fluid-filled bag. She couldn't see Mark's face. The doctor glanced up as she entered.

'Mrs Robinson?'

'Yes, how is he?'

The doctor turned to face her. 'I'm afraid the news isn't good. Your husband was one of the first patients to arrive with these symptoms. His condition is deteriorating fast. His lungs are filling with fluid so we have put in a tube to help him breathe and he has a dangerously high temperature. We have administered a large dose of antibiotics and anti-viral medication but he isn't responding to either. We haven't been able to identify the cause.'

Jenny walked passed the doctor to Marks bedside. He had a tube in his mouth and his face was red and mottled, his eyes were closed. He looked very different to the Mark she had seen just yesterday. She rested her gloved hand on Mark's chest, regretting the argument they had the night before. He just didn't see mess like she did. She'd got home to find Mark on the sofa, watching TV. The sink was full of washing up and there was a pile of dirty laundry. She'd had a hard day at work and it was the straw that broke the camel's back. She'd stormed into the lounge, raged about how lazy he was and then gone straight off to bed. Feeling guilty, she leant over and whispered in his ear.

'I'm sorry about last night, I love you, really I do. Please get better, we need you.' She lay her head on his chest. After a moment, the doctor cleared her throat, and asked to speak with her. She stood up and followed him outside.

'Mrs Robinson, did your son and husband go anywhere together yesterday or the day before?'

'Yesterday Mark took Jasper to rugby practice after school, then I think they went for a burger afterwards. Other than that, no, Mark worked yesterday and then Sunday he was out with some friends.'

'Okay. I need you to make a list of everyone he may have come into contact with.'

'Okay. Why don't I have it? I've slept in the same bed as Mark and I've been around Jasper.'

'Mrs Robinson, so far, only males have presented with these symptoms. None of the women who have come to the hospital with sick patients have shown any symptoms and the blood work from women has tested negative. The working assumption is that women have a natural resistance or even immunity.'

'Is that unusual?'

'Females can be more resilient to some infections but to be completely immune would be very unusual. I'm no expert in this field so we are seeking advice. I'll know more later today. '

'Okay. Is there anything more you can do for them?'

'Not until we identify the cause. We are already doing everything we can to head off the symptoms but a cure is some way off.' The doctor patted her on the arm and walked away.

Jenny stood between the two rooms once more. She knew Mark would tell her to go to Jasper but she still hesitated, desperately guilty that she couldn't be in two places at once. She needed Lisa to sit with Mark.

She pushed open the door to Jasper's room.

'Lisa, can you sit with Mark? I need to be in here but Mark is in a bad way and I don't want him to be alone.'

'Of course. Jenny, I just buzzed for the doctor, Jasper's breathing just got worse.'

1986

My tummy is really big, my skin stretches across it like the skin of a drum and there are bright red lines zigzagging across it. Mummy says they are the marks of motherhood and shows me her own silvery versions. She is teaching me at home because schools don't allow pregnant girls. When the baby is born I will go back to school which I'm nervous about because I don't have any friends here. When we moved I left my best friend behind, which made me really sad. Her name is Shirley and we still write to each other sometimes. In her letters, she talks a lot about their new dog Nelson. I ask Mummy if I could have one but she says that having a baby is a big responsibility and I won't have enough love for a dog as well. Mummy said that I can't tell Shirley about the baby, which I don't like because I used to tell Shirley everything. Mummy said that the baby would be 'a scandal' and we have to pretend that it is hers when it arrives.

I ask Mummy when Daddy is going to visit again. He promised he would come before he goes to America but Mummy says that he is busy packing up his house and she doesn't think he will visit again after all.

I think Daddy is moving so that he doesn't have to see me again. I have been reading the bible he gave me and I want to ask him why it says I am a sinner for having a baby outside marriage when the law says I can't get married because I'm only twelve. It seems like one of them must be wrong.

When we go out now, Mummy wears a cushion up her jumper and I wear big baggy coats and jumpers. Mummy says we are lucky because I'm quite slim so the bump doesn't show much when I'm wearing clothes. But the other day we were walking down the road and a man looked at my tummy and then said to Mummy that I was a 'dirty heathen.' I know what a heathen means because Daddy uses that word to describe people who were evil. I didn't like that man at all. Mummy says that it is better if we stay indoors as much as possible now.

2025

Medical records for Mark Robinson, completed by nurse on duty.

12:02pm: Subject regained consciousness. Complained of feeling heavy and described intense pain all over body. Presented with dyspnoea and was conscious for approximately two minutes.

1.25pm: Intubation required as patient can no longer breathe unaided.

4.55pm: Cardiac arrest, CPR administered.

5.02pm: Time of death

1986

I wake up with a start. My tummy feels like someone is clench-ing a fist inside me, it hurts so much. I scream and Mummy wakes up with a jolt. She looks at me and says 'It's time now Jeanie. You have to be really brave.' We get dressed and Mummy drives us to the hospital. Every time the pain comes back I scream because it is getting worse and the hospital is far away. Mummy is nervous because she is driving and I am screaming and she tells me to try and calm down, because she can't help me when she is driving. She says I have to breathe like she showed me. I pretend to be a train and it helps a bit.

When we get to hospital there are lots of screaming women there. The nurses know who I am and they take me straight to a private room. Mummy asked for one especially. The lady who comes in says that she is my midwife. I feel funny having a wife and I laugh at that but she says that actually it means she will help me get the baby out safely.

The midwife leaves for a few minutes and I ask Mummy 'Do you think that Daddy will come to see me now?' Mummy shakes her head and has a funny look on her face. 'No, Jean. I don't think he can afford to come all the way here to see the baby but you can send him pictures.' I lay back down glumly. I want to ask why Daddy doesn't love me but the midwife comes back just then and so I keep quiet.

When the next pain comes it is so painful and so long that I can't take it anymore and the midwife and Mummy have a worried conversation in the corner. The room swims and goes blurry and then nothing.

I wake up and lots of things have changed. I am in a different room; the midwife is here but there are about six men in white coats here too and I am naked and I am back in that house and my tummy is hurting again and I am screaming and screaming because Mummy isn't here and she said she would never let anything happen to me again. The men at the end of the bed stare and then Mummy is here and she is stroking my hair, saying 'Don't worry Jeanie, they are doctors. You are in an operating theatre and they are here to help you and the baby.' She strokes my hair but I can't stop screaming and one of the men in the white coats gives me an injection and then there is nothing.

I wake again and I am back in my bed in my room. Mummy and the midwife are here and she brings the baby over. I cry when I see that she is a beautiful baby after all because I have been worrying that she would look like the men and I wouldn't love her. The midwife gives her to me and I am allowed to hold her for as long as I want. She is the most beautiful thing I have ever seen. Mummy says that she looks just like me. I know I am going to love her more than anyone else in the world. I look up at Mummy and the midwife and I say 'Hope'.

2025

Jenny Robinson, 5.30pm

It was hours before Jenny had a chance to check her phone for missed calls. Mia had called twice and left a text;
'MUM!! Call me!'
Jenny sat heavily down in the chair next to Jasper's bed and Lisa gave her an awkward hug. 'She's probably worried. Call her so she knows you are okay.'
Jenny's voice wobbled as the call connected to her daughter.
'Mia, thank god. Are you okay?'
'Mum I'm fine but half the university has gone down with some kind of bug, it's mental here. They are closing the campus, I'm going to get a train home in about an hour's time. All the boys are sick, the girls are completely fine. I saw on the news that they think it's a virus and it's spreading everywhere. Are you guys okay?'
'I'm fine. Your brother is in hospital but the doctors here are really great and are looking after him. I'm so happy you are coming home. I'll ask Lisa to come and get you and bring you to the hospital.'
'Jasper? Oh god. I haven't even spoken to him this week. Can I talk to him now?'
'No love, the doctors are examining him at the moment. Just get home, we can talk properly then. Do you want to speak to Aunt Lisa?'
'Yes please. I'll see you soon Mum.'
Jenny handed the phone over and put her hand quickly over

her mouth. She jumped out of her chair and ran down the corridor, looking for a toilet. She saw a door and burst through it, into a store room. She collapsed to her knees, felt her stomach twist and vomited. A nearby nurse heard the noise and came quietly into the room. She bent down and put her hand on Jenny's back. 'It's okay love, happens a lot. Just breathe.' She handed Jenny a tissue and knelt on the floor with her as she cried.

When she had recovered the nurse led her back to Jaspers room where Lisa had just put the phone down. 'She's walking to the station now.'

'You know I can't even remember the last thing I said to him? We were having an argument about housework and I was awful to him, then I went to bed. I didn't get the chance to make up with him.' Jenny bent her head and sobbed.

'He knew you loved him, Jenny. Everyone fights.'

'I know, but it doesn't make me feel any better.'

They sat in silence. The tissue in Jenny's hand was sodden but the tears kept coming. She couldn't imagine how she could ever stop crying.

1986

Hope is very noisy at night. Mummy says that I don't need to get up to look after her but I still want to. At first, though, I am too tired to move. It takes a really long time for me to heal after Hope is born. Mummy says that when Hope was born the birth caused lots of damage. I bled and bled and in the end, they had to take everything inside me away, so Hope will be my only baby. I am sad about that because I wanted Hope to have a sister one day. Mummy is sad too and she cries a lot.

She thinks I am too young to look after a baby and says I should pretend to be Hope's sister instead. But I will only get one chance to be a Mummy and I don't want to pretend to be Hope's sister. I tell Hope that I am her Mum every single day and I cuddle her and kiss her all the time.

Babies like a routine so when I wake up in the morning, Mummy always gives Hope to me so that I can feed her while she makes breakfast. I like to hold Hope, she always smells like soap and milk. When I go to school Mummy takes Hope to the lady down the road, so that she can go to work. She is nice and she looks after Hope really well but I still feel sad to leave her with a stranger. Mummy says that it is a 'necessary evil' to leave Hope. She has to work so we can afford our house and eat nice food.

I go to a school just for girls now. No-one knows my real surname, which Mummy says is because we need to start afresh. I am happy to be in a new town near the sea and especially happy to live very far away from the bad place. I make friends quickly, the girls at my school are nice and they call me 'the new girl'. Some of the girls say that I am 'quirky' and I don't really know what they mean. I haven't told any of them about what happened to me because Mummy says 'children are cruel if you are different.' I pretend that we have moved here to be nearer the sea, which I suppose is true. I feel like I have been at my school forever and my teacher is pleased that I have settled in so fast. She tells Mummy that I am a 'natural leader'.

After school, it is always just Mummy, Hope and I. We don't really have visitors, or friends over for tea, even though I could probably invite a different friend over every night because all the girls want to see where I live.

Mummy encourages me to study in my spare time. She buys me books about the topics that they don't cover in school. She says she would give anything to have my brains. All I know is that I like the time we spend together, even if I do have to study. It is good to have Mummy all to myself but sharing her with Hope is okay too.

Sometimes I think about what happened with the bad men and I have nightmares. I wake up sweating and screaming and Mummy runs in, scoops me up and carries me to her room. Hope is usually there too and we all snuggle up together. I wish I could sleep in Mummy's room all the time but Mummy says that Hope keeps her up a lot and there is 'no point in all of us being tired.'

When Hope starts sleeping through the night Mummy lets me move into her bedroom all the time. I hardly have any nightmares after that.

2025

Jenny Robinson, 7.30pm

Jasper died at 7.30pm. As the life left his body Jenny's heart seemed to tear in two. She clung to her son, her mask and gloves long discarded. She stroked his face, his skin still soft with childhood and wished that she had recorded every moment of his life so that she could live it again. The boy that she had fed, watched grow and thrive, witnessed taking his first stumbling steps, bathed, cuddled and loved more than she ever thought possible. His first day at nursery and how his lower lip trembled when she left him for the first time. All the bedtime stories and the cuddles. All those funny things he used to say when he was learning to talk, his love of superheroes and video games.

She thought about the time they had spent together as a family and the games they invented. The 'Santa sleigh' made of chairs and cushions that took over the lounge, the den they made under the trampoline, the holidays by the pool, the endless water fights, the competitive races and Jenga games, the movie nights with popcorn and nachos. She remembered the big events, his first day at school, in a uniform that seemed too big for his tiny frame, his first rugby match.

She thought about the things she would never see, his first girlfriend, his wedding, his graduation and his babies. She sobbed for the things she'd miss, the new chasm in her life. 15 was no age to die, she didn't even know if he'd had a first kiss. She couldn't remember the last time thing she said to him or if she'd ever really told him just how much he meant to her. She lay her head down on Jaspers chest, her tears sinking into the thin white sheet that covered his body and it was as if time had stopped. There was nothing worth moving for.

* * *

She registered the muffled voice of Lisa talking to someone on the phone.

'Okay, don't panic, I'll come as soon as I am allowed to leave. I don't know how long it will take but as soon as I can go I'll text you. Stay where you are okay? I'll find you.' Lisa's voice was shaky.

Jenny lifted her head and looked at Lisa quizzically. Lisa mouthed 'Mia'. Lisa searched Lisa's face for signs of panic. Finding nothing, she lay her head back down.

'She's fine, she just can't talk right now, she's speaking to the doctor.' she glanced at Jenny guiltily.

'Okay, see you soon.'

Lisa sat down on the bed next to her sister. 'Mia is stuck. The train she was on has been cancelled and she is waiting at Guildford Station. We need to go and get her. You have to leave him now, we need to speak to the doctor about when we can leave.'

Jenny nodded slowly, then leaned forward and kissed Jasper on the lips. 'Goodnight, my darling. You sleep now. I love you so, so much.' Fresh tears slid down her face as she tore herself away.

The on-call doctor was sat at reception, drinking coffee, her shoulders sagging with the weight of the crisis. 'I'm so sorry for your loss Mrs Robinson.' She said gently. 'I don't know if anyone has made you aware, but your blood tests came back clear and the quarantine has been lifted so you are free to go. There are some forms that you need to fill in but you can take them with you if you like. I know this is difficult but there are so many sick people in the hospital that we need to move

Jasper now to make room for new patients. He will be taken to the morgue and when you return the forms we can discuss next steps.'

'Thank you.' Jenny replied dully. Lisa linked arms with her and Jenny felt grateful for the contact. More than anything now she just wanted to be with her daughter.

1987

Mummy and I have to go back to the bad place today so that I can give evidence in court. I have the day off school and we have to leave very early in the morning so we leave Hope with the neighbour overnight. I didn't want the men to see her and think she was theirs.

On the way to the bad place I ask Mummy if Daddy will come to court with us. She looks at me with surprise on her face and for a little while she doesn't answer. Then she says 'Jean, your father lives in America now. He can't come to court but he knows how strong you are and he knows I'm going to be right there with you, keeping you safe. He wants you to know that he loves you very much.'

I look out of the window, watching the fields and trees pass by. Then I say to Mummy 'I think Dad moved to America because he thinks I am a sinner for having a baby without being married.' Mummy leans towards me and grabs my shoulders. She says 'Don't ever think that. It was very hard for your father to accept what happened to you but he doesn't think you are a sinner.'

I ask Mummy why Dad doesn't want to see Hope and she says grown-ups are complicated and Dad finds it difficult to think of Hope without thinking about what happened to me. I am angry with him for not even trying to love her, he's never even saw her in the flesh. She so beautiful that if he saw her I know he would forget all about how she was made and just fall in love with her.

Mummy changes the subject and starts to talk to me about

what is going to happen today. She says that I have to sit in the courtroom in front of the men and tell the court what happened to me, which makes me really scared. She said that I have a 'barrister' who is there to make sure I am safe. She asked for a screen so that I can't see the men but I don't think that will help much because I'll still know they are there. Mummy says that she can't sit with me behind the screen. I have to sit there on my own. By the time we arrive I am shaking so much that I can't walk and she has to carry me. She hasn't done that since we moved to our new house by the beach. We get in a taxi and the driver takes us straight to the main entrance.

As we walk in I see one of the men who attacked me. He is standing with a lady and a girl who looks the same age as me and I can't help it, I scream as loud as I can. Everyone turns around to look at me. Suddenly everyone is moving. A lady runs up and ushers Mummy and I into a small room off the main corridor. Mummy is cuddling me but she is angry and she is shouting at the lady at the same time.

'How is this justice? Seeing him before we even get in the court to give evidence? She's a wreck and who can blame her, the man nearly killed her. I've a good mind to take her straight home.' The lady tries to calm Mummy down but all I can think about is the little girl standing with him so I try to get Mummy's attention, I pull her skirt and say 'Mummy, what about the little girl? Please tell the police to move him away from that little girl.' The lady crouches down next to me and she says 'The little girl is his daughter and the lady is her Mummy. Don't worry, I'm sure her Mummy won't let him hurt her.' She stands up and Mummy and the lady look at each other, Mummy still looks angry but now she is sad too.

We sit in the little room for a long time until it is our turn and I think about that little girl a lot. I don't pray very often which Dad used to say was sinful but today I pray that he didn't hurt her too.

* * *

I sit in the witness box. the lady we saw earlier on is wearing a silly wig, which I think makes her look old and scary. She smiles and then starts asking me questions. Earlier she told me to try and remember as much as possible and tell the court how it felt to be there. I try to remember and it feels like I'm there but everything is jumbled up.

I tell her that I waited outside school for Mummy until it all the other Mummies had arrived. A few parents talk outside.

I decide to walk home because it isn't far and I know I'll probably meet Mummy on the way.

I turn the corner and see the big blue van with its doors wide open. I see the men in the back of the van, the same men who are in court.

One of them holds a puppy and as I pass the puppy jumps out of the van and runs towards me. I bend down to stroke it and feel a hand over my mouth and then I am in the van with a piece of cloth wrapped so tightly over my eyes that it hurts my face.

I shake.

I want Mummy.

Scared.

Think I wet myself.

I hear talking and the puppy yelping.

The puppy yelps and then screams and then silence.

Is the puppy dead?

They are going to hurt me.

SCREAM loud, try and escape.

A dirty cloth in my mouth, making me choke.

Shouting.

'STOP FUCKING CRYING'

Van stopping, doors opening.

Being dragged along the ground, knees sore, hear keys and I cry and cry...

I hear the lady ask the judge if we can have a break. I open my eyes and I see my Mummy running towards me with tears all over her face and she is mad and I hope she is not mad at me.

2025

Mia Robinson, 7.45pm

Mia sat on the stationary train at Guildford Station, her chin length blonde hair tucked behind her ears. She was getting more and more anxious; the train was already half an hour late and she knew her mum would worry. A speaker in the carriage crackled as the conducted finally broke the silence.

'Apologies for the delay to this service. Unfortunately the driver has been taken ill and this service is now cancelled. Please make your way off the train and onto the platform and listen for further announcements.' The whole carriage groaned in unison. Mia cursed under her breath, picked up the phone and called her mum in the hope of a lift as the rest of the passengers began to file off the train.

When she finished talking to Lisa she looked up and noticed that the sleeping man opposite her still hadn't woken up. His head was resting against the window and he looked awkward and uncomfortable, so she reached over and tapped his shoulder to wake him.

'Excuse me, the train is out of service, we have to get off.' He didn't stir.

She shook him gently but he didn't move and when she shook him again his head began to slide forwards against the window. Panicking that he would fall onto her, she stepped away. What should she do? She tried to push him back onto the seat but he was heavy and it was difficult to move him. Her heart was racing and she felt her face grow red as she struggled.

Just then she heard movement behind her and turned to see a red-haired woman wearing a purple suit striding purposefully down the carriage. Mia opened her mouth to ask for help but the woman began to talk loudly into her phone. 'Yes, I know... there's absolutely nothing I can do about it. Look, I can't talk now, I need to find out what's going on.' She cut the caller off as she moved towards Mia and glanced down at her, still frowning. Mia quickly stood up.

'Excuse me, can you help me? This man isn't moving, I think he is sick.'

'Have you checked his pulse? His temperature?' The woman spoke quickly, as if she had somewhere else to be.

'No, I haven't had a chance.' The woman walked up to the man and put two fingers under his jaw. She paused for a moment then snapped 'Well, he is hot and his pulse is weak.' She rolled her eyes. Stay here, I'll get someone.'

The redhead turned sharply and hurried off the train as a young guard and a paramedic passed the carriage window, wheeling a gurney containing the driver of the train. Mia heard Redhead shout after them, 'Excuse me, hello? There is a sick man in here too, can you help?'

The paramedic looked over her shoulder and said 'Is he breathing?'

'Yes.'

The medic turned back to her patient. 'It would be quicker to ask someone to drive him, you'll struggle to get an ambulance now. Are you first aid trained?'

Redhead pulled her shoulders back slightly before she answered. 'Yes, actually I am.'

'That's good. Get him in the recovery position, check his airway and then find some help.'

Mia looked past Redhead and the medic to the crowd behind her, jostling for position and shouting at a member of station staff stood before them. The man held a thick book limply and appeared completely exasperated. Redhead got back into the carriage and looked pointedly at Mia. 'Let's move him.'

Between them the wrestled him onto the floor and moved him into the recovery position in the aisle. Then Redhead stood up and left the carriage again, bellowing 'Does anyone have a car? This man is sick.'

'I do.' A young man with thick, dark hair who was standing towards the rear of the jostling crowd peeled away and then walked towards her, appraising Redhead as he did. 'I'm supposed to be waiting for my girlfriend but her train is stuck in London so I'll be here a while.'

'Can you help us get this man to hospital?'

Between them they managed to manoeuvred the man off the train. A nearby couple saw them struggling and came to help. They made slow progress because of the slow-moving crowds but managed to carry the man out of the station. Some people leapt aside as they passed with fear on their faces and it occurred to Mia for the first time that she might be putting herself at risk. The other people helping seemed to come to the same realisation and they all paused for a moment.

'Can't stop now' said Redhead breathlessly. We are nearly there. Come on.' They all glanced at each other guiltily and then trudged onward.

As they moved passed the entrance, a crowd was gathering outside, next to the taxi rank, though there were no taxis in sight. As they carried the man past the crowd Mia caught snippets of conversation.

'...sick and tired of bloody waiting...' '...ridiculous to leave so many people stranded....' '...need to get back to my son...' '...really not feeling too well....' '...can't get hold of him...' 'what the hell is going on?' '...news says that hundreds have already died...' '...shouldn't stand too close to people...'

Mia could feel the anger and fear and felt instinctively that they weren't safe. At that moment, a heavily built man in the crowd regarded them angrily and began to shout;

'What the hell are you doing! Get him away from us!' He and his friends moved back, pushing the crowd towards the wall away from the group. She glanced at Redhead nervously, who muttered 'Keep going. Don't look at them.' Despite the heavy load they were carrying, all of them picked up their pace as they passed the throng.

They finally reached the young man's car. It unlocked with a click and Mia opened the back door. Between them they wrestled the unconscious man into the back, then stood back, panting.

'I'm going with them, seems safer than that.' Redhead nodded back toward the crowd. 'Are you coming?'

'No, my aunt is on her way to pick me up so I need to stay here.' Redhead opened the passenger door and as she climbed into the passenger seat she looked back at Mia and said 'Be careful. Don't stand in the crowd. Go back into the station and wait.' Mia nodded and Redhead shut the door. The car drew away from the curb, leaving Mia and the two helpers behind.

As they turned back towards the taxi rank Mia heard the sound of people screaming. A man lay on the floor where the crowd had been, struggling to breathe. A woman crouched over him crying, trying to loosen his tie. The rest of the crowd huddled a distance away watching, their faces twisted in horror. As Mia approached, the man coughed out a spray of blood, spattering the woman's white t-shirt. The crowd gasped in unison and shrank back against the station wall.

The large man who had shouted at the before clenched his fists and screamed 'WHAT THE FUCK IS HAPPENING!'

The fear in his voice seemed to jolt the crowd into action and people peeled away, running in all directions away from the station.

The woman who was helping the sick man looked up at Mia desperately. 'Please help me. He's my husband. Please!' Mia shook her head, mumbling 'sorry' and hurried past them into the station, her heart pounding. Only when she reached the relative safety of the station café did she slow her pace. Her whole body was shaking as she sat heavily on one of the chairs at the table furthest from the door. 'Hurry up Lisa' she muttered to herself. She got her phone out of her pocket and sat holding it, looking anxiously at the door.

1987

It is my thirteenth birthday. Mummy, Hope and I visit the zoo. I race downstairs in the morning but pause at the kitchen door because I hear Mummy on the telephone. I think she is talking to the lady who asked me all the questions in court. I hear Mummy say 'No, I'm not happy! Those men left Jeanie for dead! Ten years is nowhere near enough for what they did.' I wait outside until she is finished and pretend I haven't heard. When she tells me that they are all going to prison I act surprised.

The zoo is great. Hope loves the monkeys and we spend a lot of time pretending to be a monkey and looking through the bars. When we get home after the zoo Mummy gives me a letter from Dad. I am excited because we sent him photographs of Hope and I want to know what he says about them, so I run upstairs to read it. The letter isn't very long. It says;

'Dear Jean,

Thank you for your last letter. I hope that you are well. Your mother told me how brave you were in court and that the men who were tried will probably go to prison for life. I am pleased that you were brave. Always remember that God is watching over you and will keep you safe from harm. He will punish those who hurt you even if the law does not.

I hear that you are feeling a lot better now that the trial is over and that you have started a new school. I hope that you are studying hard.

I am sorry that I didn't manage to see you before I left for America as I said I would, I had to leave early as there was a lot to arrange here. Do you remember me telling you about the nice woman who stopped me feeling sad? Her name is Marion and when we got to America we got married. She has just had a baby, so you now have a half-brother, isn't that great? I have put a picture of him in with this letter so that you can see him. His name is Peter and he is a lovely, happy little boy. His hair is so blonde that it is almost white and his favourite game is peek-a-boo. If you look at the picture you will see that he is holding a blue bear. He sleeps with that bear every night, he loves it so much. I hope that one day I can bring him to meet you, when you are both older.

I have put some money in this letter for your birthday. I hope that you will spend it on something educational. You are a bright enough girl and I think you could do quite well if you put your mind to it. Make sure you say your prayers every night before you go to bed.

God loves you.
Take care
Your loving Father'

I look at the photograph of the boy. The blue bear that he is holding looks just like the one that Hope has. I suddenly hate Hope's bear, even though I know that she loves it. I look back at the letter. He didn't mention Hope once, not even to say that he had seen the photographs we sent. I put everything back in the envelope and go downstairs. I take Hope's blue bear away from her and go to the fire. I throw the letter and the blue bear straight in and I watch the bears eyes melt away and his blur fur turn black and melt into the flames. I can hear Hope crying for her blue bear but I don't turn around until it is completely gone. I will buy her a new bear.

Later Mummy asks what was in the letter. I tell her that I don't want to write to Dad anymore.

2025

Mia Robinson, 8.20pm

Mia sat in the station café well over an hour. The woman behind the counter was unexpectedly kind. Fearful of the aggressive crowd outside, she pulled down the shutters within minutes of Mia's arrival but let her wait inside. Despite this, Mia struggled to relax. She spent the time trying to reach her friend Teddy, who had been taken into hospital that morning but his phone kept going to voicemail and she worried that he was as sick as the other men she had seen.

Her mobile announced Lisa's arrival with an angry buzz. She looked up and saw her Mum and Lisa peering through the shutters. She thanked the woman in the café and waited as she lifted up the shutters so that Mia could leave.

'Mia!' Jenny squeezed her so tight and for so long that Mia was struggling to breathe. She pulled away slightly.

'Mum? What are you doing here?'

'Come on love, it isn't safe here, let's go home.'

As they walked quickly to the car, Mia noticed that most of the crowd had now dispersed, though a group of about a dozen men remained and were sitting on the floor near the taxi rank, drinking beer from cans. As they passed them the group looked up at them and one of them leered at Mia.

'Where have you been hiding?' He lurched to his feet and swayed on the spot.

'It's the end of the fucking world, the least you could do is stay and fucking talk to me.'

Her mother pulled Mia towards her and shot an angry look at the man, who shrugged and sat back down heavily.' As they walked away the man muttered something to the group, who burst into loud, drunken laughter.

They breathed a sigh of relief when they were finally in the car with the doors locked and Jenny turned to Mia. 'I'm sorry you had to wait so long, we came as soon as we could but the roads are terrible.'

'Mum' Mia asked again. 'Why are you here? Is Jasper okay?'

'Let's just get home, we can talk there.'

Lisa drove toward the motorway with the radio on low to pick traffic warnings. Jenny sat in the passenger seat, trying to find a route around the growing traffic and Mia kept trying to contact Teddy. They could hear her leaving anxious messages with friends, seeking news. After twenty minutes or so she gave up and sat miserably, looking down at her phone as if willing it to ring.

Jenny looked out of the window but saw nothing. She was thinking about how to tell Mia about Mark and Jasper but couldn't think of the right words, it felt wrong to wait but equally wrong to tell her now and she wished that she could keep Mia from the pain that she felt forever. She didn't hear the newsreader until Lisa nudged her.

'...growing public health disaster is sweeping Britain today, as thousands of people fall victim to an as-yet unidentified virus. Hospitals across the country are reporting unprecedented numbers of infected patients and it is understood that fatalities are already in the thousands...'

Lisa mouthed to Jenny 'Turn it off'. Jenny clicked the radio off and looked around at Mia, who was looking out of the window at the slow-moving traffic. A tear slid slowly down her face.

'I'm worried about Teddy, Mum.'

'I know you are. We will be home soon, it'll be easier to reach people from there.' She reached out and squeezed Mia's hand.

The cars ahead of them picked up pace as they passed the source of the traffic jam. The crumpled car at the side of the road was in full view. A young man in a leather jacket hung out of the driver side door wheezing, blood pouring from his mouth. A red-haired woman next to him was slumped forward in her seat, her purple suit stained with blood from her wounds. Jenny didn't need to look closely to see that she wasn't going to make it. The rear door was open and she could make out the body of another man lying across the seats.

Mia leant forward. 'Oh god!' She exclaimed. 'I know them.'

Jenny turned to look at her, puzzled. 'Are you sure?'

'Yes, they were on my train. The man in the back was sick, the girl helped me get him to that car. Mum, I'm scared.'

Jenny's heart sank. She looked at her daughter. 'Did you touch him, Mia?'

'Yes, we all carried him, why? Am I going to get sick too?'

'Did he cough on you? Or bleed on you?'

'No. Mum? What do you know?'

'I don't know anything, Mia. I'm sure it's fine. I'm just being paranoid. Let's just get home.'

Jenny faced forwards once more and lapsed into silence, thinking again about the list on the wall at the hospital. It was all men. She had been with Jasper and Mark all day and she wasn't sick, none of them were. They may well be okay for now but they still weren't safe. They needed to get home. Her mind wasn't working properly, the same few words were going over and over in her mind. 'We just need to get home, let's just get home.' She turned to Mia again. 'When we get home we will be safe, let's just get home, okay?'

1988

I can hear Mummy on the phone, talking to Dad. I go to my room and shut the door so I can't hear her. Mummy will ask me to talk to him but I won't because he is a hypocrite. I've read his bible and the letters, telling me to follow God's word but he has broken all the rules. Divorce is forbidden by god. He had sex outside marriage- a sin. He refuses to accept his own granddaughter. He spends his life studying the bible and is not strong enough to follow it. He disgusts me.

I don't believe in god. I have read the bible from cover to cover and it is full of contradictions. I believe in science, in things I can see and touch.

Mummy comes upstairs and asks me to speak to him. I tell her I don't want to talk to him, or read his letters or see his photographs. He can talk to his new family. She is sad that I don't want to talk to him and she keeps on at me, just to say hello, so he can hear my voice and I can't take it any more so I shout at her

'GET OUT OF MY ROOM. I'M NOT TALKING TO HIM EVER AGAIN SO STOP ASKING ME.'

She sighs as me and goes to tell him.

'She won't talk to you, I'm sorry Neal.' He must have said something back because I hear her snap at him

'Well if you hadn't left to shack up with that woman maybe you would still understand your daughter.' I slam my bedroom door. I don't want to hear another argument.

Later, she knocks my door, wanting to talk about Dad. She says that I don't have to talk to him if I don't want to but she had to ask. I tell her I am happy and I don't need anyone else, I have her and Hope.

2025

Jenny Robinson, 9.30pm

Jenny ushered Mia and Lisa inside the house and shut the door, pausing for a minute to catch her breath. She wanted to shut out the world outside and retreat into the comfort of home, but the feeling of impending doom that hung over her on the journey home remained and the house didn't feel welcoming or safe. Everything was different, the life she knew was crumbling around her. Jasper and Mark were gone. She didn't know how she would cope, a jumble of questions and problems crowded her mind. How would she afford the house? How would she pay Mia's university fees? Would they make it or were they going to get sick too? The weight of the questions and problems instantly overwhelmed her and the pressure of keeping her emotions in check in front of Mia felt like a lead weight around her shoulders. She turned to remove her coat and caught sight of Jasper's jacket hanging on the hook.
Jasper.
She reached for it, breathing in the familiar scent. Her head swam, her legs buckled and she sank to the floor, still holding his coat in her arms. Her sobs echoed in the silence of the house and she barely noticed Mia's footsteps as she came running in to see what was wrong.
'Mum? Mum, what is it? You're scaring me, what's wrong?'
The tears kept coming. Lisa came out into the hall and motioned to Mia to go into the lounge. She gently put her arms around her sister. 'Come on, Jenny. I'll tell her, but you need to

be there.'

They sat down together and Lisa took Mia's hand.

'You know your brother was in hospital today?' Mia nodded silently.

'The doctors said that Jasper was really sick. He had a new virus which spread really quickly, the hospital was full of people who had the same thing. The doctors said to us that everyone who has caught it so far has died.'

'Is Jasper going to die?' Mia eyes widened and filled with tears. She looked around the room as if searching for him. 'Is he in hospital? Why aren't we there?'

'The doctors did everything they could but they couldn't save him. I'm so sorry.'

'No...' Mia's stared at Lisa. 'But he only got sick today. How can he be dead?'

'It happened really quickly. He was unconscious most of the time. I'm not sure he knew he was sick. I'm so sorry Mia but there is more...'

Lisa's voice cracked and she stopped for a moment. Mia stood up. She felt numb. He couldn't be dead; Aunt Lisa was wrong. She walked out of the lounge towards the stairs and ran up them, two at a time. She flung open Jasper's bedroom door and saw the empty bed, unmade, covers strewn across the floor. A pile of clean clothes sat on his chest of drawers and magazines covered the desk. Everything looked...normal. But he wasn't there. Jenny came up behind her and touched her shoulder gently. Mia turned and buried her face in Jenny's chest, her tears dampening Jenny's shirt. 'Mum...'

'I know.' Jenny stroked Mia's hair, then walked Mia over to the bed and they both sat down, Jenny's arms wrapped around her. Lisa leant against the doorway, the burden of yet more bad news weighing heavily on her.

After a few minutes Mia's head snapped up and she looked at Jenny. 'Where's Dad?' Helpless, Jenny looked at Lisa.

'I'm sorry Mia.' Lisa didn't know how to say the words. She

looked down at the floor and when she spoke again her voice was flat and lifeless.

'When we arrived at the hospital we realised that your Dad was there too. He got sick as soon as he got to work and died shortly before Jasper, I'm sorry...' Lisa sank to the floor and sat in the doorway crying, her head in her hands.

The bottom fell out of Mia's world. She looked at Jenny in horror.

'Both of them?' Jenny nodded, her devastated heart breaking again for her daughter. Mia let out an anguished wail and fell against Jenny, sobbing. After a moment, she sat up 'I'm going to be sick.' She ran quickly past Lisa to the bathroom and they heard her retching.

Jenny was exhausted, she felt as if there was no tomorrow, nothing to do but lie down. She pulled Jasper's cover across her body and curled into a ball. After a few moments Mia came back in the room and got into bed beside her.

Lisa watched them for a few minutes and then left the room, closing the door behind her.

1988

I wake up with a start. Hope is lying next to me in bed which is nothing new, she does this most nights. I don't mind, I love finding her curled up next to me in the morning. I touch her face to brush her hair away and notice that she is cold and clammy. When I turn on the light she looks almost blue and she is breathing quickly, like she is having a bad dream. I shake her but I can't wake her up so I run in to Mummy to wake her.

We quickly get dressed and bundle Hope into Mummy's car. I sit beside her while Mummy drives to the hospital. It is dark and mummy drives fast, the street lights flash across Hope's face like strobe lighting. I am terrified. I sit with her head in my lap, stroking her hair and telling her not to worry but I am worried. I am so scared that she is going to die that I can barely breathe. We know it is serious because when we carry her into A&E they rush us straight through the waiting area where lots of people are sitting. A doctor meets us on the other side of the swinging doors and takes her away. We are left standing there, looking at each other and I cannot stop crying because she is my life.

When the doctor finally appears again he tells me and Mummy that Hope has developed sepsis. It happens when bacteria take over your whole body. He says it's lucky I woke up because they caught it early and she has a good chance of getting better. She had an untreated urine infection which he said sometimes happens with children. I feel guilty because I remember Hope crying when she went to the toilet yesterday.

I sit next to her in her hospital bed and watch as the antibiotics go along the tube and into her vein. The doctor gives me a leaflet on sepsis which I read over and over again. I am anxious because the leaflet says that if she goes into septic shock there is only a 60% chance of survival. Sepsis stops blood flow to your organs and limbs, leading to organ failure and gangrene. I want to ask more questions but Mummy says that I need to relax and let the doctors fix her. I want to know exactly what they are doing so I make sure that I am always there.

This shouldn't happen to a child. It is why I don't believe in God. When I think about it everything seems unfair because people like Hope get sick and people like me get hurt and the bad people who deserve to be sick get to keep walking around like everything is fine. Hope has never done a bad thing in her life but she still might die.

It seems to me that no-one ever really gets what they deserve. I read the newspapers and I know that people do bad things and get away with it. Even when we do catch them they seem to get off lightly. I read that a man went to prison for seven years which sounds like a long time until you read that he raped a woman and destroyed her life. Another man went to prison for twelve years but he killed his wife and she doesn't get another life. Prison is not a punishment when you compare it to losing your life, or being scared to walk down the street. When I hear about vigilantes who go out and punish bad people themselves, I cheer inside. If I had been strong enough and old enough I would have tracked down the men who hurt me and murdered them in their beds. They took away my innocence. They made me afraid. Two of them were never even found. The other men are in prison but they aren't really suffering. Not like Hope is suffering. Not the way I have suffered.

* * *

Hope got a bit worse last night but this morning she is a tiny bit better. The doctor says that the antibiotics are working. They are all men and when they come to check on her I can't help feeling a bit scared. I don't let them send me out of the room. I watch them, with their white coats and serious faces. They might be helping Hope but I still don't trust them. Doctors took away my lady parts. They do evil things too.

❊ ❊ ❊

Hope is a lot better today and she is allowed to go home and rest. We get home and tuck her safely into bed, then I ask Mummy if we can go to the library. I say that it is because I need science books for my homework. Mummy asks our neighbour to watch Hope for an hour and drives me there. I check out four books about bacteria because I want to know exactly what the bacteria did and whether I could have stopped it. I read them from cover to cover while I'm sitting next to Hope's bed. I learn that bacteria existed long before man and are essential to our survival. Our immune systems keep bacteria under control and some bacteria keeps us healthy. However pathogenic bacteria can kill humans. It was pathogenic bacteria that caused Hope's illness.

Infections are different to bacteria. Whereas bacteria can live and thrive outside the human body, most infections need a human host to multiply. Most infections will die without humans but bacteria are strong. For a tiny organism, they can do a lot of damage. The plague, the Spanish flu, tuberculosis, cholera and typhoid were all bacteria based. Even a small amount can reduce a man to nothing. They are more powerful than guns, or knives, or rocks. You can even engineer them to kill some cells while leaving others perfectly healthy. They are miraculous.

In the book, there are pictures of bacteria and infections up close and I carefully tear them out and pin them up on my wall in my room right next to my bed so that I can look at them at night. They are so beautiful close up and even though they are small like me, they can do big things.

I watch a programme about serial killers with Hope while Mummy pops over to the neighbour's house. Serial killers are similar to bacteria. They do big terrible things too but they are almost always men and they usually kill women and children. Men only ever seem to hurt people who can't fight back and I can't think of anything that makes me hate the world I live in more than that. If anyone ever hurt Hope like the men hurt me I wouldn't let them carry on living in this world. Just thinking about it makes me so angry it feels like there is a ball of flames in my chest. Mummy says I have to sit away from other people and take deep breaths when this happens, so I leave Hope on the sofa and go to my room. I am so angry and sad that my body wants me to scream. Sometimes when I get this angry I feel like I am back in the room with the men who hurt me, or with the doctors who took away all the parts that made me a proper woman. I have to curl up into a tiny ball, as small as possible so that they can't see me. Mummy usually knows I need a hug then and she squeezes me tight until I feel safe again. Today she isn't here so I crawl under the bed and hide until it goes away.

I am under my bed a long time.

2025

Justine walked through security, feeling more like she was walking into the 'Westminster bubble' than usual. With ten years as a civil servant under her belt, she knew how to behave when ministers born into privilege demanded advice. She could answer questions about how to minimise a public backlash while cutting public spending on benefits, or write lines on why the rise in crime wasn't really linked to cuts in police officer numbers. Today though, she was scared. The ministers she ranted about after work with like-minded colleagues over copious amounts of red wine, were in charge of the biggest disaster the country had ever seen. She knew that they all had quirks and fallibilities. They were no more able to fix this than anyone else and since most of them were men, women would have to pick up the pieces once they were gone.

She walked into the Prime Minister's office to a distinct atmosphere. The mood was bleak. Half the staff were off and the rest were preoccupied, checking texts for news about friends and relatives or watching the screens on the wall repeating the same horrifying news over and over. They knew more than most about what was happening across the country but it didn't make them feel any better.

She caught up on the nights events. Things had taken a turn for the worst, the Deputy Prime Minister was in a private ward at St Thomas' Hospital, several junior ministers were sick and the Secretary of State for Transport was in a critical condition in a hospital in his constituency. A Department of Health briefing on the virus had been released this morning which confirmed that the virus was previously unknown and predicted to be a bigger killer than the plague or the Spanish flu. All available experts in the UK had been diverted from current research to work on ways to treat it, slow down the effects or develop a cure, though they all knew this was unlikely to save those who were already sick. So far, those who had contracted it had died within 12-18 hours of the first symptoms.

To top it all, the Prime Minister, George Moore, had woken up that morning feeling under the weather. George was a cold, arrogant man. His fiery temper made his staff less loyal than they would otherwise have been and the team began succession planning that morning with a degree of enthusiasm, despite the circumstances.

Justine began pulling together a full list of female MPs, after a cursory check confirmed that only five of the twenty-one members of the cabinet were women. This reversal of a general trend to appoint more women to cabinet was entirely based on George's preferences. The five women on his team were reluctant 'tokens', more liberal than the rest of the cabinet and arguably more talented but without a real voice in the debate.

One of the Prime Ministers advisors was on the phone to the Health Secretary's office next to Justine, looking even more stressed than normal. He was a recent appointment, after the PM sacked his predecessor and was so thin that Justine often thought he might snap in two under the weight of his responsibilities.

'He's sick? What do you mean by sick? Does he have it?'
Justine pricked up her ears.

'Oh god, this is a bloody disaster. Okay. What hospital is he in? Make sure that there is security on the main entrance and try to get him transferred to St Thomas'. The DPM is there, it'll be easier to contain the story if we aren't spreading ourselves too thinly.'

He replaced the handset and looked around grimly.

'That's three cabinet ministers and twelve junior ministers so far. Two hours to COBR and I'm starting to worry that we won't have enough people around the table to run the bloody meeting. Justine, get me the Commissioner on the phone.'

The new Commissioner of the Metropolitan Police was an intelligent and ambitious woman with a razor-sharp wit. At 49 years old, Elizabeth Vinn was younger than the average incumbent which had raised a few eyebrows. Her inclusive and engaging approach was seen by many as a breath of fresh air after the last, more traditional Commissioner and even George had conceded that she was a good appointment, albeit reluctantly.

Justine held out the phone. 'The Commissioner for you.'

'Hello Commissioner. There will be a change of personnel at COBR this morning, ministers are dropping like flies. How are things your end?'

'Busy.' Elizabeth said coldly. She hadn't warmed to the new special advisor. 'We are dealing with unprecedented levels of absence across all forces. All rest days have been cancelled but that is unlikely to be sufficient. We have 36,000 female police officers across the country, just about enough to police London and too few to sustain an effective police service across England and Wales. Members of the National Police Chiefs' Council are also 'dropping like flies' as you so eloquently put it. We are exploring contingencies.'

'Talk to me in percentages. Do we need to call in the army?' His voice had developed a slightly whiny tone which Elizabeth did not respond well to.

'20%, of the workforce is off sick. You'll know already that only 11% of the total workforce are available for foot patrols on any given shift. On a normal day, that amounts to around 14,000 officers across the whole of England and Wales. Only 4,000 of those are female. Today under 11,000 officers are available and we expect that to decline as the day goes on. To answer your point about the army- my understanding is that the army is 91% male so I am not entirely clear how that would assist us. Let's discuss this at 11.'

Elizabeth replaced the handset and turned to her staff officer. 'Can you do me a favour please? Call Suzanne again, I'm worried about her.'

Elizabeth's wife Suzanne had rushed up to Leicester the night before after hearing that her father was unwell but by the time she had reached the hospital her father had already passed away. Suzanne was inconsolable on the telephone last night and Elizabeth felt terrible that she had to work when so much was going on. Suzanne said that she understood but Elizabeth knew that it would be stored away as another in a long line of important events that Elizabeth had missed because of work. The job took its toll on everyone's relationships.

In the PM's office, The Special Advisor balked as he replaced the handset. 'That woman is bloody rude.' No-one responded, their attention was focussed on one of the PM's aides who has just rushed into the room.

'The PM has collapsed. I've called an ambulance.' The special advisor put his head in his hands in despair.

The DPM died at 8.45am, 35 minutes after the PM arrived at St Thomas' Hospital. The PM's office called an emergency cabinet meeting at 9.30am. By the time the meeting convened, an hour and a half before COBR, a total of ten members of the cabinet were either sick or deceased.

1990

I'm taking my GCSE's this year. I seem to be the only one in my class still interested in studying. My friends spend their evenings with local boys and have no time for anything else. I miss them, especially now I am allowed to see them after school.

Michelle and Jennifer are my closest friends. Michelle is confident and funny, whereas Jennifer is clever but quiet, letting others take the lead. They both wear makeup and fight with their parents. Michelle calls her mum's 'old lady' which I think she got off the TV. They are interesting and they seem to look up to me, probably because I am so different to them. They talk about their bodies and famous people they fancy a lot so I haven't told them that I don't get periods because my uterus was removed. I don't talk about boys either. I don't feel like they do about them. When I see famous men on TV they might as well be aliens to me. Mummy says when you have your uterus removed the hormones that make women mad about men go away but I don't remember a time when I ever liked boys.

When I was a little girl, before that day, I had a friend called Julian but I don't remember whether he was nice or not and after what happened I didn't see him again because I didn't go back to my school. He is the only boy that I remember.

I hide all this from Michelle and Jennifer because they wouldn't understand. I haven't told them what happened to me or about Hope. I have to pretend to be someone I'm not because the truth is too awful to share. I talk to Mummy sometimes about why I am so different. She says that other girls haven't had the life I have. Lucky them.

Mummy and I argue because I want to go to youth club with Michelle and Jennifer. Mummy says that I can't go because there will be boys there and she doesn't know how I will react. She doesn't want me to get upset but I tell her that I'm not going to meet boys, I'm going so that I have something else to talk to my friends about.

I'm sixteen but Mummy still treats me like a child. I say that I am clever enough to know when I'm not safe and she surprises by saying 'okay you can go, as long as you look after yourself.'

She goes to a drawer in the kitchen and pulls out a red box with a thick black cord attached. She tells me it is a rape alarm. If a boy ever tries to touch me, I hold the box and pull the cord. She says it is really important that I keep it in my hand or in my pocket, especially if I walk home alone. I suddenly feel scared about going out, in case someone tries to take me again. I am about to tell her that I don't want to go after all but before I do she tells me to test it.

We stand in the lounge. Hope is sitting on the sofa reading her favourite book and we tell her to put her fingers in her ears.

We pull the cord and the most terrible wailing noise pierces the air.

EEEEEEEEEeeeeeeeeeeeeeeeeeeeeeeeeeeeeeeeee

It is completely unbearable. I drop the red box and put my fingers in my ears. Mummy is holding the string, groping on the floor for the red box. She fumbles to push the button at the end of the string back into the red box until finally, she manages it. The noise stops and Mummy and I look at each other and burst out laughing. Hope takes her fingers out of her ears. 'Ow. That was very loud.' She says. We laugh again. Mummy smiles at me. 'Okay?' she says. I nod. She looks more relaxed now and I feel more confident with that in my pocket.

As I turn to go and get ready, she puts her hand on my shoulder and says I should remember that if I don't feel like talking to a boy then I shouldn't feel I have to. I think that Mummy is like me. She doesn't like men either. Once, I asked her why she didn't marry someone else and she said Hope and I are quite enough to keep her busy. She works with lots of men in a solicitor's firm and so I think that if there were any nice men around she would have met one by now.

I run upstairs to call Michelle and get changed out of my school uniform. The girls have shown me pictures of the people at youth club and I know they dress up and wear makeup. I don't want to feel like the odd one out, so I pull on my favourite jeans and a t-shirt. I polish my shoes and brush my hair fifty times until it is shiny. I take Mummy's mascara and lipstick from her room and slip them into my coat pocket on the way down the stairs so I can put them on later. I am excited and nervous and I feel like a grown up for the first time.

Michelle and Jennifer call at the house to collect me. It is the first time they have been here so they want to come in and look around. I am suddenly aware of how small our house is but they don't seem to notice. They smile and are polite to Mummy, who likes them. When they see Hope they exclaim 'Look at your sister, isn't she gorgeous! I didn't know you had a sister, Jean?' They look at me, inquiringly. Mummy cuts in before I can say anything. 'Yes, this is Hope, she is four now. Come and give me a cuddle, Hope.' Hope jumps up into Mummy's arms and I feel excluded by the lie we have told. I don't want Michelle and Jennifer to see that I am bothered, so I turn away and go into the hall to get my coat.

I call from the door, 'Bye Hope, Bye, Mum.' I know it will bother Mummy that I called her 'Mum'. I want her to know that I am annoyed with her for pretending to be Hope's mum but actually I think Michelle and Jennifer would laugh if they heard me call her 'Mummy' anyway.

Michelle, Jennifer and I head out. Michelle says that we are going to meet some boys they know at the youth club, which is near the beach. I didn't know we were going to meet boys and I start to worry. What if they are horrible? What if they hate me? What if something bad happens? It is a ten-minute walk and Michelle doesn't stop talking about them. She likes

Chris who is tall with blonde hair and blue eyes and is really fit because he plays rugby for his school. His friends John and Jason are twins and are both shorter than Chris but just as handsome.

The rape alarm is in my pocket and I hold it tightly, I don't know what to expect, I am nervous but also curious. I only ever see boys in passing when I go to the doctors, the dentists or to the shops but I have seen them on TV in programmes like 'Coronation Street' and 'Grange Hill'. TV isn't real life though. Mummy once told me that boys are sometimes nice but that you need to be 'on your guard'. I know that I need to be alert once we get there, keep hold of the alarm and remember not to give much away. I don't know how I will ever relax if I have to remember all these things to keep myself safe.

Michelle asks me if I have ever kissed a boy. I don't know what to say, I don't want to say that I haven't but I don't lie, I just say 'Erm, I haven't really met anyone I like lately.'

Jennifer asks who I like off the TV. I say that I haven't ever thought about it but that seems to set her off and she scoffs 'Come on, you must have thought about it, what about Jordan Knight from New Kids on the Block? You must like him, everyone does.'

I know who Jordan Knight is but I don't have any feelings for him and I don't like the music at all. I'm a bit lost, I have always managed to sit these conversations out and it makes me wonder whether they took away all the things that made me a girl when they took away my uterus. Maybe the reason I feel so different is because I'm actually nothing at all. I just nod and I must have done the right thing because she doesn't ask me any more questions. As we get closer I can see a small group of boys waiting outside. 'There they are! God Chris is lovely. Look at him!'

I look at the boy she points at. He is the tallest in the group, with blonde hair and piercing blue eyes. His eyes make him seem cold and I can't see why she likes him. I look at the other two boys who are shorter with dark hair and so alike that I can't see a thing to help me tell them apart. The three boys smile and wave and I think they look like slathering wolves. There is a ball of fear in the pit of my stomach and I know it was a mistake to come. When we get to them we are engulfed in greetings and fuss. They know each other well and I feel like an alien so I hover at the side of the group until Chris turns to me and says;

'What's your name?'

'Jean, my name is Jean.' My mouth is really dry and I have to swallow several times after I speak. I feel sick and all I want to do is go home. He smiles and says 'Hi Jeanie. Your name is like that old TV programme, you know, I dream of Jeannie?'

I wonder if he misheard, or if he is just being mean. Only Mummy and Hope call me Jeanie and I don't think that I react very well when he uses my nickname.

'No. Not Jeanie, it's Jean.' I know that my voice sounds cold but I can't help it. His eyebrows shoot up in surprise and he shrugs. 'Jean. Okay, sorry. How come you haven't been here before?' He gestures to me to follow him inside. I don't understand why he is still talking to me. My heart is pounding and I'm worried that he is going to do something to embarrass me, so I wait for Michelle and Jennifer and follow them inside. As I do, I catch a look that passes between Michelle and Jennifer. They don't like him talking to me either. Maybe they are being protective but it didn't seem like that sort of look.

We sit in a big lounge with lots of sofas. It is quite a dark room, though all the lights are on. The walls are covered in purple swirly wallpaper and the floor is black and quite sticky under foot. There are two pool tables at the end of the room and a dance floor off to the right. Two groups of boys are playing pool and a group of girls are standing on the dance floor talking to a boy who Jennifer says is the DJ. There is also a door to a patio area out the back but it is quite cold so we stay inside. Everyone looks happy to be there but I'm not happy. I feel sick and the room is too small. I feel like the walls are closing in on me and I don't like that the room is so dark. I need to get out.

I go to get a can of coke from the machine in the corner. I just need a minute. I take big deep breaths and remember that Mummy said I don't have to talk to them if I don't want to. The can falls into the tray with a clatter, making me jump. I take a few sips to wet the inside of my mouth, then go back to the sofas. There is no space next to Michelle or Jennifer, the only space is next to Chris and as I walk up he pats the sofa next to him. I sit as far away from him as I can get but there is hardly any space and when I move I can feel his leg resting against mine. I get very hot and uncomfortable and I feel like I shouldn't be here. I can't focus on anything else except that I am in danger.

Mummy says that boys have a way of distracting girls so much that they can't focus on the important things and she is right because though Michelle and Jennifer are talking, I can't hear what they are saying. All I can hear is a rush of blood in my ears. Their voices seem far away and I feel like I might faint. I take big gulps of the coke but I can still feel my face getting hotter and hotter, so I stand up and say 'I'm just going to the bathroom.'

I lock the bathroom door and try to calm down. I might feel better if I blended in more so I take out Mummy's makeup and but my hands are shaking and it takes me a while to apply it. When I'm done I look at myself in the mirror, I look more like Michelle and Jennifer now. I take a few breaths and try to relax a little. I don't know why I am so anxious.

When I go back, Michelle and Jennifer are up at the pool table with the boys, playing a game. I don't think they noticed that I was gone but Chris looks up as I walk towards them.

'Where did you go?' I catch another quick look that passes between Michelle and Jennifer. I feel paranoid now, like everyone has had a conversation about me while I was gone. I want to leave more than anything but it is the coward's way out so I pretend I am Michelle. I smile brightly and say 'I just went to the loo. Who is playing who?'

Chris is playing Michelle and everyone else is standing around watching them. I watch the game but it is quite boring, all they do is drink pop, play pool and talk about boring things like a film they watched or a rugby game. The girls ignore me and fawn over the boys so I am left to fend for myself.

I think about Mummy. I don't think she would like any of the boys, she would see Chris's eyes and decide straight away that he was not very nice. I wonder why Michelle likes him so much. They don't have a lot to talk about.

When the game finishes we all sit back on the sofa, this time I make sure I don't leave a seat free and Chris ends up on the sofa opposite me. This is actually worse as when I look up I realise that he is staring right at me.

He leans forward

'Do you have a boyfriend, Jeanie?' I feel like he is using my nickname to get a reaction from me, so I ignore it.

'No.' John and Jason are talking to Michelle and Jennifer, no-one is paying any attention to us. I don't want to talk to him but he leans further forward until he is almost touching me.

'What do you usually do in the evenings when we are here?'

'Study mostly' I sit as far back as I and look away so he knows I don't want to talk to him. He looks at me like I'm doing something weird and then he asks me what is wrong. I don't know what to say so I just shrug at him.

'Is it because you don't know me?' I shrug again. I don't know what to say. The way he looks at me is really annoying and I just want him to leave me alone. I realise that he looks at me the way men do on TV when they love someone and I don't know what I did to make him feel like that.

I turn to the others and say loudly 'I'm going now.' Before they can say anything, I stand up, wave and start for the door. Chris jumps up. 'You can't walk on your own, I'll walk you back.' He grabs his coat and follows me out. I look back at Michelle and Jennifer, hoping they will call him back and I see Michelle's face. She is really angry with me. I worry they might stop talking to me if Chris keeps this up so I turn around and say 'I don't want you to walk me home. I'm fine, go back to the others.' I turn around and leave before he can reply and though I don't look back at him I can hear that isn't following.

I walk quickly down the road. It is quiet at night and I hear my footsteps like gunshots on the pavement. Although I am calmer now, I am still not comfortable because I don't usually walk around alone at night, so I walk quickly, keep my head down and hope that no-one notices me. After a while I realise I can hear another set of footsteps behind me. It sounds they are running because the footsteps are fast and getting louder. I put my hand in my pocket to grab the rape alarm. My heart is pounding in my chest now and I feel like running but if I do I'll look scared, so I just walk faster. The footsteps are coming closer and closer and I grip the alarm and wind my fingers around the cord, really to pull it. A hand touches my shoulder and I jump and pull out the cord with a tug.

EEEEEEEEEEEEEE!

The noise almost knocks me off my feet. It is even louder than the test in the house. My attacker shouts 'Turn it off, you're bloody deafening me!!' I spin around and realise that my attacker is Chris and he has his hands over his ears and a shocked look on his face. I back away and fumble for the cord and the alarm, both buried deep in my pocket. I pull them out and run to a street lamp so that I can see, then push the clip back in like I saw Mummy do earlier. The noise stops immediately but my ears keep ringing and the silence is almost more deafening than the noise.

I am so angry. I turn to Chris and scream 'WHAT THE HELL DO YOU THINK YOU ARE DOING?'

We are outside a house and I see the curtain twitch as some one looks out at us. Chris is standing a few feet away from me and he waves awkwardly at the person standing in the window, then looks at me.

'I'm really sorry, I didn't mean to frighten you, I just want to… to talk to you. What was that?'

'It was…my mum gave me a rape alarm.' Chris immediately takes two steps back.

'You thought I was going to attack you? I wasn't...' Chris stands with his hand on his hip. He runs the fingers of his other hand through his hair. 'God, I just didn't think you should walk home on your own.'

My heart is pounding and I shout, still a little too loudly 'DIDN'T YOUR MUM TEACH YOU NOT TO FOLLOW GIRLS DOWN DARK STREETS?'

'I'm sorry.' He holds his hands up helplessly. 'I really didn't want to scare you. I assumed you heard me coming. Look, I'll go, okay?'

But he doesn't, he hovers there, looking awkward. I look at him in the light of the street lamp and realise that he is scared. HE is frightened of ME. Probably more frightened than I am, though I don't know why. I'm not strong, all I have is a loud alarm. If he wanted to he could still hurt me. I stare at him. 'What do you want?'

'He sighs and sits down on the curb. 'I just wanted to talk to you. You seem different to the other girls.'

'I am different.' He has a face you can't forget, but I don't want to talk to him, though I am curious about why he is so interested in me. I haven't given him any reason to be, I was cold and rude to him when I did speak, which wasn't much. Now I think I could make him cry with one word and it feels...good. Weird but good. I am in control and I can hurt him, on the inside.

I say to him, 'You don't get the hint, do you? I. DON'T. LIKE. YOU. I don't understand why my friends like you because I think you are boring. Go back to the Jennifer and Michelle if you want attention. You won't get it here.'

When I say horrible things to him, his face changes. His smile drops off his face, his cheeks go red, his eyes go red and I think for a moment that he might cry. He looks quickly down at the floor and takes a deep breath, then shrugs and stands up. I don't think he's used to girls turning him down and so I wait to see what he will do next. He looks at me for a moment, then he says 'Maybe I got you wrong. See you around, Jean'. He walks away quickly and I watch him go. I don't know why but I have tears running down my face when I turn back towards home.

* * *

I meet Michelle and Jennifer to walk to school. I am desperate to know what happened after I left, whether Chris went back to the youth club or went straight home. I want know what he thinks about what happened.

Michelle is glowing with excitement and has happiness written all over her face so I ask her what happened to make her so happy. She says Chris came back to youth club and asked her straight out on a date. Her eyes are shining. I know that this is what she has been hoping for but I feel instant rage which I have to press down inside me so that it doesn't spill out.

I think about what I can do. I look at Michelle, rambling on about how great Chris is. She is stupid about boys, they have complete control over whether she is happy or not, she doesn't have a brain of her own. If I am going to be her friend then I need to teach her to protect herself, to wipe the smile off her face. She needs to hate him.

I stop walking and Michelle and Jennifer turn around. 'What's wrong, Jean?'

I catch Jennifer's eye and then I answer Michelle. 'I don't think Chris is a nice person, Michelle. Maybe you should turn him down, he isn't what you think he is.' Jennifer stays quiet. Michelle looks embarrassed then she laughs.

'God, Jean are you jealous because you didn't get hold of him?' She never usually challenges me and Jennifer turns back to me, watching the discussion like she is watching tennis. I have to persuade them both and it might take tears. I press my eyes closed and when I open them I am crying. Michelle stops smiling.

'What's wrong? Jean? I'm sorry, I didn't mean to make you cry. Are you okay?' She puts her hand on my shoulder.

'I'm okay. I just really don't think you should see him again.'
'Why not?' she demands petulantly and drops her arm to her side. 'You've only met him once, Jennifer and I have known him for ages and he has always been lovely.' She scowls at me and looks at Jennifer for reassurance. Jennifer stays quiet and looks at me. I am taking a bit of a chance but I know from Jennifer's face that I am halfway there. I take out a tissue from my bag and blow my nose loudly.

'I'm sorry. I wouldn't have said anything but I'm worried for you.' I try to act as if it is painful to talk. 'He…tried to kiss me. He didn't walk me home, I asked him not to but when I was walking he ran up behind me and grabbed me. I pushed him away and said no because I don't like him like that and I knew that you really like him… but then he got angry… he grabbed me and…' I cover my face with my hands and cry loudly 'tried to force himself on me… I'm so sorry Michelle…'

Jennifer puts her hand on my shoulder and I see in her face that she believes me. 'How did you stop him? I mean did he…?'

'No, nothing like that…I had a rape alarm in my pocket and I set it off.' I look Michelle straight in the eye. 'If you don't believe me then knock doors on the road and ask. Someone came to the window because they heard the alarm. They saw everything. I'm sorry, Michelle, I know you liked him.'

Michelle is looking at me and Jennifer, who has been watching me the whole time. Jennifer puts her arms round me.

'God, Jean, how awful for you. Are you okay? What can I do?' I hug her back.

'I'm okay, honestly. He didn't hurt me and I don't want to take it any further, I just want to forget about it. Hopefully I won't see him again.'

We both look at Michelle. I watch her as she weighs up her options, she looks at both of us. Then her face sets into a decision. She walks over and puts her arms around both of us.

'I'm sorry Jean, I didn't mean to suggest you were lying. I trust you guys way more than I ever would a boy. What a snake. I'll tell him I have changed my mind.'

Sometimes you have to lie to protect people. Chris is no different to all the other men out there. They think they have the right to take whatever they want from us. Some of them do it by turning on the charm but others will hurt us and then take it anyway. Some hurt us on the inside, like my Dad and some hurt us on the outside, like the men who hurt me. I saved Michelle from being hurt and I am proud of that.

2025

Report from Porton Down

We have ruled out all known viruses. This is an entirely new, lethal pathogen, engineered to target men, though some females may also exhibit brief, flu-like symptoms. Unlike males, females seem to be able to build a vastly increased antiviral response, which may explain why there have been no female fatalities to date.

The virus is able to survive long periods in chemically treated water, which is how we believe it has been transmitted. It has a durable outer shell that enables it to survive in water and multiply quickly. As a pathogen, it can survive longer in cooler temperatures.

Moving on to the projected rate of infection, we have the following factual data to draw from. The virus has been present in all water samples tested so far, from 300 reservoirs. We have mapped the location of reported cases over the past twenty-four hours and know that exposure to the virus is widespread, covering most of Great Britain. Young boys under the age of ten appear to have a developed immunity.

From this and from the limited data we have on the rapidity of its effects, we can conclude that as many as 80-90% of males may have been exposed to the virus over the past week, assuming that there are some men who have not ingested contaminated water. The virus is likely to prove fatal to all exposed males within seven to ten days.'

1990

Hope is four and is starting school. I find this difficult as she is my baby and I can't protect her if I'm not with her. I really want to home school her but Mummy says that it would be a mistake, she needs to make friends and be around children her own age. I am quite anxious about it and Mummy and I talk about it a lot. In the end, we agree to send her to an all-girls school. We research the girls schools in the neighbour-hood until we find one. We have to move to a new house to make sure Hope can go there. Our new house is nice but our old house was nicer and it takes us a while to settle in. I have to move away from my friends but that doesn't matter to me as much as keeping Hope safe. I don't see Michelle and Jennifer much now that they are at a different college and I can make new friends.

I drop Hope at school every day on my way to college. She skips and bounces along with her tiny hand in mine. She is such a beautiful child, her hair is darker than mine, thick and luscious, with a beautiful natural wave. Her creation was ugly and evil, yet you could not wish for a more kind and placid child. She is gentle and thoughtful, a light in my dark mind. I have accepted that I cannot have any more children which makes Hope even more special. I want to be important in this world so that she will look up to me and follow in my foot-steps. On the way to school we play games, like eye-spy, or the memory game and I sometimes talk to her about what I want the world to look like. Sometimes, I even forget about the dan-gers on the street, just for a second.

After I drop her off, I watch her join her little girl friends and go into her classroom through a door right off the playground. I wait until the bell rings and the teachers lock the gates before I go because I want to be sure that she's safe. Once I know that no-one can get into the school I go to college. I am usually late but my teacher knows that I have to drop Hope off so that Mummy can work.

* * *

Making girlfriends at College is even easier for me than it was at school. I'm studying biology, chemistry, politics and women's studies, which everyone says is an odd combination. In politics, the lecturer reads out my answer in front of the whole group and the class look at me with respect. At school, they wouldn't have looked at me like that. I have been here a term now and I am the cleverest person in the year. Being clever here isn't something that people hide like they do at school.

The lecture ends and as I walk out towards the canteen a girl taps my shoulder.

'Hi, I'm Lexi. I'm in your politics class?'

'Hi, nice to meet you, I'm Jean.'

'I know who you are. We all do. You are so good at this stuff! I was wondering... well would you study with me? I could do with a study partner, I'm struggling a bit.'

'I'd love to study with you.'

I like to pass on my knowledge. It makes me feel like I am contributing more to the world. We walk to the lunch hall and sit together while we eat. She is a nice person and seems very kind but not confident at all. She asks me a lot of questions about myself and I find out a bit about her. She lives near our house, she doesn't know many people here and she seems scared of everything.

I tell her that I am quite shy but pretend not to be because being shy doesn't get you anywhere. I'm not really shy but she is and to get to know someone quickly you have to find something in common. By the end of lunch, we are friends. She says that I am beautiful and clever which is quite rare and that I understand her more than anyone else she has ever met. I'm not sure it is helpful to be beautiful but it is definitely helpful to be clever.

The few girls in my science classes want to be doctors, surgeons or chemists. None of them want to be a research scientist and when I tell them about my ambitions they look at me as if I have already made it. The boys in my classes try and talk to me but I am very good at brushing them off and so they learn to avoid me. One boy keeps asking me out and when I tell him I don't find him at attractive or interesting he calls me a 'dyke'. Quite a lot of the boys now think that I am a lesbian. I am happy for them to believe that if it means they will leave me alone.

* * *

I have lots of friends here but I still find it hard to understand them. They are silly about boys, as if they have been brainwashed into believing that all boys are interesting and attractive. None of them see how dangerous they are. Boys find it easy to pick up a girl, use them and then cast them aside when they are done having sex with them. My girlfriends don't learn from their mistakes either. For example, Lexi tells me that she loves a boy called Steve who goes to college here. She talks about their relationship and it is clear that she followed him to this College even it wasn't her first choice. She has forgiven him many times, even though he seems cruel. He cheats on her with other girls and then tells her he doesn't love her but even after everything he has put her through she still loves him. Being a friend to her is difficult. I watch her stumble back to him and I tell her over and over to forget him and be happy in her own skin but she doesn't want to listen. It makes me so angry and protective, I don't like to see her hurt. I take matters into my own hands by spreading a rumour that he has a sexually transmitted disease. The girls at College give him a wide berth, the boys tease him about it and his grades start to slip. His parents move him to a new college and the girls in our classes tell Lexi that she had a lucky escape. It was almost too easy but I congratulate myself on a job well done.

Other girls in my classes start to ask my advice and some of them even do what I tell them to. Suddenly I am the person to go to for advice about boys and the girls gravitate towards me. It is a triumph but so many of them have trouble with boys that I wonder why they bother. It seems like a lot of energy for no reward. My friends tell me that I am amazing, they say I have real strength of character and focus. More and more they realise that they deserve better. Women are superior to men in almost every way and deserve respect and reverence, not the disdain that these boys show. I tell my new friends that I don't think boys have anything to offer me and that it is clear that they bring nothing but trouble, heartache and pain.

In my politics class I write about female oppression. Even now we are denied the opportunity to demonstrate our higher intellect. I have lots of examples of amazing women and talk about them in depth. After the class, a few of the girls approach me to ask me if I will help them form a debating group to discuss women's rights. I love the idea of a group of women speaking out about their beliefs and capabilities. Men have used their power to destroy the planet and degrade women and it is time that we show them how wrong they are.

The key is that I don't give an opinion without having examples to back it up, this unnerves even my lecturers but it is the scientist in me. It means that the other girls listen to me and ask me to guide them. I want to change the world and I think that I could make a real difference. I often think about what a wonderful world it would be if women were truly in charge.

2025

Deborah Walsh, Department of Health,
8.30am

Deborah Walsh sat in her office opposite a civil servant called Kirsty. Kirsty was the only person from her unit to make it into the office and she was nervous. She had only briefed a minister once, accompanied by her deputy director but today he was in hospital and the phone hadn't stopped ringing as her other team mates called in sick. She had struggled to gather the information the newly promoted minister had asked for and wasn't entirely sure it was right. However, with no-one around to clear it she decided that honesty was the best policy.

'Good morning Minister…' Kirsty inwardly cursed as her voice shook.

'Please call me Deborah.' The minister smiled and Kirsty thought she looked almost human which Kirsty thought was odd. The whole meeting was unconventional but the day was fast becoming surreal.

'Um, okay.'

'What's your name?'

'It's Kirsty.'

'Okay Kirsty. Relax, it's just us, just tell me as much as you can and let me know if you aren't sure about anything, okay?'

'Okay.' Kirsty took a deep breath and smiled at the minister. She was relatively new to the civil service and didn't really support the current government's policies but couldn't help liking Deborah.

Deborah looked down at the handover note provided by her office that morning. 'I don't have any current information on bed capacity in hospitals. What can you tell me?'

'Most hospitals exceeded their official bed capacity by 9.30am yesterday. The number of infected people admitted yesterday presented serious challenges for hospital administrators. Usually such patients would be isolated in secure facilities, however this protocol was abandoned early yesterday morning, when the scale of the problem became clear. All hospitals have activated contingency plans, designating whole hospitals as secure infection centres, cancelling scheduled appointments and clearing wards of non-critical patients. Yesterday afternoon, when these measures proved insufficient, infection centres were established in town halls and other community buildings. The speed of mobilisation was impressive but new centres are filling up too quickly and staff shortages are compounding the issue. The use of whole hospital infection centres is only a good tactical solution for the next 24 -48 hours and the next step is to impose quarantines in residences.'

Deborah had sat forward in her chair and was staring intently at Kirsty. 'Do you have any information on how hospitals are treating the virus?'

'Hospitals are administering painkillers and antibiotics or anti-viral medication but there is no evidence that it is having any effect and the focus is purely on pain relief. Hospitals describe a consistent pattern, with those infected falling unconscious and slipping into a coma. They lose all respiratory function within hours of first infection. This is followed by the rapid failure of all organs which ultimately leads to death within approximately 16-20 hours. The few people who have regained consciousness complain of weakness, lethargy, pain in their joints and muscles, headaches and shortness of breath.'

Deborah sighed. 'Okay Kirsty, thank you. That has been really helpful. Did you manage to pull all of that into a briefing for me to take to my next meeting?

Kirsty handed the minister a paper. 'Here is it, Ma'am... I mean, Deborah.'

Deborah looked at Kirsty gratefully. 'Quick work, thanks Kirsty.'

Kirsty closed the door behind her and walked quickly away. Since there was no-one to ask, she made an executive decision to collect her bag and work from home for the rest of the day. Deborah watched her go through the window, then turned to gather together the papers ready for the COBR meeting.

1992

Mummy speaks to my College tutor on the phone. She is talking about my essay on the male subjugation of women. I know I got an A and the teacher commented that it was very well argued.

Mummy puts down the phone and turns to me crossly. She says that my teacher thinks I hate men and wants to know if there is anything she needs to be aware of. I tell Mummy that there are lots of very good reasons to dislike men and start to list them. She interrupts me when I talk about the things that happened to me when I was eleven and says I need an outlet for my rage. She thinks that my views on men are based on narrow experiences and that I should get to know boys at college. I say that my girlfriends have all been badly treated by the boys at college and I have absolutely no intention of leaving myself open to abuse. What's more, she is a hypocrite because she has kept men away from us for years. She says that she doesn't agree with me at all and that she only kept men away because she knew they made me scared. I laugh at her. I challenge her to find a nice, kind, generous boy since she thinks that there are so many in the world. She hasn't even managed to find one for herself yet, which I think proves how difficult it is.

She is full of contradictions which I start to list. For example, she says I shouldn't assume every man is evil, just because I have come across some that are but when Hope asks to go out alone she says that the world isn't safe for young girls. I feel like she doesn't know what she believes which annoys me. I couldn't be clearer. I get so angry I just rip into her and go to my room before she can trip herself up anymore. She shouts up after me 'God Jean, you are bloody hard work'.

I don't think I am hard work at all. I am very thoughtful, I often make Mummy breakfast in bed because I know she works hard and take Hope out to give her time to herself. I don't know what more she expects of me. Hope comes to see me and gives me a cuddle. She hates it when we fight. I tell her that Mummy should just decide what she believes and then stick to it.

2025

Emergency cabinet meeting, 9.30am

Everyone around the table looked up as the Home Secretary walked in to the meeting room. Well-respected across the party lines, they were looking to him for reassurance. Usually his presence alone would give everyone more confidence but today he was ashen-faced, less polished than usual and appeared almost reluctant to sit down. A hush descended on the group as they watched him take his seat. When he spoke again, his voice betrayed his anxiety.

'You will all have heard the sad news about the Deputy PM, who passed away this morning. He is a great loss and was a good friend to me personally.' His voice cracked as he continued;

'You may not know that the PM has been taken to hospital with the same symptoms.'

A number of people gasped as the Home Secretary continued;

'This is not public knowledge, so please do not mention it to any reporters. The police are reporting widespread panic and this news will only make things worse. We need to remain focussed. Our priorities are containing the virus, maintaining essential services and keeping the public calm.'

He paused and looked around the room. Claire followed his gaze. Everyone was shaken, with some on the brink of tears. The Home Secretary snapped harshly;

'You need to pull yourselves together. The public need leadership, if we fall apart there will be anarchy.'

The minister for international trade snorted bitterly. 'We can't do anything to stop this! I don't even know why I'm here. This is a fucking waste of my time.' He stood up and walked out. Claire looked at her colleague Karen and raised her eyebrows. A number of people looking longingly after him, as if on the brink of following. The Home Secretary looked on, sternly.

'Anyone else?' The room was so quiet, you could have heard a pin drop.

'Look, I'd rather be anywhere but here right now, but if we all leave then everything falls apart.' He sighed miserably. 'Now, as a starting point we should dust off departmental disaster recovery plans, I'd like to see them by midday.'

Claire realised she was holding her breath and let it out shakily as the Home Secretary continued, 'Only men have been infected but lots of service areas are male dominated, which will leave us particularly vulnerable. We need to know where were might have problems and pull together a list of female experts in those fields as soon as possible.'

He looked around the group again and sighed once more as one of them surreptitiously brushed a tear away from his eyes and another rummaged through his bag for a folded handkerchief, which he used to wipe his nose.

The Home Secretary's voice softened a little 'Look, I know some of you are here despite the loss of friends and relatives yesterday, for which we are all very grateful. Let's just try and get through today. Another meeting will be scheduled for tomorrow. Female nominees can attend on your behalf if you are unable to because... um...well. You may already know that the Health Secretary was hospitalised late last night. The PMs office have recommended that Deborah Walsh step up to Secretary of State. She is a safe pair of hands and is currently getting herself up to speed ready for COBR later on. Does anyone have any comments or questions?'

Claire Flint spoke first.

'Do we have any news on the source of the virus?'

'There have been few developments on that front I'm afraid. All we can surmise is that it was released intentionally in multiple locations and is only fatal to men. Given how fast it has spread, we think it has been released in large quantities, which suggests either an airborne or mainstream food or water source. My understanding is that we have no intelligence about the source of the outbreak. '

The Foreign Secretary spoke next, his voice shaking a little. 'As you know, a large number of men attempted to storm a ship due to leave Southampton late last night and thousands of people tried to purchase flights out of the country. We contained last night's unrest but we need to announce border closures as soon as possible. Our allies are anxious and I have had numerous calls from foreign leaders asking for information.'

'Yes, we are briefing the press within the hour. For the benefit of others, I ordered the closure of our borders late last night, shortly after the first incident. Full briefings will be sent to heads of state after the COBR meeting this morning so those calls will be more informed from now on. Anything else? Alright then. Let's get to work.'

As everyone stood to leave, the Home Secretary seemed to sway slightly. He put his hand on the table to steady himself and mumbled, 'I don't feel too good actually'.

Then he legs seemed to crumple under him and he fell forward onto the long conference table in front of them. Claire, who was sitting closest to him grabbed his arm and helped him into his chair while the others looked on in horror. He looked at her helplessly and then his eyes rolled back in his head and he passed out.

'Someone call an ambulance!' cried Claire.

She removed his tie and loosened his collar as one of the aides ran out of the room to call for an ambulance. The minister sat nearest the door mumbled 'fuck this' and made for the door, the rest of the men jumped out of their chairs as if burnt and shrank back against the wall, as far away from the Home Secretary as possible, fear very visible in their faces.

'He doesn't look well enough to wait for an ambulance.' Karen Tonge muttered to Claire, as the Home Secretary began to gasp for breath.

Karen was the Minister for Communities and Local Government. Quieter than Claire but no less intelligent or capable, they had become close over the years and confided in each other regularly, usually over a few glasses of wine.

Claire glanced across at her.

'You're right.' She called to an aide.

'Excuse me... can one of the drivers take him? It will be quicker than waiting for an ambulance.'

'Yes, of course, I'll call them now.'

She ran down the corridor towards the exit while Claire and Karen tried to make the Home Secretary more comfortable, moving him off the chair and into the recovery position. Once they had done all they could they sat back onto the chairs behind them and looked at each other.

'For heaven's sake, look at them.' Claire said bitterly, nodding to the men clustered at the far end of the room.

'They're scared.' Karen's tone was more sympathetic. 'The virus is spreading faster than anticipated and we will run out of space in the morgues by lunchtime. Even our contingency plans are based on something far less catastrophic. Everyone is panicking and to be honest, so am I.' Her voice rose as she spoke until it reached a pitch that sounded unnatural and Claire glanced at her quickly and with some alarm before replying.

'We are all scared but aren't we supposed to be leaders?'

The men at the end of the room were whispering urgently and one of them called to Claire 'When are they coming for him? Every second we stand in this room with him puts us at risk. Fucking move him into the hall.'

Appalled, Claire stood up and was about to confront the speaker when the door opened and the PMs driver wheeled in a tired and dusty wheelchair.

'I'll take the Home Secretary to hospital. Can someone help me lift him onto the wheelchair?'

Claire and Karen looked towards the cluster of men, none of whom made any move to help.

'Don't bother asking them.' Claire snapped. Roland Bertram, the Defence Secretary rounded on Claire. 'You might sneer it isn't appropriate for us to help. The Cabinet is thin on the ground as it is.' There were several nods of agreement. None of them moved.

Claire had precious little time for Roland, who was dismissive and patronising towards his female colleagues. She'd met his wife at a conservative function and watched Roland order food and answer questions for his wife all evening. Claire had been unable to get to know her at all and formed an impression from Roland that she didn't work. She later found out that his wife owned her own successful business and her opinion of Roland had sunk through the floor.

Silently shaking her head, Claire leant over the Home Secretary and prepared to lift him. Karen stood up to help and between them and the driver, they manoeuvred the Home Secretary onto the wheelchair, then followed the driver out of the room. At the door, Claire rounded on them. 'Shame on you. He is your friend. Shame on you all.'

They walked down the corridor. Karen turned to Claire, her eyebrows raised. Claire shook her head. 'I know I shouldn't have, but I really can't abide cowardice. I'm so disappointed in them. How can they talk about leading the country through a crisis when they won't put themselves in harm's way for a friend?'

'Hmm, it's easy to judge but can you imagine how terrifying it must be to know you could die today? They may have said goodbye to their families this morning for the last time. I'm only surprised they made it to work at all.'

'True, I suppose.' Said Claire, grudgingly. They reached the car and helped the Home Secretary into the back. 'Thank you, ministers', said the driver. 'You're welcome, drive carefully' replied Claire.

Claire and Karen walked back through the doors of the cabinet office. They had twenty minutes until the COBR meeting and neither of them wanted to go back to their colleagues so they ducked into a nearby office and closed the door

'We aren't equipped to deal with this. Local councils are already buckling under the weight of the dead.' Karen sat down at one of the desks.

Claire nodded. 'I know. Over thirty thousand inmates have died or are dying and a prison officer was beaten to death yesterday after being overwhelmed by angry prisoners. I can't risk transporting sick inmates to hospital because of the security risks and none of the local hospitals have the capacity to help even if we put the protocol to one side. Prison officers are calling in sick by the dozen and we have had to resort to keeping inmates in their cells. I'm sending in medics but it all feels morally wrong to me. Their lives aren't worth any less than ours.'

Karen shook her head. 'It just feels like there is nothing we can do.' Claire grimaced. 'There isn't.' She hesitatingly asked 'Have you lost anyone close yet Karen?'

'No, my husband is abroad which is a huge relief. My girls are staying with Mum while I'm here. I'm most worried about my dad, he's so frail anyway and he lives on his own. My sister is with him but he is stubborn and he won't accept help at the best of times, so I can't imagine he is making it easy for her. I just wish I could be there as well. How about you?'

'My ex-husband is in hospital. He hasn't regained consciousness and the doctors don't expect him to live much longer.' My son seems fine but he is only young, he is with my mum. My brother is okay so far. Selfishly, I want to send them all away but there isn't anywhere safe to send them.'

Karen sighed. 'it's unimaginable, the position we find ourselves in. I don't feel I have the space to think about the people I could lose.' She glanced at her watch. 'It's time, shall we go in?'

They headed off towards the Cabinet Office Briefing Room for the meeting.

1992

I get four A-grades at A-level which means I can go to any university I want. Mummy is so proud. She didn't work as hard as me at school and college so she couldn't go to university. It's a shame because she is clever, she just doesn't know as much as me. I try to persuade her to go to university as a mature student but she says that she is too old and has to carry on working so that I can afford to go.

I decide to live at home and go to Sussex University to study politics and women's studies. Making the choice is hard as I love biology and chemistry but if I want to change the world I can't do it from a lab in London. There are lots of reasons to stay at home but the main one is Hope, I don't want to leave her and Mummy alone. Hope needs me even more than Mummy does. I think Mummy is pleased with my decision because she worries about my living alone in halls of residence.

Hope is only six but she knows how hard I have worked and is happy too, we have a little party with a big chocolate cake and Mummy lets me have a glass of wine for the first time. I don't like it. It tastes quite bitter and it makes me feel out of control and dizzy. I like to know that when I walk, my feet are going to land where I expect them to and the words that come out of my mouth will make sense. Hope is desperate to try it but I say no.

Mummy is on her third glass of wine and is quite drunk. We have eaten our cake and talked about my future and I think she seems happier than usual but then she is crying and I realise that she isn't happy after all.

She doesn't explain why she is crying very well. She says it is because I am 'growing up and becoming a woman' but I can't quite work out why that would make her upset. She says I have 'exceeded her expectations' and that I am 'the most single minded, motivated person' she knows, that no-one could have predicted that I would turn out as I have, given my past and that I am brave and fierce and she wishes she was like me. She doesn't know where I get it from because she isn't brave and my Dad was the weakest person she knew. She says that if what happened to me had happened to my Dad he probably would have just died right there.

Hope looks up when Mummy mentions my Dad and I worry that Mummy is talking about things we don't discuss with Hope. I don't want her to know what happened to me before she was born. I think if Hope ever found out how she was made she might decide she should never have been born, when she is actually the one thing in my life that isn't sad or ugly. Hope makes me happy and I worry that Mummy is going to accidentally ruin everything so I shout at her to stop it and say that she should just go to bed. Mummy stumbles off upstairs and Hope and I sit in the kitchen. I let her eat an extra slice of cake and then we read a book together. She is so clever, she can already read quite well. I think she must take after me.

While we are sitting there, eating our cake, Hope asks me why neither of us have a Dad. I don't know what to say so I stall by asking her why she wants to know. She says that all the girls at school have Dad's and that she left out.

I start with the only thing I can tell the truth about and tell her that I had a father when I was very young but then he went away to live with another woman and have babies with her. She asks why he didn't stay and I say 'I'm not really sure but for a long time I thought that he left because I did something wrong and it made me sad'.

She says in a small, sad voice 'I'm sorry that you were sad, Mummy' and that makes me feel like I am going to cry. I take a big deep breath and give her a big cuddle. I tell her that we are better off without him because he didn't deserve a family like us.

She sits for a while, picking the crumbs off her plate and popping them in her mouth. Just when I think she has forgotten about it she looks me right in the eye and says. 'Was he my Dad too?'

'No.' I tell her, then I lie. 'Your Dad died long before you were born and I don't remember much about him at all.'

She looks at me with wide, innocent eyes and asks if she looks like him. I can't help feeling horror at the thought of it and I shake my head a bit too quickly, then say 'We are both really lucky not to have a daddy because it is really unusual to have a strong family like ours. Mummy and I will always be here for you no matter what happens.'

After I put Hope to bed I tell Mummy what happened and make her promise to stick to my story. She nods but warns 'It was all over the newspapers at the time and there are court records. If she was curious and determined she could find out.' I hope that never happens.

2025

Head Office, National Grid
Extract from a situation report

Though systems are increasingly automated, to keep utilities running requires constant maintenance.
It is worthy of note that 24% of staff across the industry are female.
15% of the national workforce called in sick over the last 24 hours, many of whom are key personnel.
We have begun training female staff across the industry to perform maintenance functions but basic training will only go so far.
If there was a major failure, only a team of experienced engineers could get the system up and running again. There are only five female engineers across the UK.
Over the coming weeks, if the infection spreads as predicted we can expect frequent power cuts and potentially complete power failure...

1994

Now that I am in my final year at university I start to think about my future. I excel in the debating society and most people assume that I will go straight into politics when I leave university but I struggle to pick a political party to align myself to. Our politicians are incapable of thinking outside the box, confined to 'party lines'. This is the reason why politics is so universally hated. Having individual thought is not encouraged in politics. Political parties take a talented individual with new ideas and squish and mould them into a clone who parrots party opinion. I can't let that happen to me, I have ideas. I believe that the only thing stopping us from banning the CFC gases that are destroying the ozone is mans arrogance. The inequality that constrains us is there because our leaders want it to be. The way children are taught at school pushes girls into 'pink jobs' and boys into 'blue jobs.' There are so many things that need to change I don't know quite where to start.

I am becoming bored by the lack of challenge at university and frustrated that the system teaches us only what has gone before, not what we could become. I'm not interested in the sort of leadership that our current system provides. No-one in this country is willing to think about the sort of changes I envisage. I want to see the world move forward in great strides, not small baby steps. During the industrial revolution, the world moved from producing every single individual item by hand to using machines to mass produce and using steam or water power to drive progress. That happened in just eighty years, can you imagine where we could be if we could make such strides today in areas where reform is needed? Wouldn't it be amazing to see true equality, an end to pollution, war, poverty or violence against women within a lifetime? The things I want require huge step changes and you don't get those by changing laws or holding up banners. All the half measures and promises to achieve something 'in the next ten years', are depressing in their lack of imagination. The Equal Pay Act came into force in 1970. Twenty-five years on and we are still miles away from achieving it, because the law is toothless. Where is the punishment? Where is the incentive? It's all half measures, a limp effort to keep a lid on women's indignation. We need to act NOW and punish dissenters.

It is so obvious to me that men are not interested in this type of change. They make money from wars and the processes that cause pollution. They are too lazy to build wind farms or eradicate plastic. They benefit from ensuring that women stay in middle management roles with no influence. The few women who make it to the top do it despite the men in the world, not because of them. They don't care enough about our legacy and young people are just beginning to understand the problems that previous generations have left them to fix.

If I go into politics now I will be part of a system that thrives in the status quo. I just can't do it to myself. I would rather die than see the world remain as it is and I haven't yet worked out what is needed to change it. It needs to be huge.

I go back to my scientific roots because it may be the only way I can make a difference right now. If I can't change the world for women yet then I will focus on something smaller that I can change for us all. I find a part time job as a lab assistant in a breast cancer research lab. Studying is easy for me so I can work at the same time and it means I'm making money which I will save for when I can make a change.

1995

It is my twenty-first birthday.Mummy takes us on our first ever holiday. I don't know who is more nervous about taking Hope away for the first time, me or Mummy. Sometimes when we are alone I have to remind myself that Hope is only nine but when we go outside I am painfully aware of how innocent she is. She is very like me, her thick, dark hair is the only real difference, mine was thinner and less beautiful.

We go to the Lake District because Mummy says there are plenty of great things to see in this country and that people who go abroad rarely take the time to appreciate what is on their own doorstep. I am disappointed that we aren't going somewhere more exotic, I have never been abroad but I read a lot about other countries and I would love to visit somewhere like Tibet. Women of the Mosuo in Tibet run households and property is passed from female to female but it doesn't feel quite right because they appoint male leaders and men handle the politics. I haven't found anywhere where women run everything which I think is such a waste. I believe men have had their chance and it is obvious that they have completely messed it up. Women should be given an opportunity to lead, sooner rather than later.

We are in the Lake District. It is so beautiful here, I feel my heart swell when I am in the countryside and it fills me with joy. It is something special to breath fresh air and feel the wind whip through your hair and across your skin. I take the time to look around at the wild flowers and watch the birds. I take Hope over to the edge of a stream and tell her to dip her fingers in the cool moving water. We watch a dragonfly dance across it, its legs brushing the surface of the water, leaving a tiny dent of a trail across it. Hope's hair is picked up by a gust of wind and it dances around her face before it flies across her face and into her mouth. We laugh and I pull long strands away from her face and stroke her soft skin. When we are somewhere like this I can forget that the world is a dangerous place for a while. Today we plan to climb to the very top of Helvellyn and eat our mint cake at the top. As we walk Mummy tells us about other beautiful and quiet places in Britain that she has visited. She has the same reaction to the outdoors as I do and Hope has the same light in her eyes. We are all happy today, away from home. I wonder why Mummy chose to move us to a town all those years ago when she could have moved us somewhere like this. I guess it was about work but I it would have been lovely to live in a place where you see more trees and bushes than people.

I love my country when I am out in the countryside like this. I feel connected to it, as if I am growing out of the ground instead of standing on top of it. I feel the same when I stand on a deserted beach and feel the sea wind whip across my skin, leaving salt on my lips that I can taste. It feels as if the sea has given me a salty kiss and left behind a piece of herself, just for me. Sometimes I think that nature is the only thing that can fill the void that the men left behind when they violated me. I breathe deeply and the air that fills my body temporarily takes away the pain. When I go back to college and see all the boys walking around like they own the place the pain will flood back in.

I remember a bible story from my childhood. It feels as if I have always known this story and I think Mummy must have told me it. In the story, the world was full of sin and God sent the rain to wash the sin away. He told Noah to build a boat and save two of every living thing in the world so that they might inherit the earth after the rains stopped. I look around and suddenly there is clarity. The world is full of the sins of man, it covers the earth in a dirty, smelly sludge that chokes the women and children, kills the animals and birds and stifles our growth. It makes us slow and lumbering. It gets inside our brains and makes us believe that sludge is a necessary part of the earth and it is where we belong, sunk up to our necks while the men sit in boats, sailing past us.

I try and explain this to Mummy on the way up Helvellyn but she says that the best way to change the world it to start with yourself and work outwards. I tell her I have spent my life doing that, the sludge in my brain is gone and my heart is full of possibility.

She doesn't understand, her sludge is still there so she can't see what I can see. It is my job to make her and all women understand. We spend a while talking about it. Mummy is a good debater, she would go far in my university debating team. But she says that she finds it all exhausting to listen to sometimes. Her mind is not ready.

We get to the top of Helvellyn, open our mint cakes and sit down to rest and enjoy the view. I decide to teach Hope about feminism. Hope looks at me with wonder when I tell her about how the suffragettes chained themselves to railings and jumped in front of race horses in pursuit of their cause. For some reason Mummy is angry and says that I am ruining the day with my obsession. She tells Hope that it is more important to be happy, warm and safe than it is to change the world. I don't agree with that at all, it is important to have ambition. To resign ourselves to just being happy, warm and safe really means giving control of the world to someone else.

I tell mummy and Hope that if we rely on other people to do all the work then we can't be cross when things never change, or if we don't like what is happening in the world because what we are really saying is that we don't care when women are abused, when men lead us into pointless wars, or when young girls are sold into prostitution. If we can't take action ourselves then we should at least actively support those who do. Men have had control for so long because women decided it was fine to sit at home and knit socks or cook apple pie all day long. She laughs at that and then Hope laughs too. But I wasn't joking.

2025

Meeting of 'COBR'

As Claire listened to the briefing from the Health Minister, Deborah Walsh, she glanced around the room at her colleagues. Roland Bertram had assumed the chair and was aggressively facilitating the meeting, he seemed in a hurry to get it over with. Some of her other male colleagues were pale and visibly shaken and most of the women were trying hard to avoid eye contact. Karen had tears in her eyes. Claire mind wandered to her male friends, colleagues and family members and she had to force herself to concentrate as Deborah continued.

'...we are already 10% down on staff numbers and based on the current rate of infection 60-70% of the adult male population could require hospital treatment over the next three days. The system simply cannot cope. We recommend putting in place home quarantines immediately, along with clear advice on handwashing, disinfection and disposal of contaminated items, use of face masks and gloves and consumption of boiled or sanitised water only as soon as possible.'

Roland Bertram looked sternly around the room at those who were struggling. 'Are we all agreed?' there were subdued nods from around the table.

'Okay, we knew this was going to be a tough meeting but we need to crack on. Can we move on to the intelligence briefing please?' The head of MI5 nodded and picked up his briefing notes.

'Porton Down have, this morning, confirmed positive test results on all tap water samples received so far. They believe that contamination could have occurred as part of the treatment process as the virus appears to be able to survive in chemically treated water and can replicate itself without a host. CTC are trawling CCTV footage for evidence of tampering but this is not a small task as there are a large number of facilities where purified water is stored for consumption.

This information does tell us something about the organisation and reach of the terrorists involved. They have managed to acquire the virus, contaminate water across the country and evade all intelligence efforts to detect and monitor such activity. Until yesterday I would have said that it wasn't possible but there were no flags, no early warnings or chatter of any kind. We didn't see this coming, nor have we been able to find any evidence to link this to any known terrorist organisations. Whoever did it was clever enough to cover their tracks.'

We are working on three theories. Firstly, a known terrorist group has attacked us and had discovered a new method of communicating and organising itself that we haven't been able to detect. This is the least likely scenario as the mode and method of attack doesn't fit the profile of any known groups.

Secondly, a new group has formed that we weren't looking for. Given the planning involved, it is likely to have been in place for a number of years but its ideology is unknown. Its ability to recruit is also unknown but the scale of the attack suggests a strong ideology, founded on a strong distrust or loathing of men. This fits more with our assumption that the immunity that women and children enjoy is no accident.

Lastly, a group or foreign power have targeted British men in order to remove our leadership and weaken our ability to recover and retaliate, leaving a vacuum into which a new order could thrive.'

Claire glanced around the room. All heads were turned towards the Head of MI5 and their expressions varied from fear to horror. The head of MI5 concluded 'Any of these three scenarios are possible and we should prepare for a follow up attack in any eventuality.'

Roland cleared his throat and when he spoke his tone was contemptuous. 'it is profoundly disappointing to me that we have no intelligence at all on this. Resorting to guesswork is not really good enough.' Elizabeth Vinn, the MET commissioner, leant forwards and those around the table perked up, anticipating a spat between them. 'The MI5 briefing is based on behavioural science, Minister. The investigation is in its infancy. Let's give everyone time to do their jobs, shall we? I believe that I am next on the agenda.' Bernard looked indignant but sat back and waved his hand to indicate that she should go ahead.

'Thank you, minister. Early figures suggest that around 20% of police officers across England and Wales have failed to report for duty in the last 12 hours due to illness and we expect numbers to decline sharply at the next shift change. This is a significant issue, particularly given the high probability of unrest. We have called in all available police personnel and are looking at other contingencies but we need to be realistic. If the only available resource left were female police officers, then the maximum available for duty at any one time across the country would be 4,000, nowhere near enough to provide an effective police force. Where possible, forces are doing what they can to prepare for the impact of the virus on communities. Usually we would hold community meetings to try and resolve issues like community unrest but given the risk of infection we are considering alternatives like social media and community notice boards in the short term.

At present, the main security concern, outside the virus itself, are growing pockets of unrest centred around hospitals and involving grieving relatives. We are prioritising the ongoing investigation and policing any unrest. Anything outside those priorities in unlikely to be resourced unless there is a risk to life.'

Claire nodded to the Commissioner, who she knew well. 'Hi

Elizabeth. Nearly a third of the prison population have contracted the virus. We are isolating sick prisoners in specific wings but staff shortages mean that prisoners who are not sick are becoming difficult to manage and I am concerned about the risk of significant unrest. Usually we would rely on the Territorial Support Group for assistance. I'm assuming that is not a possibility?'

'I'm afraid not, Claire. I recommend isolation and immediate withdrawal of staff if there is the slightest prospect of unrest. We don't have the resources to provide any aid.'

'Thanks Elizabeth, that's what I thought.' Claire sat gloomily back in her chair.

As the agenda moved on, all hope in the room ebbed away. Misery hung like a cloud and many people around the table became preoccupied by the safety of their own families and friends. The information provided in the meeting was highly confidential but that didn't stop most of the group thinking about who they were going to tell or how to keep loved ones' safe. No-one was really paying attention to the agenda anymore.

The Immigration Minister was a heavy-set man with a chin that wobbled when he talked and a suit that strained across his ever- expanding waistline. He was sweating even more than usual. He cleared his throat and then reached for a glass of water in front of him. As he was about to touch it his hand hovered in mid-air for a moment, and he glared at the water as if it were poisoned then snatched his hand back. The whole thing seemed to unsettle him and he cleared his throat repeatedly before speaking.

'All travel in and out of Great Britain has been suspended to prevent the spread of the virus overseas and this will remain in place for the foreseeable future. We are experiencing unrest at airport and ferry terminals, many people are stranded and a group of foreign nationals have been forced to remain here after a layover between flights. We closed all surrounding roads and are directing traffic away from ports and airports but this is difficult to contain without police support and people are gathering at various border points. Some members of the crowd have been violent and abusive to airport staff.'

'We estimate that some 300,000 British nationals are stranded overseas and are working with the Foreign Office to ensure that Consulates and Embassies are able to provide advice and emergency assistance to British Nationals who don't have travel insurance to cover their extended stay. As you can imagine, embassies, consulates and immigration centres have been experiencing high call volumes in the past few hours and we expect this to increase as people wake up to the news across the world.'

Roland Bertram nodded to his colleague. 'Please continue to work with the Foreign Office, concerns have already been raised through diplomatic channels about the group stranded here. You could divert any available border personnel to the phones, which might help in managing demand.' There was resentment in his voice as he added 'Those stranded abroad appear to be the lucky ones- it may be worth pointing that out if they complain too loudly.'

The Foreign Secretary spoke next. At forty, he was the youngest man in the room, an expert negotiator and a handsome man. He was usually full of confidence and charisma, keen to make eye contact with every woman in the room. Today he avoided eye contact and appeared barely able to maintain his composure. His hands shook and the front of his hair stuck to his forehead, wet with perspiration. Claire had spoken to his wife numerous times and recalled he had a fifteen-year old son. As he began to speak his mobile lit up, indicating a phone call. He glanced nervously down at it and then reluctantly began.

'A number of our allies have expressed concern at the lack of available intel on those responsible. Despite our border closures they remain anxious about the potential for the virus to be released abroad and have asked that we share all relevant intelligence with them immediately.'

'Approximately one hundred thousand individuals have fallen ill after taking flights out of Great Britain. The infected, all adolescent and adult males, are in isolation units across 30 countries and all travelled within the last 24 hours. All cases have been contained and so far, the virus has not spread to the general population. Most countries are now trying to locate everyone who travelled from Great Britain in the past three days to find out if they are symptomatic. We don't know much about the incubation period of the virus but can assume that the risk of a further outbreak originating from Great Britain will diminish with each passing day.'

He finished speaking and finally looked around the room. Claire saw then that his eyes were dull, his usual twinkle was gone and there were signs that he had been crying. She caught his eye and smiled, sympathetically. It was hard for everyone.

'Well there's nothing more we can do that we haven't already done to halt the spread of the virus overseas. We will share as much information as possible but should be mindful of the fact that we still don't know where it originated and can't rule out a foreign aggressor. Deborah, please provide a sanitised version of the briefing on the virus for us to release to our allies.'

Roland Bertram assumed his role as Defence Secretary to lead the next item. He seemed relatively unaffected by the mornings briefings compared to others in the room, something which surprised Claire slightly. His voice boomed out across the otherwise silent table.

'Military chiefs have modelled several scenarios, focussing on the counter measures Britain would consider if there were a similar outbreak in Europe and have raised concerns about the prospect of nuclear air strikes by countries seeking to protect their own nationals. We would undoubtedly consider similar measures to contain such an aggressive outbreak in a neighbouring country. Their objective would be to prevent the worldwide spread of the virus but the outcome for the British public would be complete extinction.'

'Military chiefs are of the view that the threat is very real and being discussed. Our surface to air missile system is operational and all personnel have been put on alert. As the majority of personnel trained to maintain the missile system are male, we are training a small female cadre to take control of the missile system should the worst happen. We are also maintaining open back channels to try and neutralise this risk.'

Some were unable to keep the anger and disbelief from leaking onto their faces at this news. 'Have we received any specific intelligence indicating a threat, or is this just speculation?'

'No specific intelligence and if it were raised it may be dismissed just as quickly but we need to prepare for the possibility that it is not.'

Roland sat back in his chair and looked around the room, his face crumpled and he let out a huge, defeated breath. 'This has been a tough morning. I think we need a break. We still have a fair amount to get through and I need fifteen minutes just to let what we have heard so far sink in. Refreshments will be made available next door.'

They stood up and filed out silently. Some went straight outside to get some air, others disappeared down the corridor alone. The group naturally separated into men and women without discussion or particular organisation. Claire followed a few of her female colleagues into the room next door, where refreshments were being hastily laid out. As she looked around at people she had known for years a wave of complete helplessness hit her, as if an invisible burden had shifted irrevocably onto her shoulders. Sympathetic to her male colleagues, she felt uncomfortable about approaching them, for fear of igniting an emotive response. All the women present knew that they were likely to survive, all the men knew they would die. The meeting must have seemed futile to them. It was difficult to imagine how they must be feeling. Karen, Millicent Cain, the Secretary of State for Education and Claire joined Deborah in the queue for a coffee, as the men hung back in small groups.

'This is horrific, I feel completely out of my depth.' Karen picked up a coffee and walked with Claire over to a table nearby.

'We all are. I feel like I'm part of a horrible nightmare and I can't wake up.' said Claire. Millicent and Deborah walked towards the table with their coffee and Karen and Claire fell silent as Millicent's angry voice cut through their conversation. '...I was visiting a senior school when some of the pupils suddenly started to fall ill. I went with the head teacher to the hospital and saw how quickly those young boys succumbed to the virus. I watched their parents break apart one by one, as the boys got sicker and sicker and I was with them when their children died. I can't tell you how bloody angry I am. I would really like to find myself in the same room as the people who did this. I can't even begin to imagine what their motivation could be. Watching what those children went through broke me, so I cannot imagine what it did to their families. If we ever catch them we will have a security problem on our hands. There will be a long queue of people who want to dole out a fitting punishment and I'll be at the front of it. Life in prison won't even come close to what these people deserve.' Deborah touched Millicent on the shoulder and said gently 'It must have been awful. I'm so sorry you had to go through that.' Claire opened her mouth to ask if Millicent was okay but before she could, Roland's bulky frame appeared at her shoulder. 'We will be going back in in five minutes, you can bring your coffee along. Important to press on.' Roland hadn't read the mood of the group before joining them and there was an awkward pause in conversation which Claire broke just as it became uncomfortable. 'Okay, thank you.'

Roland cast his eye around the group with an odd expression on his face. 'I suppose this must be easy for you women.' Claire felt the resentment in his voice keenly. 'We were discussing how difficult it is to be here when our focus is on our families but for you, well you just have to wait it out.'

Karen shot a worried glance at Claire, who felt a growing sense of indignation. Roland blundered on, almost spitting out his words as his neck flushed a deep red. 'I just pray that you know what you are doing. It's a lot of responsibility to shoulder, far too big to manage on your own, you'll need to bring in outside help, assuming they are willing to provide it.'

Claire fought the urge to respond as Roland concluded '…there are so many things to think about. I'm sure it feels overwhelming but you have no choice, you'll be here afterwards and we won't. I don't intend to stay after this briefing is over and many of my colleagues feel the same. We need to spend time with our families now, so we will hand the baton to you.'

Roland nodded brusquely, turned and walked away. The group collectively exhaled and looked at each other in bewilderment as the implications and tone of his comments sank in. It was difficult to accept but in a few days, if the briefings were accurate, the group at the meeting would soon be a third of its size. Deborah looked around the table and wrinkled her nose, then vocalised what they were all thinking. 'I guess we really are on our own now.' Claire nodded grimly and they returned to the meeting room quietly to ready themselves for the second half.

1996

I have finished my course. Politics is a field I enjoyed but political change is not fast and I get impatient even studying it. The best modules involved strong women who have changed the world, like Joan of Arc, who led the French to victory during its occupation by the British, or Elizabeth I who lead the country through economic and societal change, or the suffragettes who changed women's rights forever. I aspire to do something great like them and politics seem to be the only way to do it.

I miss study a lot so I start a degree in microbiology with the Open University. Biology is still my passion and I love my new course. Studying how a tiny organism can alter a host by either destroying or changing it is so interesting that I could watch it all day. Mummy is not happy about my choice and says I have to fund it myself, as it is an indulgence rather than a career choice, so I get two-part time jobs, one as a research assistant working for my local MP and the other as a lab assistant. Mummy doesn't understand that the way into politics is hard and grumbles about the low pay but if you don't have connections then you have to work your way up from the bottom. She does like the idea of my going into politics, she thinks it will give me direction and force me to listen to the people, rather than deciding for myself what's best for them.

She is naïve because the people don't know what they want or what is best for them. They need to be shown. The best leaders in history broke new boundaries, challenged current thinking and forged ahead, often at great personal risk. Look at the suffragettes. Emmeline Pankhurst fought against the tide for the rights of women and Emily Wilding Davison martyred herself in the name of the movement. Many women didn't know they needed more rights and if asked, would probably have said they liked their lives the way they were. Years on and the suffragettes are celebrated and revered. Opinions only change when they are actively challenged.

I see the research job as a means to an end. It is mundane, dull and unimaginative. The man is no innovator and nothing I'm asked to do challenges me in any way so I use the time to get an idea of how the system works. How the local MP got elected is beyond me, he is the most tedious of men with no charisma and no original ideas and his appearance matches his personality, flabby and unkempt. He is far too old to understand current culture and harks back to the 'good old days' regularly. He is clumsy with women, he can't decide whether to be a flirt or a father figure, both make me sick to my stomach.

He is unaware of my contempt for him which amuses me and I enjoy the act of concealing my true feelings. He regularly stands behind me while I work, resting a hand on my shoulder and doesn't seem to notice or care that my whole body stiffens. He calls me 'Jeanie' (a name I have come to detest) despite my protests. He has an overwhelming need to be admired by women and believes that all women need to be rescued which is not only ludicrous, it is propaganda to stop women taking control of their own lives.

I need the job but that doesn't mean that I have to put up with his ridiculous pawing. I decide to tackle it through his wife who has a little more about her than him. I keep a diary of every inappropriate comment he makes, particularly when constituents are involved. When I am alone with her I show her the diary and explain that I wanted to show him how easy a woman would find it to ruin him. I pull my best innocent expression and tell her that we must protect him from scandal because he puts himself at risk every day. I suggest a quiet word in his ear and reassure her that he probably doesn't even know he is doing it. She is grateful. She speaks to him that evening and the next time I go to work I am given a pay rise. My job as a lab assistant is interesting, it renews my interest in science and I skip to work, I am so happy to be there. I love the precise nature of the work and that the results are clear, even if they are unexpected.

2025

Meeting of 'COBR'

Roland opened the second part of the meeting with a speech to the group.

'Before we begin, I wanted to say that I expect all men to stand down from their roles after this meeting. It isn't reasonable to expect our male colleagues to continue to work after what we have heard today. I am not alone in feeling that my priorities have shifted away from politics. I want to spend my last hours with my wife and daughter and I am sure other colleagues feel the same. I have given my life to politics and made many sacrifices to serve my country and I deserve the chance to say goodbye with some dignity.' He lifted his chin with a look of defiance and continued.

'The country will undoubtedly fall apart when we are gone and we will not be here to save you. You women must focus on continuity and building resilience.'

Claire looked around the room. Most of the men were nodding in agreement while the women looked aghast. Elizabeth caught Claire's eye and, almost imperceptibly rolled her eyes. In Claire's view, it was a dereliction of duty. She saw no point in beating around the bush anymore. She stood up, indignantly. 'Roland! It is highly inappropriate to have this discussion now. You are the chair of this meeting and...'

Roland rounded on her, slamming his hand on the table in front of him. 'When should we have it Claire? We've just heard that we could all drop dead at any moment. Every minute that

I spend here is one I lose with my family. You're very lucky I'm still here.'

'Should we all go home too? We have fathers, sons, husbands and friends in exactly the same position as you. Don't we deserve to spend time with them? Why not just leave the country to fend for itself? For god sake Roland. You were elected to represent the people. You have a responsibility.'

Roland raised his eyebrows, his temper beginning to show through in his eyes. He spoke with venom and Claire watched, repulsed as spittle formed in the corners of his mouth.

'How dare you. You women will inherit EVERYTHING we have built. For years you lot have moaned about equality. You on the side lines criticising, nit-picking our decisions, requesting more rights and more say while condemning our behaviour as inappropriate or sexist. You got the vote, you got equality, we gave you a seat at the table and still you wanted more control, more say. Well, now you have got it. Good luck, you'll need it.'

He flung himself back in his seat and folded his arms across his expansive stomach, out of breath with the exertion of his rant. Claire was furious. She opened her mouth to speak again and then closed it as she felt a hand on her arm. Elizabeth, who was sat next to her, muttered in her ear 'This is not a fight you can win today.' Claire nodded reluctantly and sat back, taking a few deep breaths to calm herself down.

Roland smiled, slightly smugly and looked around the table, studiously avoiding the gaze of several angry women. 'Shall we move on?' There was a new type of tension among the group, fuelled by resentment and frustration.

'Err...okay. 'The Minister for Transport stuttered, his eyes darting from left to right nervously. His hands shook slightly as he grasped his briefing notes. 'Erm, we have suspended all rail travel to limit passenger movement and reduce the risk of spreading infection. Local buses are operating a reduced service but this will cease this evening. The likelihood is that people will use their own vehicles to travel rather than staying put so we should expect congestion. Current supplies of petrol and diesel are likely to run out in approximately two to three days.'

Claire spoke up again. 'Where is your evidence that the virus is airborne? We have heard that it was spread through the water supply. All we are doing is preventing people from reaching loved ones, I think we should run transport for as long as possible...'

Roland slammed his hand down on the table once again. The whole group jumped and looked at Roland, who was leaning forward in his chair. At first, they thought he was showing symptoms of the virus but when he stopped holding his breath they realised he was just angry. His eyes blazed as he glared at Claire, who responded by staring back at him, unapologetically. The minister hesitatingly responded to Claire, his voice trembling a little. 'We...err, we don't have any evidence that the virus can be spread that way but, following a risk assessment we have concluded that we don't know enough about the virus to rule it out. In any case, will be unable to sustain services by the end of today if projections from the DOH are accurate.'

Claire was still staring at Roland, willing him to challenge her but they both kept quiet this time and the agenda moved on. Karen was next up and shot a nervous look at Roland before starting.

'Vital local services are still just about operating, though many local councils are running a reduced service as the availability of council staff is variable. Social services are experiencing high call volumes as concerns are raised about the children of sick parents and vulnerable elderly men. Social services have diverted all available staff to carry out visits but there are far too many to cover and some will undoubtedly be missed.'

'Thanks Karen. We should ask members of the public to look in on any neighbours. Any comments from the room?' Roland looked pointedly at Claire, who did not have any to make, though she was sorely tempted to comment just to irritate him.

'Let's move on then.' Roland raced through the agenda, his regard only for his own circumstances now barely concealed.

Millicent Cain was next on the agenda. 'Secondary schools have closed. A handful of primary and preschools are still open but we expect many parents to start keeping their children at home as panic sets in. We have included lines in the statement due to be released, encouraging the public to check on lone male parents.'

'Thank you, Millicent. Please close all remaining schools. Any objections?' No-one spoke. 'Claire, you are last on the agenda.' Roland almost spat her name through gritted teeth. Claire tried to rise above it. 'Thank you, Roland.' She slowed her voice down a fraction and lowered the tone of her voice quite deliberately in an effort to slow the pace of the meeting down a little.

'Male prisoners make up 87% of the prison population. The total number of males in prison before the virus stood at 79,750. So far, more than thirty-thousand are symptomatic or deceased, a number that is rising by the hour. We cannot transport prisoners to hospital because of security concerns and lack of hospital beds, instead isolation wings have been created to treat the sick.

There are significant pockets of unrest across the estate, in three prisons this has become unmanageable and tragically a staff member has been killed by a group of inmates at Wormwood Scrubs so we have taken the decision to pull all prison staff back to the perimeter. Two thirds of prison officers are male and there is a high probability that we will lose control altogether in the next day or two if staff absences continue to rise as predicted.'

Roland asked 'Is there an increased risk of escape?'

'Not at this stage, though as things progress we may see a marked increase in attempts.'

Roland raised his eyebrows. 'How do you propose to manage

that?'

'Well, short of shooting potential escapees, I have no contingency plan for that at the moment Roland. We are unlikely to have the staff to mount a man hunt but equally, any freedom that escapees might enjoy is likely to be short lived.'

Roland glared at her but didn't bite back. 'Thank you, that concludes the meeting. Male attendees should provide the name of a female successor before they leave.' Claire stood up and gathered her things quickly. She was angry and disappointed in her colleagues and needed to get outside for some air.

Outside the meeting room, Elizabeth caught Claire up and pulled her to one side. 'I know how you feel, Claire but you expect too much from them. Most people can't control how they will respond to a crisis and none of us are perfect. You know where I am if you need me.'

Claire nodded. 'I know you're right. I'm just disappointed.'

As she walked back to her car, the information they had been given swirled around her head and she felt lost in the hopelessness of it all. The meeting felt like an exercise in futility and while usually she felt comforted by knowing the whole picture, today she almost wished that she didn't.

1997

It is Hope's 11th birthday. She is now the same age as I was when I was taken and I think about it all day. Last night I dreamt about my 11th birthday.

Mummy, with red puffy eyes, carrying an arm full of presents smiles through her tears and says 'Happy birthday, Jeanie!' I open each present with a painted-on smile, pretending that they are the best presents ever. She makes French toast and gives me fizzy pop. She brings in a huge pink cake with icing flowers. I know Mummy loves me because she always has, but all day I watch the door. Daddy promised he would come but I haven't seen him since he left us.

Mummy distracts me with sweets and cake and little presents she hides in her pockets, or in my shoes.

It is night time and I know he isn't coming but I stay awake as long as possible, just in case he is late. I fall asleep and when I wake up it isn't my birthday anymore. In the dream a card arrives, I open it and it says 'Happy Birthday. I don't love you anymore. Your Father.' I wake up with a start.

What happened in that dream is almost the same as real life, except that my father didn't send a card at all. I do not have a single good memory of that year.

We throw Hope a party in the church hall. All the little girls arrive in pretty puffy dresses, like princesses. I watch the little girls kiss their fathers' goodbye and I wonder if Hope feels like me when she sees her friends with their fathers. They look so happy to have a father to cuddle and kiss. They don't know that it is all a lie and their fathers will leave just like mine did.

They will learn that the only person they can rely on is themselves but I want to run up to those little girls and warn them not to love their fathers because it hurts when they leave.

2025

Government Press Release

'The Government is actively managing the emergence of a new virus, early symptoms of which resemble the flu. Men in particular may experience persistent headaches, a sore neck and aching limbs, a cough or cold, high temperature, difficulty breathing or periods of lethargy. Women and children appear to be at lower risk at this time, though we cannot rule out the possibility that symptoms may develop in slower time.

As many hospitals and treatment centres are stretched, members of the public with emerging symptoms should remain at home and call the virus helpline on 111. Staff on the helpline are trained to provide advice on making yourself or your loved one more comfortable. You should remain in bed, drink plenty of treated water, eat if you feel able to and take paracetamol or ibuprofen to ease the symptoms. If you have an unrelated illness please contact your GP or, in an emergency dial 999. If you have elderly or frail neighbours or know of single men with dependants at home, please make sure that they are okay and have sufficient food and boiled, cooled water to last at least a few days.

We believe that the virus may be present in our water system and, as a precaution, advise members of the public to boil tap water, add purification tablets or drink bottled water if it is available.

Though we do not believe that the virus is airborne, the government is taking extreme measures to limit further infection. All flights have been grounded and borders closed until further notice. Stock market trading is suspended and we urge employers and non-essential services to close or allow their staff to work from home if possible. Travel within Great Britain on trains, tubes and buses is subject to cancellation and suspension. All public buildings will be closed until further notice, though essential services will continue to operate. Food banks are stocked with supplies and will be open to anyone who needs them. Supermarkets may be open, however if you do go out to get essential items please follow the online guidance to prevent the spread of the virus.

There have been reports of violent unrest outside hospitals and at ferry and airport terminals. Feeling unsettled and fearful is understandable, however violence and looting will not be tolerated. Police and security personnel have been advised to treat all such incidents harshly and offenders are warned that such behaviour increases their risk of exposure to the virus.

As women appear to be resistant to the virus, we are asking women with skills or experience in key sectors such as engineering, health, utilities, security and emergency planning to make themselves known to the authorities by registering at the www.virusaction.gov.uk within the next 48 hours. Please check the website for a full list of the skills required.'

1999

Hope is hard work. Mummy and I have to team up a lot to manage her because she wants to go out with her friends all the time and she is obsessed with pop music. She likes 'Boyz II Men' and 'The Backstreet Boys' and she has posters all over her walls. The music is just terrible, the lyrics objectify women and the music videos consist of men sleazing all over young girls. What really gets to me is no-one seems to care that we are allowing young girls to be brainwashed into believing that this is how people should behave.

I want to rip the posters down and take away Hope's radio but Mummy says if I do that I will just alienate her from us. I am enraged by Hope's sudden interest in this vacuous rubbish and can't help telling her how disappointed I am. She usually falls into line when I tell her off but it is not working anymore, she just sighs and tells me that I'm too old to understand. Maybe she is right, I wasn't like this when I was her age so I don't really understand her at all.

I talk to Mummy about it when Hope is asleep. She says I missed out on my childhood and it makes her sad to think about it. All I remember about being a teenager is studying. Hope does study but she doesn't spend nearly enough time doing it, preferring to talk on the phone to her friends all evening. What they talk about for so long is beyond me. She is a puzzle.

2000

We reach the millennium, I think about what has changed in the world since I was a child. I read the headlines in the pile of newspapers stacked in the corner of our lounge.

A male doctor is imprisoned for killing fifteen elderly patients and is suspected of killing far more.

An enquiry into child abuse receives 140 allegations of abuse in children's homes across North Wales.

A young child is abducted from a field near her home and murdered.

A young girl is tortured and murdered by her guardians after a man of the cloth convinced them the child was evil.

A young boy is murdered by a group of teenaged boys on his way home from school.

There are hundreds of others that don't make the front page. I can't understand why we are not indignant about the crimes of men. Women go about their daily lives, oblivious to the evidence. Men beat us, demean us, rape and murder us. They start wars, commit genocides and pollute the world and we close our eyes. I am so angry that I want to shout and scream in the street, but ironically it is likely that I would be arrested for that.

Hope distracts me from my anger. She has her period and comes to me for advice. I only ever had two periods and struggle to help her. She speaks to Mummy who is apparently very helpful. I am frustrated and bitter and go to my room to escape it all. Hope is growing further and further away from me with every day that passes and I struggle to relate to her. I watch her lead the life I should have had and I feel as if those men ripped away everything that made me normal that night. All that remains of Jean is an outer shell. Everything else is full of their poison.

Mummy says I should be happy that Hope has her period. She can get married, have babies and live a fuller life than Mummy or I ever will. She says to want a better life for your children is instinctive, as if I don't already know. She forgets that Hope is mine, not hers. Of course, I want Hope to have a better life than mine, I want her to be successful and happy but I don't want her to get married. Marriage is only beneficial to men, why would I want that for her? I tell Mummy that and she sighs. She says that marriage can be beautiful if two people love each other but she forgets that her marriage wasn't like that at all. My father was a religious fanatic and a hypocrite and he left. He didn't love Mummy and he didn't love me. If he had he would have stayed with us. Mummy has been on her own for years and years. If she thought marriage was that great then wouldn't she have done it again?

Come to think of it, my father didn't have the feelings Mummy describes about me either. He didn't want me to have a better life than him because he doesn't send Mummy any money, he doesn't visit to check that I am okay and he doesn't even call. He could be busy with his new family but I don't think so. I bet he left them too. I don't think feel the same as mothers about their children. You can only feel love like that if you have carried a child inside your body. Fathers who stick around probably just pretend they love their children until they convince everyone it's true.

2025

Claire was on the way back to her office when she got the call she had been dreading. 'Claire, it's Carrie Townsend.' Claire drew a sharp intake of breath. She had never been able to hear Carrie's voice without having a physical reaction. 'Hello Carrie, what is it?' 'It's James, He's gone, Claire.' Claire shut her eyes and took a deep breath. 'Okay.' She could hear Carrie's muffled tears but couldn't bring herself to be kind, even now. 'Thank you for letting me know, Carrie.' She cut off the call and said to the driver 'Can you take me home please.'

She sat in the car, numb, as they drove out of the city. There was barely a car on the road and though abandoned cars made the journey more challenging for the driver, they still made good time. She looked out of the window as the city fell away, thinking about how to tell Ben about James.

The car drew up to the house almost too quickly and with little chance to absorb the news, she had to pause for a moment to compose herself. She leant against the wall of the house and breathed deeply. James had been her life for fifteen years before she discovered his affair. Every memory of him now was tinged with his betrayal and cowardice. She had endured months of media interest in the story, each bringing fresh pain, anger and revelations about his character. Over the years his presence in her life continued to evoke a twinge of the pain, anger and resentment she had experienced. Counselling had dulled it but it would always be a part of her.

She waited outside until she was calmer, then got out her keys and opened the door. As she did so she heard the sound of her mum crying and panicking, hurried into the lounge. Ben was sat on her Mum's lap, cuddling her while she sobbed. 'Mum? What is it?' Her mum looked up. 'Thank god you are here, Claire. I'm sorry but I need to go. Your brother has it.'

Claire froze in the doorway as a wave of despair washed over her. Her mother looked up at her with a strangely resentful expression and Claire suppressed an urge to defend herself for failing to provide any words of comfort. She stood inadequately in front of her mother, cursing herself. No solutions presented themselves, she could find no skills to draw on and couldn't even manage a tear. Her mother wiped away her tears and stood up, lifting Ben gently onto the floor.

She brushed past Claire, mumbling 'I have to go.' and climbed the stairs to the spare room to pack her things. Claire followed, guilt spurring her into action.

'Mum, we can drive you to see Martin. If you want to stay I'll come back and get you when you are ready to come home. I'd like to see Martin, before...'

She stopped herself abruptly. Finishing the sentence would destroy her mother.

'No.' her mother snapped, looking her daughter in the eyes. 'I don't want you to come.'

Claire's heart dropped. She knew what was coming was going to hurt. Her mother was resolute.

'There is no point denying that you have a terrible relationship with Martin. If you come with me I'll end up in the middle of it like I always do. I want to be with him without worrying about you. Besides, you can't take Ben anywhere near him, what if he is infectious? It's better for everyone if you keep Ben at home.'

She turned towards the wardrobe, grabbed her overnight bag and pulled open the drawer where she had placed her clothes the day before.

Claire nodded miserably. She wanted so much to be support-

ive to her mother but when she opened her mouth intending to say something supportive, she blurted out, 'James is dead.'
Her mother's mouth dropped open and she sat heavily down on the bed.
'Oh, my goodness. Poor Ben.'
Childish resentment clouded Claire's judgement and she eyed her mother with a flash of bitterness as she struggled to control the feeling that her mother's concern, while freely given to Martin, was never on offer to Claire.
'How did you find out?' Her mother stood back up and started folding the clothes for her overnight bag.
'Carrie.' Her mother looked at Claire briefly then and a glimmer of pity passed over her face, then she turned to finish packing. Claire hovered, reluctant to leave and feeling small and selfish for wanting her mother's attention at such a difficult time.
As her mother zipped up her bag, Claire spotted the fresh tears sliding down her mother's face and strode over to give her mother a hug, breaking the tension between them. 'I'm sorry, Mum, I shouldn't have told you about James right now. I can manage, go to Martin, he needs you more than I do.' Iris allowed herself to lean into Claire for a few seconds in recognition of the apology, then pulled away. Claire sighed. There was always tension between them when Martin was mentioned. She drifted back downstairs to see how Ben was doing and sat on the sofa with him on her knee while he watched TV, thinking about her brother.
During their childhood, they were very close but as Claire began to excel at school, she left him trailing behind and with every passing year he'd become wilder, less controllable and more inclined to rebel against their strict parents. At sixteen he fell into drugs and Claire could only stand by and watch as her parents struggled. Her successes were dwarfed by Martins behaviour, culminating in an accidental overdose when she was just 20. When her father succumbed to a heart attack the following year Claire had unreasonably blamed her brother

and cut him off entirely. Since Claire's divorce they had reconciled but it was a strained relationship and they often fell into old arguments, her mother was right about that. Claire found it difficult to be around him and Martin referred to her 'perfection' as if it were an affliction. Hearing that he was ill was hard for her, she knew she would regret staying away but it was the right thing to do, for her mother if no one else.

She looked down at Ben. He was such a gentle, loving child. His face was beginning to lose the chubbiness of childhood and in the last year or so he had grown so much sometimes she forgot that he was only nine. He had a sensitivity that she didn't recognise in herself or in James. She stroked his hair, surreptitiously feeling his forehead for signs of a temperature. Normal. She breathed a quiet sigh of relief. She wondered how he felt about his uncle Martin being sick. Ben was obviously worried for his Nanny but she doubted that Ben had many fond memories of Martin to speak of.

She decided not to tell Ben about his father just yet. He seemed a little tired and she needed time to plan how to talk to him about it. Despite her own very mixed feelings, she was heartbroken for Ben. He idolised his Dad and would be utterly devastated. She sat, cuddling him, silently crying for her lovely son, who did not deserve this on top of the upheaval the divorce had caused. Ben looked up 'What's wrong, Mum?' 'Nothing, just thinking about your uncle Martin.'

Her mum came downstairs, packed and ready to go. She gave her daughter a hug, Claire squeezed her extra tight. 'I'm sorry Mum. I have made this harder for you than it needs to be. Will you be okay?'

Iris nodded and bent down to give Ben a cuddle. 'Take care of my grandson, won't you?' She said. She straightened up and looked at Claire. 'None of us are perfect, Claire. Not even you. Don't beat yourself up while I'm gone.' She turned around and walked out of the front door, shutting it behind her without a backward glance. Claire ruffled Ben's hair. 'Come on Ben, let's get you some tea.'

2001

I finally finish my degree in microbiology and am awarded a first. Mummy says she is proud but it feels phoney as I know she didn't want me to do it in the first place. Hope tells me she wants to be a veterinarian when she grows up. I am pleased that she is choosing a biology-based career, I can at least understand her interest in that. She has always loved animals but Mummy has never let her have a pet, which I don't agree with. I can't see the harm in her having something to look after and love.

I pass a pet shop every day on my way home from work, so I stop in and ask if they have any kittens. The woman behind the counter says that she knows someone who has kittens that are just about ready to leave their mum. The address on the card she gives me is only a few streets away so I decide to go there right away.

When I get to the house I suddenly feel scared. I can't walk up the path to the front door but I have no idea why. I wish I had asked Hope or Mummy to come with me. I stand in the street, paralysed, like a child. I see the curtain twitch and after a few minutes, the door opens and a woman comes out. She looks at me with an expectant expression and says 'Can I help you with something?'

I don't know what to say, so I just stand there staring. She scratches her head nervously. 'Are you here about the kittens?' she asks hopefully. I nod quickly. 'Ah, okay, do you want to see them? Come on, they're in here.' She beckons me inside but all I can see behind her is darkness. Suddenly I am eleven and

I don't believe that there are any kittens inside. Nausea makes me mute, I feel like all the moisture has been sucked out of my mouth and there is no oxygen left in the air. I turn around and I run away as fast as I can.

Hope doesn't get a kitten after all.

2025

DAY 3, 2,000,000 confirmed dead.
Witness testimonial, Amelia and Jack Foster

Amelia woke up, yawning and stretching. She had never woken up before Daddy! She ran to wake up her brother. 'Come on Jack! Time to get up.' Jack turned over in his bed and groaned. 'Amelia, go away, I'm still sleepy.'

Amelia decided to make breakfast. She ran downstairs to the kitchen and got out eggs and a bowl while trying to remember how Daddy made scramble. She cracked four eggs into the bowl and used the whisk from the drawer to beat the eggs. 'Whisk, whisk, whisk!' she sang to herself. Some egg splodged onto the table. 'Oops, naughty Amelia, don't make a mess.'

She put the eggs into the microwave and pressed the button to make it start like Daddy did. The microwave lit up and the bowl started to move, she pressed her nose to the screen. 'Just like TV' she thought.

The microwave beeped and she opened the door. She gave the eggs a stir, then called up the stairs 'Jack!! Breakfast! I made you eggs.'

She got two plates from the cupboard and shared out the eggs. A bit more for her because she was bigger.

Jack stumbled in, his hair messy and pyjama bottoms on backwards. 'Look at you, silly Jack!'

They took their plates to the lounge. Amelia put the TV onto the cartoon channel and they ate their eggs on the floor, right in front of the TV, too close. Daddy didn't let them do that but he was asleep, he wouldn't know.

Matilda came in, mewing, Amelia gave her some eggs which Matilda sniffed, as they watched Matilda turned her nose up and stalked off, tail in the air. 'Silly cat. Eggs are lovely.'

They watched TV for ages and ages. Amelia said to Jack impatiently 'Where IS Daddy? Shall we jump on him?' They ran upstairs into Daddy's room and leaped onto the bed, bouncing. 'Daddy, Daddy, wake up, wake up!!'

Daddy didn't wake up. Amelia sat on Daddy's tummy. 'Fat tummy, Daddy' She poked his cheek. He didn't move.

'Jack, Daddy is playing dead! Jack laughed and peered at his Daddy's face. 'Come on Daddy, we want to go to the park.'

Daddy still didn't wake up. Amelia sighed. 'Jack I'll have to be your Mum today.' Jack looked at her, eyes wide. 'But Mum is in heaven, with the angels. You can't be Mum, I don't want you to go and play with the angels.'

Amelia hugged her brother and stroked his hair, like Daddy did when Jack was sad. 'It's okay, Buddy.' Jack wriggled away and they ran downstairs again. 'Hey Amelia.' Jack said 'If Daddy is asleep we can have chocolate!'

Amelia dragged a chair over to the worktop in the kitchen and climbed on it. She stood up on the worktop. 'Be careful Amelia, don't fall!' Jack said anxiously. Amelia reached up to the top shelf and just managed to touch the big box of treats. She moved it with her fingers closer and closer to the edge until she managed to grab it. 'Jack, I've got it, she said triumphantly.' She pulled and the box fell off the shelf and burst open, spilling bars of chocolate and packets of crisps all over the floor. 'Oops. Naughty Amelia.' They look at each other and laughed. Amelia clambered off the worktop and they grabbed as many treats as they could carry into the lounge. 'Hey Jack, carpet picnic!'

* * *

After they had eaten as much as they could, Amelia and Jack sat on the sofa. 'Amelia, I'm bored.' Amelia thought for a minute. 'I know, how about some Lego?' She dragged out the box of Lego and tipped it over the lounge floor. Jack gasped 'Amelia, we aren't meant to do that. Put it on a tray!'

Amelia looked at the floor. There was Lego everywhere. She started to cry. 'Daddy will be really cross now.' Jack patted her on the back. 'It's okay Amelia. I'll say it was me. Let's build a rocket.' They immersed themselves in building. It took ages as all the pieces were mixed up.

It started to get dark. 'Daddy has slept for a really, really long time, maybe he is sick.' Jack said.

'I know', said Amelia. She remembered what Daddy said once. 'Daddy always goes to see the next-door neighbour if he is in a fix.'

'I don't want to see her, she smells funny.'

Amelia thought about it some more. 'I don't want to go outside anyway, it's too scary.'

They sat huddled together, in the darkening lounge.

'Amelia, it's too dark.'

'I know, Jack. I can't reach the light.'

2002

I am alone with my boss, the local MP. He is talking to my breasts instead of my face. I loathe him. I imagine leaning forwards and poking out his beady eyes with a pencil. I wonder what that would feel like and how easy it would be.

One minute he is standing there, the next he is on the floor, foaming at the mouth. I think he is having a fit and it feels like all my hatred has jumped out of my body and into his. I stand there watching him thrash on the floor, wondering what is happening to him. As he thrashes and writhes it occurs to me that he might be about to die and I feel like I have power over a man for the first time in my entire life. I don't think he knows I am standing here, his eyes are rolling in his head and he is clutching his chest.

He stops moving, it is weird because suddenly his whole body relaxes and for the first time since I have known him his face looks kind. I walk slowly to the phone and call an ambulance. When I put the telephone back down I sit down on a chair next to him and wait.

The ambulance arrives and the men come into the office with a stretcher. They feel his pulse, then they look at me. 'He is gone.' They say. 'I know' I say. They lift him onto the stretcher and take him away. I go home. I think I just lost my job.

* * *

It is Hope's sixteenth birthday. Mummy decides that we should have some fun and wants to take us out for dinner and

154

drinks by the beach, to a new restaurant with a small dance-floor. I am nervous because we don't go out much. Mostly we spend time together at home, any day trips we have are quiet and safe like to the zoo or walks along the beach during the day.

Mummy is excited to do something different but that is nothing compared with Hope. She is bouncing all over the place. For her birthday, Hope has been given a new dress and her first proper makeover. It is a chance for her to practice being a grown up for the first time. She is ready to go out at least an hour before we are due to leave. Her long dark hair is cut into a style that makes her look older than her sixteen years and she has makeup on. Her dress is pretty but high-necked and reaches down below her knees, something Mummy insists on. As we walk down towards the beach from our house we link arms, with Hope in the middle. It is a lovely spring day so we take our time.

The restaurant is intimate, there are three groups of people at other tables in the restaurant and we are directed to a table in the corner at the back, next to the dancefloor which opens out onto the beach. We can hear the sound of the sea while we eat and as the sun goes down we toast Hope with a glass of 'bubbly' which is Hope's first ever alcoholic drink.

'Happy birthday darling.'

'Thanks Mummy, well, actually thanks 'Mum's'. You are both amazing, I love you so much.'

I smile and look at my daughter. So young, with so much time ahead of her. It doesn't seem so long ago that she was a baby but soon she will want to find her own way in the world. It terrifies us. The world is a horrible, evil, cruel place and she is such an innocent girl. Men have never been a part of our lives but lately we have both started to notice Hope glance at young boys in the street when we are together and we see the flush in her cheek. It is a worry. I have spent a lot of time explaining to Hope how dangerous the world is but she just smiles when I talk about it and I wonder whether she is just humouring me.

'Can I go and dance Mummy?' she asks. We look up towards the dance floor. It is quiet and we will be able to see her from the table. Still, it is getting dark already.

'Let's all go.' Mummy says.

We leave the table and go to the centre of the dance floor. I realise I have never danced on a dancefloor before. Sometimes on Saturday nights Mummy plays music and we all dance around the lounge but I have never danced around strangers. Mummy is comfortable dancing in front of strangers and as I watch her I see a glimpse of a woman I don't know at all. This woman sways and swings her hips in time with the music and she looks beautiful. She has her eyes closed and is savouring the music. I realise I don't know much about her life before me and I wonder what she was like. I look at Hope. Pink cheeks, eyes wide, laughing at me as she steps from one foot to the other. 'Dance Mummy, dance!' she says, eyes dancing along with her feet.

I start to move. I am so awkward. I close my eyes and I pretend I am Mummy, as she is right now. I listen to the music. I begin to move in time to the beat, then open my eyes and join hands with Mummy and Hope. I feel happy today.

2025

Buckingham Palace Report. Author: Private Secretary to the Queen, Evelyn Carey

This is a summary of the current position:
The following male members of the royal family are symptomatic;
The Prince of Wales
The Duke of Cambridge
The Prince of Cambridge
The Queen suffered a heart attack and was admitted to hospital at 9.45am. Her symptoms are not related to the viral outbreak. She is currently in a serious condition.
When considering succession planning for the purposes of post-virus planning, we are now excluding males. Given this, the Princess of Cambridge is expected to become heir to the throne. She would require a Regent to support her until she is of age.
It is proposed that the role of regent be offered to the Princess of York. The Duchess of Cambridge is content with this arrangement.
We are proposing that 'Operation London Bridge' be set aside. The Queen advises that a state funeral would be distasteful under current circumstances. She proposes that members of the royal family be buried in in private ceremonies on the royal estate.

2002

Hope and I have a day to ourselves. Mummy is working and there is no school or college today. We go for a long walk in South Downs National Park, which is 20 miles away from our house. I drive Mummy's car, I am nervous because I have never driven without Mummy in the passenger seat. Hope is so excited, as she always is when we do something new. It's a hot, sunny day and by the time we arrive I am sweating from the nerves and from gripping the steering wheel too hard but I feel proud of myself for getting us here unscathed.

We walk the longest route around the park, I carry our picnic all the way. It is heavy but Hope wanted lots of different choices and we so rarely go anywhere special that I wanted it to be nice for her.

I had hoped that the park would be quiet but there lots of families and people with their dogs here. Every time we pass a dog, Hope runs to stroke it. The first time she does my heart races and I tell her not to but she looks so happy that I decide to concentrate on the owners. If the owner is a woman I will let her go, if the owner is a man I will stop her. I don't tell her why I worry about men with dogs because I would have to tell her how I came to be pregnant with her, instead I talk to her about how you can't trust men. I explain that they think differently to women, they are motivated by sex and don't see a girl or a woman, they just see something they can take and own. If Mummy were here she would change the subject, she often limits my time alone with Hope, so that she can control what Hope hears from me.

Hope doesn't agree with me. She says that she knows boys who are kind and nice and wouldn't dream of hurting her. She has made more male friends than I thought and when I tell her they are tricking her she gets quite upset. We find a spot to have a picnic and lay out our blanket. We eat in silence, I am thinking about how stupid I have been and how I must be stricter. We have let our guard down with Hope and have allowed her too much freedom. I will speak to Mummy about it.

* * *

After a while Hope looks at me and says, quietly 'I'm really sorry if I have upset you, Mum.' I realise that I have been frowning to myself. Hope doesn't call me Mum in public because we had to pretend I was her sister when she was little and I smile a little bit at that. I pull her into a hug and try to make her feel better.

'Don't be silly. I just worry about you. You are very innocent and you don't know what the world is really like. I don't want to scare you but I need to keep you safe.'

'Okay Mum. I understand. I'll try to be more careful.

As we walk back to the car we see a man with a dog. Hope looks at me and takes my hand. I am happy about that. She is learning and I have kept her safe.

2025

Mary Bertram, wife of the Defence Secretary

That morning, my husband woke up early and took himself downstairs. He made himself a large bacon sandwich and a cup of tea and was eating it at the kitchen table when I came downstairs. When I asked him if he was okay he nodded. 'I'm fine. I was just thinking that this could be my last bacon sandwich.' I glared at him and left the room. Comments like that were especially upsetting.

It quickly became clear that he intended to spend the day in his pyjamas. While I got dressed upstairs, I heard him crashing about in the lounge, then the opening credits to 'Full Metal Jacket' blared out over the TV speakers.

I stood on the landing for a few moments, torn. I wanted to spend time with him before there was no time left but my business was struggling in the wake of the outbreak and I could not afford to pause recovery efforts. I know that sounds heartless but my husband was a very selfish man and after years of living with someone like that you have to think of yourself because no one else will. I was still deciding when I saw him wander through the hall with a glass of scotch and some popcorn. One of his most unattractive character traits was to drown himself in alcohol at the first whiff of a crisis. I spent many nights pouring him into a taxi or apologising to friends and relatives on his behalf and I didn't want to spend the day with that person. I'm still a little ashamed to say that it made up my mind for me. I finished dressing and slipped out of the house. I could tell it was going to be a difficult day.

I popped back at lunchtime to make him lunch as I had been feeling guilty all morning. He didn't acknowledge my arrival and when I walked into the lounge with his favourite lunch I saw an empty glass and a quarter-full bottle of scotch on the table. I sighed and gave him his lunch. As he took it, he winced, put the plate down and looked at me.

'I have a headache.'

I sat down next to him. I meant to be kind but couldn't help myself, quipping 'Three quarters of a bottle of scotch will do that to you.'

He didn't even crack a smile, in fact he looked thoroughly miserable. I took his hand. 'Does your head feel heavy?'

'I don't know.' He slurred. 'You are right, I have had a lot of scotch.'

I relaxed back into the sofa, feeling even more guilty for working. I could take the afternoon off. I looked up to see what he was watching.

'Falling Down? Not really a feel-good film, is it?'

He snorted. 'No. I guess not. What would you suggest?'

I stood up and cast my eye over our collection. 'What about Forrest Gump?'

He grimaced. 'I don't think so. Stay and watch this with me for a while.'

He watched the film and I watched him. We had been together for so long, I didn't know what it would feel like to be alone. I sat thinking about it until the credits rolled and a fat tear rolled down my face. He turned to me and looked at me like he was seeing me for the first time. He wasn't usually one for sentiment but he smiled at me fondly and pulled me towards him for a cuddle. I leant into him, thinking 'Wow, this is actually nice.'

Then he ruined it. 'This might be our last cuddle' he said miserably.

My face fell and I pushed him away. 'Can you bloody stop it? It's so morbid. You're ruining the time we have left.'

'Okay, Sorry. Come back. Please?'

I sat there with him, being held. The screen on the TV went blank. After about fifteen minutes, he sat upright and said 'I really don't feel good.' I went out to the medicine cabinet in the kitchen to get some painkillers and when I returned he was lying down on the sofa. He was sweating, his hands were shaking and he looked terrified. He sat up to take the tablets and his face turned purple with exertion. He was struggling to breathe and before I could reach him, he passed out with a wheeze and fell backwards onto the sofa. I ran to him, checked he was breathing and then sat for a moment, wondering what to do. In the end, I called my daughter. Her relationship with her father was difficult but I thought she might regret it if she didn't see him now.

'Hi Gillian, it's Mum. Your Dad has it. Will you come over and be with him? Please?'

'Oh Mum, of course I'll come. Did he ask for me? Actually, I don't need to know the answer. I'll be there in ten minutes. Okay? Sit tight.'

I replaced the handset and poured my first scotch in fifteen years. I set it down on the table and popped to the kitchen to get a damp cloth for his forehead. Then I put Forrest Gump on the DVD player and sat next to my husband, sipping my scotch. I pulled his head onto my lap and stroked his forehead, gently.

As I looked at him, I tried to recall the moment I had stopped loving him. I was fond of him and knew I would miss him but we'd been together a long time. The world had changed beyond recognition but he was still the man I met thirty years before. He hadn't adapted and couldn't see how talented his daughter was or how successful I had become. He saw a daughter who despised him and a wife who couldn't look after him. I felt terrible in that moment, because instead of the grief I should have felt, I felt a flicker of excitement. I put it down to the scotch. It was very strong.

2002

I am sitting on the floor reading about the latest gene therapy cancer research. Mummy is on the sofa, reading a book. The doorbell rings and she looks at me, quizzically. 'Hope?' she asks. I shake my head. 'No, she isn't due back until 5pm.' We let her catch the bus to and from College alone now. I spend nervous hours watching the window, waiting for her ponytail to bounce past.

'Wait there.' She goes to the door and opens it with the chain on. 'Hello?' I hear her ask. Then almost immediately I hear her exclaim 'Oh!', so I stand up and peek around the doorframe. Mummy has swung the door wide open and I can see two policemen standing on the step. Mummy is asking for ID. They draw out warrant cards and present them to her and she steps aside so that they can come in. They are the first men to enter our house in over ten years.

They tramp through into the lounge in heavy boots and sit down, looking expectantly at Mummy and I. I am uncomfortable and don't want to sit down so I hover near the door, ready to run. Mummy looks at me and says shakily 'Jean, it's okay, sit.' I sit next to her, holding her hand.

'Do you have a daughter called Hope?' We both nod and I glance across at Mummy crossly. I have told her to stop it plenty of times, I am old enough to be Hope's mum now.

The policeman continues. His face is pale and pinched and he looks more serious than anyone I have ever seen. 'We found the body of a young girl at lunchtime today in an alley close to the College. Identification in her pocket indicated that the body was your daughter. I'm so sorry.'

I feel a wrench, as if someone is tearing and scarring my insides and then I hear a noise. A horrible wailing. It is terrifying, like an animal fighting for its life. I look at Mummy. Tears are running down her face but her mouth is closed, her hand is on her chest. I look at the policemen, who are looking right back at me and I realise with some surprise that the noise is coming from me.

2025

Cabinet Office, 10am

The Government was in crisis. The PM and the Home Secretary were dead. Six healthy ministers remained, all of whom were women. The PM's special adviser, who would usually have called an emergency cabinet meeting, had died that morning. Justine, a reliable but overlooked aide, arrived in the office to find the Cabinet Office in complete disarray. She called Victoria Buxton-Smith to ask for help, concluding that since everyone involved in the decision to sack her was now dead, no-one would really care if she came back to work. Besides, they needed her. No-one else knew what to do next.

Victoria was fired by the Prime Minister at the turn of the year. The official explanation to the press was that she was fired for insubordination but in reality, the Prime Minister had been informed about a disloyal comment she'd made to someone who was not as discreet as she first thought. A public sacking like that, however unfair, left her with few options and she was running out of money.

The day before, her partner of two years had left to be with her parents but Victoria's father was sick and she had chosen to stay with him. He'd passed away at home the night before, leaving her numb and alone in his house. She'd wandered around the property, unsure of what to do and still reeling from the pace of his decline. When the phone rang she had just decided to join her partners family and was preparing to leave. Usually she would have jumped at the chance to redeem herself but that day nothing felt as important as losing her father and she uncharacteristically paused for a few moments, wondering what her father would say at such a quick return to work. She could almost hear him.

'For god's sake, go. What are you waiting for? Staying away won't help anyone, least of all you. You need to keep busy.'

She agreed to go in.

She arrived at No. 10 and immediately called the six remaining ministers to a cabinet meeting at 11am. She called the Palace to ask them to prepare for the temporary appointment of a new PM to reside over the crisis. She wrote a short press release for publication immediately, concise, factual and devoid of any tributes or sentiment, which she doubted would be well received.

'At 3am this morning, the Prime Minister, George Moore, passed away after contracting the virus. He is survived by his wife, Charlotte and their two children. At 3.35am, the Home Secretary also passed away. He is survived by his wife, daughter and three grandchildren. Several members of the cabinet have been taken ill and an emergency Cabinet Meeting has been called. Surviving members will recommend a temporary appointment to Prime Minister along with appointments to other vacant ministerial posts. The new Prime Minister will remain in post until the situation stabilises and a leadership election can be called. The new Prime Minister will address the nation tomorrow morning at 9am.'

* * *

Claire arrived early and waited for her colleagues in the meeting room. Two hours ago, her mum had returned home, inconsolable after the death of Claire's brother Martin. Claire felt emotionally inadequate and it was Ben who consoled his granny while she cried. Claire sat on the sofa next to them, wondering why she felt as if she were in a bubble, surrounded by grief but unable to feel any of it for herself.

When Victoria called Claire had looked to her mother for per-mission to leave. Her mother said dully 'Just go Claire. It's fine.' She felt terrible about leaving her and couldn't shake the feel-ing that she was in the wrong place.

She looked up as Victoria and four of her ministerial col-leagues filed into the meeting room. Victoria closed the door quietly.

'Good morning.' Victoria began. 'Does anyone know where Nancy King is?'

Karen nodded sadly. 'Her husband has it, she is at the hospital with him now. 'Claire shook her head. 'George? God. I went to university with him.' They sat silently for a moment, taking in the news.

Victoria was the first to break the silence. She looked around at the despondent faces of her colleagues and said softly. 'I am sorry I had to call you in, I'm sure there are people you would rather be with but we have no Prime Minister and a cabinet of five. You need to nominate a new leader from among this group, who can assume the position of Prime Minister until a leadership election can be held. The new Prime Minister should appoint cabinet ministers into all of the vacant seats.'

Claire grimaced. 'Don't we have to consult the party?'

'What party?' Victoria exclaimed. 'They are all sick or dead, there is no-one to ask and we don't have a functioning gov-ernment. We need to address that quickly if we don't want the country to descend into anarchy. There is no precedent for this, we must appoint a temporary leader as soon as possible.'

Claire sighed. 'Okay. Does anyone here want the job?' All eyes darted around the room but no-one answered. 'I can't imagine why.' said Karen wryly.

Victoria looked at Karen. 'Why not you, Karen?'

Karen sighed. 'I've never wanted it, I'm not robust enough and I wouldn't know what to say to comfort the pubic or give them strength to carry on. I'm barely functioning myself.'

Claire looked at her. 'Karen, I've known you for years. You do yourself a disservice. You are one of the strongest people I know.'

Victoria turned to Claire. 'And you, Claire? What about you? I know you have ambitions for the top job.'

'I would certainly think about it in ten years or so but I'm not ready for it. I'm eighteen months into my first ministerial role. I don't have the experience to lead the country through something like this. I'd feel like a fraud and I wouldn't know where to start.'

'That's what advisors are for, Claire. You wouldn't be doing it alone. We would be here to support you.' She turned to Deborah. 'What about you, Deborah?'

They all looked at her. Deborah was a fiercely bright woman in her late forties and they all knew that they only reason she hadn't been promoted before now was because the PM had felt threatened by her intellect. She looked at them in surprise. 'I'm the least qualified here. I have been a Secretary of State for a matter of days. I won't deny that I have ambitions but right now I would prefer to play a supporting role. Besides I'm the Health Secretary, I don't think the timing is right to replace me. The department needs consistent leadership and I understand the issues better than anyone else there.'

Victoria nodded. 'Okay, I understand that argument. Millicent?'

Millicent Cain, the minister for Education, looked around, shaking her head. 'My husband is okay for now but we all know he probably won't make it and I don't know how I will cope when....' Her chin wobbled and she paused for a moment to compose herself. 'Look, we are all ambitious but no-one wants the job right now. We just need to choose. Any one of us could do this, we just need to pull together but I'd rather not put myself forward, I'm not the right person.'

Victoria smiled wryly. 'You know, if you were men you'd have all put your hat in the ring.' She gave each of them a piece of paper. 'Vote for the person you think has the strength to lead us through the crisis.'

Claire didn't hesitate, she wrote Karen's name down and folded the paper in half. They gave their votes to Victoria, who opened them all and lay them out in front of her.

'Okay, one vote for Karen, five votes for Claire. Congratulations Claire.'

She looked at Claire's horrified face and said gently 'It's only until the situation stabilises enough for a leadership election. '

Claire was aghast and felt instantly overwhelmed. She couldn't see an end to it, the country would not be stable enough to call a leadership election for months. Justice Secretary was her first cabinet post and when she took the job, it was made abundantly clear to her that she was only appointed because George Moore wanted a qualified barrister to appease the judiciary who were scathing about the appointment of ministers with no legal qualifications to the role. George was a bully and under his leadership she'd been undermined and belittled. Her confidence had diminished and she had no idea how to manage a crisis of this magnitude.

Around the table the other women looked visibly relieved. Karen grabbed Claire's hand and shook it warmly. 'Congratulations Claire. You have my full support and I will help you in any way that I can.' The others nodded emphatically in agreement. Claire swallowed her fears and looked around at the others determinedly. 'I'm surprised you chose me but I appreciate your confidence. We need to work together though, I need all the help I can get and I don't want to do this on my own.'

Deborah leant forward and touched Claire's hand. 'Of course, we are here for you whenever you need us. '

Victoria turned back to her notes. 'I have convened a COBR meeting at 1pm but only eight of the seventeen people due to attend are fit and well. There are the four of you, Nancy, Elizabeth Vinn, the Head of MI5 and the Foreign Secretary. The remaining nine men are either in hospital or deceased. Claire realised that Victoria hadn't mentioned Roland Bertram. 'What about Roland?'

'He died this morning. His wife and daughter were with him.'
Claire nodded sombrely and Victoria continued.

'I have a list of stand-ins but they are all relatively junior. Expertise is scarce, almost half of all civil servants are off work and the rest are finding it difficult to travel because public transport has ground to a halt. Most people are working at home, if at all so new ministers are unlikely to be well briefed on the current situation.

There are intermittent issues with all utilities across the city. We have seen an increase in the number of power cuts, as there is a severe lack of personnel available to detect and repair problems before they become issues. Back-up generators have been installed in some of the recently refurbished government buildings but in others power cuts have meant that Ministers have been unable to communicate with officials at all. Each department has a continuity plan and I am drawing those together.

All this means that it may become difficult for central government to function as effectively as it normally does. We need to focus on providing clear plans to local councils, along with emergency funds so that they can execute them. Do you have any questions?'

Claire had barely heard Victoria's words. Despite her colleague's words of support, she felt like an imposter with the weight of the world on her shoulders. She stared at Victoria numbly, then said, 'Victoria, can you please get us all a coffee? We need to come up with a plan.'

2002

Hope's murder is changing everything. The rage I have pushed down inside me all these years is bubbling to the surface. It spills everywhere, I can't control it. It burns everything it touches. Mummy either watches me cry and rant or sits, staring into space. Saying nothing, doing nothing.

A police woman named Sheila is assigned to us and is always here, like part of the furniture. She tells us Hope was strangled and they suspect a man in his early twenties. They question Hope's friends at College, who say this man was always on the bus to College and seemed obsessed with Hope. Though Hope was shy and innocent she was also too nice to ignore him, even though he was a bit weird. As soon as she died he stopped getting the bus.

The police have issued an E-fit of him and they give me a copy. I pin it next to my pictures of bacteria and viruses and study it. His face is etched on my brain like a scar. He has dirty blonde hair and dark, hooded eyes. His face is narrow, long and gaunt, like he hasn't eaten in a while. The dark circles under his eyes make him look old. He looks like someone I would cross the road to avoid.

Sheila arrives with news. She says they have arrested a man for questioning and hope to charge him within the next 24 hours. When Sheila leaves I go to the police station and sit in reception. I need to see the man who killed my daughter. A police officer comes out from behind the desk and asks me who I am. When I tell him, he tells me to go home but I don't.

Sheila comes to reception and sits with me. She understands

why I am there but she says that I can't see him. If he is charged he will be taken straight to a remand prison so there is no way I can come face to face with him until the case goes to court. She tells me to go home, so I do.

I go to the shed and get Mummy's axe. She uses it to cut the thick parts of the hedge away and sharpens it a lot. I put the axe in my coat and set off. When I am back at the police station I sit outside the back gates where the police cars go in and out. It gets dark but I don't move. At 10pm the gates swing open and a car edges out. I can make out the man from the E-fit through the window. I stand up and pull the axe out from my coat and try to lift it so I can hit the door but is heavy and I am too slow. A police officer jumps out of the far side of the car and runs at me.

'You really don't want to do that, do you?' He says. He grabs my arm and take the axe away. I'm watching the window and I see the man in the car peer out at me with a horrified look on his face. I feel the rage again and I thrash at the policeman, but he is strong and holds me so tight I can't escape. Everything goes black.

Sheila tells me later that I threatened to kill him and that it took three policemen to restrain me. I get in trouble for that but I only care that I missed a chance to look into his eyes and drive that axe into his skull.

2025

Jenny Robinson

Jenny, Lisa and Mia sat in the lounge, watching the news unfold on TV, unwilling to watch but unable to tear their eyes away.

As the hours dragged on the reports became more sporadic, less organised. When a reporter collapsed in the middle of his interview, the screen went temporarily blank and then news reports began to play on repeat with only a live tickertape to display new information. They watched numbly as the messages ran along the screen.

'...The Deputy Prime Minister dead and several other cabinet ministers in hospital with virus...'

'...Prince of Wales and Duke of Cambridge at St Thomas' Hospital, sources close to the Royal household confirm...'

'...Three Sky reporters die after falling ill while covering events as they unfolded yesterday...'

'...So far there are no reported cases of women falling ill...'

'...NHS hospitals overwhelmed as sick patients continue to pour in...'

'...SOCO release statement: 'The investigation is ongoing and we urge anyone with any information to contact the police. We are particularly interested in anyone acting oddly near treatment facilities or covered reservoirs in the past week....'

'....Virus NOT airborne, officials confirm. Public urged to avoid exchange of bodily fluids with anyone suffering from viral symptoms...'

'No new information about the virus, government confirms...'

'...Questions need to be asked about the competence of this government- Head of the Opposition...'

'All police leave and rest days cancelled after thousands of officers taken ill...'

'...All airports, ports and railways closed in an attempt to contain the virus. Members of the public urged to avoid travel wherever possible. Checkpoints introduced throughout the country...'

'...Estimated 2,000,000 British men dead and thousands more sick as the virus spreads. Angry public call for answers...'

'...New Minister for Health, Deborah Walsh, visits King's College Hospital today. 'Doctors and nurses here are working around the clock. They are angels in the darkness.' Additional resources confirmed for palliative care...'

After what seemed like hours, Jenny glanced up. Mia was no longer in the lounge. Her heart leapt and she looked at Lisa in alarm. 'Where is she?'

'Relax. Mia went to her room about half an hour ago. I think she needed a break. She's fine, she just needs rest.'

'Okay.' Jenny sank back onto the sofa again.

'Have you called the school?' Lisa shook her head.

'The head text me, it's still closed. Thirteen more pupils have died.' Lisa spoke in a whisper, not wanting Mia to overhear.

Jenny turned back to the screen and Lisa wondered if she had heard her at all. After a few moments she looked at Lisa, anger flashing in her eyes. 'I need to do something. I can't sit here and watch TV while people die. I want to help.'

Lisa sighed, her expression resigned. 'You have just lost your husband and your son.' She said gently. 'You have barely eaten or slept since they died. Claire can manage without you for a day or two.'

'I don't think she can. I'd like to think that we are close friends but I haven't even told her about Mark and Jasper and I'm worried about her and her family. If she does needs me then I want to go in. I can take Mia with me.'

Lisa shook her head. 'No, Jenny. Taking Mia outside at the moment is not a good idea' She indicated towards the TV screen where earlier footage of an angry mob outside a hospital was being repeated.

'I knew you would say that but the virus isn't airborne and women are immune anyway. I know there is unrest but, as long as we are careful, there isn't any practical reason why we can't go.'

Lisa raised her eyebrows. 'You're set on this, aren't you?'

Jenny nodded. 'I am, if Claire needs me. Look, I know you are worried. I have my work laptop here. If you really don't want us to go out then I can at least offer to help her from home.'

'I know you, Jenny. As soon as you speak to Claire, you'll go in. For the record, I don't think anyone will expect you to turn up for work two days after losing your husband and son. If you are doing this for yourself then okay but don't push yourself too hard.'

Jenny stood up and made for the door, then turned back to her sister briefly. 'Aren't you angry, Lisa? Don't you want to know who did it? What leads they have? What the government is doing about it? Sitting here watching TV is like watching the world end from my sofa. I can't do that, I'm going bloody insane. In my job, I usually know everything that's going on. Sometimes that's a perk, sometimes a curse. But not knowing is far harder.'

Lisa sighed. 'okay, I get it.' A news report flashed onto the screen and Jenny and Lisa turned to watch it.

'At 3am today the Prime Minister, George Moore, passed away after contracting the virus. He is survived by his wife, Charlotte and his two children. At 3.35am, the Home Secretary also passed away. He is survived by his wife, daughter and three grandchildren. Surviving Cabinet Members will shortly recommend a temporary appointment to Prime Minister along with appointments to other ministerial posts. The new Prime Minister will remain in post until the situation stabilises and a leadership election can be called. She will address the nation tomorrow morning at 9am.'

Jenny looked at Lisa. 'I'm calling.'

2002

The monster who killed Hope is charged and remanded in custody to await trial. All there is to do is wait for the hearing. Mummy and I are a little bit lost. Hope's body has been released to us and we plan a memorial service for her. Her murder is all over the newspapers and everyone in Brighton knows. Mummy says it was the same when I was taken and it will be difficult for me because our lives will not be private anymore. She is right. When I go out of the house people look at me and sometimes they even say things like 'I'm so sorry for your loss.' and 'That man should be hung for what he did to your sister.' When they say 'sister' I want to scream in their faces 'SHE WASN'T JUST MY SISTER, SHE WAS MY DAUGHTER!' but I don't because Mummy really wouldn't like it. She hasn't been out in a while and so it is up to me to do the food shopping and the cooking.

The memorial service is ruined because so many people turn up uninvited. It is so full that there are people queueing outside the church and when they realise that the church is full they wait outside. Some of them hold candles or lay flowers. I am angry because none of them knew Hope and it feels like they are just being nosy. Or maybe they feel guilty because everyone avoided the monster who killed her but no-one bothered to stop him. I can't look at them or talk to them after the service so I just leave. I don't care that I look rude.

I have to go back to work in the lab to pay for food and bills because Mummy isn't working now. I like being in the lab because the people who work there know I don't want to talk about Hope so they give me lots of work to do.

When I work I think about all the ways that the monster could be punished for what he did. Nothing the courts could do to him is quite enough. I need to feel that he got what he deserves.

2003

I sit in court every day of the trial watching HIM.

He is emotionless as my daughter's injuries are read out to the court. The expert on the stand says Hope's injuries were consistent with an initial impact from behind. She was hit over the head and then dragged a short distance, evident from scratches on her legs. The expert says that there were indications of sexual assault and she fought her attacker, whose skin was found under her nails. After that ordeal, he strangled her, then stabbed her several times in the chest. The body was not moved after the attack and she was found approximately thirty minutes to an hour later. The expert is very matter-of-fact about her attack, showing no emotion at all, much like HIM. I watch these emotionless men with tears running down my face. I don't have enough tissues for all the tears. The lady next to me cries too. Some of the women in the jury cry and I am pleased because at least they care.

Mummy is not in court with me. She says she heard enough about the terrible things men do to girls at the last trial and it almost broke her. She wants to remember Hope as the lovely, energetic girl she was. She spends a lot of time in bed and she still isn't working. I try to make her change her mind every day but she tells me to leave her alone.

I have to come and hear what happened to Hope. I need to know if it was as terrible for Hope as it was for me. Even though she wasn't raped, the way that he hurt her means that she may as well have been and I think she is better off where she is now because living with what happened is worse. She wouldn't have been the girl I knew anymore, she would have been like me.

The court hears all of the evidence and the jury retires to consider their verdict. I think it is an easy decision for them to make because the evidence against him is overwhelming. Hopes blood was on his clothes, his DNA was under her fingernails, eye witnesses saw him get off the bus at the same stop as Hope and her friends gave evidence about his unnatural interest in her. I expect the jury to come back quickly but they actually take hours to decide. Tortuous, painful hours. I sit in the coffee shop across the road waiting, with a cold cup of tea in front of me.

When the verdict comes back it is as expected- GUILTY. He is sentenced to life in prison. I go home and research what it is like in prison and what 'life' means. I discover that 'life' doesn't mean he will die in prison, he will be released one day. When that happens, I will find him and make sure he doesn't hurt anyone ever again.

2025

Hertfordshire
Witness Testimonial, Violet Brown

Violet sat in her lounger, studying her husband. He sat in his chair with his mouth hanging open, his tongue lolling on his blue cheek. She spoke loudly enough for him to hear. 'You really are dull these days.' She laughed wryly at her own joke and got up to make tea. It wasn't as easy as it used to be and as she shifted forwards gingerly in her chair and levered herself up she muttered 'Come on Violet!'.

She stood up on wobbly tired legs and shuffled out into the kitchen to put on the kettle. As she gathered a cup, teabag and milk she wondered how long it would be before anyone came. She thought again of her big, strong son David who would find it easy to lift Stan.

When she'd settled back in her chair with the tea, she picked up the telephone and tried her son again. Still no answer.

'Where could he be?' she asked Stan. 'Maybe at work?' Stan didn't answer, so she picked up her book and carried on reading. It was a good yarn.

Later, she turned on the television to listen to the news.

'Claire Flint was today appointed temporary PM and will chair her first COBR within the hour. In the meantime, the virus continues to spread unchecked. We understand that she has not yet been formally sworn in by the Queen, who is rumoured to be in hospital...'

Violet switched off the TV with a snort. 'Bloody politicians, always making a drama out of nothing. I'm sure it is just the flu.' She lay her head back in her chair. 'I'll go to the shops to-morrow, Stan.' Stan didn't reply.

2004

I go over and over my conversations with Hope, trying to work out where I went wrong. I am wracked with guilt that I couldn't keep my daughter safe. I told her that men were dangerous so many times but she still spoke to him. I speak to her friends at College and ask how many times she spoke to him and what she said. They say she tried her best to ignore him but he was persistent and she was too nice. She didn't encourage him, she only ever replied to his questions, she never initiated a conversation.

I think about the sort of person who would kill an innocent girl. Even if she'd been rude to him, he would still have followed her. It wasn't her fault, she didn't do anything wrong. She was in the wrong place at the wrong time. It was all him.

I hope that Hope didn't spend her last moments thinking that I would be angry with her. I am angry that men believe they have the God-given right to do what they want with women. I am angry that he was allowed to exist but I'm not angry with Hope.

I should have told her what happened to me. If she knew why were so protective she might have told me about the odd man on the bus. Then I remember that if I'd told her, she would have known she was the product of a rape and that would have hurt her. But if I had hurt her, maybe she would still be alive.

I try to talk to Mummy about it but she shouts at me, she doesn't want to talk about Hope. When I start to cry, Mummy holds me and says 'There isn't anything we could have done, Jean. These things just happen. Some men are just evil. You couldn't have known. You need to let it go and move on with your life.'

I need to be busy. I spend most of my time at the lab. There is a lot to do and the nature of it keeps me occupied. We are working on a cure for the common cold. I love watching particles of a virus attach to a cell and take it over. I am not supposed to love the virus, I am supposed to protect the healthy cell but I like to watch it do its work and imagine that it is wiping out all of the evils of this world. It is the only thing that distracts me from this hell that I am in.

2025

Rt. Hon. Claire Flint MP.

Claire had been up most of the night compiling a list of suitably qualified and experienced women to fill the cabinet posts. If the briefings were to be believed, her male colleagues wouldn't survive the week. It was a difficult job; George Moore had suppressed the female talent in the party only her five female cabinet colleagues had any real experience. She looked at the hand-written list she had so far.

Home Secretary- Karen Tonge. Experienced, sensible, talented.
Foreign Secretary- Katrina Ironside. Junior minister in FCO, good, experienced.
Chancellor of the Exchequer- Millicent Cain, experienced economist.
Health Secretary- Deborah Walsh, clever, good with public.
Defence Secretary- Sarah Hammond, junior minister in MOD, served in military. We might clash?
Justice Secretary- Nancy King, experienced lawyer, women and equalities experience.
There were lots of empty spaces left but she was too tired to fill them. She put down her pen and closed the book. She needed help. Jenny had agreed to come back into work in a few days but Claire felt terrible for even asking that so calling her now was not an option. She resolved to gather her colleagues together again in the morning to help, it was too big a chal-

lenge to do alone.

2004

Hope's murder wasn't the only murder in 2002, far from it.
The same year, three little girls were also murdered, all by men. I think about what happened to me and what happened to Hope and to the other girls. I want to go outside and scream at the top of my voice
'ARE YOU ALL STUPID? CAN'T YOU SEE WHAT IS HAPPENING HERE?'
Why are we all pretending that the world is fine? It's not fine. It's broken and violent men are the reason. They should all be locked up. Why do we let them walk the streets and eat the same food as us? Why do we let them run companies and countries? Why can't anyone else see that this is wrong?

2025

Meeting of 'COBR' (based on minutes)

All faces turned to face Claire the moment she entered the room. She sat down trying not to appear nervous. It was her third appearance at COBR but only her first as Prime Minister and her stomach was churning with nerves. All of the newly promoted Ministers were there, plucked from the back benches of parliament and clutching hastily prepared briefings.

The head of MI5 sat next to her and was the only man in the room. She had been expecting the foreign secretary as well and looked quizzically at Victoria who had just walked in. She hurried over to Claire and leant forward to whisper in her ear. 'The Foreign Secretary has been taken to hospital. He collapsed in his car on the way here.' Before she could stop herself, Claire mentally scanned the list of women who could step into vacant posts, trying to remember who her back up was. She felt immediate shame and her cheeks flushed slightly. 'Okay, keep me posted on his condition. Have you asked Katrina to join us?'

'She is just entering the building now.'

She cleared her throat and looked around the table. 'Okay everyone, shall we begin? This is my first COBR in the chair so please bear with me. Shall we do a round of introductions?

As the group gave names and roles, Claire readied herself. She wanted the meeting to be pacey and decisions to be taken quickly. When the last person had spoken, Claire began.

'Okay, What is the latest intelligence picture? Do we have any suspects?' Claire felt as if she were role playing on a stage but no-one seemed to notice. The head of MI5 nodded at Claire and began.

'At the beginning of our investigation we focussed on water treatment facilities and reservoirs and found very little evidence of anything untoward. Yesterday we shifted our focus to chemicals and fluoride added to the water.' He saw one or two puzzled faces around the table and added 'The addition of fluoride to our treated water is now mandated, following an extensive health study a few years ago.'

He continued 'We have found a significant piece of CCTV footage, following a trawl of CCTV in over 500 facilities. It shows five masked individuals entering a fluoride production company using keys and entry codes. It took them almost an hour to enter, unload barrels and exit.'

Claire interjected. 'Do you know anything about these people?'

'Well, by their gait, height and build we have reason to believe that they were female but we have no intelligence on their identity.

'And we only have one piece of evidence, after three days?'

'I'm afraid so. My theory is that this method of entry was the exception, rather than the rule and that they gained access to other facilities during working hours.'

Claire thanked him and turned to Victoria.

'I'd like to gather a group of senior executives from the water companies as soon as possible for a meeting, can you arrange that please?' She turned back to the Head of MI5.

'I assume you are already investigating staff with the necessary access to fluoride and to the water treatment process itself?'

'Yes, Ma'am. We are interviewing everyone of interest.'

She nodded. 'Okay, What's next?'

'Elizabeth Vinn, ma'am.' Claire smiled at her. 'Our command structure ensures that all policing operations are conducted with proper authority and are co-ordinated effectively. Across the country this command structure is breaking down. Officer numbers over the rank of inspector are dwindling those that remain are struggling to maintain order. Local forces are relying on the heroism of individual female officers and unless there is a concerted effort to plug gaps in command and co-ordinate the resources we have left we risk a complete breakdown in law and order.

We have instructed the most senior female officer in each force to contact the Association of Police Chief Constables and will attempt to co-ordinate activities through them in the coming days. We are using retired and ex-police officers as well as officials who can be redeployed and have some relevant training, like prison officers and immigration officials.

Locally, forces are reporting less crowds on the street as public messages about avoiding close contact have the desired effect However, there remain pockets of unrest and looting, so we must not be complacent. We are preparing local policing plans based on the assumption that there could be significant unrest once the outbreak has subsided.'

'Okay thank you Elizabeth. I am concerned that you are so under resourced but until we can bring troops home from abroad to assist I don't think we have any other immediate options. I'd like to hear from Health next please, Deborah.'

Deborah cleared her throat and nodded at Claire.

'Not good news I'm afraid. For every patient admitted, we have turned away another nine because of lack of capacity. Based on admissions alone we estimate that around two million men have died and a further three million are infected. Those figures do not include those being tended to at home. Most hospitals are operating a 'one out, one in' policy for new patients.'

She turned to speak to Claire directly.

'Claire, I would recommend issuing strongly worded public guidance asking the public not to attend hospitals if they can be cared for them at home. There are only 142,000 NHS beds in Britain, and even with the emergency centres we've set up there are still nowhere near enough beds. We are issuing virus information packs and the virus helpline is working well. I recommend focussing more effort on that type of activity.' Claire nodded her agreement.

'There was one more issue I wanted to raise.' Deborah hesitated for a moment and Claire got the impression it was a tricky subject. 'The NHS is running low on supplies and many are considering the withdrawal of palliative care. There are concerns that border closures mean palliative medications like painkillers will not be replenished. It would be my preference to ensure that we do what we can to continue palliative care, especially to patients in their teens but given the pressure on resources, I would welcome your view on this point.'

'Thanks Deborah. On your first point, please put together as much information as possible about home treatments and make that available to the public. On your second, I don't agree to the withdrawal of palliative care. It is unacceptable to let patients needlessly suffer. Please provide a list of medication that we are running low on. We are currently negotiating airdrops of aid and we can ask for extra supplies to be included.'

'As you wish, Claire.' Deborah made a note of the request and sat back, as Claire moved on to the next item.

'Department for Energy and Climate Change. Ma'am. Electricity supplies are intermittent in some areas and female engineers are in short supply. Those available are being asked to travel long distances to fix problems and carry out essential maintenance work across the grid. At the moment, the position is manageable but we don't know for how long. The CEO of the National Grid, who many of us know, died this morning. Wendy Matthews, formally executive director, has temporarily taken over as CEO.

There are also issues arise with gas suppliers, though incidents have been managed well and breaks in supply largely avoided. On water, tests are being carried out every few hours to determine the extent to which the virus has dissipated. It is still present in the water supply in most areas, in some cases in large quantities. It is resistant to heat and chemicals. We continue to run water through the purification system but it may be some time before it is drinkable again so we recommend reinforcing public messages about boiling and purifying water.'

'Okay thanks. I'd like to see a clear plan for purification of the water supply to drinkable levels and projections on that as soon as possible. I'd also like similar plans on the maintenance of the power supply. What's next?'

'Katrina Ironside, Foreign and Commonwealth Office. We are in continued contact with our allies. We believe that the immediate threat of the virus spreading beyond this country has been neutralised as there have been no new cases for 24 hours. However, serious concerns remain about our ability to contain the virus, given the rate of infection and our failure to apprehend the culprits. Our borders remain closed and we have requested airdrops of essential medical supplies, fuel and foodstuffs. Those requests have been accepted and airdrops are being arranged.'

'My colleague from the Department for Defence will no doubt cover the threat of attack in more detail but I am concerned that, despite the open channels in place, there remains a significant risk that attempts will be made to neutralise the threat, by potential aggressors or even our allies. Conversations are stilted to say the least. Maintaining diplomatic relationships with foreign leaders is vital and this government is now an unknown quantity. We may want to consider a news blackout as the constant commentary from reporters is doing little to put anyone's mind at ease'

'Thank you. I'll make contact with all foreign leaders today. Victoria, get me a list of states and contact numbers in order of importance. I'll take the point about a news blackout under advisement but I'm not sure that it will do much to put anyone's mind at ease and taking over control of reporting smacks of a dictatorship. Does anyone else have a view?'

The new Secretary of State for Defence, Sarah Hammond raised her hand. 'Ma'am I agree it won't help. A media blackout may make foreign aggression more likely but the press could assist more in managing messages.'

'Okay thanks. Anyone have any other views?' Again, there was silence. Claire looked around and saw grief, defeat and horror on the faces of her colleagues. She had been so focussed on her own inexperience that she hadn't noticed the mood in the room. When she spoke again her voice had lost the tone of authority and there was a slight wobble to her voice.

'Look, we have all lost people and I know how hard this is, but we need to focus.' she took a breath. 'Karen, I think you are up next.' Karen nodded.

'Local authorities are responsible for the disposal of bodies. Emergency legislation has been prepared which will allow families to bury their dead in designated places, including on their own properties with permission. The legislation will also allow local authorities to collect bodies and dispose of them by mass cremation. Councils are now designating the first public spaces for mass cremation.'

'Thank you. That sounds sensible. Do you have any data on the scale of the issue, or any information on how the logistical arrangements required to transport bodies?' Karen shook her head. 'Not with any degree of accuracy at the moment. I'll know more tomorrow. '

'Okay, Thanks Karen. Moving on to defence please?'

Sarah Hammond spoke briskly. 'We are on high alert, all ground to air missiles are operational and we have trained female personnel to operate them. Three of our four vanguard submarines containing trident missiles are at sea and personnel on board have been updated. Our troops abroad are preparing to return home as soon as it is safe to do so.'

'Thank you, Minister, unless anyone else has any comments, I believe that is all. COBR will remain active until the position has stabilised. We will hold daily meetings but if there are urgent matters that need addressing please call my office immediately.'

The group filed out of the room, silently. When they had all gone Claire turned to Victoria. 'We need to do something. Everyone is waiting to die or mourning the dead. We need to make them act.'

2004

Mummy is unwell. She doesn't eat, she just sits at the table, looking at old photographs. There are a few pictures of Hope on the table but mostly they are of me. I look at them over her shoulder, then turn them over one by one and read her writing on the back.

'Jean, aged 2, on Daddy's lap'.

'Jean, aged 5, with Mummy in Manchester.'

'Jean, aged 8, in nan and grandads garden.'

'Jean, Mummy and Daddy, Lulworth Cove, Dorset'.

I am confused by this. She can look at me now, I am right here. I don't know why she wants to remember these times. I can barely remember them.

I ask her why she is looking at them and she says 'These pictures were taken back when you were a happy, carefree child. It's nice for me to remember that.'

She means they were taken before Daddy left and the men took me. I find it difficult to think about these times because back then I was naïve. I didn't know what the world was like and I thought there were men out there who were good. I thought my Daddy loved me. I thought a lot of things that weren't true.

When she goes to bed I pack those pictures away and hide them. It doesn't do any good to pretend.

2025

DAY 4, 6,000,000 confirmed dead

The lights flickered and died across swathes of the land. Televisions went dark. The virus invaded cells, homes and families, plucking out men like errant hairs. Women left their homes, bearing the bodies of their dead as the death trucks rolled by to collect them. Others dug graves and buried their loved ones in the garden, then worried about the virus seeping up through the soil. The first funeral pyres were lit, filling the skies with smoke and an unfamiliar smell. Grief pervaded the souls of women, twisting and blackening them forever.

The boy cried, he did not understand this new world with no lights or entertainment. It was full of bad smells, hot tears, wailing sounds, bland tinned food and his sick father, confined to his bed in a locked room. His mum spent more time holding him and she cried a lot more than before. She let him go only when he wriggled away. There was a lot more washing with scalding water and Mum made him scrub his hands until they were raw, which made him cry.

She was scared of men now. They didn't go out much but when they did, she shied away from the men in the street, pulling him towards her and covering his face. He wasn't allowed to play with his friend next door anymore. The mummies talked over the fence, hands covering their mouths and they cried together. Mum passed food over the fence to his friend's mum, who had nothing.

He overheard his Mum say 'No-one will come. We have to bury

them ourselves.' He wondered what they were burying. He took a trowel from the garden shed and started to dig.

2004

I have the most wonderful dream. I dream of a world where only women exist. Hope is alive, Mummy is happy again and the weight of my life's experiences is lifted. There is no war, the world is beautiful and the air is clear. I wake up crying with joy and then realise that I am not there anymore.

It makes me think about what is required to make the world a better place. Powerful women rarely talk about war or deny climate change but they do talk about equality, or empowerment. Women are mentally tough but few have the necessary status to make the changes the world needs. I am one of very few women with the vision and will to make it happen.

Any change must be transformational. It must propel women into power and it must be unstoppable. Unfortunately, we will always need men to procreate, they cannot simply be removed but they do need to be 'put low'. I know that women cannot win a war against men so any plan to put women in control must be elegant yet swift. I spend a lot of time thinking about this.

Mummy is back in bed again. I go into her and talk to her about my dream. She smiles sadly at me and says 'It is a lovely dream, Jean. But it is not real. Hope is gone. The world isn't a nice place and you can't change that. You need to move on.' She lies back down and turns her back on me. I think she is tired.

2025

Birmingham Children's Hospital: Briefing for Department of Health.

'Paediatricians and virologists at Birmingham Children's Hospital have discovered a pattern in the infection of children. There is a clear age line, the majority of boys under ten do not present with viral symptoms.

There are notable exceptions to the age line. Six males aged between five and nine years old have contracted the virus in the local area. Study of their medical records indicates that all six families declined the MMR vaccine.

We are testing the MMR vaccine. Early results indicate that the vaccine contains antibodies to the virus...'

2005

Every year since the millennium I have written a list of major crimes committed by men that year.

Today I compile my list for 2005 to date.

Four men bombed public transport in London, killing 56 and injuring 784 others. (It is hard to write that down as a single event, it makes it seem insignificant when it wasn't.)

A female police officer was shot dead

A young model was murdered by a known sex offender

A man was kicked to death by a large group of youths.

A man was beaten to death by two men who believed he was gay

A Pakistani woman was stabbed repeatedly by a male member of her family while other men in her family stood by and watched.

A man was murdered by two men in a racially motivated attack.

It is hard to find details online, one could almost deduce that the crimes of men are hidden from the public. There were over 600 murders in Great Britain this year but only a handful made headline news. Men write the articles and own the newspapers, so it is easy for them to cover it all up. The media focus only on a few shocking cases that can't be ignored. It is as if we accept male violence as a part of life that must be tolerated. Well, I do not tolerate it, I am full of rage and indignation and I refuse to believe that I'm the only one who cares.

Mummy doesn't debate with me anymore. She watches me as I talk and I think I am finally persuading her. Sometimes I pace back and forth and pretend I am speaking to all women, not just Mummy. I talk to Mummy about the bold decisions we must take to create a better world for women and she actually smiles at me. She believes in me, I know it.

2025

Rose (Based on a note provided by an anonymous donor)

Rose lay down her spade, her tears mingling with the sand on her face. She looked down into the hole. 'Deep enough and wide enough', she thought. The harsh wind whipped her hair across her face as she returned to the car. She drove wearily back to the house and went upstairs to their bedroom, where she watched her beautiful sleeping boys. She lay with them, stroking their hair and kissing their cool cheeks.

She remembered that day at the beach. The boys pushed the dinghy out to sea, the sand clung to their hair and the wind flushed their cheeks. They laughed and shouted to her as they rowed out to the rocks and she sat on the beach, smiling and laughing with them but always quietly worrying. 'What about rip tides? What about sharks?' She remembered removing her shoes and feeling the sand between her toes as she readied herself to swim out to them and then watching as they expertly rowed the dinghy back to land. Of course, they were fine, they were taught by her husband, the expert.

She collected the things she needed. Two quilts, favourite items, her bag, the note she wrote to her sister. One by one she carried her boys to the car. They were almost too heavy, gangly legs hung across her arms as she summoned the strength to make the last few steps with her second son. She laid each of them gently on the seats and locked the house, then thought to herself 'How foolish! There's no-one left to break in!'

The drive was different with the boys in the car. She smiled as she drove and wound down the windows to feel the sea air on her face. 'I'm happy we moved here, we've had so much fun.' She told her sleeping boys.

They arrived at the beach. The wind blew harder, she heard the sea thrashing against the shore and tasted the salt on her lips. She took a deep, cleansing breath and smelt the sea air. She taped the note to her sister on the windscreen and then took the quilts and their favourite things to the hole. She made them all a bed and when she was finished she stood back and checked to make sure it looked cosy and warm. That done, she carried her boys down the beach and placed them in the hole, one at a time, then went back to the car.

She unzipped her bag, laid the tablets out on the passenger seat and counted them. One hundred, double strength. She swallowed them, a few at a time, with the water she brought. then locked the car, went down to the hole and stepped into it with her sons. She lay between them, put her arms around them both and pulled the heavy quilt over them all. 'You are so cold boys! We are all safe now.' She told them. She shut her eyes and feeling a wave of sleep, she let it take her.

2006

When I am not at work I study in my room. I have a lot to do. Mummy and I don't talk much these days. She has a computer set up in the dining room and she sits at it, staring at the blank screen.

In my room, I am busy gathering all the evidence I can about men. It is a really big job and I want to catalogue everything. I fill folders with clippings and printouts of all the evil things men have done. I highlight key passages and I have amassed hundreds of articles, all the facts. I don't need to write anything myself as the evidence is there for anyone to see if you look for it. Murders, rapes, violence, frauds, robberies, massacres, wars, greed. Always men. Sometimes I forget to sleep, it takes up so much of my time.

2025

Statement from the Palace

'The Queen passed away at 10am after a short illness, unrelated to the viral outbreak.

The Prince of Wales passed away at 10.35am after suffering the effects of the virus.

The Duke of Cambridge passed away at 1.45pm after suffering the effects of the virus and his son, the Prince of Cambridge, passed away shortly after his father. The next in line to the throne is the Princess of Cambridge and will be crowned Queen in due course.

As she is not yet of age, legislation will be passed allowing for the appointment of a Princess Regent. After some consideration, the Palace has taken the decision that this honour will be bestowed on the next in line to the throne, the Princess of York.'

2007

I think of a brilliant plan. I am giddy with excitement, though I don't have the expertise to make it happen yet. My plan is to create a bacteria, virus or disease that could purge the country of men, not all of them but enough of them to bring them low, so that women can rise up and take control. I know it sounds implausible and already I see all of the potential problems that I must overcome, the biggest of which is ensuring women are left unscathed. I would be inconsolable if even one of us were to die as a result of my actions, we have suffered enough already.

I research how to make my idea a reality. I'd like to start with a virus or disease that already exists but anything that lethal is stored so securely that it would not be possible for someone like me to gain access to it, even with my qualifications. I either need access or I need to create something new. I may have to commit to further specialist study in order to progress.

2025

DAY 5, 16,000,000 estimated dead. Buckingham Palace

A grey cloud of smoke hung over London, smelling acrid and stinging the noses of the women and children. Too quickly, the smell became normal, just another part of death and grief. London's streets were quiet apart from the death truck that rolled past each day, ringing its tell-tale bell. For the women who brought their loved ones into the street and watched them disappear into the vans like refuse, it was a jarring insult to the memory of their beloved husbands, sons and fathers. But it was necessary. Their hands were raw and blistered from digging graves for those they had already lost, their bodies were too weary and minds too broken to dig any more. The truck rolled past, stopped, collected the dead and rolled away. Outside Buckingham Palace, members of the public had placed flowers on the gate in mourning for the Queen and her family. Those flowers were already limp and dying, an unnecessary reminder of the fragility of life.

Inside, staff lingered in mournful groups. The Princess of York, now Princess Regent, had moved to Buckingham Palace with the Princess of Cambridge and her mother. She wore traditional black and was quiet, having lost her grandparents, her uncle, several cousins and her father, the Duke of York. She mourned them all in silent fury, their deaths unnoticed by a country enveloped in their own grief and loss. She could not vocalise her anger for fear of upsetting the staff and other members of the family so decided not to speak at all.

She had been told that there would be a coronation for the Princess of Cambridge. It would be a simple occasion and would be held once the country had stabilised. As Regent, she would be part of the ceremony. She would rather not have the job of Regent at all. The life she had out of the spotlight suited her. She enjoyed the perks of Royal life without the expectations placed on her cousins. Being heir to the throne was not the life she wanted and she'd barely acknowledged her position in the line of succession. Even when the Prince of Cambridge passed away she did not for a moment believe that she would be considered as regent. The Princess Royal or the Duchess of Cambridge were more appropriate choices in her view, but the Princess Royal was extremely unwell and the Duchess of Cambridge was not of royal lineage. There had been several heated discussions about the role of Regent in recent days. She wasn't like her grandmother, she wasn't dutiful or regal and she didn't give rousing speeches. Evelyn Carey has committed to helping her through the difficult times. 'Evelyn would do this job far better than I ever would' she thought privately.

Evelyn's son, Finn was staying in the palace with Evelyn. A quiet boy, he was sweet and affectionate and captured the Princess Regent's affection far more quickly than the young princess she was to advise. To watch him roaming the halls of the palace, finding delight in the smallest of details that the family took for granted, was a fair distraction from the horrors of the world outside.

They sat on the floor in one of the private rooms, playing with Finns trucks. He pushed them around the room, stopping them every few feet, 'to load them'. The Princess Regent asked 'what are you loading, Finn?' Finn replied. 'All the daddies.' She took a sharp intake of breath and quite unexpectedly began to cry. She stood up and moved quickly away from the child, hiding her face from his gaze. As she looked out of the window at the rising smoke she realised the scale of the task ahead. These people were her people and they were dying.

2008

Mummy asks what keeps me locked in my room so much. She says she misses me. I haven't told Mummy about my plan, though I usually tell her everything so today I decide to share it with her. Verbalising it makes it real and at first, I worry that it sounds implausible but the more I say aloud the more perfect it seems. Just telling Mummy is enough to help me find answers to the questions that have plagued me, like 'How would you make sure all the men caught the virus?' or 'How will you persuade other people to help you?' I talk for so long that I almost forget she is there.

When I do finally stop and look at her I see her reaction for the first time. It is not what I expected, she isn't proud, her face is full of horror. I ask her what is wrong but she will not answer me. I am so confused and I start to wonder if she even heard me. She looks very ill.

Mummy is in bed. I try to make her eat and talk to me but she won't. I call our doctor who prescribes her antidepressants. She says Mummy needs to be hospitalised for a while and thinks this has been coming for a long time. It is a delayed reaction to Hope's death which happens a lot after the loss of a child. An ambulance arrives and takes Mummy away. She will be back in a few weeks, the doctor says. She just needs a break from everyday life, somewhere quiet where she can get some help to recover. I am sad about Mummy but I am relieved that she isn't sick because of me.

While she is away, I really focus on the details of my plan. I need to create a virus or bacteria that can thrive in the air or in water, otherwise some men might survive. To do that I need to recruit an expert, I am good but I am not a virologist. I know people in the industry from university and from working in the lab, so I will start there.

I know I need a large quantity of the virus and I will need to store it somewhere secure and find a way to distribute it. I need money for that and I don't think Mummy's money will be enough, so I need a good job. I am saving my wages but I only have a few thousand saved.

I must also focus on what I will do after I have released it. The country will need me to lead them out of the darkness and into the light. I am the only one that can do this. No-one else has the vision and I know from experience that grief can paralyse a person. It will make you lose your mind, so I need to keep the women focussed because they will grieve for the men that are gone. They are so entrenched in the life that men have created for them that they will not want to lose it. That will be the hardest thing to change.

2025

Jenny Robinson, 8.30am

Jenny drove the short journey into Westminster, the lack of public transport made it the only way to get into London now. She didn't use her car much and usually wouldn't dream of driving in to Central London but today the roads were clear, with the exception of a few abandoned cars that had been pushed to the side of the road. Mia sat in the passenger seat reading 'Wuthering Heights'. She selected the book the day before from the bookshelf at home and had been reading it ever since. Jenny thought that was probably a good thing but Mia was so quiet that it was hard to tell. She asked to come with Jenny that morning and a change of scene seemed like a good idea, though the dull ache that had settled in her own stomach since Mark and Jasper died made her question whether either of them really ready. Mia wanted to help catch the people who did this and Jenny rationalised that resources were so scarce, Claire would probably be grateful for an extra pair of trusted hands, security cleared or not.

They reached the gates of Downing Street and Jenny showed her security pass. It was hard not to be nervous, as advisor to the Prime Minister she would have a lot more responsibility than she used to. Her involvement in politics still felt like a privilege and she still had to pinch herself sometimes. Compared to her colleagues in the party she came from a modest background and was proud of how far she had come.

The guard nodded an acknowledgement, they were expecting

her. As a young woman, No. 10 was her ultimate goal and, despite the terrible circumstances, she felt a flutter of anticipation as the gates opened, quickly replaced with guilt as she drove through the gates. She owed it to Mark and Jasper to do the best job she could.

Mia looked up from her book as the car drew to a halt. 'Are you nervous, Mum?'

Jenny turned off the ignition and opened the door as Mia unbuckled herself.

'Very. Are you?'

'Nope!' But as they reached the doors to no. 10, Mia reached for her Mums hand

'Well, maybe a bit.'

A policewoman opened the door and they stepped inside. As instructed they removed their phones, left them on the table next to the door and headed up the wide staircase to the white drawing room, where the Downing Street staff met.

Claire was there and greeted Jenny with a huge hug. 'My god, I'm so glad to see you! How are you both?'

Jenny smiled at her friend's warm welcome 'We are okay, Claire. It's good to see you too.'

Claire hugged Mia, then stood back and looked at her. 'I'm glad you've come, Mia. Let's sit down.'

They sat on the plush sofas and Jenny said to Mia gently, 'If you want to, you can read while we catch up.' Mia nodded but then Claire called out to Victoria who, it seemed, was waiting outside the door.

'Can you bring us some snacks and drinks please?' she turned to Mia.

'Mia, would you like a tour? It's not every day you get to see inside Number 10?' Mia's face lit up briefly.

'Yes please, Claire, I'd like that.' She managed a small smile, her first in days.

'Victoria, why don't you take Mia with you and show her around?'

Victoria smiled and beckoned to Mia. 'Come with me, I'll

show you all the places normal visitors aren't allowed to see.'
They left and Claire turned to Jenny. 'How is she? How are you doing? She looked at Jenny intently and her face fell as she saw the misery in her eyes.

'I'm so sorry about Mark and Jasper. I don't know what to say.' Tears welled in her eyes and she quickly brushed them away. 'I don't know how you are here, but thank you for coming.'

Jenny nodded, unable to answer. She cleared her throat. 'How is Ben?' Claire's eyes flitted up to the ceiling. 'He's...okay. He's upstairs, Mum is with him. Since we told him about James he has cried a lot but he doesn't want to talk, at least not to me. Mum stays with him while I work and I'm trying to get upstairs to see him every hour or so. I feel so guilty for being dragged away when he needs me. I didn't even want this job.'

Jenny leant forward and touched her friend's arm. 'It's easy to be self-critical Claire, just remember that everyone feels the way you do. they just don't have your job on top of it all. It's okay not to be okay.'

Claire nodded.

Jenny pulled out a notebook and pen from her bag. 'Now, what's first?'

'Are you sure you are ready for this Jenny? If you need more time...'

Jenny interrupted her 'I'm ready, I need this. I can't sit at home anymore, all the memories... it's just too upsetting. I want to be busy, I need these people to be caught.'

'Okay. I'll tell you where we've got to.' She lowered her voice as if worried about who would overhear, even though they were alone. 'Current figures put the total number of victims at just over sixteen million males, from age 10 upwards.'

Jenny gasped. 'Oh my god, that many? I saw bodies on the street on the way here and I have been watching the news but I didn't realise it was that bad.'

Claire nodded, grimly. 'We haven't realised any figures to the media. The bodies are a huge issue. Karen is trying to co-ordinate local councils to retrieve them but they are too many bodies and not enough people to help. It will be a while before we can get on top of it.

She held out a report for Jenny. 'This will provide you with more detail of the issues we are facing, it's a summary of all the briefings I have had today. It makes grim reading.' Jenny took the report and put in on the low table in front of her.

'Do you know who did this?'

Jenny almost held her breath waiting for the answer.

'No. But we know more than we did and we know a lot about the virus. Were you aware that younger boys don't seem to be affected?' Jenny nodded.

'A handful of children under ten have died. The rest seem to be immune and experts have been trying to work out why. Yesterday, a paediatrician at Birmingham City Hospital noticed a link between the children under ten who were sick. None of the children received the MMR vaccine. One paid privately for separate individual vaccines for their sons, the others chose not to vaccinate at all.

'Twelve years ago, the government decided to stop using multiple suppliers of the MMR vaccine, procuring it through one national contract instead. The decision was controversial. The contract was awarded to a firm called Cruise Pharmaceuticals, a well-established company with a good reputation. All those who received the MMR vaccination from this supplier are immune to the virus. The virus is engineered to target men. If the vaccine hadn't been provided, all male children under ten would also have died.'

Jenny was confused. 'I don't understand. How can they have developed a vaccine for a virus that has just been discovered? Was it an accident?'

Claire shook her head. 'We don't think so. We are investigating the people responsible for developing it now. The good news is that the vaccine can be used to prevent the virus from spreading any further, but it doesn't help the people who are already infected.' Claire took a gulp of water from a glass on the table and continued.

Jenny slumped back in her chair, it was a lot to take in. She looked at Claire, puzzled.

'But this means... I mean, doesn't this mean that it was planned, years in advance?'

'I think it means exactly that.' Claire watched as Jenny caught up with her. 'God. I can't believe it. It would take years of planning. Who would do such a thing?'

'We have a lead. The virologist who developed the vaccine resigned from her job at Cruise Pharmaceuticals about a year ago. The police have tried to trace her but she has disappeared without a trace. Her house was sold shortly before she resigned. She told her neighbours she was moving closer to family but she has no close relatives. She was estranged from her brother. He died three days ago. Her ex-husband died yesterday.'

Her background is complicated. She filed for divorce several years ago, citing unreasonable behaviour. Police reports show a pattern of domestic violence in the home. In 2009, she was hospitalised with a fractured skull, fractured cheekbone, broken arm and collar bone. Her husband was arrested and charged with rape and attempted murder. Shortly after that she filed for divorce. He spent four years in prison and when he was released she took out a civil order to prevent him from contacting her which he breached several times. The last time was shortly before her house was sold. She might have disappeared to escape him and we are keeping an open mind but she is our number one suspect.'

Jenny raised her eyebrows. 'It's quite a story but it isn't uncommon to be a victim of domestic abuse. That doesn't make her a murderer.'

'I know, but it's all we've got. Whoever did it didn't act alone. There is CCTV footage of a small group entering a factory that produces fluoride. We believe that the group added the virus to the fluoride, which is how it entered the water supply. Security services believe that the group responsible is small but utterly committed, even indoctrinated to their cause. They also believe that the group are all women.'

Claire looked at Jenny's shocked face. 'I know. It's a lot to take in, isn't it?'

'I find it difficult to believe that a group of women are responsible. What on earth could motivate them? It doesn't make any sense.'

Claire shrugged 'It's been on my mind too.'

Jenny let out a breath, then shook her head in disbelief. 'How did they get away with it?'

'I've asked that, no-one can explain it. There was no obvious build up to this. No internet chatter, no call to arms, no street demonstrations or emerging political groups. Remember that violent women are a rarity. Our prisons are full of men and research shows that female offenders are almost always victims as well as perpetrators. As a society, when we think about threat, we think of men. We just weren't looking for them.'

Claire stood up and went to the window, looking out at the deserted streets.

'The impact is truly terrifying. London is a ghost town; all the hospitals and emergency centres are full. There are thousands upon thousands of bodies to be disposed of. We have two weeks of emergency medication stockpiled and no foreign imports arriving. Border as closed. We will run out of food if we can't reopen them.'

'How quickly?' Jenny felt as if she wasn't in the room anymore. Nothing seemed real. It was as if Claire was speaking to her through a veil and the sounds were muffled.

'60-80% of the food we eat is imported from other countries, we also export a lot of food that isn't popular with British consumers. If we had to rely on stored food or things we produce ourselves we would run out of many types of food within a few months, maybe a little longer. If the borders don't re-open quickly, people will starve. We have to introduce rationing of cereals, fruit and vegetables, dairy products, beverages, meat and seafood. DEFRA is looking at a rationing scheme but it will take time to put in place. We rely heavily on men to farm the land and work in food production plants so we would need to put people to work in those industries to make sure the food doesn't go to waste.'

Jenny took a gulp of water and then stood up leaning on the back of the sofa to steady herself. She began to mentally scan her cupboard at home, thinking about how much food she had and how long it would last. She joined Claire at the window. Claire looked sideways at her. 'Are you okay? Shall I stop?' Jenny shook her head. 'Keep going, I need to know.'

'Okay. As you might expect, our economy is crashing through the floor. Industries that rely on a male workforce will almost certainly collapse. The national grid is vulnerable, a small number of qualified women are travelling huge distances to keep the power on. Water is still tainted with the virus, though most people who aren't sick by now are probably immune. The public will be reluctant to drink tap water for some time so water purification tablets will need to be rationed as well.'

Claire looked at Jenny, who saw the sheer exhaustion on Claire's face. She continued.

'This isn't the worst of it. The world is watching with great concern, they don't want the virus to spread abroad and will do anything to stop that from happening. We believe that some foreign powers are exploring nuclear options. They are considering wiping out the virus, along with our people, in an effort to prevent a further outbreak.'

Jenny gasped and clasped a hand across her mouth. 'How could they even consider that?'

Claire shrugged miserably. 'Intelligence sources suggest it has been actively discussed and I'm not sure it is off the table yet. We are rushing out the news about the vaccine which might help. Cruise Pharmaceuticals are producing 10,000,000 units of the vaccine and have stockpiled existing supplies. They are being very co-operative as you can imagine and are keen to distance themselves from the outbreak. Their main concern is reputational damage and the safety of their staff. We have offered state protection in return for their cooperation and priority access to supplies.'

Jenny stopped Claire. 'You didn't tell me the name of the virologist, the one who worked for them?'

Claire hesitated a moment. 'Do you really want to know?' Jenny nodded vigorously.

'Her name is Professor Nicole Moreland. We are considering releasing her details but it is a risk. I have a task for you, Jenny, if you are up to it?' Jenny nodded. 'Please, I'll do anything.'

'We need help. We expect the outbreak to peak over the next few days and then slowly peter out. We need volunteers to remove the bodies and get essential services running again. We also need to distribute the vaccine to anyone who isn't already symptomatic. Can you think about how to appeal to the public to help? We need to reach as many people as possible. You're here, something made you come in, even though you've lost Mark and Jasper, what was it?'

Jenny shrugged. 'I don't know. I just couldn't sit at home. Can I ask Mia to help? I need to give her something to focus on.'

'Of course. She's a bright girl and we need people her age to pitch in.' Claire stood up as the door opened and Victoria entered, bearing refreshments. Can I leave you to it? I have work stacked up and I want to pop up to see Ben quickly.' 'Of course.' Jenny sat back down on the sofa, ignoring the food that Victoria placed in front of her. She expected to feel more in control by going back to work but struggled to contain the growing anxiety she felt. She took a deep breath to calm herself down and opened her laptop to start work on a speech.

2009

I am late and I know that Mummy frets, so I am rushing and out of breath when I get to the front door.

As I turn the key I notice a shadow through the frosted glass. It is on the stairs. I stop in my tracks. I cannot fathom what it is but my heart races because I know it isn't supposed to be there. It could be an intruder, a man in our house. I am shaking and I don't know what to do, a knot of fear forms in my belly. Mummy is in there and she might be in danger so I look around our front garden for a weapon. I find a piece of wood, the leg of a chair that was supposed to go to the tip. I pick it up, feel its weight and swing it back and forth to get a feel for it. It is wet and a splinter from it pierces my skin but I don't let go. The knot eases a little and I feel a bit more confident but my heart still races and my legs are shaky. I look back at the shape, he is still there. Odd that he hasn't moved at all. Does he know I am here? Is he waiting for me to turn the key? I take a deep breath, turn the key and fling open the door.

The piece of wood drops out of my hand, I hear it clatter on the doorstep but it sounds far away.

All I can see is her face. It is purple and her eyes are wide open, one of them bulges out of its socket. I shut my eyes to stop seeing her but her face is still there in the dark behind my eyelids. I feel like I am going to faint and I grab hold of the doorway to steady myself.

Breathe.

Breathe.

I open my eyes. Don't look. Don't look.

Her feet are only a few centimetres away from the step. I need to get her down. I make my feet move and run up a few steps so that I can reach her. I try to lift her up but she is heavy and she sways a bit when I touch her.

Do something.

The rope is tied the bannisters at the top of the stairs. I have to let go of her to untie it but I don't want to hurt her. I squeeze past her and run up the stairs, I need to be fast. I try to tug at the knot, then I remember the knife I have hidden under my mattress in case intruders come in the night. I run to get it and saw at the rope until it snaps. I didn't think about what would happen to Mummy then. She crashes down the last few steps and lands in a heap.

I run down to her. Her neck looks livid and burnt when I loosen the rope and her skin is cool but not cold. I can't help pulling my hand away because her skin feels waxy. I can't save her. I am too late. She is gone because I was late home. I don't know who did this to her but I wasn't here.

I sit down and put mummy's head in my lap. All I can feel is my own heart pumping so hard it might explode. I rock backwards and forwards, trying to stop it.

Our neighbour sees the open door from the street. She comes through the gate and up the path. She calls out, cautiously. 'Hello? Everything okay? Your door is ope...oh my goodness!' She sees us through the crack in the door and in a flash, she is kneeling next to me looking down at Mummy. 'Jean. Oh god Jean, your mother...' I look up at her to explain what she is seeing but I can't because I don't know myself.

'She was hanging... I thought she was a burglar...I cut her down... and she fell. I can't save her. I was late...'

My neighbour stands up and runs to her house, shouting 'I'm going to call an ambulance. You stay with her, I'll be back.' I stay here. I have nowhere else to be.

2009

I find the note as I get into bed. She tucked it under the quilt for me to find. No-one killed Mummy. She killed herself. She left me all alone. The note says:

'Dearest Jeanie'
'This will be hard on you and I am sorry to leave you alone, but everyone dies at some point. I am so tired and I don't know what to do to help you. I love you very much but I have spent my whole life worrying about you and Hope. Keeping you safe was my priority but I have failed you in other ways.
I don't have any regrets about spending my life with you and Hope, in many ways it has been an absolute pleasure, you are my world and when Hope was alive I loved coming home to you both every night, but I made poor choices about your up-bringing which I deeply regret.
The day you were abducted, I was supposed to collect you from school but I was late because I was arguing with your father about the divorce. By the time I got to the school the teacher said that you had already left. She looked surprised to see me which made me angry with her because I always picked you up. I drove the route home really slowly, peering out at every person I saw to check if it was you. My heart was pounding and the closer I got to our house the more I worried because I knew that you couldn't have walked that far in the time. I burst through the front door but I knew that you weren't there because you didn't have a key.
I called all the mothers I knew to see if you went to their

houses. I drove all the routes you could possibly have taken and then I drove to the police station and reported you missing. The police reacted so quickly that I wished I had gone to the police station sooner. They sent everyone they had out looking for you. The policeman in charge called your dad, they thought that you might have run away because of the divorce but I knew that wasn't you.

No-one found you. They didn't know about the men in the van, no-one saw you get taken. The missing hours felt like years. I couldn't eat or drink, I felt sick. I was hot and angry and my heart pounded so hard I felt I might die. I couldn't sit down even for a second, I paced the floor like a caged animal. I wanted to walk the streets looking for you but the police made me stay in the station and answer lots of questions which they said would be more helpful. They sent police officers to the house to get photographs of you and then one of them waited there in case you came back. Your Dad came to the police station and sat with me, looking at me with angry eyes. I knew he blamed me, like I blamed him for keeping me on the phone too long.

It was hours before the old couple rang the police and said you'd knocked their door. The police said you were miles away from home but I wasn't listening, I was so relieved, I even hugged your Dad. I didn't realise what it meant.

Later they told us how injured you were and what those animals did to you. My heart broke then and there. I would have offered myself up just to take the pain away from you. Your Dad was so upset, he couldn't even come in to the hospital room with me. He sat outside, wringing his hands and praying for your soul. I was the one who sat and watched as they tried to reset your broken bones and sat with you while you screamed in pain. I saw your reaction to strange men, any men and I knew that I needed to keep you safe forever.

When we found out you were pregnant, I wanted them to abort it. I thought you would hate her and she would always represent what they did to you. Your Dad said it was God's will and that she was put inside you for a reason. He refused to consent so Hope stayed. I am not grateful for many of your Dad's actions but I am grateful for that. Can you imagine our lives without her? What a blessing she was, her short life filled me with happiness and I know she made you happy too.

Fear made my choices after that. Fear of prolonging your suffering or feeling as I did when you were missing and I didn't know if you were alive or dead. I wanted more than anything to keep you safe. We moved house because I thought you needed a fresh start away from your school, where everyone knew what happened. I wanted you to be able to walk down the street without hearing whispers. I put you in an all-girls school so that you would feel safe. I kept men away from the house so that you could relax. I was scared to start a new relationship in case he turned out to be a paedophile. I was scared of my own judgement.

All those poor choices I made have shaped who you have become and the things you believe. I have failed you as a mother and I feel the weight of that every second of every day. Women deserve equality and to be treated with respect but I do not believe that the world would be better without men, or that they should be 'purged from the earth' as you so eloquently put it. I regret keeping men away from you, I wish I'd sent you to a mixed school and encouraged you to meet boys, so that you could see for yourselves that most of them have good qualities. I am so sorry that my actions have caused such distrust and loathing in your soul, it was never my intention.

Please believe me when I say that not all men are bad, or evil. Most men are kind. Most men do not kidnap or rape children, or abandon them, or treat them badly, or murder them. The events that shaped your life are horrific but they don't happen every day or even every year. Everyone else just reads about these stories in the newspaper, they don't experience it like you have. You, my courageous girl, have seen more evil than anyone should ever have to endure but you mustn't allow it to define who you are, or turn you into a monster.

I hope that my death saves you. You need to seek out new opportunities and see the world through untarnished eyes. Find new friends, look for the positives, meet a nice man who can show you that there are good people in the world. Find some joy, do things that make you happy every day. Go and see the world outside this small town, use that wonderful brain to help people, not to hurt them.

You might also consider getting in touch with your Dad. His address and telephone number are listed in my address book. I kept him updated on your life even though you didn't want me to. He may not feel like a father to you anymore but he would like to be part of your life if you let him. He is a pastor now and he lives just outside Texas. Your half-brother is in his early twenties now and I think he owns his own business. It might be nice for you to visit and meet him. America is a big place, you could move there. The world is your oyster.

I will miss you and I know that you will miss me. I will go and find Hope in heaven now and together we will watch over you.

Goodbye my beautiful girl

Love Mummy'

2025

DAY 6, 23,000,000 estimated dead. Rt. Hon.
Claire Flint MP

Claire stood in front of the cameras, nervously brushing invisible dust off her dress. It was her first speech as Prime Minister and she was scared. Some of the women out there had lost their whole family and she was terrified of saying the wrong thing. She wanted to run away but everyone in the room was waiting for her to say something comforting or to provide answers to their questions.

Jenny had asked the networks to play Claire's speech as much as possible over the next few days. The power was out in a number of areas, so Jenny had printed out transcripts to display in town halls.

Claire ran over her speech in her mind. If she got this wrong she could make things worse. They needed the women to help move the bodies and transport food and safe drinking water to children and the elderly. She didn't have a 'Plan B' if this didn't work out.

She took a deep breath as the cameraman in front of her began the countdown. Five, four, three two, one...

'No-one would choose to give this speech. To stand before you all in these circumstances is beyond appalling.'

Her voice cracked and she took a deep breath before she continued.

'...This week has been the worst in human history and like

you, I am stricken with grief and despair. What happened to us is barbaric and inhumane, like a nightmare we cannot wake up from. It feels as if we may never smile or laugh again. I am new to this role and I don't mind admitting that I am scared. I feel the enormous weight of this tragedy, as I know you do. I don't know where to start, there is so much to do and yet I am tired and consumed with crippling grief. It is difficult to find the strength to think about our survival but we must.

How can we move forward?

Where will our food come from when the borders are closed?

How can we protect our children?

How will we afford to clothe, educate and protect them?

How can we make sure that they are not irreparably damaged by this tragedy?

How will we pay our mortgages now that our husbands have gone?

Will we lose our homes?

With no electricity, how can we keep our children warm?

How do we find the strength to get out of bed every day?

Isn't it easier just to give up?

Most of all I think about how many people it took to keep the power on, the water flowing, the roads safe, to farm our land, stock our shelves with food and build our homes. Before this tragedy, hundreds of thousands of men and women made it possible for us to switch on a light, turn on a television, open a fridge full of food and heat our homes every night. How will these things work now that half of us are gone?

These are all questions we have to answer and it is overwhelming and terrifying in its complexity. I lie awake, night after night, angry, fearful for my child and our future, grief stricken for those I have lost and devastated for our communities.

As I lay in bed, worrying about our future I realised something important.

We. Are. Still. Here.

Women are strong and capable, we are survivors. We have big

brains, lots of skills and we rise to difficult challenges. We multi-task, running homes, raising children and working. We tend to the sick, perform surgeries, run businesses, clean up messes, pay bills. We are amazing.

Yes, we are angry, sad, fearful and broken. But we will endure for our children. We know we can survive these dark days because women have consistently overcome difficult challenges throughout history. In the second world war, when our soldiers were fighting for our futures, our great grandmothers worked in factories, making weapons, ammunition, tanks and clothing for our troops. They sat on the ruins of their homes, drinking tea, they made sure that the country continued to run, kept the war effort alive and made sure the next generation was safe. When the men came home from war they found our great grandmothers forever changed, more resilient, determined and resolute. Strong when our men were broken.

We can do this. Today we grieve for our fathers, our husbands, our sons. We are allowed to cry. Tomorrow, we must find the strength to pick ourselves up and carry on for our children.

Like you, I feel lost and scared but I am here today because I am full of rage. I want to know who did this. I want to find them and make them pay. That got me out of bed today and it will get me out of bed tomorrow. It makes me determined to bury our dead, restore power, feed our children and get our country back on its feet. Because if we don't do it then they have won.

I promise you that I will do everything in my power to find the monsters who did this. They have poured poison into our communities, our homes and the bodies of our precious children. I won't leave this job until I find them and give you justice. I will do my best to lead our country back from this indescribable nightmare into a future that is full of hope once more. We are stronger as a team and I need your help so tomorrow, your local council doors will be open wide to welcome you. Please contact them, tell them what you can do to help. They will record your skills and match them to the work that needs to be done to raise our broken country from the ashes. In return for your hard work, all families will receive enough money and food to sustain your family until we recover. Together we will make sure that our great country endures.

We will do this in memory of our men, our fathers, our boys, our friends and our colleagues and as a tribute to their lives. We will not let them die in vain.'

2009

It is Mummy's funeral, a difficult day for me. Mummy and I have lived here for about twenty years but I don't even know our neighbour well. A group of women arrive at the church and tell me they knew Mummy from work. They tell me things that I don't know about Mummy and I feel angry because I don't like the idea that Mummy had a life which didn't involve me. It feels like she hid things.

A man talks to me about Mummy and I feel betrayed that she associated with him, knowing what happened to me. I wonder if she hated him as much as I do when he looks at me with his greedy eyes. I hate Mummy for dying. She left me with so many questions that I can't get an answer to, like why she carried on speaking to my father about me even though I asked her not to and why she thinks I would ever visit him or his stupid son.

Our neighbour is here, along with a few other people who live in our road. She is nice but some of the people with her have come because they want to see how broken I am now that Hope and Mummy are both dead. I keep myself to myself, smile tightly at the strangers and remember that they didn't know Mummy like I did. They think they are sad and they have the right to cry for her. I am her daughter, the one she loved best in the world. I am the one who should be crying, but I don't.

The vicar says some things and then looks at me because I am supposed to speak next. I come forward to the front of the church. The vicar told me that I should try to give everyone an idea of why she was so important to me, but to do that I have to pretend to be like everyone else. I put on my best face, the one that seems to make people like me and I say;

'I had the best mother in the world. Our house was our sanctuary. She protected me and she kept me safe, sheltering me from all that is ugly. She would say was too protective but no mother can ever do too much to protect her children. She loved and understood me. She was the best mother I could ever have and I really hope that she can hear me because I want her to know that.

As many of you know, we lost Hope when she was just sixteen. I know that she is here today too. When we have finished saying goodbye to Mummy they will hold hands and dance by the sea. I know that the world Mummy and Hope have gone to is beautiful and safe because I saw it in a dream. One day I will see it again but before I do I want Mummy to know that I will make the world a better place. I owe her that. Rest in peace Mummy. I love you.'

I go to sit down and people come up and hug me. I don't like it but I know that they expect me to hug them back, so I do.

We go to the place where Hope is buried and I watch as Mummy's body is lowered into the ground. She is lucky because she will see Hope again, I am a bit jealous about that. But I know that I have to stay, I have work to do.

Mummy leaves everything she owns to me. It turns out that Mummy saved a lot of money and she already had an inheritance from when Nanny and Grandad died. I knew she was good at saving and investing money but I am surprised that there is so much. It is good to have options.

I know I need to move house, so I start to look for something smaller in an area where people don't know my face or my business. I don't like the pity that passes across people's faces in the street. It makes me feel weak when I need to be strong.

2025

DAY 7, 25,000,000 estimated dead.
North Hertfordshire. Joanne Mitchell, volun-
teer.

Dark, foreboding clouds of smoke filled the air and even with the windows shut the smell was acrid and earthy. Joanne tried to breathe through her mouth as she drove the truck up the narrow road. The field came into view as she rounded the corner and she couldn't help a sharp intake of breath as she saw it for the first time. The grass around the edge was still green and luscious but after a few metres the ground softened and then dropped away. The trench that had been dug out was deep, dark and gloomy but she could see the outline of bodies, piled unceremoniously one on top of the other. She turned the van and reversed up to the edge of the field as instructed. She heard the women in the back of the van jump down onto the grass, open the doors and drag out the bodies. She put her hands over her ears but not quickly enough to avoid hearing the first body slip into the ditch. It felt callous and brutal. She closed her eyes and thought of her husband, whose body could easily have been here if she hadn't gritted her teeth and dug up the back garden. She looked at the blisters on her hands and felt grateful to have them. She knew this was necessary because there were too many bodies but it would never be okay. She thought of her son at home with the neighbours and prayed he would never see this.

Her new colleague Mabel came to the window.

'All done. Only seven hours and five trips to go.'

Joanne looked at her with tears in her eyes. 'This is awful. How are you okay?

Mabel leant on the van door. 'I have been doing this for four days. On the first day, I picked up the first body and threw up. One of the girls came to this field for the first time and broke down because her husband was taken here that morning. She went home and didn't come back.

On the second day, we bought masks and gloves, thinking it would be easier. Joan and I picked up a man, his mouth fell open and a bug crawled out. I screamed so loud that the driver jumped out, thinking we were being attacked.

On the third day Jan saw someone she knew in the pile of bodies and cried so much that the driver swapped with her.

Yesterday the police sent in cadaver dogs to find the bodies that we haven't been able to access and as they searched a road, I realised that I had stopped thinking about them as bodies and started thinking about them as rubbish to be removed. That night I went home and wrote down the names of every man that I've ever known. It took me all evening. I needed to remember that the people in the road aren't rubbish.

None of us are okay. I don't think we ever will be again. But this has to be done and if we cry all day it will take longer and feel worse. One day soon, all the bodies will be gone and then we will do something else. The speech that the new prime minister gave, it was right. We are all that's left. If we don't do this, no one will. You ready to go?'

Joanne looked at Mabel with admiration and nodded. 'If she can do this then so can I.' she thought.

2010

I live alone now and I quite like the solitude. Mummy and I had a particular Saturday routine which I like to carry on in memory of her and of Hope. I get up early, so as not to waste the day. I make myself a coffee, put a croissant in the oven and sit down with the Saturday paper which I always have delivered to my front door.

I never read the front page of the paper first. Today I begin by reading an article on page six. The article is about a 12-year old girl who was murdered earlier this year. Her uncle was convicted of her murder in the autumn. He lured her to his house, drugged her and then sexually abused her. When he was done he strangled her. The journalist raises the growing problems associated with pornography and how it contributes to violence in men.

I turn to page eight and read an article about an undercover operation to expose a paedophile ring. They groomed and abused over a hundred girls in one city.

I flick through the rest of the paper. A story about a missing woman who police believe has been abducted, an actress's struggle with her weight, a story about the rise in domestic violence, a two-page article about the new Prime Minister.

I turn back to the front page. A man is on the run, armed with a sawn-off shotgun. He shot his ex-girlfriend, her new partner and a police officer and is being hunted by police officers.

I put the paper to one side and turn on the radio. The host is joking to his female co-host about the size of her breasts. I turn off the radio and go to get dressed.

* * *

I walk to the shop to get bread. A builder whistles at me, telling me to 'cheer up'. When I pass without comment, he shouts 'suck my dick'.

* * *

In the supermarket, I hear a man talking to his wife in a low voice. 'No, why don't you ever fucking listen to me? Just do as you are fucking told.' His wife walks away from him, her face burning. He yells after her 'Don't you fucking walk away from me when I'm talking to you.' As he catches my eye, he mumbles 'Fucking cunt'.

* * *

At the checkout, I see a little girl drop a bottle of orange juice and watch her father say 'You really are a stupid, clumsy girl. You can't do anything right.'

* * *

That night I switch on the TV and start watching a programme about policing the streets on a Saturday night in the city centre. I see a group of drunk men kick another man repeatedly in the head and then attack the police who come to arrest them.

* * *

As I go to bed, I hear my neighbour screaming at his wife, then the unmistakable sound of him hitting her. Again.
I call the police for the third weekend in a row. One word repeats itself over and over in my head, drowning out my thought-

s. ENOUGH.

❋ ❋ ❋

I write to Mummy. I know I can't send it but I hope she is up there watching me because I want her to know why.

'Mummy, I love you so much and will never forget the note you left me. I understand why you left me alone, though I wish that you hadn't because I don't see what you see. When I look around I see that men have broken the world. We are lead to believe that we are equals but it is all a lie. They rape, they kill, they hurt women, children and each other every single day. They wield their power with a sense of entitlement, expecting to have it forever and we do not challenge it. We cower before them, they are stronger, they have money, they control the water, gas and electricity, what we watch on television and how laws are made. They wreak devastation and they don't care that they are destroying the planet, killing off whole species in their pursuit of money, power and control. They are greedy, selfish and blind to the devastation that they cause.
I know in my heart that you see these things through my eyes now. This must be stopped. I don't want to do this but I need to. Our world is worth saving and if there were a God then he would do it. If there is a God then maybe that's why I am here. I'm the only person who knows what to do and how to do it.
We all die in the end. All I am doing is accelerating that for some men, so that the rest of us can survive and thrive. They are doing so much damage, they deserve to be punished for it. Punishing a few now will save billions in the future. It is a kindness to humanity. Enough is enough.'

2025

The doorbell rang. Violet grabbed the lounger arms and gave herself a shove forward, then eased herself up. 'Old bones' she grumbled. She shuffled off to the door where the shadow of a woman darkened the hall through the frosted glass.
Not David.
She called out 'Hello?' The woman at the door answered.
'Hello there. I'm Jan, from the council. We are doing some house calls. There's a funny smell coming from your house, are you okay?'
'Well, I'm fine.' Violets voice broke as she called through the glass.
'The funny smell is Stan, my husband. He's dead. Been in his chair for days. I can't move him. I was waiting for my son David to come and do it but I can't get hold of him. Do you want to come in?'
'Oh. Erm, yes please.'
Violet took the chain off of the door and opened it a crack. She looked suspiciously at Jan.
'Do you have ID?' She asked.
Jan took out her council pass and handed it to Violet. Violet studied it for a moment. She didn't really understand the point of asking for ID as she wouldn't be able to tell a fake from the genuine article but David told her not to let anyone in

without it so she pretended she knew what she was doing. She handed the ID back to Jan and opened the door wide. 'My name is Violet.'

* * *

Jan stepped inside. The smell assaulted her senses. She wrinkled her nose and said to Violet, gently. 'How have you managed? The smell is overwhelming.'

Violet shuffled back into the lounge. 'I don't have a great sense of smell anymore to be honest. Though I have to say I have started to feel a bit queasy when I look at him.'

Jan followed Violet into the lounge. Stan's body was slumped in the chair. Jan estimated that he had been dead for around six days. The smell was overpowering. His body was bloated and his flesh was shiny and greeny- grey. His face looked odd, as if it was starting to melt. Jan gagged and quickly turned away. She looked at Violet who had returned to her lounger and was looking up at her. She crouched next to her. 'We need to move your husband and get you out of this room for a while. Is that okay?' Violets face sagged a little with relief. 'That would be good. I need to find my son David.'

Jan helped Violet out of her chair and guided her towards the small kitchen. 'We need to have a bit of a chat. Have you been watching much TV over the last few days?'

'Not really, no. the news depresses me. It's all bad news. We don't even get a cheeky good news story at the end anymore.'

Jan smiled sadly. 'That's what my mum says. Come on. Let's see if we can make a cup of tea. I'm just going to pop and tell the ladies I'm here with what I'm doing.'

'Can you fetch my handbag for me?' Jan popped back into the lounge to collect it, shutting the lounge door firmly behind her. In the street, she signalled to the crew outside. Mabel hurried over. Jan spoke quickly and quietly. 'Her husband's body is in the lounge. He's been there for about six days I would think. It's pretty awful. You'll need masks and gloves. If you try and move the body off the chair I think it will break up.' Mabel wrinkled her nose. 'Sounds great, Thanks for that! Is she okay?'

Jan shrugged. 'I don't know. The poor woman has been sat in there for days.'

Mabel watched Jan go back into the kitchen, then called the others. Joanne had come back for a second day. Mabel liked her. She had started to get out and help at each stop. For her first day of lifting and shifting, she was doing pretty well. 'This is a bad one. We need to move the whole chair. Nose plugs and masks for this one. Don't forget to put the Vicks under your nose.'

Jan put the kettle on while Violet sat at her kitchen table. 'Violet, have you managed to get out to the shops?' Violet shook her head. "I meant to go but it's a trek without help and my legs aren't what they used to be. I've been using up my tins. Don't need a lot of food anyway and there wasn't much point cooking for one.' Jan nodded. She found some tea and powdered milk and made a strong cup with plenty of sugar for Violet.

They sat in the kitchen while the women moved the body. 'You must miss him.' Jan said, quietly. Violet snorted and tears rolled down her face. 'He was very lazy. But you are right, I do miss him.' Her face sagged and she said to Jan. 'Do you know, I had to sit with him for five nights and watch him rot in that chair. Forty-nine years we've been married and that is the last memory I have of him. I'm glad you've come. I never want to see his face again. I don't think I'll ever be able to remember how he was when he was alive. All I can see is his face, slowly slipping off his bones.' Another tear slid down her wrinkled face and she brushed it away with her sleeve.

She looked at Jan. 'Didn't you want any tea? Or are you one of those coffee drinkers?'

'I just had one.' Jan looked at Violet, sipping her tea. She wondered how much Violet had taken in about what was happening outside.

'If you haven't been watching the news then I think I might need to tell you what's been happening. You see, Stan isn't the only person who got sick.'

Violet interrupted. 'I know, that's why I need to see my son. I think he's sick, because he usually comes over every day and if he can't come he always calls. He's such a good boy. I can't think of a time that he didn't come. When he goes away he sends a carer to help us instead. He hasn't been round for over a week. I just need to know.'

'Okay.' said Jan. 'After you've finished your tea we will call social services and find out what's going on. Okay?'

'Thank you.' Violet slumped a little into her chair. Finally.

2011

I am thinking about my plan. I think about it for hours every day, especially if I'm not working. I know that my capabilities will only take me so far. It would take me a lifetime to develop, mass produce and distribute a virus and I would probably get caught trying. I need to find an expert to help me but that will be challenging. How do I make another person understand why this needs to happen? Even my own mother struggled.

Anyone I bring in to help has to be completely committed or I risk exposure. It's a challenge that keeps me awake at night. I am no fool, it's easy to close your eyes and believe that things are okay. Most women think they are treated well. They believe the lies men tell us and will assume I am crazy, a psychopath, or even a narcissist if I try to recruit them. I will likely find myself in prison before too long if I try. Unless you have experienced what I have, it is hard to understand what motivates me.

However, there are thousands of women who have been broken by men, many of them damaged beyond repair like me. Those women might understand what motivates me. I need to research my targets and choose the right people.

I am self-aware enough to know that I can be persuasive. In the past, I have used my knowledge to mould and shape the views of others. At university, I was a master debater. I can hold a room, I once made a whole lecture hall full of students turn away from the lecturer and towards me. I was given that gift for a reason. I need to get to work.

2025

Witness Testimonial, Amelia and Jack

The doorbell rang. Amelia looked at Jack and whispered 'Shall I answer it?'

Jack was scared. 'Daddy told us not to answer the door to strangers, Amelia'

'I know but Daddy is sick and he smells funny. Besides, we are hungry.' Amelia took a few steps towards the stairs and looked back at him. 'Coming?'

'Okay.' Jack grabbed her hand and Amelia lead the way down the stairs. She opened the letterbox and peeked through it. 'Hello, is someone there?'

The lady on the other side of the door bent down and looked through the letter box at Amelia and Jack. Amelia could see her eyes. They were smiley.

Hello' the lady said 'My name is Kate, what's your name?'

Amelia waggled her fingers through the letterbox to wave. 'Hi, I'm Amelia and this is Jack.' She paused. 'My Daddy says I'm not allowed to talk to strangers.'

Amelia moved so that she could see the lady's whole face through the letter box. 'Well, is Mum or Dad there with you now?'

'Daddy is upstairs but he has been sick for a long time. He smells funny.' Amelia crinkled her nose.

'Okay, is there anyone else home?'

'No, just us and Matilda the cat.'

'Do you want me to come in and see how your daddy is? I expect you guys are hungry, aren't you? I have some food in my bag.'

Amelia looked at Jack eagerly and then stood on her tiptoes and opened the door. The Kate-lady was very tall, she had brown curly hair like Aunt Susan's and a big smile. Amelia thought she looked nice but Jack was shy and hid behind her.

'Hi guys, aren't you brave?' Why don't I get you a drink and something to eat first? You look really hungry.' Amelia nodded quickly. They had eaten most things in the fridge, except the cucumber. They had eaten all the sweets, crisps cereal, fruit and bread in the cupboard. Amelia had tried to open a tin this morning but she couldn't use the tin opener, even though she had watched Daddy do it. They had been drinking the water from the tap after they ran out of orange and juice boxes.

The Kate-lady found a bar of chocolate in her bag and gave them half each. As they ate she rummaged through the cupboards, boiled the kettle and poured the hot water into a pan to cook some pasta she found. She made them each a cup of hot, sweet tea with milk which she had in her bag. They had never had tea before. It tasted really nice.

When the pasta was ready, she sat them down at the table in the kitchen and watched while they ate. Jack was really hungry and ate too quickly. The Kate-lady said to him, 'You need to slow down a little bit. I know you are hungry but you don't want to make yourself poorly do you?' Jack looked at her with wide eyes and shook his head. He thought she was a beautiful lady.

After they'd eaten, the Kate-lady said. Can you go to your bedrooms and collect two of your most favourite toys? I'm going to check on your daddy, okay?'

The children ran off to their rooms. Kate went to the main bedroom. As she opened the door, the smell confirmed what she already knew. She quickly checked the other rooms for other people but the children were alone.

She leant against the wall for a second and took a deep breath, blinking away the tears that threatened. It wasn't the time. She went back down stairs and searched for an address book or letters which might help her find one of the children's other relatives. She found a mobile phone but the battery was flat so she put it in her bag and called the children. They ran down the stairs. Amelia had a soft toy, a notepad and colouring pencils. Jack had a soft toy and a truck.

'Okay guys' Kate said brightly. I'm going to get someone to come over and see Daddy because I don't think I'm the right person to help him. I need you to think about other people in your family that we could go and visit. Can you remember any names?

Amelia thought about it. 'We had a Mum but she died when Jack was a baby. Our aunty lives in America, we visited her there and she comes here sometimes. She has a big house with a pool and lots of doggies who Jack didn't like. We had a Nanny last year but Daddy stopped talking to her. We have a babysitter called Mia. She's really nice, she's at college now. Anyone else, Jack?'

Jack shook his head. 'Daddy had a friend called Barbara but we haven't seen her for ages because Daddy said that she was a bit weird.'

'Okay. Do you remember Mia's second name?'

'No. I know that her Mum is quite famous though.'

Kate raised her eyebrows 'Really? Does she live near here?'

'I don't know.'

'Okay, I'm going to take you to my office for a little while, is that okay?' Amelia and Jack looked at each other.

Jack said questioningly 'what about our Daddy? We can't leave him here.'

Kate sat down next to the children. 'Daddy was very sick which is why he couldn't get up to play with you. I can't help him and we need to get someone else to come and see him. I think it would be best if we try to find someone who knows you to come and see you but I can't do that from here, I have to go and talk to a few people first. Will you come with me?'

Amelia whispered to Jack 'Jack I think we should go.' Jack looked at Kate suspiciously. 'Can we take our toys with us?' Kate nodded.

'Okay, let's go.'

2011

I give up my job in the lab. It isn't helping me to focus or move my plan forward. I take a role working as a crisis case worker for a charity that specialises in finding shelter and work for homeless women. I use the role to look for women who might be persuaded to join me. I focus on victims of domestic abuse because it is easier to persuade women with nothing to believe in my cause. I find women who are desperate and I give them hope. I listen to their stories, nurture them and become a friend for life. I pay to secure accommodation for them out of my own pocket and help them find jobs. I help them retrain, suggesting skills that will be useful to me later. It works well, the women I find are grateful for my compassion and support and I reveal some of my own tragedies so that they know I understand them.

I meet 'Anne' by chance. Every Friday lunchtime I go to the same coffee shop for lunch. I have the same thing every Friday so the woman behind the counter doesn't even need to ask me my order. As I sit down a girl to my left looks at me with such acute interest that I feel she must know me. I am well known in the homeless community so at first, I assume she needs my help. I turn to her and say, as kindly as possible 'Do I know you?'

The girl replies 'You don't, yet. But I know you.' When she stares at me I feel irrationally exposed, as if I have been stripped bare and I laugh nervously. She very distinctive to look at small, wiry and no older than twenty by my estimation, though she has a look on her face that suggests wisdom and experience beyond her years. She has long, almost white hair and bright blue, piercing eyes that seem to see underneath your skin. When she moves, her hair slips back and I notice a long, thin scar down one of her cheeks. She is unnerving. I look down to see what she is eating and notice that she has the same long thin scars across the backs of her hands.

I find my voice. 'How do you know me?'

She smiles. 'I know a lot about you. You have quite a past.'

Now I am scared. I have hidden my past from everyone around me, but she doesn't look like a liar. She looks like someone with a past of her own. I hold out my hand and take a chance. 'Then you will already know that my name is Jean. You are...?'

'I'm Anne.'

I talk to her while I eat my lunch, she hasn't given me much of a choice but at the same time I am intrigued by her. She clearly knows things about me and though that is unnerving she could be useful. She seems strong but has a vulnerable quality that makes her endearing and likable despite her appearance and I feel a surprising connection to her. After my initial scepticism has passed, I relax and she starts to tell me about her childhood. Anne's story is not a typical one. She grew up in a well- known crime family. Ruthless and unforgiving, they are famed for their brutality and even I have heard of them. Her father and his five savage sons are notorious and operate throughout the county but I have never heard of a daughter. From what she describes, she was the brains behind their entire operation but instead of protecting her they abused and bullied her. When she was sixteen she escaped, changed her identity and made them believe she was dead.

To be able to conceal herself from such a powerful family is not a small feat and this interests me. Despite my desire for privacy and Mummy's efforts, a lot of information about my life is in the public domain. Anne has done her homework and others will follow. My past is a barrier to my plan, people might think I am too damaged and broken to be placed in a position of power. Becoming someone else would open doors for me. It is easy enough to dye and cut my hair and there are plastic surgeons abroad who can change my face. I could become the sort of person that can move in circles that Jean cannot. I could pass the vetting process required to enter politics which thus far has been the only thing holding back my plan. I have been searching for an answer to this problem for some time and I believe that I have found it.

I arrange to meet Anne again. I need to know if I can trust her.

2011

'Anne Sanders'

Anne was born 'Ruth Madding'. She quickly learnt that the name 'Madding' bred fear across the local community. The first time she noticed that her family were different was her first day at school. The class was asked to draw a picture of their home and then tell the class about it. The other children drew mummies and daddies, brothers, sisters, pets, colourful houses and lots of smiling faces. Anne drew a dark room with a bed and a man with a red angry face. Her new teacher asked a lot of questions and her father was called into the school to discuss it. when she got home, she was punishment for her indiscretion.

As the weeks went on, she saw the other parents arrive at the gate every day to collect their children and realised things at home were not how they should be. Her mother died when she was just eighteen months old, her father and five brothers were all she had. Her brother Tom collected her from school every day and while the other children were receiving hugs and fuss he would turn his back and snap 'Come on, keep up.' He made her carry all her bags home, even on PE day when they were heavy.

Her 'family' were violent, uncaring and had no reason to bond with a small slip of a girl. Her brothers treated her like a slave from the moment she could walk. Her father took her to robberies, using her to gain entry through small windows. She regularly acquired cuts and bruises from falling through them. Once she broke her wrist and it took her father three days to take her to the hospital. When she got too big to fit through windows, he 'gave' her to Eleanor, who was one of his girlfriends. He gruffly suggested that Eleanor find something 'the girl' was good at. Anne was seven.

Eleanor was kind but not too bright. She took her home and for a while things were better. She let Anne sit at her work laptop in the evenings. She taught her what each of the buttons did and loaded games onto it for her to play with. She gave her treats and bought her clothes that fitted properly. She even gave her the odd cuddle, contact which Anne found oddly comforting having never received cuddles or affection before. Anne was a fast learner and enjoyed being in front of a screen. It felt good to be in control and, her interest sparked, she started going to computer club at lunch and break times. At first it was an opportunity to avoid loneliness as other children found her difficult to relate to but she quickly developed a love for computers. When the IT teacher picked up on her interest and natural aptitude, she offered to teach her the basics and then Anne started to really excel. By the time she reached her eighth birthday, Anne was using the school computers to learn new skills and Eleanor's work computer to test them. She hacked into the company's customer accounts and accessed personnel records just to see how far she could get.

Eventually, Eleanor was 'moved on' by her father, who had tired of her and Anne was forced to go home. It was a difficult parting. Eleanor bought Anne a computer as a parting gift, hoping that she could use it to avoid contact with the Madding men.

Anne returned, hating her father for taking away the only person who had ever shown her any kindness. She spent her time in her room, teaching herself IT skills. She was neglected, dirty and undernourished but her father and brothers quickly forgot she was there. As long as they had food and beer they didn't care about much else.

That all changed on the day her father burst into her bedroom and caught her hacking into council tax records. At first, he couldn't quite understand what he was looking at and snapped 'What the fuck is this, girl?'

She never knew how to predict what would anger her father and her hands shook as she shrugged and said quietly 'I hacked the council tax system.'

She expected a hiding but instead her father sat down next to her. All of a sudden, the girl was more interesting. 'You can do that?'

She nodded cautiously. 'Yes, it's easy.'

His eyes lit up. 'Show me what else you can do.' She showed him proudly, believing that he might actually take an interest in her for once.

That was the start of it. For almost eight years she was forced into illegal on-line activities to fund her family's lifestyle. She barely registered birthdays, the only 'present' her father ever bought her were computer parts. He allowed her to go to school to keep social services off their backs but for the rest of the time she was a prisoner in her own home. Her brothers enjoyed bullying her and her father regularly beat her if he thought she wasn't working quickly enough. She grew up quickly and learnt to avoid their attention but her world was very lonely and grey. She was a bright girl but had few friends and no social skills and, apart from Eleanor, a few of her teachers and the people she met online, she had never known real kindness.

She jealously observed other girls at school. They wore their hair in neat plaits, styled by their mothers whereas her hair was long, dirty and rarely brushed. Their parents collected them from school with cuddles and bundled them into warm cars in the winter. She walked home alone now, whatever the weather. Their clothes were replaced when they got too small while she had to trawl around the charity shops herself on her way home, looking for school uniform to fit. She wanted something different to the life she had but she didn't know how to look for it. The only thing she knew was that she would never be happy at home and hated her father and brothers with a passion.

When she was ten she encountered someone in a chat room who required the services of a hacker. It was easy work and though she knew it was wrong, there was no risk that her father would find out. She got paid £1,000 for her first job and used the money to buy kit for her computer, some food which she stored under her bed and a new uniform for school. She felt alive and free for the first time in her life and lay in bed that night, thinking about what she wanted and how to get it. She needed to find Eleanor, maybe she could go and live with her again. She could easily fit in two or three extra jobs a week. She didn't know what to charge at first and inadvertently undercut those with similar skills but even so, in three years, she made over £150,000. No-one noticed when she bought shampoo and conditioner and started washing her hair every day, or when she wore jeans for the first time, or the day she decided to get her hair cut, or even the day when she started wearing makeup. Her family only saw the money.

Over time the mood in the house began to shift. Her family was greedy and lazy and began to expect bigger and better. They researched bigger scams that involved stealing or exploiting vulnerable people. She wasn't comfortable with the changed and when they instructed her to design a site to sell trafficked women to online buyers, she refused. The scars on her face and hands were from the thin, burning needles that her father pressed onto her flesh while her brothers held her down. She was just fifteen.

As she recovered, she started taking a few extra of her belongings with her to school in her school bag each day, storing them in a lock up she hired in Eleanor's name. She left just enough to satisfy her father if he happened to pop his head around the door. A new computer was delivered straight to the lock up and she left her old computer behind, along with any evidence of the crimes she committed in the family name. On her sixteenth birthday, she left for school knowing that she would never return home. For the first few days she lived in the lock up. It was dark, cramped and with no power for her computer, she felt a little lost. She stayed in hostels for a few days while she looked for a small flat, but her age made this more of a challenge than she expected and all the while her fear of her family finding her grew.

The solution was right in front of her, she went to an internet café and created a new identity for herself, something she had done a thousand time before for other people. Sixteen-year-old Ruth Madding disappeared and nineteen-year-old 'Anne Sanders' emerged. She created a birth record, a full history in education, qualifications, attendance at ballet lessons, a full social media history and an employment history. A flat followed shortly after.

Next, she looked for Eleanor and was devastated to find that she had moved overseas and had a daughter of her own. There really was no-one left to care about her. Her online friends kept her in work and she wasn't short of things to do but when she realised she missed the sound of her brothers' fighting, she knew she needed something more.

Jean was working in the area and Anne heard her name from the people who ran the local hostels. They talked about the girls she had rescued and suggested that Anne might find her helpful. One day Anne looked her up to see what all the fuss was about and found one of her university essays on the subjugation of women, published on her university website. As Anne read, she felt something click into place.

'...It has been decades since the equal pay act and the sex discrimination act promised change, yet women and girls remain second class citizens. Young girls continue to outperform young boys at school in almost every discipline, yet are expected to slow down to the pace of the boys. Gender segregation of children in schooling is becoming less and less common, despite the obvious benefits for girls. There are blatant and concerted efforts by the establishment to ensure that boys are given every opportunity to outperform girls by the time they reach sixteen.

In domestic life things are no better. I conducted a small survey of 200 households with young children to test the extent to which parental expectations reinforce gender stereotypes. In the sample, girls were given gender typical chores (e.g. cooking cleaning, ironing and washing up) while boys were more likely to be excused from chores altogether, or given stereotypical male chores such as mowing the lawn. Girls spent on average 3 hours a week longer doing household chores than boys of the same age.

As a society, we knowingly retain gender roles despite all the evidence that girls, if allowed to do so, could flourish, both academically and in the workplace. It is a crime that we habitually perpetuate...'

Anne had never associated her treatment at home with gender, though in hindsight the connection was obvious. She researched Jean in earnest, finding Hope's death straight away. Her kidnap and rape as a child was harder to uncover, though still easy enough if you knew where to look. It was all over her school and social service records.

Anne was intrigued. She began to watch Jean from a distance and saw her help women out of poverty into shelter and employment. She noticed that women looked at Jean with complete trust and gratitude, listened to her talk and followed her advice without question. She also saw how Jean brushed off male attention with disdain and felt a bond that she couldn't explain. Jean had been through more than she had and yet she was strong and capable. Anne craved a female role model and felt drawn to this woman who seemed so capable and powerful. By the time Anne met her, she knew she would follow Jean wherever she wanted to go.

2011

Anne is an odd girl. I have met her a handful of times yet she treats me as if she has known me forever. It is a little disconcerting that she seems to know everything about me. I had no idea that I was so easy to find. Information about me is available to anyone who has the skills to find it and that scares me. The way she looks at me makes me feel as if she can read my mind.

She has very few friends or acquaintances and I think she struggles to relate to people. She has hidden behind a computer for so long that she thinks you need to research people to get to know them. Conversation is sometimes challenging as she isn't used to one-to-one engagement and tends to say whatever comes into her head, jumping from topic to topic at random. Having said that, her naivety about the world is endearing and I find myself anxious to protect her.

I would like to see her work so I can see how she found out so much about me but that feels some way off. She only meets me in public places and her eyes dart around like a frightened deer. It is as if the world is unfamiliar to her. I am fascinated enough to put a bit of time into this relationship. I think she may be useful to me.

2025

Rt. Hon. Claire Flint MP, 10 Downing Street

Claire was attempting to clear her evening box of submissions but was exhausted after a day of community visits. She had seen the devastation first hand and felt more daunted than ever. A group of doctors she'd met spoke angrily of feeling as if they had been abandoned in a warzone, with dwindling supplies and no hope. She listened but could provide no comfort. No-one knew if or when this would end.

She'd instinctively rolled up her sleeves, holding tearful mothers, listening to angry relatives as they demanded answers and all the while feeling as if she was presiding over chaos. By the time she left she felt closer to the tragedy, yet more helpless than ever. The tears finally came on the journey home when, after days of holding it together, she finally allowed herself to dwell on her personal losses. Her ex-husband, her brother, colleagues, friends, neighbours. People she had barely had time to even think about, yet alone grieve for. The weight of the crisis was overwhelming. By the time she got back an hour later her eyes were puffy but her resolve strengthened. They needed to find those responsible. She spent the rest of the afternoon on the phone to the French and German governments, requesting further air drops of aid.

She looked up from the report she was reading on food supplies and noticed that her office had darkened. The huge pile of papers in front of her loomed and the prospect of working into the night made her feel all the more overwhelmed. She wanted to go upstairs and give Ben a hug but Deborah Walsh was on her way in to see her. Claire had known Deborah for a while, though not particularly well. As a junior minister, she'd been one to watch and Claire thought she was purposefully held back by George Moore's misogyny. She knew just how to respond to the endless questions about the virus and had coped with being thrust into the spotlight remarkably well. Claire on the other hand, felt as if she were drowning. She wondered how Deborah was doing it, she exuded authority, making Claire feel even less prime ministerial. Deborah was everything Claire aspired to be.

Just then, there was a knock at the door, which Claire assumed was Deborah. She stood up, feeling as if the walls were closing in on her. She needed a change of scene. She went to the door to greet Deborah, who seemed surprised not to be called in.

'Hi Deborah, shall we go and find somewhere a bit more comfortable to have a chat?'

Deborah smiled serenely. 'Yes, that would be great, I've only ever been in that room, or the board room, it would be good to see a little more of the building.'

Claire led the way down the hall towards the small dining room.

'George wasn't great at hospitality, was he?'

'You could say that. I didn't care for him much. He was a bit too fond of his own voice and I don't think he liked women much, especially me. He either hated my ideas or claimed for his own.'

'I don't think you were alone there. He didn't have many friends in parliament in the end. Here, let's sit in here, it's a little more comfortable.'

Claire showed Deborah into the small dining room and closed the door. They sat together on a sofa opposite a low table in the corner of the room. Deborah looked at her expectantly.

'So, you wanted to see me?'

Claire nodded. 'Yes. I know I haven't been as available as I'd have liked in your first week. I wanted to check you were okay.'

'I'm...okay.' Deborah shook her head grimly. 'I don't deny my ambition, but I would never have chosen this. I'm lucky though, I have a good support network. I'll be fine.'

'That's good, you'll need it.' Claire hesitated before asking 'Did you lose anyone?'

Deborah looked at her quizzically for a moment. 'Yes. I've lost people. Haven't we all?'

'Sorry.' Claire mumbled. 'Stupid question. I can't quite believe that it has only been eight days, it feels never ending.'

Deborah 'I can imagine. I admire your courage. Not many people could lead the country as well as you are under the circumstances.'

Claire raised her eyebrows, surprised at the compliment. Her fears almost tumbled out. 'Well if it seems that way I'm glad, though it certainly doesn't feel like it. I am just as exposed and vulnerable as everyone else. I'm stunned you chose me. Any one of you would have been a better fit.'

Deborah frowned a little. 'I don't think so, Claire. You have more experience in office than any of us. The public like you and everyone agrees with your approach. You know that, right?' Claire shrugged, feeling a little embarrassed at the compliment.

Deborah leant across and hesitatingly touched Claire's hand. 'Are you okay?' Claire shook her head. A lump formed in her throat. No-one had asked her that since she took the post and she realised she really wasn't.

Deborah looked at Claire sympathetically. 'You look exhausted. She paused and then said cautiously 'Would you mind very much if I gave you some advice, purely in an effort to help?'

'Not at all, please do.'

Deborah chose her words carefully. 'The public doesn't know how it feels to be criticised by the media, or stabbed in the back by colleagues you thought were friends. Politicians are held to extremely high standards and most of us don't have a hope of living up to them. Words like 'dishonest' 'arrogant' 'out of touch' and 'power hungry', are banded about until we start to believe them for ourselves and the people who let the side down don't help. It is a wonder that any of us ever want to stay.

What strikes me is the way that the women in politics react, compared to the men. We spend an awful lot of time and energy criticising and second guessing ourselves, whereas men are confident enough to ignore it. It makes me sad because we are often more compassionate and willing to listen than men. We ask other people for their opinions and genuinely listen to the answer, qualities that make us better at our jobs. Don't doubt your own abilities or belittle your achievements to others. You're here because despite the barriers, you were a strong enough character to make it this far. Then, in a crisis, when there were only a handful of us left, you were the one we knew would do the best job. You don't have to shoulder all of the country's problems on your own though. Accept you are one woman and ask for help.'

She nodded to Claire's pile of papers on the table in front of them. 'They can wait, nothing you can do about anything in there this evening. Go and see your son. You must worry about him. He's young, isn't he?

'He's nine.'

Deborah smiled. 'So young and innocent. Treasure him.'

Claire sat in stunned silence. She felt chastised and empowered all at once. 'I don't know what to say... thank-you, Deborah, it means a lot to me to have your confidence.'

'You're welcome, I'm here if you need me. You have a hard job and you need friends, just be careful who you show your underbelly to. There are still wolves out there, circling. They just look a little different now.'

After Deborah left, Claire sat for a few minutes before she went upstairs to see Ben. She realised that she had spent much of the week worrying about her own abilities rather than focussing on the task in front of her, yet the only person who had been critical of her decisions so far was her. As she walked upstairs to Ben she decided to start believing in herself a little more. She also realised with a stab of guilt that she hadn't asked Deborah a single question about herself.

2012

Anne and I meet daily, though I am still not permitted to know where she lives as she is cautious about her safety. I ask few questions. We always walk around the park a few streets away from my work, where we cannot be overheard. We talk as we walk and slowly I get to know her a little better.

She is angry that her father and brothers are still free men, she doesn't like knowing that they are out there somewhere and could find her if she let her guard down. She wants rid of them, their cruelty is all she has ever known and her hatred is palpable. She speaks of a woman called Eleanor who she loved but she is no longer in her life.

She seems lonely, she lives her life through a computer screen and watches the world through a tainted lens. In many ways, she reminds me of a younger version of myself, her life consists of four walls and she is still a prisoner even though she is free.

She did not enjoy school as other children did not warm to her, she describes them the way you would describe a film or a book. I imagine watching other girls with normal lives and families was extremely painful for her. She left as soon as she could and rejects formal education, preferring to learn by herself. She is practically a recluse, if it weren't for me she would not have a soul to talk to.

However, she is also completely brilliant.

A few months passes and I am confident enough of her loyalty to speak cautiously of my plan. I talk about it as if it is just a wild idea or a dream, but she immediately relates it to her brothers and father and talks about how much she dislikes them. She says she imagines burning their house down with them inside, so that she can be free.

Over time we create an elaborate 'fantasy' where we rid the world of men. She talks about how grateful the local community would be if she were to 'free them' from her family. We turn it into a game, like one of those video games where you decide what the world inside looks like. Eventually I talk about what happened to me, how badly I was treated and how many women I have met through work who have suffered at the hands of men. I tell her that I wish I could rid the world of the cruelty and pain men cause. One day she arrives for our meeting and says 'I want to do it for real. They don't deserve to live.' I feign horror and try to talk her out of it but slowly allow her to talk me around.

We talk about how we would do it and what comes after. These conversations take weeks and require me to play the long game.

I share how difficult it will be to achieve and how much I worry that the wrong person will take control of the country and turn all the women into slaves.

She believes that I am 'the perfect leader in waiting' and questions why I haven't already put myself forward for election.

I point out my past is such a stumbling block to a career in politics that I gave up on that idea at a young age.

She thinks of ways around my chequered history. She knows her own abilities, she thinks she could turn me into a politician with an unblemished record, creating a back history that is credible and water tight.

She is so convinced of her skills that I tell her to do it, she has extreme focus and determination and gets onto it immediately, leaving me to think about other parts of the plan.

My list of problems is slowly being resolved.

2025

'The French government began air drops of aid to Great Britain today, just days after the first deaths from a deadly virus now sweeping Great Britain. The virus targets men and adolescent boys, leaving women and children unharmed. A shocking 28 million males have died in just over a week and news out of the country has slowed to a trickle in recent days. Witnesses describe scenes reminiscent of the black death with heat, water and power now luxuries and food running low. Hospitals are overwhelmed and as the dead pile up, there is a real risk of disease, with local councils struggling to remove the bodies before decomposition sets in. It is clear that the British Government, itself crippled by the virus, has lost control and, with no sign of a cure, there is nothing to do but let it run its course.

Deaths outside Great Britain are miraculously limited to those who travelled in and out of the country in the days leading up to the outbreak, a miracle borne only from Britain's geographic isolation.

The majority of the British Government, including the country's Prime Minister, succumbed to the virus in the first few days of the outbreak. After a scramble to re-establish executive control, the new Prime Minister, Claire Flint, took up post but with little experience she is struggling to manage the crisis. Very little is known about the rest of the skeleton administration but it is unlikely that they possess the military, or crisis management experience required to grip a catastrophe of this magnitude.

With no sign that spread of the virus is slowing, the rest of the world can only watch, as the risk of spreading the virus further prevents the deployment of ground support.

There are serious questions to be asked and no-one left to answer them. To date the British intelligence services have failed to identify the person or persons responsible for these atrocities and with police resources under 30% strength, the priority in Great Britain has to be stabilisation.

In the meantime, the knock-on effect of this disaster is already being felt across the world as financial markets slump to an all-time low. The British economy has collapsed overnight and the effect on the rest of the world is more of a flood than a ripple. Even if the virus has run its course, the effect of this crisis on the western world will be felt for decades to come.

2012

Anne makes progress. It is as if a higher power is removing the obstacles in my path but one large problem remains. I do not have the means to rid the world of men, I have tried to create a virus but I don't have the experience or expertise to create something so highly engineered that it only kills men. I cast around for other options but there is nothing that would work as well or deliver as quickly.

I ask Anne to look for someone with experience, who might be pliable. I think that this is impossible but after a few weeks, she presents me with a virologist named Professor Nicole Moreland who is highly regarded in her field.

I am sceptical about whether someone like her could be persuaded to help. I don't know what I can offer her. Then Anne shows me what she has discovered about Professor Moreland's past. The more I read, the more I see possibilities. She is vulnerable, has had a terrible life and has a looming problem that needs to be solved. It is as if the pieces of this puzzle were scattered years ago for me to find. My plan is supposed to work. It is my destiny.

2025

Claire looked out of the rear window of the car she was in, as the gates to Buckingham palace swung open. She was nervous, the new Regent was an unknown quantity. As 'minor' royals, her and her sister had stepped back from official royal duties to pursue careers when Parliament reduced the sovereign grant. Claire knew very little about her character, interests or intellect. The Regent had been 7th in line, far enough away from power to avoid the attention of the media. Claire felt sorry for her now. The idea of being thrust into the position of Regent without warning or preparation reminded her of her own fate.

Claire couldn't help her expression as she was led through the palace to the room where she was to meet the Regent. Every room was cavernous, with high, gilded ceilings and elegant furnishings. She took note of the tiniest details, the exquisitely carved bannisters and beautiful, probably priceless pieces of art on the walls. It was easy to forget why she was here among all the splendour and she realised with a jolt that the aide she was following was speaking. She guiltily refocussed her attention.

'When entering the room, please curtsey, address the Princess Regent as Ma'am and don't turn your back in her presence.'

As she walked through another set of tall, gilded doors the Princess Regent rose from a chair in the corner and came to greet her. Claire curtseyed and she immediately said 'Please don't. I really do hate it.' Claire looked up, surprised and the Princess Regent smiled. 'Please sit down' she said, gesturing to the chair next to her. Claire sat and looked at her expectantly, unsure of how to begin.

'Well, I'm happy to meet you. You must feel much the same as I do. Being thrust into a position that I didn't apply for, in the middle of the worst crisis in human history with no support and very little advice wasn't part of my life plan and I'm sure it wasn't part of yours either.' Claire laughed, surprised at her candour. 'No, Ma'am.' She replied. 'Well let's see if we can help each other, shall we? First of all, I suppose I should formally appoint you as Prime Minister.' The Princess Regent rose and Claire quickly stood up. 'I hereby appoint you as my Prime Minister' she declared grandly. 'Please, sit.' Claire sat.

'I'd like you to talk me through what has happened and what I can do to help. We are, after all, the women in charge. Between us, we should be able to work through most problems, don't you?' Claire nodded. At thirty-six years old, the Princess Regent seemed older and wiser than Claire was expecting and she immediately felt she had an unexpected ally.

The Princess Regent listened as Claire summarised the chronic problems she was facing. She gave advice and offered her assistance in diplomatic talks with foreign powers, which Claire gladly accepted. At the end of the meeting they stood and the Princess Regent took Claire's hand. 'I would like to do more to help. I feel useless sat in this place doing nothing when outside, the people are suffering. I need something to occupy me, is there anything you can think of that I might usefully do?'

Claire smiled. 'There is a lot you can do. You could visit communities, give speeches in town squares, give the women left behind something to hope for. Your great-grandmother did a fabulous job of rallying public spirit during the second world war doing similar things. Communities need to see familiar faces.' The Princess Regent smiled. 'Well I can certainly do that.'

2013

Anne and I talk about how to move me into a position of power. I have contemplated the creation of a new persona, someone who can walk the corridors of power without attracting attention. Anne takes notes and lists the problems she must overcome. She says she needs a full history of my life. I have diaries which will help, though I am reluctant to open myself up like that. She is insistent- she cannot help me without them, so I give them to her. I have to trust someone. She says it will take a while but she is confident that I'll be happy in the end.

Next, we start recruiting Professor Moreland. Anne has limitless resources and more money than I would know what to do with, yet she lives frugally. She has acquired access to a wealth of information about Professor Moreland through an online source, so we know every detail of Moreland's life. She was married to an abusive man and nearly died by his hand. He was released from prison recently and an injunction prevents him from contacting her. She attends a support group for survivors of domestic abuse and has never dated another man. Though she is the best in her field she has been overlooked for promotion. Professionals in her field seem to be divided into two camps, those who sided with her and those who didn't. Her ex-husband- also a scientist- went to great lengths to discredit her after they split up and even her boss believes that she exaggerated her injuries. Her parents are dead and her only brother sided with her husband. She lives alone apart from a dog called Bella and orders a takeaway every Friday evening.

She attends counselling regularly but has recently carried out several internet searches for a replacement counsellor which suggests that she isn't making progress.

It is easy to flood her life with reminders about how different the future could be if only men were not in control. There are ways to get inside anyone's head if you know how to press their buttons. I need to be particularly persuasive with Nicole as she is arguably one of the brightest women in the country.

I don't know how far she remains brainwashed by the myth that there are 'still good men out there'. It does astound me how many women continue to believe it, even when they have been treated like animals by every man they have ever met. All men are programmed with a sense of entitlement through thousands of years of conditioning and evolution. I need Nicole to decide that they need to be brought down, in order to ensure the survival of our planet and our species.

Anne and I organise a conference in London, using my work as a cover. It is designed purely to recruit Nicole, though it attracts a surprising number of other women who may be useful. The agenda is simple and the advertising written just for her, based on everything we have been able to find out about her life.

9-10am- Why Successful Women are Attracted to Violent Men
An exploration of why intelligent and successful women are drawn to abusive men and why violent men seek them out. Speaker: Louise Drake, CEO and Founder of Free Women from Abuse.

10.30-11.30am- The Psychology of Abusers
Eminent psychologist, Dr Frances Wilkes, who has worked with abusive men for thirty years, discusses why men turn into abusive partners.

12-1pm- Surviving and Thriving after Domestic Abuse (workshop)

Attendees will have the opportunity to participate in a workshop hosted by the leading authority in the psychology of domestic abuse Professor Sophie Brown.

2-3pm- The Power of the Female Voice
Human Rights Lawyer and activist Dame Marie Macaulay on how women recover their voice after surviving abusive behaviour.

330-430pm- Re-discovering your Freedom
Modern-day feminist and political commentator Judy Faulkes rounds off the day with an inspirational speech on the power of women.

Attendees are invited to attend an evening reception following the event, where they will get an opportunity to meet the speakers.

We send the advertising to her directly and flood the local area with leaflets. We also target her support group and counsellor. A few days later she books onto the event. Success.
The speakers are well known and attract all the right people. Talented and intelligent women who do not fit the traditional mould. Anne is tasked with recruiting others with the skills we need. I focus my attention on Nicole. Already I see her pliability. She wants to believe that there can be something better. Conveniently, her husband starts to stalk her again just before the conference, so I know she feels helpless and alone.

* * *

The day arrives. The hotel has prepared well for us and women are starting to check-in. The speakers are in a separate room and I go to greet them. Though they are extraordinary, fascinating women who I would usually covet, today I am distracted and anxious to find Nicole. I have spent so long studying her background, history, current movements and interests that I feel I know her intimately.

Finally, I find a reason to escape and go out into the main hall to cast my eye around for Nicole. No luck. I go out into the reception area and see that she hasn't collected her name tag. The first session starts in fifteen minutes and I start to worry that she isn't coming. I call Anne, who answers and immediately admonishes me.

'Jean, relax. I am tracking her, she is two minutes away. Go back inside and look natural, you don't want to scare her away.'

I stand just inside the door, so that I can see her walk in to reception. After a minute or so I spot her. She is more impressive in the flesh, her long, auburn hair falls in waves down her back and she is dressed in a light grey trouser suit with a cream shirt underneath. She appears to be a confident, self-assured woman but I see the cracks. Her eyes dart left and right, looking for danger. She hesitates at the front desk before giving her name, then picks up her name tag and hands over her luggage. I position myself with a group of women who have just arrived and I smile at her pointedly. She comes towards me gratefully and I finally meet her.

It is an exciting moment, I know who she will become with my guidance. She doesn't know how amazing she is because her husband has taken away her soul and made her forget how magnificent and talented she is. As I shake her hand, I resolve to bring her back to life again.

2014

While Anne is busy setting up a support group for selected women from the conference, my task is solely to recruit Nicole. She is understated, timid and lacking in confidence which is surprising given her professional reputation. I encourage her to talk about her job because I find it fascinating and gives her a reason to open up to me. She takes great pleasure in her work, when she talks about it she is animated and engaged and I see a glimmer of the confidence she must have had before her husband took it away. I take particular notice of the stories she tells about her peers because the industry she works in is male dominated and her colleagues undermine her constantly. I don't think she sees it.

I stop her in the middle of one story about her boss and ask why she allows her male colleagues to treat her that way. She disagrees with my assessment that she is being treated badly because she is a woman and is a little angry with me when I point out examples. I tell her that women are undermined, not by one major act but a thousand tiny ones. We often miss the signs. She leaves abruptly but as she says goodbye she says she will think about what I have said.

* * *

We meet for coffee. She has forgiven me. Her boss met with her and listed all her past mistakes, one after another after another until she felt beaten and incompetent. He didn't mention her accomplishments despite the numerous awards she has won this year. She got home, drank wine and wrote down her achievements to remind herself that she is not a failure. I am angry on her behalf. I ask her how she feels about our last conversation. She sighs and says that I may be right after all. She is beginning to understand the true nature of men.

* * *

I meet Nicole for a drink after work and tell her about my past. She is the second person I have told (Anne was the first) and I find it easier this time. When I tell her about being in the van and about the men killing the puppy she asks me to stop. She is crying but I know that I must carry on so I tell her that I need to tell someone I trust. By the time I have finished she is overwhelmed with emotion and her eyes are full of pity. I talk about the court case, moving house and my father leaving us and she touches my hand and says that she had no idea that I had such a difficult life and how much she admires my strength. I haven't told her about Hope or my mother's death yet which I hold back for now.

She tells me about her husband which takes a lot out of her. She is ashamed and scared, she lost herself in the relationship and allowed him to control her without even noticing. He even controlled where she worked, preventing her from seeking a better job because she 'wasn't talented enough'. He stopped her publishing a new research paper, saying it would be 'ripped to pieces' by her peers. She tells me about the violence he inflicted which was much worse than the police reports indicate. They only give an outline, the colour is in her description of the hatred, violence and horror that she suffered in between the bruises.

Anne walks into the bar. I act surprised to see her but this has been engineered by me. I want Nicole to hear Anne's story while she is vulnerable. Anne has her laptop, which contains reams of evidence. She shows Nicole NHS records, photographs of injuries and school reports as well as newspaper articles about the hold that the family has on the community. She paints a terrible picture and Nicole is compassionate and instantly maternal. It is a relationship I suspect they both need.

❊ ❊ ❊

Nicole's local support group is small and she believes that the stories she has heard there, while terrible, are exceptional. They are not exceptional at all and it is my job to expose Nicole to the truth. I take her to see the women who I have helped find refuge and they tell Nicole how men ruined their lives, beat them, left them to raise children alone or stole from them. When she isn't working she starts to volunteer with my organisation and I see her begin to question the belief she has that most men are good.

Nicole is persuaded by real people, facts, evidence and patterns. The volunteering has an impact but it is painfully slow and I need to move things on more quickly. I decide to show her the evidence I have collected. It is voluminous, I have added things to this collection almost every day for years, thousands and thousands of articles cut from newspapers and a hard drive full of evidence. Every article describes crimes committed against women, children and even other men. The crimes of men in power show that they are damaging our planet through their greed, pointless acts of war, vengeance or lust. This is my life's work, I knew I would need it one day but to use it in pursuit of my plan is poetic and I am excited for her to see it.

I take Nicole to my study, saying that there is something I want her to see. On one wall, I have fixed shelves that go from floor to ceiling and are full of newspaper articles bound in indexed folders. I give Nicole a cup of tea and one of the folders, then leave her to it, pretending that I have some work to do. She is there for hours and when she surfaces her face is mottled and it is clear she has been crying. She says she read five folders from cover to cover. I know how that feels, I have sat in that room for days doing the same thing. One of the articles is about her and her husband. I wonder if she read it but I don't ask.

She sits at my kitchen table and she says to me 'Okay, I understand your point. The world is a terrible place if you are a woman. This country is considered progressive and yet women are still treated appallingly. What I don't understand is why you are doing this. What would you have me do? I can volunteer more, I can even provide rooms in my house for victims. Is that what you need? Come on, Jean. I know you want something I just can't work out what.'

She isn't ready to hear my plan so I tell her that I want to open her eyes. Women have normalised the stories about men raping women, or abusing children. They are drip fed to us, one or two at a time, easily dismissed as exceptional events until you realise just how many there are. I can't normalise them anymore because there is a clear pattern of violence against women that we ignore at our peril.

Nicole begins to notices things on her own. A colleague asks her out on a date and is aggressive when she turns him down. A neighbour is overheard calling his new girlfriend 'fucking frigid' during a late-night fight. A colleague admits that he no longer loves his wife, just before they announce that they are having a child. She begins to tot up these events in her head, just like me.

I set out my future vision to her one night over dinner. I am careful not to tell her how it might be achieved, that comes later.

I ask 'Imagine how much better it would be if the world were run by women? Men have had countless opportunities to make the world a better place yet they chose to rape and torture others. They go to battle in pursuit of money and power, justifying millions of deaths as 'casualties of war'. Don't you think we deserve better?'

She doesn't disagree so I go on. 'You and I are survivors, we know the arrogant, entitled nature of man. They are programmed by our society to want money, power and control. Baby boys are not born wanting to take over whole continents, conquer the oil industry or belittle and rape women. These attitudes are taught, ingrained in our development over generations of male dominance. Someone needs to be brave enough to stop it. We need to step in and teach the next generation that we are born equal, so that our daughters can fulfil their potential and our sons can learn to be kind and respectful.

She agrees wholeheartedly but cannot see how to make this a reality. The laws put in place by men constrain her thinking and she lacks the imagination required to make this happen.

I conclude my argument. 'The only way to bring about such monumental change is for women to rise up. A revolution is required now, incremental changes don't work. Women have been trying to effect change for generations and yet have barely scratched the surface. We have the vote but equality is decades away. Men possess the arrogance that comes from being at the top of the tree and having never been effectively challenged by women, they don't believe that we are capable of it. Watch them at work. They allow us to sit next to them at the table, to be their deputies but they don't value our voices, they might allow us to speak but then they slap us down. They throw us the odd bone but they don't allow us to really thrive or recognise our talents. Watch them at home with their families. They still expect their wives to cook and clean, they might encourage them to work but roles aren't equal. They need to be challenged and we need to find a way to do it that is swift and effective.'

She is excited, she wants to know my plan and thinks I should start a movement, or run for prime minister. I am exasperated.

'That won't work. Even when we had female prime ministers they were distracted by male priorities like war or power and surrounded by men ready to leap into their spot as soon as they put a foot wrong. There has never been an all-female cabinet, though there have been countless all-male ones. Why do you think that is? Men vote for men and women are conditioned to believe that men are better leaders, so they vote for men too. We will never see that kind of change in our lifetime without action.

'Then what, Jean?' I don't answer because I can't, yet. She isn't ready. She has to think it for herself.

* * *

The police have put a woman named Suzanne in touch with my organisation. She is in hospital, recovering from the horrific injuries that her ex-husband has inflicted on her. I go to the hospital and look through the glass door to see how bad her facial injuries are. Her husband threw battery acid in her face and then beat her to a pulp while she was screaming from the pain. The bandages cover her entire face but the nurse on duty says that her injuries are the worst she has ever seen. She has a lot of internal injuries too and is about to go into surgery. I call Nicole from the hospital phone and say that I can't interview the girl, I have too many other women to see. She agrees to go and take the details.

* * *

After a few days of silence, I visit Nicole's house. She has been to see Suzanne in the hospital daily and she is angrier than I have ever seen her. She shows me 'before' and 'after' photographs of Suzanne. Her injuries are shocking and I cannot help the noise I make. She is so badly injured there's a chance she won't make it. The police have a guard posted on the door of Suzanne's room because the husband is still at large and it's not the first time he has attacked her.

Nicole blurts out 'He deserves to die. Every man who hurts women like this deserves to die.' I raise my eyebrows at her and she stops talking. She focusses on the coffee cup in front of her, saying nothing. I sit with her quietly and wait for her to speak again, on tenterhooks.

Finally, she looks up. 'I don't know what I'm doing, Jean, the world isn't what I thought it was. We must do something.' I nod vigorously, my plan is on the tip of my tongue but I must be patient. Timing is everything.

'What are you thinking Jean? Trust me and just tell me.'

I am careful with my reply. 'Something big has to change. The small things just don't work.' She nods curtly and is quiet.

I wait a few minutes, watching for despair to hit her, then I say 'I don't think men want women as equals, they prefer us to be subservient. I know not all men are violent but they all buy into a system that makes them 'better' than we are, they don't value what we bring to the table. I keep thinking about what the world could be like if men had been raised to treat woman as their equals, things would be so different! It's difficult to envisage how we could ever get to that place with the system the way it is.'

I stand up abruptly. 'You need to think and I'm tired.' At the front door, I turn and say to her 'If you think of a solution, I'd love to hear it.'

* * *

Nicole goes straight to Suzanne's bedside from work every day, sitting with her until visiting hours end. Sometimes Suzanne wakes up and talks to Nicole, she wants a new life but she is scared. Nicole shares her own experiences and arranges a place for her in one of my refuges. I think she reminds Nicole of herself and so I observe with interest.

* * *

I am in bed reading and my doorbell rings. Visitors are unusual so I am instantly on my guard. I pull out the knife from under my pillow and head downstairs cautiously. There is a shadow at the window and I am instantly reminded of the day I found my mother. The person on the other side of the door is breathing heavily. I call out 'hello?' and hear a voice I recognise, though her response is inaudible. I open the door on the chain and see Nicole, with tears pouring down her face. Only then do I put away the knife and open the door.

I manage to piece together the events through Nicole's tears. Suzanne died of her injuries which was probably inevitable. Nicole is calming down now and I can speak to her properly. The husband still hasn't been caught, the police think he has fled the country. Nicole is angry.

'Right now, I could kill them all.' I am sympathetic, I make her tea and we sit down in my lounge. We talk about poor Suzanne and then I tell Nicole about losing Hope, I feel the time is right. I show her photographs of Hope and the newspaper articles about the monster who killed her. I tell her about the time that I sat outside the police station waiting to kill him and about watching him during the trial. Then I tell her about how Mummy died and how alone I felt afterwards.

We talk all night and are as close as it is possible for two women to be. I have found my equal at last. She knows everything about me and yet she is still here, closer than ever.

I decide that now is the time. 'Nicole, I think you and I have met for a reason. Look at what we have been through. I think we were supposed to meet, don't you?!' She nods, smiling.

I pause, then I go for it. 'Wouldn't it be great if... no, don't worry, it's stupid.'

She looks at me, amused. 'Come on Jean, if what?'

'Well we are clever women. What if we created a virus that made men so sick that they had to relinquish power? Is that stupid?'

I look at her, eyebrows raised, then I laugh as if I am joking. 'Oh, ignore me, is a pipe dream, it probably isn't even possible!'

She goes into work mode immediately. 'Oh, I don't know, sounds like a challenge! It would have to be gender specific, which is tricky... and to make them incapable of working... hmm. Of course, you wouldn't want it to affect children because the risks are too high. Something to think about... where on earth did you get that idea?!'

She looks at me, her eyes are shining, it is a theoretical challenge for her. She doesn't believe in it yet.'

'Oh, I don't know, it just popped into my head. It would have to be long term and untreatable otherwise the men would recover too quickly and we wouldn't get a chance to make a difference. Isn't it fun to think about?'

Nicole is off on a theoretical mission to make something that works and all I have to do now is keep working on her until theory becomes reality. If we ever get caught I know most people won't understand but Nicole and I are not mad, damaged, or broken. We are brave, strong and inspired. I have given her something to aspire to and work for and, quite unexpectedly I have also found a friend.

* * *

Anne, Nicole and I are a team. I am the leader but each of us have our strengths.

Anne provides technical genius. She really is like no-one I have ever met. She can access any system, create and delete people at will, hack into someone's life and turn it upside down, all before breakfast. She gives me access to everything I can possibly need. She has also managed to bring together a group of women with the skills we need to execute the plan. It will be my job to persuade them to join us but for now we bring them together often and encourage them to forge friendships.

Nicole and I are the creators. She is almost where I need her to be, close to the belief that this is inevitable and necessary.

She challenges me, actively testing my theories and views but I like that. We are on the brink of greatness.

2025

Nicole Moreland. (Diary entry)

If anyone ever reads this, then I'm sure they will wonder 'Is she insane, perhaps a psychopath? Why would an intelligent and sane woman create a virus like that? What possessed her to do something so despicable? How does she sleep at night?'

I have agonised over those questions and I can't answer them. All I know is that I tried to live in the old world, I joined support groups and had counselling, I tried to be productive but I was so scared that I was a prisoner in my life. I couldn't walk down the street or go shopping without looking over my shoulder, I was afraid of my own shadow. Even when I was safe from my husband I still experienced discrimination, sexism and bullying from men who believed that women were objects to toy with rather than equals. Jean opened my eyes, to it all. The women I respected were treated like second class citizens by husbands who were blind to their value. The media reported assaults, rapes, murders and abuse every day. My colleagues were harassed and ignored at work. Once you open your eyes and actively look for it, you really do see it everywhere.

I was normal before I met my husband Tim, a professor at my university. He was an intellectual and I was young and impressionable. When he started paying me special attention it felt like Christmas. He made me believe my research mattered and coached me through my degree and PHD. I even went to him for advice when I considered specialising in virology. I adored him and was blind to his flaws.

We became a couple the year when I completed my studies, he swept me off my feet and insisted that we make things official as soon as possible. We married less than a year later and I didn't have time to see the classic warning signs. My friends were critical, spotting his arrogance and vanity way before I did. One of my friends labelled him a narcissist after a particularly bruising exchange in front of our other friends. I spent a lot of time explaining him to other people which I shudder to recollect. I'd say 'You don't know him like I do.' or 'There is a vulnerability to him that only I see.' or even 'All those things just make him more exciting to be around.' My friends sighed, nodded and slowly drifted away, realising that we came as a package deal.

The first time he hit me was on a Sunday morning in 2003, about a year after we were married. We got home from a function about 3am and fell into bed. The next day Tim woke up with a fierce hangover and a temper to match. He crashed about in our room until I woke up and then insisted I cook breakfast right away. I felt terrible and took my time getting up which only made him grumpier. I should have seen it coming. When we finally sat down to eat Tim launched into a critique of my conduct with one of his peers, a professor at the university, saying that I behaved appallingly. I recalled only having a lively discussion with him about my research over dinner but Tim accused me of flirting. It was ridiculous, he was a leading expert in his field and I was simply asking his professional opinion.

Sensing that something was going to happen, I tried to make light of the conversation by teasing Tim about 'professional jealousy'. His reaction was immediate and vicious. He overturned the kitchen table, sending our breakfast flying across the room. A shard of glass embedded itself in my right foot, severing a tendon. It was excruciatingly painful. As I bent over to examine the injury, he grabbed a handful of my hair and slammed my face into the upended table leg. It all happened in a split second, my face seemed to explode and I later learnt that the force of the blow smashed seven of my teeth out. Fragments of my teeth were lodged in my cheek, which split open. I fell to the floor and as I passed out I remember him stepping over me to leave.

I came to a few minutes later and dragged myself over to the phone in the hall. There was a mirror on the wall and as I picked up the phone I caught sight of my face, a mess of blood and flesh. I sat there shaking with the phone in my hand but no idea who to call. I remember thinking how difficult I would find it to explain away my injuries.

In the end, I stuck a gauze patch across my cheek, wrapped a bandage around my foot and drove myself to the hospital. By the time I arrived I knew I wanted to leave Tim. The hospital contacted the police on my request and referred me to a plastic surgeon to repair the tendon in my foot and stitch my cheek. I transferred to a private hospital after the first surgery and spent three days there having new teeth screwed into my gums.

The nurses talked about moving to a women's refuge and brought me leaflets and information packs about domestic violence. They tried to persuade me to speak to friends and family but instead I checked out of the hospital, bought new clothes and toiletries and checked into a hotel. I was too ashamed to ask anyone for help and struggled with the label of 'domestic violence'. In my mind that sort of thing didn't happen to people like me.

A few days later Tim turned up at the hotel. I don't know how he found me. He begged me to come home, I can still hear the excuses, he was stressed at work, he was jealous of his colleague, he was worried that my head would be turned by someone better than him. He promised to go to the doctors or to counselling for anger management, whatever I wanted, if only I would come home. My resolve was weakening and I didn't have the support network in place to keep me on track. I began to convince myself that I'd provoked him.

After six weeks, the wounds healed and the stitches were removed, the swelling went down and my teeth stopped aching. I was staying in a short term let a few miles away from home and agreed to go to marriage guidance counselling with Tim. He was contrite, remorseful and active in his attempts to win me back. He attended an anger management course and went to the doctor, who diagnosed depression and prescribed antidepressants. After three months and a marked change in his behaviour, I weakened, thinking I'd seen true remorse. I moved back in.

Months went by without incident and the memory of my injuries faded, though there were times when I felt flashes of fear, mostly during arguments when Tim's temper flared. The second incident happened at Christmas in 2009, shortly after I started working for Cruise Pharmaceutical's. I had been out to the company's Christmas party, a strictly employees only event. I had a great time, my colleagues were hard workers and it was a novelty to have some fun together. I confess I was enjoying myself a bit too much and didn't realise how late it was until I booked a taxi home. I texted Tim at the same time to let him know I was okay but he didn't answer so I assumed he was in bed.

When I got home I tiptoed to the kitchen to make a snack and found Tim sitting at the kitchen table. Several empty bottles of beer were stacked on the table in front of him. My heart lurched but I smiled at him and swayed slightly, putting my hand on the wall to steady myself. 'I'm making toast. Do you want some?' Tim looked at me contemptuously and his lip curled as he snarled 'Where the fuck have you been? Fucking your colleagues, I imagine. No wonder you didn't want me to come.' He jerked out of his chair and in one move was on top of me, I had no time to react. He forced me down onto the kitchen floor, smashing my skull on the ground. Pain shot through my head and my vision swam. I knew I was in trouble. I summoned all of my energy to reach up and try to push his face away from me. I remember shouting 'No Tim! Stop it, don't do this.'

He punched me in the face hard and pain seared through my skull as my cheekbone shattered. Blood filled my mouth and I sagged back onto the floor. I fought unconsciousness as I felt him pull my arms over my head and press down on my wrists. Inside I was screaming 'NO' As he ripped away my underwear but I was too weak to fight him.

After he violated me, he sat on the floor next to my limp body and looked down at me. 'Not so fucking great now, are you?' he sneered. I couldn't reply. I looked up at him through the pain and searched his face for regret, finding nothing but hatred.

'Don't even think about leaving me, I made you what you are and I can take it all away.' He stood up to leave and then everything went dark.

When I woke up it was daylight. The house was quiet, all I could hear was my heart racing as I strained to listen for any sign that he was still in the house. I tried to sit up but the pain forced me back down, I couldn't even tell where it came from. I remembered that my bag was on the kitchen counter and tried to pull myself across the floor towards it. I pulled myself into a sitting position using the same table that he upended and smashed my face into all those months ago. I felt stupid. I reached for my bag, pulled out my phone and dialled 999.

I remember very little after that. The police told me that Tim was in the house when they arrived at the door and answered the door in his pyjamas, claiming they had woken him up. He let them in without protest. In hospital, I was asked if I wanted to press charges and this time I didn't hesitate.

The trial was difficult. It amazed and upset me that so many of our friends came forward as character witnesses for Tim. Some waxed lyrical about his good character, the importance of his research, how charitable he was and how dedicated to developing talent in his field. Others talked about how calm he was and how much he loved and respected me. Even my own brother gave evidence.

The prosecution barrister provided photographs of the injuries I sustained in this attack and those I sustained in 2003. I described the attack and the history of our relationship in detail and wrote a victim's personal statement describing how the incident had affected my day to day life.

He was convicted but the sentence was shorter than I'd hoped for as the judge took his previous reputation and charitable work into consideration. He received seven years. My solicitor said it was 'one of those things.'

I recovered, finalised the divorce and got on with my life. My career flourished, I made friends and expanded my social life. I got back in touch with old friends and life improved. Then, four years in to his sentence, Tim was released from prison on licence. Though his licence conditions prevented him from contacting me, he found ways to bump into me at work functions, social occasions and even the supermarket. He invaded every aspect of my life, each encounter was more sinister than the last and I believed it was only a matter of time before he did me harm.

Every time I saw him I recorded the incident and called the police. The police kept each incident on file but proving that the encounters weren't accidental was impossible and his probation officer wasn't persuaded to recall him to prison. I even tried a civil injunction but enforcing it wasn't an easy process and the law didn't appear to be on my side. I felt hounded, victimised and completely defenceless and became a recluse. I installed burglar alarms and a panic button and spent months waiting for him to attack me. Shortly after I met Jean, something changed. I don't know what happened but he suddenly stopped pursuing me. I sometimes wonder if Jean and Anne had anything to do with that, with Jean, anything is possible.

It is hard to describe how Jean made me feel, you have to meet her for yourself to know. She was compelling. Life treated her cruelly, yet she was engaging and articulate. Her vision for the future was inspirational and she made me feel special. She seemed to have unique access to a place where women could take control of their own destiny and would be respected for the contribution they made to the world. That kind of vision was enthralling. She made me believe that it was possible to change my destiny. When I'm not with Jean, I feel afraid but around her, I am invincible.

She persuaded me to volunteer with women who had escaped abuse like me. She had to build up my confidence because I didn't think I had anything to offer them at first. After all, how could I help them when I couldn't help myself? Women who have been in an abusive relationship sometimes find it difficult to see a way out and over time I realised that I could show them it is possible to create a new future for yourself. You just need to be brave.

Suzanne was brave. She was going to leave her husband before he got to her. He deserves to die for what he did, the acid destroyed half her face, he broke sixteen of her bones and caused her massive internal injuries, all because she dared to go out and get a job. I was there when she saw her face for the first time and I don't think anyone could have prepared her for that sight. I remember the grief that I felt when I looked in the mirror and saw my own face after my ex-husband slammed it into the table leg but my wounds were superficial compared to hers. She was so brave though. The doctors said to her that they would refer her to a plastic surgeon who could start to rebuild her face but that she would never look like she did before. She was devastated of course but she was determined to leave her husband and make a life for herself.

Suzanne reminded me of myself and I wanted to save her, I really did. I spent all my spare time at the hospital talking to her about the support she could get. I told her about what happened to me and how far I'd come since leaving Tim. I wanted her to be safe, so when she died I think it affected me more than I expected. I realised that this isn't an isolated matter. There are many men who believe that it is okay to hurt women, it's so commonplace that we put in place refuges for women to hide from their abusers and the emergency services have to be trained to respond appropriately rather than dismiss domestic abuse as a 'private matter'. Her death made me realise that my life was just as precarious as hers. My husband was out of prison, he could come to my house and attack me anytime he liked. The protection the law provides isn't worth the paper it is written on. On my way to Jean's house that night I passed a group of men in the street. I remember looking at them, standing there talking, with the arrogance of entitlement. All I wanted to do was wipe the smug, self-important smiles off their faces.

After Suzanne's death, it was easier to understand Jean. She wanted the same things I did, she was just further ahead than me. Over time I came to see that it wasn't enough to stop men for a while, everything had to be reset. I know this doesn't explain what I have done and I'm not really sure that I will ever be able to do that, because I find it hard to justify to myself. all I know is that I suffered for decades and then Jean saved me. All I tried to do was to save the rest of us.

I still believe that Jean is the answer. I haven't seen her since we released the virus and I probably won't see her again for a long time but I know she is thinking of me. Jean is the reason I don't regret the part I have played in this. The children left behind will have hope and Jean will provide the guidance they need. Our success means that the little boys we saved will not be raised to behave towards women as their fathers and grandfathers did before them and the little girls won't be treated badly anymore.

Despite the horror of it all, I know deep down that I had no other choice. I often wake up at night, sweating and screaming because of what we have done but when I turn on the light and really think about it, I know in my heart that we did the right thing.

2014

Nicole and I are in her lab, an annex at the rear of her property. Away from prying eyes and completely enclosed, it is the perfect location for our work and she has converted it well.

We are working on our virus. For someone who a few months ago was not entirely on-board, she is enthusiastic in her research, though I remain unsure whether she is wholly inspired by my vision as her motivation appears to be the professional pride that comes from creating the deadliest virus on earth.

Though I consider myself an expert on bacteria and viruses, she is far superior to me in her brilliance and has thought long and hard about our plan. Creating a virus deadly to men, without attracting any attention whatsoever, is a big ask. The bacteria and viruses that cause death in humans on the scale that we need are closely guarded. You can't just acquire them, even if you are a renowned scientist like Nicole.

She comes across a potential candidate, a Lago virus responsible for causing a highly lethal disease in rabbits. It causes liver necrosis and haemorrhage, a condition known as Rabbit Haemorrhagic Disease Virus (RHDV). The peracute form causes sudden death without clinical signs. It is transmitted orally. It is a non-enveloped virus and is very stable in the environment, crucially it is resistant to inactivation by heat and chemicals which means it may survive in tap water.

Because RHDV doesn't affect humans there are fewer controls on laboratories storing or handling it so Nicole acquires some samples. It's so exciting to watch her work and I am a willing lab assistant.

We are contemplating how to engineer 'our' virus to cause a similar disease in humans. We are so enthused, so completely in tune in our thinking that I feel sure it will not be long before we crack it.

It is wonderful to work with Nicole. I confess that I have grown fond of her. She is the sister I never had and has made living without Mummy and Hope more bearable. I hope she feels the same way about me. Our work together is beautiful.

2014

Anne and I meet in the café where we first encountered each other. She has been quiet lately and I worry she is going to tell me she can't create me a new identity but she is smiling when I arrive so I relax. Before I even have chance to say hello she is grasping my hand and exclaiming excitedly. 'I've done it, Jean. I have created the new you.'

She takes me through her work and I cannot help but be impressed. If this goes to plan I will be under intense scrutiny, I need to be good but not too good to be true. It has taken Anne time to get it right but she seems to have created a fool-proof identity that will stand up to even the most meticulous scrutiny.

She has deleted anything that might link me to my new identity, though she says hard copy photographs may still be a problem. Mummy kept me out of school photographs after we moved house but there were pictures of me on-line and old newspaper articles about Hope's murder which she had to erase or change. My appearance can be altered so I am not worried about photographs. It is enough that she has managed to alter records and destroy a large number of hard copies. It is no wonder that it took her a year to do it.

Anne has made this look easy. She has created a better version of me, clean and untarnished, with a new name and a history free of rape and murder. It is the life I would have chosen for myself if I'd had a choice. I am delighted. Anne is beaming, she enjoys impressing me.

'I don't know how to thank you Anne.' I say. 'Is there anything you need?'

She is resolute. 'Just make sure you don't forget to give my father and brothers a dose.'

We talk some more but my mind is elsewhere, I am busy planning. I will stand in a local election, I will finally be the person I was supposed to be. Change is part of life, Jean was my caterpillar and soon I will be a butterfly. My past is a cocoon that I have been trapped in, when I finally shed it, I will shed my grief and pain too. I don't want to feel the pain of a lost daughter and a lost mother or dwell on how unjust my life has been. I want to think of Hope and Mummy and know that they are in a better place, where men cannot hurt them.

I am working towards something so amazing, so transformational, that I cannot help but be grateful for my journey to this place, however challenging it was.

❊ ❊ ❊

I am with Anne in a private medical unit in Brazil waiting for surgery. After the operation, I shall be quite unrecognisable. My travel plans were tricky, I left Britain as Jean but I must return as someone else. My new passport is concealed in the lining of Anne's luggage. It contains a replica of the exit stamp in my passport on the way here. After our flight landed Anne changed the records, deleted my old passport and switched the record of my flight here to my new identity. When I get home, she will wipe all records of our flights. She really does think of absolutely everything.

When I get off the plane I will go directly to my new house in Kent, where all my things are waiting. Records show that until recently I lived in a busy high-rise block in Manchester. My new-found wealth comes from my recently deceased mother, a wealthy landowner who spent most of her life abroad.

Records show that I am an active campaigner for survivors of domestic abuse and have years of experience. I am also an active supporter of my local political party. The move to Kent ties in very nicely with an upsurge in political support for the party in the area. I will immerse myself in local politics as soon as I arrive.

Everything is planned to perfection.

* * *

It is done. I am heavily bandaged but today I see my new face. I stand in front of the mirror and unwrap myself. I feel like I am emerging from an ugly damaged shell. I am pink, fresh, clean, undamaged by the horror of my past. I am no longer Jean, I am better than she ever could be. In this body, with this new skin, untouched by the foulness of male hands, I will achieve everything I've dreamt of.

2025

March, National Remembrance

The gathering crowd in Hitchin Town Square were sombre and respectful. They had gathered to listen to the Princess Regent speak. With the power off across most of the town, the news of her visit had been spread through word of mouth. One woman said that she heard the princess had been touring the country talking to people. Another talked about how strong she must be to do it in the face of her own grief. The older women in the crowd were reminded of her grandmother and great grandmother before her. As the Princess Regent approached the makeshift podium Joanne and Tate joined the rear of the crowd, straining to catch sight of the princess.

'I am grateful to you all for coming out to see me today.' the Princess began.

'Across the country our communities have endured unprecedented loss. I see heartache and devastation in the eyes of everyone I meet. None have been left unscathed. We have earned the right to mourn and it feels as if the grief will have no end. It is hard to find comfort in life or seek solace from our remaining loved ones. It is easier to succumb to the anger and grief and let it swallow us and there is no shame in that.

However, I want to share with you some of the things I have seen in the hope that it may bring you some comfort. During my visits, I have met extraordinary people who have given me reason to hope. I have met courageous women who are helping to recover bodies and lay them to rest. They work hard to make sure that we can emerge from these dark days, bruised but enduring.

I have met women who are learning how to be farmers, electricians and plumbers so that they can help their communities get back on their feet.

I've seen young women restore power to a hospital and watched a woman inside that hospital give birth to a baby boy.

I have watched with enormous pride as our people show bravery and dignity in the wake of such tragedy.

I am humbled by you all and I will do all I can to help. This country is ours and the responsibility to heal it lies with all of us. No-one would choose this life but we are here and we are strong. The world watches with pity but they will see that there are still things we can teach them. Our strength and survival will be the enduring legacy of the men that we have lost because while we survive, there is always hope.'

Joanne watched as the Princess Regent walked amongst the women and children in the square after her speech. She shook the hands of mothers and small children bearing flowers. She sat on a bench in the square and embraced a woman who broke down while telling her story. She seemed sympathetic, engaging and human.

She stayed long after the visit was scheduled to finish and when she finally did leave, several hours later, Joanne noticed that the other women did not go home as they usually would, nor did they avoid their neighbours or cover their mouths. She sat in the square, watching Tate play and talking to the women around her and through the grief, felt a new sense of unity with the people in her town.

2014

I lead two lives. By day, I work as a local party activist. I am 'discovered' by my local MP who wants to help me navigate the 'cut-throat world of politics'. She is a good politician but has a soft side which will make it difficult for her to progress. She is interested in my (manufactured) past and sees enough talent to put me in touch with her ministerial friends. I meet officials from the Home Office and the Department of Health to discuss my work with survivors of domestic abuse. They are writing a new joint strategy and I give them plenty of ideas for early intervention policies. They are grateful and I have new contacts. Win-win.

The men I meet in this job are odious. One in particular irritates and upsets me. I guess he is in his late fifties, he has a powerful role in the local party and it is clear that that power is what drives him. He can be quite charming and has undoubtable expertise but he wears his experience like a general wears a dress uniform. He uses it to undermine his peers and creates an atmosphere in board meetings that sometimes tips into hostility. He has the arrogance of a man who has never experienced real hardship or been effectively challenged. He is rigid in his beliefs, behaving more like a dictator than a leader. He gives the outward impression that he is inspiring the young people in the team, who are ambitious and want to succeed in the cut throat world of politics but in reality, he uses his role to subtly belittle and undermine those who he doesn't care for. He picks his favourites (usually but not always men) and emphatically praises them, sometimes this is deserved, sometimes it is not. For those he does not care for he fosters fear, picking holes in their work, ignoring their successes and making snap personal judgements about their attitude, competence or beliefs. He rarely asks about the personal lives of his staff and dismisses personal issues as irrelevant to the 'good of the party'. The team respond accordingly. There is a culture of long hours and many of the beleaguered members of the team are so desperate to please that they bend over backwards to make him happy, to no avail. I have seen many of the female staff crying in the toilets after a particularly bruising meeting.

I observe him with one of the younger women, a bright and accomplished girl who is unafraid to speak her mind. Over the course of just a few weeks he reduces her to a nervous wreck. He meets her too frequently and scrutinises her work in a way that is rarely seen in any industry, let alone politics. He makes her feel small and worthless, nit-picking continuously until she is scared to commit anything to paper. His behaviour causes her to change her own. She becomes obsessed with pleasing him, she seeks validation from him in every piece of work she completes and when it is not forthcoming, she is devastated over and over again. She retreats into herself, works long hours, neglects her personal life and allows him to become part of every waking moment.

I decide to help her. Though I could just ruin him of course, I want to see if I can alter him first. I approach her and ask if she would mind participating in a test to see whether his critique is personal or related to her abilities. She readily agrees. I send a piece of her work in my name and wait. His response is wholly positive, praising the drafting, structure and strategic thought that went into the work. He asks why I have strayed into that policy area and what interest it holds for me.

I catch him at his desk, bending down so that only he can hear me. I say 'The piece of work you admired so much wasn't written by me. It was written by Nina, the girl you have reduced to a wreck through bullying and intimidation. She is talented but I have watched you destroy her confidence. I suggest that you change your approach because she has enough evidence to make a bullying and harassment claim against you and of course, no-one in the party wants to lose you.'

I straighten up and smile sweetly. He is shocked but his ego kicks in and he looks at me smugly. 'I can't imagine what makes you think that a threat like that would frighten me. I have spent my career trying to get the best out of people and my approach works. She may feel uncomfortable for a while but in the long run she will come to see how much better I have made her. I have a lot of experience of this dear.' He dismisses me with a wave of his hand.

I decide to ruin him after all and give the task to Anne, who relishes such things. Within a week his 'good name' is splashed all over the local news. A series of internal emails have been leaked to the media which evidence a campaign of bullying and harassment directed at over a dozen female employees and lasting well over a year.

I watch as he clears his desk. He walks past me and his lip curls into an ugly snarl. 'I know this was you.' he hisses.

I smile back at him. 'This was entirely your own doing. You'll find no evidence of my involvement. Bullies have a way of tripping themselves up, dear.'

* * *

By night I am Jean. I travel to Nicole's to help in the lab, time that is precious to me. We share a passion for science and have wonderful, engaging conversations that give my life meaning and purpose. I know she feels the same. We are as close as sisters and I am happy that I have a friend. We are in the middle of a major breakthrough in the development of our virus. It is 3am and I really should go home but it is too exhilarating. She is using genomic segments from a Sapovirus to try and make the recombinant virus zoonotic, which means it will have an

effect on humans instead of rabbits. It is the breakthrough we
need.

From now on we treat the lab like a fortress. Tomorrow Nicole
will buy and fit combination locks on the door to the lab and
the gate to her garden, just in case. It would be a tragedy if it
were released before we are ready.

2025

Record from Hansard, 8th March 2025

Volume 650

[Authors note: Parliament was in session. Inside the House of Commons two hundred and six Members of Parliament waited for the parliamentary session to begin. Four hundred and forty-four seats were empty, a stark reminder of the impact of the crisis. The Speaker of the House was dead, there was no-one to call order.]

Claire Flint (Hastings and Rye) (Con)
'Order, Order. Good morning my right hon. Friends. It is good to see you all today. The past few weeks has been bleak and I confess to feeling very alone through much of it. These unprecedented events have altered the course of history forever. We mourn our families, our colleagues, our friends. None of our lives will ever be the same.

I could spend this session paying tribute to our fallen colleagues, friends and loved ones. However, given the scale of loss and the problems facing the people of this country, it is an indulgence that we simply can't afford. In this House, we must take urgent decisions about the future of the country.

We must, as a matter of priority, nominate a new speaker. Written nominations will be made to the Commons table office tomorrow morning. A secret ballot will take place tomorrow afternoon.

Immediately after this session, I will be approaching all party leaders to propose forming a grand coalition of all remaining MPs to begin rebuilding our country. Traditionally this place has been divided, a place of debate and opposition, now we must come together. It is our duty to rebuild the confidence of the women and children remaining, so that they feel safe to leave their homes, visit friends, work, buy food and engage with their communities.

We must urgently conclude the recovery and burial of those who perished. Bodies lie in houses, hospitals and in some cases, on the streets, destroying the spirit of the country and posing a serious risk of disease. Local councils are using volunteers from across the country to help collect and dispose of them. It is a difficult and distressing job and those who are doing it on behalf of the rest of us should be commended.

We must reopen our borders. Continued isolation leaves us cut off from food supplies and unable to easily receive support and assistance from our friends and allies. Airdrops of aid are insufficient respite from this crisis and we face a humanitarian and economic crisis beyond compare if we do not act quickly to reassure the world that our country is safe.

I can confirm that a vaccine for the virus has been discovered, our allies have been made aware this and several pharmaceutical companies are now mass producing the vaccine, which will be a prerequisite for male entry to Great Britain from now on. In a month, once sufficient supplies of the vaccine are available to support travel to Great Britain, I propose reopening our borders.

In the meantime, we are vaccinating our armed forces stationed abroad, so that we can bring them home to assist with the recovery. Thirty thousand British troops are stationed in more than eighty countries across the world. We need them far more than they do right now, so we propose to recall all thirty thousand. A vote on this issue will be held tomorrow, after the speaker has been elected.

I propose the establishment of committees to deal with the acute issues of; Disposal of bodies, Disease control, Food supplies, Restoration of utilities, Resolving personnel shortages in key sectors, The economy, Internal Security, Foreign affairs, Migration, Health and wellbeing.

Membership of these committees will be the first order of business of the new coalition, if formed.

We have a new Queen and a Regent who will advise the government until she comes of age. A coronation will be held in a few months. I do not believe that the public would want this to be a lavish occasion, given the circumstances. However, our new Queen deserves to be recognised in her role and the public needs something to help them heal. Our Regent has offered her assistance and counsel to us. I believe she will come to be a symbol of hope to the public. The final committee I would like to form will be responsible for assisting with organisation of the coronation and establishing the Princess Regent's role in our recovery, working with her aides.

I open the house up for questions.'

2015

Nicole and I work on the virus nonstop. The virus has been able to target and infect humans for some time, though we have yet to test its effect on a human host (I have several people in mind). The problem has been limiting its effects to men only. Today Nicole inserts genetic material from a Retrovirus and it elicits a clinical response similar to an HIV infection, with higher viral loads in men and an increased antiviral response in women. This is the breakthrough we were waiting for! I am beyond excitement!

Alongside this work she develops a vaccine, a necessary part of our plan. In a matter of weeks, we will be ready to begin.

I tell Nicole how keen I am to test the virus on a live host but she says that there are weeks of lab tests to be done on cells and even then, it will be impossible to test on a live host without flagging its existence to the medical community. It is true that it would be a disaster if the virus came to light in time for research to be done and a cure found. It will have to be done as close to the day we release it as possible. She says I must be patient no matter how challenging I find it.

* * *

At work, I make another breakthrough. The local MP, Judy Bridgeman, decides not to stand in the election next year. She is a good person but has lost any ambition to go further after some negative publicity about her family and will instead spend more time with her husband, an odd ambition but one that she assures me she wants.

Of course, the publicity was orchestrated by Anne. We discovered Judy's Achilles heel early on- she is completely devoted to her husband. The newspapers often mention their deep love in articles, something I find a little nauseating. Anne dug around but couldn't find any dirt on him at all, however his adult son is easy pickings. Unlike his father, he has dabbled in women, alcohol and drugs for most of his adult life and it only takes a small amount of effort to turn him from an occasional drug user to a habitual addict who supplied drugs to his friends. Anne feeds the story to a journalist who is slap dash enough not to fact-check and the story explodes. Judy's popularity is based on her squeaky-clean image. There is a significant drug problem in her constituency and she often speaks out about the 'scourge' of suppliers who target young, impressionable young people. The fallout from the story is catastrophic for Judy and her husband. The son has done well for himself and works in the renewable energy industry. He immediately loses his job. Judy's husband takes a leave of absence from his role and travels to his son's house in Kent to support him. Judy is left to manage the media and salvage what she can of her reputation. That evening, her and her husband have their first major row in years over the phone, a conversation that Anne listens to after hacking into Judy's calls. Her husband blames his son's misfortune on her job, an accusation she strenuously denies.

Over the course of the following week the media get more vicious. The gutter press run a story claiming that Judy caused the breakup of her husband's previous relationship, sending his son off the rails. All trashy and untrue of course but that didn't matter, it backed up her husband's argument. Judy begins to feel that she may have to choose between her job and her family. It is very distressing for her. By the end of the second week she has reassured her husband that she will stand down before the next election. Job done.

Judy has decided to keep this news to herself for a while, so

I use the time to shore up my position. She and I have grown close over the past few months and I have met several ministers on her behalf. I have also received some positive local media coverage of my role supporting survivors of domestic abuse and feel I am in a good place to 'up the ante'. I tell Judy that I think I have found my calling in politics and ask for some mentoring to help me progress. She tells me she wants to delegate more anyway and assigns bigger projects to me. I accompany her to meetings in London and get more involved in local events. It isn't long before I am identified as a rising star, so when Judy steps down there is very little discussion about the party's choice of successor. The decision is already made.

2015

Finally, things are moving quickly. Nicole now heads the development and quality assurance of vaccines for Cruise Pharmaceuticals, a prominent global company. Her position at Cruise is key to the plan and thankfully her reputation means that it wasn't difficult for her to secure the role. She has managed to insert the vaccine for our virus into Cruise's new combined measles, mumps and rubella vaccine without detection. We were worried about the rigorous testing process but a little teamwork between Anne and Nicole ensured our success. The company begins to market the vaccine, so the next part of the plan falls to me.

Thanks to my political activity, I have a growing number of contacts in central government and I scout around for someone I can influence who is a position to help me. I need to do this before the election and it doesn't take long to find a young girl called Ashley who works for the Department of Health. She is highly ambitious, as demonstrated by her linked-in profile. She is bright, articulate and overlooked, like most young women in her position. Anne creates a young people's mentoring scheme online, enabling me to legitimately contact Ashley with an offer of six free guidance sessions to help her progress her career. She is attracted by my experience in politics and science and we instantly connect when we meet.

After a few sessions, I make Ashley aware of a 'commission' I have been given, linked to her role. I feign a reluctance to divulge too much but she is super keen and assures me that I can trust her, so I eventually agree to let her read it, citing it as an example of how to effectively frame an argument. I give her a position paper outlining the benefits of a new national contract for the MMR vaccine. It is well researched and focuses on the benefits of three vaccines in one and the particular strengths of the vaccine that Cruise produces. She takes the information away with her and then I wait.

* * *

Ashley meets me for coffee and confesses that she used an anonymised version of my argument in a report she wrote for the Secretary of State for Health. He was persuaded by it and has begun a national procurement exercise to select a single supplier of the MMR vaccine. I scold her, she is deeply apologetic. I tell her I am very concerned that I may be accused of using my relationship with her to further my client's interests. She assures me that she has covered her tracks well and goes into some detail about how careful she has been. I reluctantly believe her but tell her that on principle I feel I must terminate our arrangement.

* * *

Today an announcement is made.

'Following a rigorous procurement exercise, Cruise Pharmaceuticals has been awarded a national contract to supply Britain with the MMR vaccine.'

Once the stockpiles of other vaccines have been used up our vaccine will begin to inoculate all children across the country. I am so happy, nothing about my plan has proved particularly challenging so far and I sometimes feel as if an unseen force is clearing my path. Without the vaccine, I think that Nicole would have stopped her research. Persuading her to create a virus that might prove fatal was a difficult step forward and I only achieved it by assuring her that we would protect children. I am sensible enough to know that the human race needs man to survive, all I am trying to achieve is a seismic shift in the balance of power. The next generation of boys will become men under the careful guidance of womankind alone.

2025

April. Testimonial, anon.

I helped clear the bodies. We became accustomed to the terrible smell of death all too quickly. Imagine the smell of a dead animal. Then imagine a house full of dead rotting animals that have been there for months. That's what the air smelt like. We tried gloves, protective clothing and bleach but nothing could mask it. It got under our skin too, despite the vapour rub we wiped under our noses and the lemons we rubbed onto our skin. It seeped into our clothes and into the fabric of the vehicles we drove. The smell was stronger in some places, like outside a house where a man lived alone or within a mile of the funeral pits and it lingered long after the bodies were removed.

Most of the bodies had been taken away from inner city and affluent areas by April but in the poorer areas there were still bodies everywhere for us to find. We had a list of places to check, which was compiled by the women in the council call centre, who responded to complaints about the smell. Sometimes the police brought the cadaver dogs to help but other times we had to follow our own noses.

A lot of the bodies we found around that time were rotting and liquefying across the ground underneath them. The smell wasn't the only thing to worry about, moving those bodies required a shovel, bleach and a scrubbing brush. The pits were filling up so the burnings happened daily as the women in the pits tried to reduce them down to ash. Crematoriums were working around the clock and the smoke hung across the whole country. I remember feeling as if it would never end. The government estimated that there were still 10 million more bodies out there and for those of us helping to clear them, it was relentless. I still dream about it, a never-ending memory I can't erase and a smell that lingered for longer than it took to wash our bodies clean.

2015

Today the people of Britain vote in the general election. I am standing in my local constituency as odds on favourite to become a member of Parliament.

This has not been an easy road, and I tend to underplay the complexity of the task I have faced to Nicole. I worked in politics for years as Jean but it was always going to be a challenge to make all that hard work relevant to my new identity. Anne is the one who has made this possible. She has done an amazing job of both covering my tracks and opening doors that would have been closed to Jean.

The party have confidence in my abilities as an orator, a strategist and someone who understands how to engage and inspire people. I have to be 'palatable' of course so I tone down my opinions and mould myself around the party majority. Sometimes this goes so much against the grain that I worry I am letting myself down. I go home with headaches that force me to lie down in the dark.

I read books on how to engage effectively with men because most of the people who can help me get into a ministerial post are male. Another irony. I read that men respond better to women who do not wield their intellect like a sword. I find this hard but downplay my intelligence with men enough to make them think I am pliable and easy to manipulate. With women, I do the opposite. They need to know that I am someone they can count on to speak for them. I teach myself how to flirt and listen to men witter, without trying to beat them. It is excruciating but when I feel I may buckle, I think of my goal.

It is worth it. I am on the brink of greatness. All I need to do is hold my nerve.

* * *

I am now a member of parliament! My party also won the general election and the Prime Minister is now selecting his ministerial team. I don't expect to be selected but I am elated to get as far as I have.

* * *

Anne, Nicole and I meet for a celebratory drink at a small bar out of town. We all stay in a hotel nearby and it occurs to me that it might be the last time we can meet in public together, now I am a public office holder. It wouldn't do to be recognised or photographed with Anne and Nicole, it puts us all at risk of discovery.

We have a lovely evening, Nicole buys some champagne and I have a couple of glasses. I can count on one hand the number of times I have had alcohol and the bubbles go straight to my head. Nicole finds this funny, she is used to drinking and a couple of glasses doesn't seem to affect her in the slightest. I find myself talking far more openly than usual and admit that Nicole and Anne are the closest people I have to family. I think I call them 'my people' and I may well have slurred my words a little. Nicole leans over and kisses my cheek. 'We love you too' she says. I don't think I have ever felt happier.

I am on the way home when another terrible headache hits and I don't leave the house for two days. I worry about myself because the headaches feel like knives, scratching at my bones. Perhaps it is because being with Anne and Nicole reminds me who I am. Sometimes when I have to be someone else all day long, I forget that I am also Jean, but when I am with them I feel like I have two people inside me. It's exhausting.

2025

Hertfordshire
Testimonial, Violet Brown

The sign in the shop window read:
'The Department for the Environment, Food and Rural Affairs has introduced rationing of certain food supplies. This will ensure that every individual receives enough food to eat until we can reopen our borders. Every adult and child must attend the council offices to register and receive a ration book containing stamps which can be exchanged for essential items at participating shops.
Rationed items include; meat, sugar, tea, coffee, dairy products, preserves, eggs, tinned and dried food, soap and soap items, fuel, bottled water and chlorine tablets.'
I joined the supermarket queue to exchange the stamps for food. It reminded me of standing in line for meat with my mother. I was ten when rationing ended in 1954 and while I don't remember it fondly, I do remember that everyone pitched in. I used to think that spirit had gone but it turned out that it hadn't. I'd moved in with my friend Edna, who was younger than me but just as willing to have a joke. It was good to share a house and having two ration books made meals more appetising. I liked working out how to make the food last and we took it in turns to cook.
I must have been muttering to myself about recipes because the lady in front of me started asking me how to make the food last. Her name was Joanne and she had a little son Tate, who

was hopping from one foot to the other. Joanne rolled her eyes and muttered that she thought he needed the toilet, though he insisted that he didn't. She said she thought Tate was going through a growth spurt because he ate a lot but he also wasted food which made her cross. I told her that my mother used to eat our leftovers rather than cooking a dinner for herself and sometimes she didn't get any food, because we were all so hungry. I explained how we used to bulk out meals with beans or vegetables, or thin them out with water to make them go further. She nodded but I could tell she was still fretting about how she would manage with so little. She told me she was part of the team clearing all the bodies, like the women who came to take Stan. She said that sometimes she would find cupboards full of food and said someone should go around and collect it all up because it seemed wrong to scrimp when there was so much food just sitting there going to waste. I didn't know what to say. My house was empty and there was no food left in there when I moved out.

2018

As a local MP, I use every opportunity to speak in the House of Commons and it finally gets me noticed. I am promoted to a Parliamentary Private Secretary role, working for the Education Secretary. With experience in central government I could be a few months away from a junior minister role. I am lucky to work for the Education Secretary, she seems to be a good person and it is good to work with a woman again. I am so sick of working with the pompous men in the party and sometimes have to go home and scream at the top of my lungs just to release my frustration. Luckily these days I live in a detached house!

I enjoy this work. Educating our children in preparation for the future is of great interest to me. My vision is a return to single sex schools. It angers me that girls are still taught in mixed classes despite the evidence that girls are disadvantaged in this environment. I talk about this with the minister, who is a great advocate of women's rights and together we try and influence teaching practices to empower girls. I oversee some great initiatives, like the introduction of new topics like 'ground-breaking women throughout history' and 'Equality and what it means'. My reach grows weekly and I am preparing the ground for what is to come, these children will be alive after the virus, the government is unwittingly giving them to tools to help them cope with life in the new world.

* * *

Nicole and I spend all our free time on refining the virus. I am happier than I have ever felt. I just wish that Hope and Mummy could be here to see how far I have come. If she were still alive I think Mummy would be proud of me. I think she might even have come to believe in my vision. I think she imagined I would end up in trouble and I wish I could show her how wrong she was.

2020

I am a junior minister. It took some doing but I now operate efficiently in this environment. These people would think nothing of stabbing you in the back, so single minded is their pursuit of power. To be effective I must emulate them.

I play a waiting game. Ideally, I will be a Secretary of State by the time the virus is released but it is of little consequence if I am not. The current Prime Minister promotes his male cronies and a few token women, which ironically plays nicely into my hands as it will leave an open field once they are all dead. Just one Secretary of State is female, after the surprise resignation of my old colleague, the Education Secretary. Officially she wanted to spend time with her family and focus on constituency issues but it is rumoured that she was forced out. A few of my female peers have what it takes to make it and I am careful not to alienate them, I need them to believe in me if I want a seat at the table when the time comes.

2025

Testimonial, Rt. Hon Karen Tonge MP

My husband, Alex was stuck abroad when the outbreak hit and after frequent altercations with foreign reporters his temper was wearing thin. As a government minister, I was of great interest to international reporters after the outbreak and Alex was overwhelmed with hacks who had tracked him down, hoping for an exclusive. The stories written about our family since the outbreak were penned without his permission and with precious little factual data behind them but they were brutal, hurtful and everywhere. The foreign media did not care for a government staffed entirely by women and was making its feelings clear.

Alex had been in New Zealand on business when the outbreak hit and at first focussed on getting as close as possible to home. He booked a flight to France but was forced to submit to blood tests at Wellington Airport and missed his flight waiting for the outcome. He was removed from the next flight after clearing his throat during the safety message and then when he finally arrived in France he was quarantined on arrival in France pending more tests. After his release, he stayed with our friend Christophe, who worked for the French government. Alex said he learnt more about the outbreak from Christophe than he managed to extract from me and challenged me continuously about it on the phone. He didn't understand that I couldn't share any information outside British borders without involving the Foreign Office and was infuriated by the suggestion that he wasn't trustworthy. Conversations became more and more fractious between us and he became angry about everything, his business which was nose-diving in his absence, the children who he missed and worried about, and me, who he increasingly saw as the enemy.

Christophe eventually arranged for Alex to be immunised by the French government, but the borders remained closed so he was still unable to travel. He felt that I was part of the establishment preventing him from coming home and, as I listened to his ranting, what really upset me was his lack of empathy. Life had been incredibly difficult for all of us over the three months he'd been away but his focus was on his own misfortune. I found his incessant complaining insulting, both to the millions of people who died and to those of us who had to watch it happen. In the end, I stopped missing him and could only hope that things improved between us once he was back home.

2021

We campaign in a snap general election. It is driven by a political scandal (orchestrated of course, by Anne) and a subsequent successful leadership challenge. There may be an opportunity to secure a senior position here but our new leader George Moore does not respect or promote intelligent women so I need to play the game well. I sit around the table with these men, discussing policies and talking of the future as if they will be a part of it. They are woefully under qualified to run the country when compared with me but it is a cross I must bear. I have my eye on the prize, as Mummy would say.

2025

Rt. Hon. Claire Flint MP

Jenny walked into the room and closed the door. 'The German Chancellor is on the line now.' Claire nodded to Jenny, picked up the telephone and switched on the speaker.

'Good afternoon Petra. How are you?

'We are good, Claire, how are things there now?

'It's been challenging but we are making headway. The government is functioning, women have started to return to work and daily life is less bleak. However, there is still a long way to go. We remain heavily reliant on aid drops, particularly food and medicines. I'd like to formally thank you for that, it cannot be understated how helpful that has been and how much we continue to need them.'

'Please don't thank us Claire, it's is the very least we can do and an inadequate response in the circumstances. We want to help, what more can we do?'

'We need to open the borders in May, Petra. The threat has passed. We haven't seen a new case in more than ten weeks. I don't expect there to be a great clamour to come to the UK but restarting trade would help our economy recover. It would be really helpful if European leaders could publicly support that move. '

The line was silent. Jenny and Claire looked at each other anxiously. Petra finally spoke hesitantly 'We will need some assurances...'

'Of course, Petra.' Claire almost tripped over her words in her rush to respond 'It goes without saying. Vaccinations are a prerequisite to entry for all males, exports will be thoroughly checked for risk of contamination. We are aware of our responsibilities in ensuring that the virus does not spread.'

'Then of course, we will support you however we can. Do you have the support of other leaders?'

'Within Europe, yes. Outside Europe we have had some challenges. It is unlikely that China, Japan or the USA will support direct flights at present but we are confident we can re-establish them within weeks, once it is clear that the threat has passed.'

'Okay, we will do what we can to help with that.'

'I appreciate it Petra. Thanks for the call.'

'No problem. Bye.'

Claire sighed and looks at Jenny. 'Well that's something, I suppose.'

'Something? It's great Claire!'

'I know. I am not sure I'd be so forthcoming if the roles were reversed.'

'We are part of Europe, it isn't in anyone's interests to keep us isolated. The rest of the world doesn't have the same economic interest in our recovery.'

'No, I suppose not. When is the announcement going to be made?'

'Tomorrow morning.'

2021

A setback. We win the election, of course but the idiot in charge decides not to promote me in the reshuffle, instead rewarding more white, upper class, misogynistic men. There are only three women in the cabinet which sickens me. He is a buffoon and a relic of a bygone era. I can't wait to see his demise. I have to defer to his inferior intellect on a daily basis and the words stick in the back of my throat. He is a smug, self-righteous, moral-less man. I find myself imagining him, writhing on the floor, slowly dying, just to get myself through the day. I rage to Anne and Nicole, who listen patiently.

We come up with a new plan. I will remain a junior minister. I will still be exceptional in my role but I will stop showcasing my ambition. It clearly threatens him when I show what I can do. Instead I will be the Mary Poppins of politics. Practically perfect in every way, immaculately turned out, innocent, un-threatening, demure. Hard to believe, isn't it? I can act and I am pretty good at it actually. It is easy to pretend when you know you are the one holding the cards.

2022

Our attention shifts towards planning the distribution of the virus. Our approach to mass infection is inspired. Fluoride is added to all treated water in the UK. We are going to add the virus to batches of fluoride as it is sent to water treatment facilities. We have engineered the virus to be highly resistant to chemicals. Moreover, it thrives in water and will quickly replicate itself, spreading quickly through water without detection. Within 48 hours of exposure to the water at a treatment facility it will achieve the quantities required to kill all men who drink it.

This is a military operation, requiring skills and attributes that Anne, Nicole and I don't have and it is time to bring the support group Anne has established into the fold. Anne has spent years warming this group of women up to the idea of a world without men, but it is for me to set out our ultimate goal. It must be done carefully and they need to be enticed in. These women have very few attachments, except to each other. If I can convince one then I may be able to convince all. I research the psychology of cults. I need to bring them in quickly and there are very effective techniques to do this.

* * *

We remove them from daily life, promising a peaceful and healing weekend retreat. Before the event they are instructed to fast for 48 hours before the event in order to cleanse their bodies. By the time they arrive they are hungry and tired but are not allowed to rest or eat. Anne explains that these techniques allow people with painful and troubled pasts to truly heal.

In the early hours of the morning they are blindfolded and taken through an exercise to put them into a meditative state. We introduce the sounds of abuse into the room, awful noises and screams that make even me anxious. A strange thing happens. Some of the women become almost psychotic. Anne indicates that this is my cue. I enter the room and I begin to talk about my vision. The sounds of abuse fade away and all the women can hear is my voice. I describe, how wonderful my world is without men. I talk about this for hours. Then I allow them a short rest. This exercise is repeated every few hours for several days, using a recording of the first session.

By the end of the retreat the women are committed. Anne and Nicole take up the mantle and my role is limited to daily sermons, communicated through a secure link. I am now a goddess to them. They revere me. I tell them that they are social reformers and this is a revolution, with necessary casualties.

Though our group is technically a cult, I would argue that the more damaging cult is the world we live in now. Women who have been successfully brainwashed by men would never dream of fighting back. My group know the truth through bitter experience, they were not 'successfully recruited' by society, all they know of men is brutality. Men did despicable things to them, destroying their innocence forever. Now they are part of something so transformative and revolutionary that their wounds are healed by it.

* * *

Some of the women are now posted where we need them to be. Two women work in the factory that makes fluoride, another is the manager of a water treatment plant and one supervises the warehouse where we keep the virus. Nicole says that making the virus in the quantities required is the biggest challenge of all. I know little about the logistics of this, I have been distant from it, Nicole runs that part of the operation and I trust her completely to manage it. She tells me that we are halfway, the pre-prepared virus is stored in freezers controlled to -80°. My inheritance paid for the land and the freezers. The virus is hidden in plain sight, in a nondescript warehouse on the outskirts of a small town. People barely notice it as they drive along the A-road next to it.

Everything about our work is hidden from the rest of the world by Anne, the architect of our deception. I question the competence of our security services, who have not managed to detect us at all. I ponder over this for some time and conclude that the system is built by men, to protect men from other men. This makes sense to me, men are arrogant, they ignore fifty percent of the population who have been oppressed for centuries. They do not see that we could be the biggest threat to their cosy, entitled lives.

2025

International news

'Great Britain is open for business! That was the message from Claire Flint, the country's new Prime Minister, as she declared Britain's intention to reopen the borders after two months of isolation. In a televised address, she said;

'The British public has suffered indescribable pain over the past two months. The consequences are far reaching and will be felt for decades across the globe. However, we remain a strong country and we are now on the road to recovery. The virus has run its course and having purified and vigorously tested the water, our top scientists have concluded that there is no further risk of reinfection. It is time to begin reopening our borders. This will be done in stages, starting with returning British Nationals. A programme to immunise the thousands of British Nationals currently stranded abroad is already underway and the first flights for retuning British Nationals will start later this month.

At the same time, we will re-open our borders to trade. We are aware of the significance of this step and are introducing a new international immunisation policy for everyone travelling to Britain. The vaccine has been made available internationally. All those transporting goods to and from the UK will be required to produce a certificate of vaccination at the border to gain entry to the UK. All exports will be thoroughly checked and certified as free from contamination.

Finally, we will allow commercial airlines to begin transporting passengers to and from the UK. New migration policies are being drawn up to ensure a sensible approach to long term migration, in order to fill some of the key skills gaps created by the impact of the virus.'

The world has reacted to this news with trepidation. China and the USA quickly declared that direct flights would remain suspended until further notice and many other countries have subsequently followed suit. European leaders have been working closely with the British administration and have publicly welcomed the news as a significant step forward in re-establishing normality in the region. However, with Europe appearing to be Britain's only ally, they have some way to go to reassure the rest of the world that the threat has passed.'

2023

I meet Anne and Nicole. We do not see each other often these days because I am too busy, so it is a joyous occasion and I feel like I am visiting family. I love them dearly, they understand me and I am able to be myself for a few hours. Sometimes I feel very alone. I am surrounded by the very people I despise the most and every day is a struggle. I survive by focussing on small gains, such as the policies I have introduced that will endure once we release the virus.

These people are truly odious. George Moore in particular makes me sick to the stomach. He is the worst of men, a scourge on the earth. He climbs over the bodies of the people he has ruined to reach the top and cares little for the lives of others. His policies push women low. The few female cabinet members he appoints are token gestures, designed to appease us. He destroys anyone who may be strong enough to challenge him. He publicly humiliates his wife by openly sleeping with other women. The whole of Westminster knows about it. After meetings with him I have to meditate just to calm down. It is that, or scream out loud and I can't do that in this job.

2025

Claire looked at the vast pile of paperwork in her overnight box and sighed. Numerous decisions were required of her now that the government was beginning to function again, the most pressing of which was an offer of ground troops and infrastructure support from the USA. It was something that Claire instinctively baulked at and she had taken a challenging call with the President on the subject. He was trying to railroad her into accepting the long-term presence of troops, which she considered less like assistance and more like an invasion. She was about to meet the Foreign Secretary, Katrina Ironside to discuss the issue.

She couldn't deny that they desperately needed help across all sectors. There were acute shortages across the farming industry, the national grid and policing to name a few and she could see the arguments for accepting foreign aid, but intuition told her to resist.

Intelligence reports indicated that although the threat of a foreign attack may have reduced, aggressive policies against British nationals had not. The tone of conversations with foreign leaders remained tense, and 'unauthorised British travel' was a major concern. Despite her assurances that British nationals were not carriers of the virus, many countries were refusing to re-establish flights, for fear of a resurgence of the virus. Reopening the borders was essential to the recovery effort and UK businesses were piling on the pressure. Industry supply chains had ground to a halt, food was scarce and there were significant calls for foreign workers to plug gaps across all industries. She felt the weight of these problems acutely but the last thing she needed was a further security risk brought about by an ill-thought through migration policy. Luckily, most MPs agreed but overall patience was wearing thin.

There was a knock at the door and Claire called out. 'Come in.' Katrina entered the room, smiling at Claire. 'Hi, how are you?' Claire smiled back. She had developed a good rapport with Katrina, who had young sons around Bens age. Claire felt grateful for the opportunity to be more relaxed for a moment after yet another difficult day. The ministerial team as a whole was tight knit and supportive, something she really valued and distinctly different from the atmosphere in parliament before the virus. Claire hoped it was not a temporary truce. 'Well I liken it to standing in the middle of a tornado with the occasional house hitting you in the face. How about you?'

Katrina laughed. 'I'm alright, though I am growing tired of negotiating with men who believe that women are incapable of running a country without the benefit of their great minds.'

Claire smiled. 'I can see how that might be a bit draining. Speaking of such things, I took a call from the President of the United States today, he has made us an offer of 20,000 army and security personnel to Britain to assist in re-establishing key services, deter foreign threats and boost local police force numbers. I wanted to get your view on this before I formally respond.'

The horror on Katrina's face betrayed her emotion and she immediately responded. 'It would be extremely unwise. Under a different administration it might be a more attractive offer but this is not a man to relinquish control to. He is ruthless, egotistical and unstable. He has an innate disdain towards women and is likely to use any personnel on the ground to destabilise this administration, chipping away at our ability to self-govern.'

Claire nodded in agreement. 'I agree. I wanted to check my reaction wasn't based just on the way the offer was put to me. I find him difficult to work with at the best of times. I'll find a tactful way to reject it.'

'Can you turn it down but request something else? We need fuel, food and medicines. He could also restart flights to and from the US so that our nationals can come home.'

Claire nodded. 'Will do. Do we have any other offers on the table?'

Katrina shook her head. 'As you know, the UN is poised to send in humanitarian assistance, including support from the Red Cross but we have agreed that sending foreign troops in now would send the wrong message. Bringing our own forces home will help more.'

Claire nodded, 'Where are we with that?'

'I spoke to the French government today. Our forces have assembled at key locations in Paris, Berlin and Nicosia and British Nationals who want to return home have also gathered there. Immunisations are well underway. The first flight is a British Airways flight from Paris and leaves in a few days' time. The crew are all British nationals stranded abroad when we grounded flights. Airlines are reluctant to put foreign nationals on flights, even as crew, so it is likely that we will only be able to fly our own nationals home for a while.'

'I understand the nervousness. Reassuring people will take time, we need to publicise arrivals and make sure that we track everyone returning home for signs of the virus. Can you work with the Home Secretary to coordinate that please?'

'Okay.' Katrina stood up. I hope you are managing to get some rest?'

Claire sighed. 'Not really, no. But my son is here and that's what matters.'

Katrina smiled, 'Yes, my children do focus my mind on why we are doing all of this. Take care Claire.'

As the door closed behind Katrina, Claire stood and stretched.

She headed towards her private quarters where Ben and her mum were cooking dinner. As she drew near she could smell chicken cooking, a novelty under the rationing policy. Her stomach growled in response. Like many others, she was feeling the effect of a restricted diet, both in her waistline and energy levels. She opened the door and paused, watching Ben as he set the table for dinner. He looked up and a smile spread across his face.

'Mum!' He ran towards her, abandoning the cutlery on the table.

'Hi Ben, how are you feeling today?' She enveloped him in a hug.

'I'm okay but I'm very hungry, Nanny has been cooking chicken but it's very small.' Claire smiled as she drew back from his embrace. 'It's not forever, Ben. What have you guys been up to today?'

Ben glanced at Claire's mum and Claire recognised the look her mother gave him back. A secret.

'Oh, nothing. Well we have a surprise for you so I don't want to say.'

Claire's mum laughed, rolling her eyes affectionately 'Ben, you really can't keep a secret!' He rushed out of the room, a secretive smile still on his face and Claire looked at her mum anxiously.

'How is he?'

'Better. He is talking though he can't quite bring himself to talk about James yet.'

'And how are you, Mum?'

Her mum replied too quickly. 'Oh, fine.' She turned away but not before Claire saw her chin wobble.

She walked up behind her. 'Mum, it's okay not to be okay. You lost your son. Do you need some help with Ben?'

Her mum turned and Claire saw the tears in her eyes. 'No. Ben is a blessing right now, he distracts me. I'm just worried about you. All this responsibility. Don't get me wrong, I'm very proud of you, I just don't know how you are doing it.'

'Neither do I to be honest!' Claire gave her Mum a much-needed hug.

'I really am so glad you are here, Mum. '

Ben rushed back into the room, a small cupcake in his hand. 'Mum, we made you this.' Claire smiled and took the cake, pulling him towards her for another hug. 'Thanks Ben, my favourite. Why don't we share it?'

2024

Another frustrating meeting with George Moore. I walk along Whitehall to clear my head. When I walk the streets in London I feel as if I belong. This is my destiny and power is within my grasp. I walk around the city and imagine it without all the men walking around. It will be quieter, there will be fewer cars, the pavements will be emptier, the women will be the ones walking around with their heads held high, in powerful jobs. The streets will be cleaner and safer. There will be no pollution and it will have the lowest crime rates in the world. I love my vision of London.

2025

Rt. Hon. Claire Flint MP, Buckingham Palace.

Claire and the Princess Regent took a seat in the palace gardens. They had met several times over the last few weeks and had a natural rapport that you couldn't fake. Claire trusted her and was always entirely honest about the issues she was facing. The Princess Regent looked at Claire and smiled. 'So, how are you?'

'I'm okay ma'am, a little tired but things are starting to turn around.'

'Good. Let's start with the border.'

Claire pulled out her notes. 'We are preparing to bring home British nationals stranded abroad, including the 30,000 troops stationed overseas. Everyone is making their way to Europe, for onward journeys to the UK over the next few weeks. In addition, trade vessels will start to bring in imported goods, though rationing will remain in place for some time.'

'How self-sufficient are we?'

'Pre-virus, we imported far more than we exported, a deficit of £6bn worth of trade. The biggest shortages come from fruit, vegetables and meat. Rationing of those items remains essential. However, our population has also dropped by almost half and with investment in food processing we could reduce our reliance on imports. Farming in the UK has been heavily hit by the virus but this is recoverable, if returning males pitch in.'

The Princess Regent raised her eyebrows. 'Are you planning to mandate that?'

'Absolutely. We need help with security, policing, farming, manual labour, utilities, engineering and electrical roles. We have to deploy people where we need them the most.'

The Princess Regent leant forwards and lowered her voice slightly, though the room was empty. 'You may want to prepare yourself for some challenge from returning army chiefs. Their world is built around men, men in power, men to command, men to defeat. They see women as something to protect, not to obey and will have views on our recovery that are quite different to yours.'

Claire nodded sagely, recalling her last conversation with the US President. 'Speaking of men in power, The US President offered us 20,000 ground troops to help with the recovery effort. We have declined his offer but that has not been received well.'

'I can imagine. It is fortuitous that the offer was made and declined before military personnel return home. The last thing you need is our military wading into the debate.'

Claire raised her eyebrows in surprise. 'Why would they? Surely they wouldn't support the deployment of US ground troops? Wouldn't it weaken them?'

'Well, even if it did, its recoverable, but it would weaken your administration more.'

'Hmm, I didn't think about it like that. Thank you, Ma'am.'

'That's quite alright. Shall we get some tea?'

2024

We are on the home straight. I shore up my position, subtly making myself known to all my female colleagues. I want them to know me when the time comes. Although I am still a junior minister I know am perceived as talented and feel I am ready.

Anne and Nicole are also busy and we speak often, usually late at night after my sermon to the group. It is difficult for me to resist engaging in the detailed planning, I need to be sure that everything is perfect. They insist that they are in control and scold me for my interference. I am too important and they do not want my time spread too thinly.

2025

*Rt. Hon. Deborah Walsh MP, Secretary of State
for Health*

Deborah sat at her desk, a large pile of official submissions stacked before her. Her department was depleted but the few civil servants left were doing a good job of keeping her updated on the status of local health provision now that the virus had run its course. The report she was reading covered the acute lack of mental health support for women. A huge advocate of mental health services, she had passionately disagreed with the previous Health Secretary, an old-fashioned man who referring to mental health provision privately as 'services for the mad, the bad and the sad' which she found particularly offensive. She closed the submission and wrote on the cover, ordering an expansion of mental health services for women, focussed on dealing with bereavement and adjusting to life after the virus.

After a year watching research grants go to causes like prostate cancer, testicular cancer and heart disease, she had come into this job with some pet projects of her own. The department had just published a report on health risks affecting the post-virus population and she'd used it to justify refocussing funding to support research on ovarian and breast cancer.

From the moment that the virus struck she had been inundated with work and stayed late most days. Being able to finally give real direction to the department was a real turning point for her. She wanted to ease the suffering in communities, it was the least they deserved. Her civil servants had rallied round, and the department was beginning to feel like a team. She'd put effort into reforming the stuffy practices she'd witnessed as a junior minister and wanted people around her who could build something better from the ashes.

She stood up, stretched and walked around the empty offices in the building, passing desks adorned with personal items. A photo of two young children, a drawing penned by a child, a post-it reminder about a 9am meeting. She took a sharp intake of breath as she spotted a shrine to the victims of the virus. She was growing accustomed to other people's grief but occasionally things still got to her. She turned away and headed in the opposite direction.

She wandered around for a while, her mind turning to the cabinet meeting she had attended earlier that day She was growing uneasy with Claire's handling of the recovery. The plan to open the borders felt premature and she didn't believe that the country was ready for an influx of men. The country was enveloped in grief and seeing men again was likely to cause many people pain. She had expressed a strong view that the borders should be closed for at least another three months but it had fallen on deaf ears as the cabinet was focussing on the economy. She took only a small amount of comfort from the fact that the suggestion of allowing US troops into the country was dismissed as quickly as it was made.

She wasn't the only one with concerns. Deborah always had her ear to the ground and had seen signs that the political truce Claire had secured was beginning to break down, with some MPs questioning Claire's approach to the recovery. She liked Claire, but saw her insecurities and knew it was only a matter of time before her grip on the coalition fell apart. She walked slowly through the building, her mind racing. Change was coming, it was inevitable.

2025

New Year's Day

This is the year. I am ready. I sit in the storage unit that Anne moved all my things into when I change my identity. My diaries, research, books, everything that made me Jean are here. Hope's things are here, her clothes were vacuum packed by Mummy after she died and when I open a bag, the smell of Hope fills the tiny room. I breath it in, and the tears come. It is as if she is here with me. I pull out a photograph of her.

'Hope. I miss you so much. I know you are safe now but I still wish you were here. I'm sad that I didn't get the chance to be the mother I wanted to be.

Everything I have done, I have done for you. Soon I will be able to give you the justice you deserve. He will pay for what he did to you.

I am sorry I didn't tell you what happened to me. I thought it would hurt you to know where you came from. You understand now what it feels like to have a man destroy your life. I was so young but I remember every second. Sometimes I relive each terrifying back in that cold room on the hard, concrete floor.

Mummy used to say that what happened was rare and most people go through life never experiencing the terrible things I did. She was wrong, it isn't rare, it is everywhere. It happened to me and to my own daughter. Women are silenced, they don't tell the police, the media doesn't report it and the world closes its eyes to our horror. So many of us have been destroyed by men, I meet them every day. That's why I need to do this. I don't want any more women to suffer at the hands of a man.

This year concludes years of planning. It will be a relief to finally see it happen. I know you understand why I am doing this, Hope. I feel your pain and am excited that the man who took your life will finally know that pain too. He will feel the life drain from his body as you did. I hold onto that because a lot of people will think me a monster if my identity is ever discovered. It will be years before they see that this country is a better place, free from the control of men who believe that women are inferior. My work will define the next generation. I know we are a small country but our influence is significant. This change will cause a ripple effect that will be felt across the world. When women in other countries see what I have created they will rise up and take control of their own destiny. I have been chosen to create a female utopia which will make wake women up and make them believe that they can lead the world to a new and better future. Men have had their day, Hope. Now it is our turn. I love you so much, Hope. I want to make you proud.'

2025

Rt. Hon. Claire Flint MP

Claire was on her way to Jenny's constituency in Finsbury Park after reading a heart-breaking letter from a local charity about the problems in the area. During the car journey, she read a selection of other letters she had received from local constituents. She felt more remote from the real issues than ever and missed the days when she had time to spare to speak to local people regularly, something she'd shared with her team before this visit. As ever, she felt she was spread far too thinly.

She knew that Victoria and Jenny were worried that she was becoming a one woman show but still insisted that community visits should take priority. Today Jenny and Mia were joining her and Claire suspected this was a tactic to stop her running over schedule. Her thoughts turned to Mia, who was helping out more and more and had become Jenny's shadow of late. She seemed lost to Claire, who knew that Mia's real passion was in health. She wondered whether focussing more on her own interests rather than following her mother would help with her recovery. It was a tricky subject but she resolved to speak to Jenny about it.

She arrived at the community centre and was met outside by Jenny, Mia and an official from the local council who introduced herself as Melissa.

'Morning Prime Minister, it is an honour to meet you. I'd like to give you a little context before we meet the children if that's okay?'

'Of course. I'm sure it will be useful to hear some of the background.'

Melissa took Claire, Jenny and Mia through to a small room just off the hall. They sat down around a desk and Melissa picked up the folder in front of her.

'This folder contains some case studies about local families which you can take away with you.' She handed it to Claire.

'The virus has amplified some of the issues that were already very much part of life in this community. Single parent households dominated this community before the virus, many with complex needs that the council struggled to meet. Alcoholism, drug abuse, poor parenting and neglect were commonplace and we had high numbers of looked after children compared to other London boroughs. The virus has exacerbated the situation. Many children and families who were doing well pre-virus are now struggling. Mental health issues amongst women have tripled and rationing means that in some cases children are not being provided with enough food to meet their basic nutritional needs. Even competent mothers are struggling to provide their children with sufficient nutrition here because food that isn't rationed is completely unaffordable.

A large number of children have been orphaned by the virus, putting additional pressure on an already creaking system. The council can't meet all of their needs with the resources available to it and relies heavily on volunteers. We are struggling to recruit sufficient numbers and there aren't enough incentives for women to come forward and help out. The children you will meet shortly are the tip of the iceberg. They are staying in children's homes but need the security of a family environment. Some of these children lost their fathers to the virus and their mothers to suicide. Two of the children spent four days in the family home alone with their dead father. The schools that have reopened are not resourced to cope with these issues and it feels like we are just passing the problem around.'

Melissa drew breath and Claire took the opportunity to cut in. 'I do understand your concerns, I would like to know what you think we should do to help.'

'We need money, staff and volunteers. We need extra help in schools so that we can get our heads above water. Volunteers should get an allowance or extra rations, which would grease the wheels. Many of them are struggling to pay rent and mortgages now that they have lost a source of income and homelessness is make these problems worse.'

'Okay. Thanks Melissa. Shall we go and meet them?'

Melissa led Claire, Jenny and Mia into the hall. A group of around 60 children were sitting on a carpet, listening to a story. When the doors opened all of the children turned around, startled by the noise. A young blonde girl jumped up ran towards them, shouting 'Mia!!'

Mia's face lit up and she bent down and opened her arms as the little girl ran towards her, closely followed by a small blonde boy. Claire turned to Jenny, a quizzical look on her face.

'Amelia, Jack! What are you doing here?' The children clung to her and then the tears came.

'Daddy didn't wake up, he was asleep for a really long time and we ate all the food. The lady came and now we are staying in a big house with lots of other children but all our toys are still at home. Daddy hasn't come to get us and the nice lady went away.'

Mia turned to Jenny.

'Mum, these are Harry's children, Amelia and Jack.' Then she turned back to the children.

'Let's go and sit down over here and you can tell me all about it.' She took them over to some chairs at the back of the hall, closely followed by one of the social workers.

Jenny turned to Claire, visibly shaken. 'Mia used to babysit Amelia and Jack, before she left for university. Harry, their father, was a friend of Mark's. They lost their mum eighteen months ago. Mia babysat once a week so that he could have a break.'

Melissa, who had been watching the exchange, drew closer.
'Amelia and Jack are the children I mentioned earlier. Their father died in the house and the children were alone with the body for four days before one of the council clearance teams found them. Fortunately, the cupboards were well stocked and Amelia was old enough to know how to make basic meals. They were found just in time, food was running low by the time the clearance team got there. They are lovely children but have been through a bit of an ordeal and have no close relatives left to care for them.'
Jenny looked at Melissa 'Harry had a sister, can't she help?'
'We have contacted her but she lives in America and it hasn't been possible to reunite them.'
Jenny looked over at Mia, who was sitting down with both children in her lap.
'You know, I could take them in, until their aunt can get here. We've known their family a long time and Mia dotes on them. How easy would that be to arrange?'
Melissa smiled for the first time since they'd arrived. 'Well you'll have to go through a fostering assessment before you can take them but it sounds like a great idea.'
Claire left them discussing the practicalities and joined the other children on the carpet. After a few minutes, some of the children started to edge closer to her and a little girl whispered 'What's your name?'
Claire whispered back 'I'm Claire, what's your name?
'I'm Sophia. This is my little sister Emma.'
'Hi guys. What's this story about?'
'We don't know, we aren't listening. We were talking about the biscuits that the lady promised us if we were good and sat still while the Pri-mister was here.'
'Ah okay. What's your favourite biscuit?'
'Chocolate chip cookies are mine but I haven't had a biscuit for a million years.'

'Well we had better be good, maybe we will get one.' The little girl rested her head on Claire shoulder and Claire put her arm around her. As they listened to the story, Claire glanced around at the other children. They were so small. Some were holding hands, or hugging but a few sat alone. It was heartbreaking to watch them. Yet again she felt powerless- an all-too familiar feeling those days.

Mia walked back over to Jenny and Melissa. 'We can't leave them here, Mum. Can we take them back with us?'

'I'm already looking into it, Mia. We have to apply to be foster parents and I need to get in touch with their aunt. Don't discuss it with them until we know we can do it, I don't want to get their hopes up. Melissa can we visit them?'

'Of course, goodness, please do. They are a little lost right now, particularly Jack. He is Amelia's shadow. Having each other helps but they retreat into their own little world when they are scared. They need lots of cuddles and a bit of structure in their lives.'

Storytime was over. Claire stood up, stretching as the children followed the social worker excitedly, talking about the biscuits they'd been promised. She called over to Jenny.

'Jenny, are you coming back to the office with me in the car?'

'If you don't mind, Claire, I think I'll stay here. I have some paperwork to fill in and Mia would like to spend a little more time with the children.'

'No problem. Let's talk tomorrow morning.'

In the car, Claire took out her laptop and emailed The Minister for Communities and Local Government, asking for options on providing orphaned children with more support and on the sustainability of local services for families. Then she looked at her inbox and inwardly groaned. The weight of the job was taking its toll and she worried that she was too busy to focus on her son, who still desperately needed her. She decided to work for the rest of the journey and opened the first email. Over the next thirty minutes she engrossed herself in a report on household debt and the escalating banking crisis. As the car pulled up in Downing Street she resolved to spend the evening with Ben and her mum.

2025

January

I am breathless with anticipation. No matter how much they try, Anne and Nicole cannot talk me out of my plan. We have a working virus and I need to witness the true impact before we release it. I know it is a huge risk, given my position but I have to do it.

Anne has been tracking him for me. He was released from prison on licence a few months ago and we have since discovered that he is a creature of habit. He is a perfect test subject, he has no job and no friends or regular acquaintances. No-one will notice that he is missing. He has a probation officer but his next appointment is scheduled to take place after the virus is released so to put it bluntly, he won't have a probation officer by then.

I have a great disguise. My wig is blonde and elfin, I have false front teeth which change my whole face and I apply far more makeup that usual. When I look in the mirror I almost don't know myself. I am not Jean, or me. I am someone else.

I go to his favourite café to watch him. He is interested in the girl behind the counter and watches her constantly. When she comes over to fill up his cup he keeps her talking. She is a kind girl and is obviously comfortable around him, she must have served him before. She doesn't know that she fuels his perversity but I can see it. I watch what he orders, a cup of tea and two packs of biscuits which he eats greedily. He dips each one in his tea and shoves the whole biscuit into his mouth in one go.

A day passes and I go back to the café. He is already here. It is busy and there are no tables so I take my chance and ask if I might sit with him, since he is alone. He doesn't recognise me at all and reluctantly shares his table with me. I order tea and then take a pack of biscuits out of my bag. They are the expensive kind and look delicious. I unwrap a biscuit and bite it, making quiet, contented noises as I chew. He glances up from his phone and I smile at him.

'Gosh, I'm sorry. Don't tell the waitress, I don't think you are allowed to bring your own biscuits but these are my favourites.' He smiles and looks leeringly down at the pack. I pretend to hesitate then pass the pack over. 'Go on, I shouldn't eat them all anyway. You'd be helping me out.' He takes two and dunks the first one in his tea. I watch as he pushes the whole thing in his slack, disgusting mouth and then picks up the second one. Perfect. I put a large dose into every biscuit in the pack to make sure it works quickly. I look at my watch to confirm the time. It is 5.20pm when he puts my virus into his body.

He leaves the café at 6pm and walks home. I follow at a distance and when he gets to his house I go to my car opposite and wait. At 8pm I decide to go in. I walk up the short path to the front door and pause there for a few moments, listening. I can hear a TV blaring and there is a light on in the front room. I quietly push the key that Anne gave me into the lock and turn it. The door opens easily, I oiled the lock earlier that day. I let myself into his house quietly and close the door with a small click behind me. My heart is pounding so loudly I can hear it in my ears and I am quite breathless. I feel I am loud but there is no movement from the front room. The television on so loud that I am sure his neighbours can hear it through the wall. I peak through the crack in the door. He is there, lying on the sofa.

Deep breath.

I charge in and rush at him, brandishing the bat that I brought with me. His face registers surprise and then a flash of complete terror. He raises his arm as I bring the bat down hard so my first blow hits him on the forearm. I hear the bone shatter with a crunch and he screams and clutches it in pain. I raise my hands and hit him again quickly, on the head this time. The second blow hurts him but doesn't knock him out so I raise my arm again and bring it down fast onto his nose. I hear a sickening crunch and he slumps forwards. I stand back, breathless. His face is a mess and he is out cold but I don't think he will be out long so I grab my bag and pull out the cable ties. I bind his wrists and ankles with three cable ties like Anne showed me. I shove a cloth into his mouth and wrap duck-tape over his mouth and around the back of his head a few times, careful to keep his bloody nose uncovered. After a few seconds, I realise he can't breathe. I need him alive so I cut the duck-tape, rip it off his face and pull out the cloth. If he were conscious that would have hurt but he doesn't move. He is breathing again. I turn the TV up a little more and change the channel to the news. I am sweating and breathless with the exertion so I sit on the chair opposite and retrieve my knife from my bag. I watch TV while I wait for him to wake up.

A reporter is talking about a speech the Prime Ministers gave and the camera pans around the chamber in the House of Commons. It is a speech from yesterday. I scan the rows until I find my own face, six rows back. I watch my face as he talks. I remember how I felt at the time. Angry, resentful, tired of listening to him ramble on. My face shows none of this, I look interested, engaged, supportive. I smile to myself, reminded of how good I am at playing my role.

❊ ❊ ❊

After a while he moves a little and begins to wake up. I turn off the television and focus on him. He is groggy so it takes a few moments for him to realise he is bound at the wrists and ankles. He opens his eyes and begins to struggle; the cable ties are good and tight and he can't move much. He notices me in the chair and freezes, then begins to shout.

'You're fucking crazy. Let me go! HELP! Somebody help!' I shush him quickly, raising my bat in warning. He closes his mouth. 'You broke my fucking nose!' he whines. He is angry but I can see in his eyes that he is also scared.

'First of all, we need some ground rules, Adrian. If you shout, or scream, I'll stab you in the eye with this knife, okay?' I gesture to my knife on the table. He looks at it, fearfully and looks back at me. He nods quickly.

'Good. Do you know why I am here?' He shakes his head.

'Twenty-two years ago, you murdered my daughter, Hope. Do you remember that?'

I see the penny drop. Now he is terrified.

'You do remember me! Good. I look different, don't I? I don't think you looked at me much in court though, so maybe my face isn't seared into your brain like yours is in mine. I remember every expression you pulled when the barrister read out what you did to my daughter. I know exactly how sick and twisted you are. I know you enjoyed killing my daughter. I know you want to do it again and that you have your eye on that pretty young girl in the café. How long have you been planning to attack her? Have you decided to just rape this one, or kill her too like you killed my baby?'

He is crying now, snot is running down his face, mingling with the blood. He shakes his head at me, miserably.

'How dare you shake your head at me. I KNOW YOU ARE EVIL! I SEE IT ALL OVER YOUR FACE!' I take a breath. I can't lose my temper with him, I don't want to stab him or beat him to death, I want him to know he is going to die. When I am calm again I talk.

'Don't make me lose my temper with you. I need you alive. You are useful to me.'

I reach into my bag, pull out Nicole's notes and read the symptoms quickly. Nicole can only really guess how the virus affect the human body in the early stages, so this part will be interesting.'

'How do you feel? A bit sick? Weak?'

He nods.

'Does it feel like the beginning of the flu?'

He looks at me, quizzically, not understanding yet.

'Hmm, interesting.' I write a note next to Nicole's notes. 'weak, sick, no flu-like symptoms yet.'

Five minutes pass and his breathing is more laboured and wheezy. He looks at me, breathless, he can't shout anymore so I tell him.

'You aren't feeling well, are you? I know why! Would you like to know what I know? I walk towards him and kneel down in front of his face so that I can whisper. 'It isn't the flu!' I smile at him, I know he is scared now because he has wet himself.

'You are going to die today. I expect you want to know how I infected you. It was so easy! Do you remember the biscuits I gave you in the café?'

He nods.

'Well they contained a virus that I created, just for you. It's deadly, by the way. There's no cure, so you won't get better now, even if you manage to escape. I watched you eat the biscuit and it was so hard not to laugh in your face! You made it too easy! My friend Nicole thought this was too risky. She worried that you might recognise me, or that I might not be strong enough to knock you out. She worried about your neighbours but I doubt they even know who you are. I can't believe that you didn't put up a fight though, what a disappointment you are.'

I look at him again. He is really struggling to breath now and his eyes are starting to roll back in his head.

'Does it hurt? I hope so.'

I should feel much happier than I do. Perhaps I will feel better when he coughs up blood, or when his organs start to fail.

He makes a noise, a whine, like a dog would make if it were hungry.

'Stop making that stupid noise, no-one can hear you but you are beginning to irritate me. I can still hit you over the head or stab you and that will hurt even more. SHUT UP! That's better.'

He is getting sicker now. I want to see how long it will take. I take pictures for Nicole and then film him for about a minute so that she can see him wheezing.

* * *

An hour passes and the virus still looks like a bad case of the flu. I've stopped talking to him. He can't answer me back and I don't have much to say to the man who killed my daughter, in the end. When he is able to focus on me I find the terror in his eyes deeply satisfying. I have his life in my hands.

* * *

Two hours and he has just passed out, his breathing is much more laboured than it was an hour ago.

* * *

Two hours and fifty minutes in, a gurgling noise comes from deep inside him. Nicole said his lungs would fill with fluid and I think this is it. I watch him closely and see death coming. It is one thing to look at the microscopic images of my virus but to see the devastation it causes up close is my life's ambition realised.

* * *

Four hours and his organs completely fail. He dies silently at 12.10am, six hours and fifty minutes after I infected him. It is disappointing. His death is so quiet. I make sure he is dead then have a look around his house. In his bedside cabinet, I find a folder full of photographs of women, taken without their knowledge and presumably without consent. I recognise the girl from the café in one of the photographs. She will never know how lucky she was. I take photos of them for my records and then put them back. I leave his body on the sofa but remove the cable ties. I turn off the lights and make sure all the windows are closed and locked. People who pass the house will assume he isn't home. I wipe the door handles and things I remember touching, just in case anyone finds him too early. When I am sure that I have covered my tracks as best I can, I leave, closing the door behind me with a quiet click. It is 2am.

2025

Heathrow Airport

The plane touched down onto the runway at Heathrow and instead of a traditional cheer there was a muted silence, the passengers peered out of the window, expecting to see bodies lined up on the runway. The plane coasted into the terminal and came to a halt, all too quickly for some. The passengers were suddenly very attached to the plane and its crew, a last safe haven from the poisonous world outside.

The plane doors opened and everyone seemed to take a collective intake of breath, as if taking their last breath of clean air for some time. The pilot left the cockpit as the passengers exited the plane but could think of nothing to say to ease their nerves.

At border control, each passenger handed over immunisation documents for examination and their blood was tested for the vaccine. Once clear, the passengers drifted through to arrivals, the airport eerily empty.

The women and children waiting at arrivals did so in silence. As they heard the first footsteps of the returning passengers, heads collectively snapped up and faces broke out into collective smiles. The men caught the first glimpses of their loved ones, saw the smiles and wondered for a brief moment whether things were as bad as they had been led to believe but then they noticed the gaps in the crowd, the teenaged son and the missing dad and sad, sad eyes of the women and the realities of life here began to sink in.

2025

January

Today is the day that the virus is released. I am on tenterhooks and have not slept in days, I can't rest and struggle to think about anything else. I go from meeting to meeting in a daze, completely ineffective for the first time in my life. My life has followed an inevitable path to this point since I was eleven.
I speak with Anne and Nicole. Anne is poised to wipe records, correct errors, open doors, close down security systems and is as excited as me. Her role requires her to be locked away from prying eyes at a computer terminal, mine requires me to be as visible as possible but the adrenaline is pumping in us both.
Nicole is running the operation. She is fired up and has become close to her team. I miss her, I haven't seen her in months. She confirms that everything in place. I am redundant for the time being. They are all ready.

❊ ❊ ❊

It's working. The virus has been in the water for three days and men are getting sick. George Moore is one of them and I can't wipe the smile off my face. It takes all of my acting skills to pretend I am as shocked and distraught as everyone else.
They are dropping like flies. I was worried that the water would dilute it too much but Nicole thought of everything and the virus is perfect. All the years of planning and sacrifices I have made to get to this point are suddenly worth it. It is

beautiful to watch even in its horror and I do know it is horrific, I am not a monster.

A headache flares and I fleetingly worry that I am infected. My head is heavy and my vision swims. This time it feels like the is someone inside my head, in my brain, ripping it apart from the inside. I wonder if this is how it feels to be a man this week.

2025

Testimonial, Rt. Hon. Karen Tonge MP.

I sat in front of the mirror applying concealer to my eye and cheek. The bruise was fading but still visible through my makeup if you looked closely enough. I got up at 5.30am every morning to cover the bruise so that the girls didn't see it and hid the news reports about my husband's arrest from the girls, wanting to protect them for as long as possible.

I don't think I am the only woman to stay in a bad marriage for the sake of her children. Like most people in long marriages, the things I once loved about my husband became irritating over time. The charm that attracted me to him was reserved for others and the jokes I used to laugh at were repeated until they became humourless. He used intimate knowledge to belittle me in front of my friends. When our eldest daughter was born his jealousy made life unbearable. He insisted on regular sex just a few weeks after the baby was born, making no allowances for my exhaustion. He stayed out after work later and later, leaving me to shoulder the demands of a new baby alone.

Over time I started to fall out of love with him and only occasional flashes of the man I first met kept me in the marriage. I learnt to see the outbursts coming and talk him down before he erupted. I tried hard to coax out the man I had loved and when things were good, I seized on those memories, pushing the darker times out of my head.

When the virus hit and Alex couldn't come home I was grateful he had been spared and sad for our children who missed him terribly. I began to feel lonely when the girls went to bed at night and I missed his advice, which I couldn't ask for because of security concerns. I felt that I needed him and planned his homecoming as a happy occasion.

For weeks Alex had been asking me to use my role as Home Secretary to get him on the first flight home. I told him that I couldn't use my position in that way because it wasn't fair to everyone else who was waiting. I think he assumed I was joking.

He arrived at the airport in Paris early expecting to be on the first flight home and was immediately surrounded by reporters clamouring for a story. The cameras flashed incessantly and airport security were forced to intervene, pushing the reporters back to a safe distance. He reached the counter a few minutes later, probably still flustered and was told he had been allocated seat on a much later flight. I imagine it was the last straw. Amateur footage was televised the following day, he was filmed standing at the check-in desk, shouting at the woman behind the counter, his face filled with a sneer of pure hatred that warped his face.

He raged at me from the airport lounge phone, accusing me of all sorts of betrayals. When I tried to defend myself, he slammed the phone down on me. The flight was an hour and fifteen minutes long and I'd hoped it was long enough for him to calm down but as soon as I saw him appear through the gate I could tell that his mood hadn't changed. He masked his anger when he saw that I'd brought the girls but not in time to hide the curl of his lip. I saw the contempt, directed solely at me.

The girls ran towards him, shouting 'Daddy, Daddy, we missed you!' and his attention was diverted with kisses and cuddles for a few minutes. Then he stood up and looked at me and a snarl fixed on his face. I tried to smile and leant towards him for a hug but he looked away, grabbed his bag from the floor and said to the girls 'Let's go home, shall we?'

The car journey wasn't much better. He insisted on driving

but hadn't driven a manual in years and crunched through the gears as we left the car park, making me wince. He drove too fast but when I asked him to slow down he snapped 'Oh, fuck off. You can't be in control of everything.' and clenched his fingers hard on the steering wheel. I realised this was about far more than just the flight.

Once home, I started dinner and made a conscious effort to cook something he would like, not easy with meagre rations. My efforts were wasted. He looked down at his dinner with disdain. 'Your cooking has gone downhill since I left, Karen.' The girls took their cue and refused to eat it so Alex pointedly made them all toast, leaving me to eat alone.

When the girls went to bed I tried to talk to him about food. 'Things have changed since you left, Alex. Rationing is tough. I was saving the bread you ate for breakfasts this week. We can't afford to be wasteful now.'

He suddenly snapped and all the pent-up rage he had been holding in came tumbling out. He lurched at me, screaming 'Rations? You're talking to me about fucking rations? For three months, you have kept me in the fucking dark, I don't matter to you, the only things that matters is your precious job. You are so fucking full of yourself. 'Everyone is laughing at you and your precious government. You're a joke. You've made a complete fucking mess of everything. Do you even read the news? While you panicked and procrastinated, the media were filming the bodies, piling up in the street. You let those men die and you can't even catch the bitches that did it. You've set us back 200 years! I wouldn't be surprised if you and Claire planned the whole fucking thing. I give it a week before you lose your job. You might even be arrested.'

I couldn't respond, I just stared at his snarling, hateful face. He had no idea what we'd all been through. The man I fell in love with all those years ago had gone. This man was not my husband. He wasn't the man who was there when I worked a hundred hours a week in my constituency, or understood what my job had cost me and why I still wanted it so much. In that moment, the last speck of love I had for him died. I stood up, turned my back on him and walked away. As I opened the door I felt a rush of air and then he grabbed a handful of my hair and yanked. I staggered backwards and his fist slammed into my face.

He pressed his face up against mine, his hand still gripping my hair. 'Don't you fucking turn your back on me. How dare you. You think you're fucking better than me, don't you? All of a sudden you all think you are in charge.' He threw me onto the sofa and stormed out of the room.

I called Elizabeth Vinn for advice. She sent two female police officers to the house to arrest him. As he was escorted out of the house I remember saying 'Maybe we did mess it all up but we are in charge now. I will never let a man do that to me again.' I closed the door behind them and watched through the window as they took my husband away.

I still wish we had kept the borders closed.

2025

February 2025

The country is in shock. The virus ran its course in a wonder-fully predictable way. All the men are dead. I pinch myself. It seems like a dream. I am at work, I practically live here now. We are in 'crisis mode' but there is a plan. Mostly we focus on clearing the bodies. There are so many, they seem to be every-where. In the city, the roads are just as I imagined them to be. There are no cars, and the pavements are clear. I feel like I can breathe for the first time in my life.

2025

British life
Testimonial, anonymous

Sightings were rare but occasionally a man was seen on the streets. Some men walked with a confident swagger. Some men cast their eyes right and left, like children in a sweet shop, their faces full of expectation. They arrived home expecting to take their pick of the women left behind. Fresh off the planes, they began to hunt.

They soon realised that grief had changed everything. Women reacted differently now. They stared at the men as if they were something to be feared. They walked quickly passed, eyes down. They cried a lot. They crossed the road to avoid them. The neighbours didn't say hello, they eyed them with jealous anger. A group formed. They called themselves 'Mothers in Mourning'. They hissed insults at new arrivals and handed out white feathers to men on the street.

'Our sons died and you did nothing, you cowards.'

The returning men were quick to judge. They whispered to each other. 'They've all gone mad. They've seen too much. They need counselling.'

By the time they had been back a few weeks, most men avoided going out alone, taking wives, sisters or children along with them. Safety in numbers. They avoided large groups of women for fear of confrontation.

Watching television, they noticed other differences. The programmes they once enjoyed were cancelled mid series. Channels were discontinued because of 'low viewing figures.' The news took on a new focus. Households ran without their input, and women grew used to existing without men. The Prime Minister issued new legislation, requiring returning men to register with local councils for recovery work. They were offered roles in plumbing, utilities management, fire services and banking. It felt like conscription. They lay awake at night, wondering how things had come to this.

2025

April

Things are beginning to settle down.

There is a new, more organised routine in Whitehall now, with clear recovery plans in place. Claire has done well to get us to this position so quickly, I don't think even I could have done a better job.

Outside of the parliamentary bubble, everyone is still grief-stricken, there are lots of tears in departmental corridors and some civil servants clearly aren't coping. It is to be expected and I have to keep reminding myself to be subdued and fit in. In reality, I couldn't be happier but I manage to convince people that I am as distraught as the rest of them.

A terrible smell lingers across London. Going outside is a challenge, the smell makes me gag and I hold a handkerchief over my nose and mouth to mask the smell. I'm told it isn't just confined to London, but we have been particularly affected because there were so many people living and working here- bodies are hidden away in corners and every nook and cranny must be checked.

Inside Westminster we talk about how we might move the bodies more quickly. We are shown photographs of decaying bodies which are honestly so disgusting that it makes the smell seem like nothing at all. If I had been able to plan in advance I would have prepared for this eventuality, as it is I can do nothing but watch. I am itching to take control.

2025

July

My contact with the group makes me feel less alone.

It is in all our interests to stay engaged. Without my direction, they may begin to doubt our plans. As long as we are one, we are all protected from exposure.

The time to introduce real change has arrived and I am on the cusp of greatness. People will remember this and when I am known, I will go down in history as one of the great reformers of our century. The world will be in awe of what I have achieved. I have hidden myself amongst those in power and despite the odds, no-one has discovered my past. I feel invincible.

2025

Press Release, July

The government has released a national census which every household is required by law to complete.

The government will use it to collate information about the national population so that it can understand the true impact of the virus. Questions cover the financial, social, educational, nutritional and health needs of the population.

You are required to complete the census on the 10th July. For more information about the national census please visit www.gov.uk/nationalcensus

2025

August

The national census excites me. It will confirm the effect of the virus and I need to know how many people died and how many young boys are still alive. I will need to think about what to do with them once I am in control. They will need special handling because of their association with men. Some of their traits and influence will undoubtedly have rubbed off. Ideally, they would be taught together and drilled on how to behave properly, but I must be careful not to alienate the mothers, that would be like throwing the baby out with the bathwater. I have time to plan this and I need to make sure that I have covered all eventualities.

2025

Extract from an intelligence report, August

<u>Summary of progress</u>
The results of a country-wide census are back. A long list of missing women is being developed, with names checked against social security, tax and other systems.

Extensive facial recognition searches for images of Professor Nicole Moreland have been completed. There were several possible matches in the north of England and Scotland. The last potential sighting was six weeks before the outbreak and pattern analysis suggests that she was heading north.

Police Scotland have begun to search local towns in the North of Scotland, though at this time there is no intelligence to suggest that she is still in the area.

2025

August

I hear stories about the men who have returned to Britain and are throwing their weight around. I am furious but at the same time had expected this, I didn't want the borders to reopen. It was a mistake to bring our armed forces home. Perhaps I should have taken control sooner, Anne could have manufactured an opportunity for me. Hindsight is a wonderful thing. I will clear this mess up when I take control because men need to learn their place.

2025

Extract from an incomplete draft of handwritten minutes, taken by the Secretary to the Chief of the Defence Staff

Item 2: continued...

Chief of Defence: The current situation in this country cannot be allowed to continue. These are extraordinary times, and though there is no precedent for this, national security concerns must be addressed. The current government is amalgamation of individuals elected under different circumstances with no mandate. They appear in no rush to hold a general election and very real security concerns are not being addressed.

2ⁿᵈ In Command: What you are suggesting is akin to a military coup. Where is the justification?

Chief of Defence: look around you. There is no co-ordination of the collection and disposal of rotting corpses, there is no coherent plan to regain the confidence of our allies abroad, the economy has crashed through the floor and the people are starving.

[role]: Theoretically, if we were to do this, what are the chances of success?

Chief of Defence: We have received intelligence from the US that suggests a high degree of support internationally, along with firepower if needs be.

[Role]: And the monarchy? We do still serve the monarch, don't forget. I'd be surprised if there were an appetite for this.

Chief of Defence: Our queen is a minor, I'll handle the regent myself.

[Role]: Should we be discussing this now? [*Nods to minute taker*]

Chief of Defence: We can trust her, she has been in my employ for over twenty years.

[Role]: Even so, I'm uncomfortable that this discussion is being minuted. It's completely inappropriate.

Chief of Defence: Very well.

[Minutes end]

2025

Downing Street, Rt. Hon. Sarah Hammond MP

The Secretary of State for Defence, Sarah Hammond tapped her foot impatiently, her anger bubbling just beneath the surface. She was waiting to see Claire and had bad news to share. She had not had an easy time in her new role. When the virus hit, all the Chiefs of Staff in the country were killed. A few senior military chiefs were stationed abroad at the time and had since returned to Britain. She had established a new chief of staff committee but her ability to lead them was limited. They didn't respect her, she was the first female Secretary of State for Defence and her military experience did not count for very much. They dismissed her views, disagreed with plans to recruit and train women, despite a desperate shortage in personnel and had openly criticised her lack of experience along with that of the Prime Minister. Today's news was the last straw.

The door to Claire's office opened and the Foreign Secretary, Katrina Ironside walked out, nodding acknowledgement to Sarah. Sarah stood as Claire came to the door. 'Hi, come on in.'

'Thanks Claire. How are you?'

'I'm good, thank you. Are the chiefs still causing you difficulties?'

'Yes, the situation is escalating. I have it on good authority that a group of military chiefs are planning a rebellion, backed by the US. It came from a source close to the Chief of Defence and I trust them.'

Claire gaped at Sarah, astounded. 'My god. Do they have the backing of the Royal Family?'

'I doubt it, but that may not stop them acting. We need to act quickly and expose their disloyalty, get the public on our side. The ringleaders should be arrested for treason. Without the Chief of Defence the rest of them will crawl back in their box.'

Claire, sighed, suddenly exhausted. 'Okay' she said, wearily. 'Prepare a case. I'll call Elizabeth, I want her advice on handling this.'

As Sarah left, Claire picked up the phone to call Elizabeth, resigned to a battle. Up to now people had pulled together in response to a crisis but it felt like they were entering new territory and it didn't feel comfortable at all.

2025

August

I feel vindicated. I knew that men would rebel at some point, but didn't anticipate that it would happen quite so quickly. Claire intervenes in the nick of time and conversation at cabinet turns to protecting ourselves against further treachery. It is good to see women begin to recognise that men have opposing motives. They aren't interested in the wellbeing of the people, they are only interested in protecting their own self interests. Finally, they begin to see things from my point of view.

2025

Local news report

Police officers from six forces raided several homes across the south yesterday morning as part of an ongoing investigation into a plot to overthrow the current government.

Six men have been remanded in custody, charged with treason and charges are expected against a further four in the coming days.

Sources suggest that the plot was led by a group of returning British military chiefs. No. 10 officials have so far declined to comment in response to the arrests. However, there has been a strong reaction from the public, with chiefs widely criticised for what has been coined an 'opportunistic attack on our country in a time of great crisis.'

2025

August

Although I have influence, I do not have infinite patience.
Our recovery is long and painful but finally, green shoots appear. More women return to work, outbound flights restart this week and our government is functioning again. The grief, though palpable, is normalising and the coronation is an event to look forward to. I am in a strong position with influence and a reputation as a 'safe pair of hands'. In this place people admire strength and stability in times of hardship and I have mastered the art of acting. My peers believe that I am horrified by the tragedy we have experienced but resolute and in control of my brief. My acting skills are really quite good.
Claire is on top of the recovery but seems tired and weary and I suspect she wants to quit. However, no-one in the party has the slightest interest in succeeding her, should she step down. It is a stressful role and a thankless task, far harder than running a country under normal circumstances. I am content to keep her in power a while longer. I am influential enough to make a difference from here and will intervene when the time comes. I haven't yet decided how I will do that but assume that favourable conditions will present themselves eventually.

2025

August

I see a man on the street. He is the first one I've seen since we released the virus. I stare as he walks past because I want him to look at me. I want to ask him lots of questions. How does it feel to live here now? Do you realise that women are in charge now? Are you scared? You should be.

He feels my eyes on him and glances up then nervously looks away. His demeanour reminds me of the way I used to behave when a man stared, catcalled or remarked about my appearance on the street. I am delighted with his reaction; the country is already changing.

2025

September

Women are leaving on the first flights out of the country. I want to scream 'Don't leave! The hardship is temporary? It will be wonderful here if you just hang on for a year or two?'
Of course, they can't see it. They don't know what I know but I realise I cannot sit in this role forever. I need to start thinking about how I manoeuvre myself into No. 10. The job is taking its toll on Claire and she is missing time with her son so there may be an opportunity here. I call her to 'see how she is feeling.
She is grateful to have someone to talk to I think. She used to confide in her advisor Jenny, but she lost her husband and son so Claire feels she can't burden her with more. She is tired and there lots of problems that she is trying to juggle, including tense international relationships. She does not feel she has grown into the job and says if someone else wanted it she would happily step down.
I am careful. I can't be sure that I am the only interested party, people in politics keep their cards close to their chests. I tell her she is doing a great job, but if she needs support I can be a good sounding board. She is grateful and says she will take me up on it.
I know I must bide my time, but am confident she will step down before an election can be held. To carry on in the role would break her. Time to move myself into position.

2025

Jenny Robinson

Jenny pulled on trainers and a jacket and grabbed her bag from the hall table. The door swung shut behind her and the sound of Amelia and Jack playing with Mia faded away. She used to go out for a walk when Mark and Jasper were alive to get some peace and quiet. She would give anything for that same noisy, messy house now. Mark's mess and Jasper's music blaring. She still woke up on her side of the bed every day and felt for Mark, hoping it was all a dream. Jasper's room hadn't changed since the morning she called the ambulance, all those months ago. She knew she hadn't dealt with her grief but she was okay with that. She didn't know anyone who had coped any better and sometimes wondered whether there would ever be a time that she didn't expect to hear Jasper's feet on the stairs or long for just one last hug.

She didn't know how she was managing to get up, get dressed and leave the house everyday but somehow, she was. Her job felt even more important now and Mia, Amelia and Jack kept her occupied when she wasn't there. The nights when they were all asleep were the worst. She hated the silence and the empty space where Mark used to be. She still cried herself to sleep every night and paused at Jaspers bedroom door every morning but most of the time she felt like she was just about managing.

Her strength came from the resilient women around her, especially Claire. Jenny didn't know how she was managing to lead the country but somehow she was doing it brilliantly, though Jenny suspected that she was dealing with some inner demons of her own.

As she walked, she people-watched, passing a woman carrying a ration bag, another holding the hands of her two children and then two women arm in arm, talking intently. She passed a woman pruning her hedge while her daughter mowed the lawn and turned the corner onto the main road that ran alongside the park.

She peered through the bars of the fence and saw a group of children kicking a ball around and a woman walking her dog. Things were deceptively normal.

As she reached the hardware store she remembered a broken kitchen drawer and went inside. She was surprised to see a young boy of around nine behind the counter. As she stepped forward an elderly woman bustled over to join them.

'Hello there' she called. 'What can we do for you?'

'I'm looking for some advice about how to fix my kitchen drawer.' It had been broken for ages, a note reminding Mark to fix it still scrawled on their white board in Mark's messy handwriting.

'Right, let's see what we can find to help you.' They walked down the aisle in front of the counter until they came to brackets, runners and screws. The little boy, Tom, stepped forward and picked out a packet.

'Does it look a bit like this?'

'Yes, but I think the screws are bigger. The woman picked up something else.

'How about this?'

'That looks like it, yes.' Tom looked at the elderly woman and smiled.

'Okay then.' She said brightly. 'Let's go and get you settled up.'

As Jenny was paying she said to the woman wistfully 'I used to love coming in here, you know, before. The man who ran it was lovely.'

The woman smiled, wistfully. 'My husband, Bob' she explained. 'It's funny, I thought I knew nothing about DIY but it turns out he taught me a lot. Between me and Tom here, we manage okay.'

When she got home, Jenny fixed the kitchen drawer. She went to the white board and traced Marks writing with her finger one last time, then wiped Mark's note away, fetched some bin bags and went upstairs to her bedroom.

This was going to be hard. She opened Mark's wardrobe and slowly pulled clothes from hangers, folding them carefully. She put the good clothes into a bag for charity and the rest into a rubbish bag. Marks favourite jumper was the last item left, it wasn't in the wardrobe, she slept with it most nights but it still smelled faintly of him, washing powder mingled with a hint of his aftershave. She left it on the bed and stood in front of the empty space where her husband's things used to be. A tear rolled down her face and she whispered, 'I'll always love you Mark.'

She picked up the bags and headed downstairs to see the kids, closing the door quietly behind her.

2025

September

I make progress. I find lots of opportunities to ask well-placed and ambitious colleagues whether they want the top job. I am met with a resounding no, one almost chokes on her lunch, looks at me as if I am quite crazy and asks;

'Only a fool would want the job right now. Claire has aged ten years in six months. Would YOU want it??!'

I quickly say no and say I'm just worried about Claire. She tilts her head a little and looks at me. She isn't sure if I'm being honest.

'You know, I think you would be good at the job if you did ever decide to go for it.'

'Thanks' I say 'but I don't think I am quite ready yet.' She is satisfied with that answer and goes back to her lunch. It seems I am the only one who wants the job and has a clear vision of where we need to go.

2025

September

The Coronation is tomorrow.

I worry about the future of the royal family. I don't know how much support I will get from them when I take power. The Regent is an unknown quantity and I can't help thinking she is a weak link in my plan. Since Claire and I are in the habit of speaking on the telephone regularly I decide to call her and ask a few questions.

I bring up the Coronation. She is pleased with the plans and believes that it may mark a turning point for the country. I casually ask her what the Regent is like. Claire is a reasonably open person and it is easy for me to get her talking. She feels very supported by the Regent who sounds quite savvy. She picked up on the potential threat from the army and the US president more quickly than Claire. I am relieved but still cautious. Nothing can stand in the way of my plans.

2025

Coronation

The Queen stepped out into the sunlight from Westminster Abbey, her crown glinting in the sunlight. A special crown had been made to fit her eleven-year-old head and the ceremonial outfit she wore looked like fancy dress on her small frame but she had an air of confidence nonetheless. Evelyn had prepared her well. Her mother followed, along with the Regent, both eyeing their young charge protectively. The Queen smiled and waved at the crowds outside. Women attended with children of all ages, looking for fun and excitement after months of hardship. They stood in the crowd, holding their children in the air, pointing out the new Queen and the surviving members of the royal family. They talked about what it meant to be a Regent, how it was different to being queen. Children watched in awe and imagined themselves as kings and queens, they waved their flags and wore crowns made of paper.

Claire surveyed the crowds, happy to see such celebration. The new Queen was an asset, a sign of hope. That she was a child made it all the more poignant. On a day like today Claire dared to believe that they would be okay. She'd worried about the public reaction, desperate for the day to be a success. Early accusations about the timing of such an extravagance had been made by the media but had faded away. Evelyn and the committee had pitched the tone well, minimising the cost and taking account of the Queens tender age. The crowds were closer than normal and the Queen stopped often to talk to other children lined up along the route. Every police officer was on duty but after a discussion with Elizabeth Vinn, many of them were in plain clothes rather than dress uniform. Claire was proud of what they had achieved. It was beautifully appropriate.

Inside the Abbey, members of the public filled the aisles after the public ballot to win a seat inside was overwhelmed with applications. The service was a tribute to the many men lost to the virus and signalled a new era. As they made their way outside the mood of the crowd was sombre and reflective but at the same time, hopeful.

2025

Westminster Abbey, October

I sit in Westminster Abbey, dressed in my finest clothes, as my country welcomes the new Queen.

I am elated, it is as if I am the Queen.

We have reached another milestone on this journey, I wish that Anne and Nicole were here to see it. This Queen, so young and impressionable, will be our figurehead as we embark on the most rapid change since the birth of the industrial age. As she passes the aisle next to me, I put out my hand and allow my fingers to lightly brush the folds of her gown.

Soon my vision will become a reality. I am so close that I can almost touch it. I sit among colleagues and imagine the day that I become Prime Minister. Not long now.

2025

Downing Street
Rt. Hon. Claire Flint MP

The Cabinet listened intently as the intelligence officer continued his briefing.

'Nicole Moreland attended a conference in 2013 about surviving domestic violence. It was held in London and organised by a woman named Jean Smith. Over 200 women attended and within a year of the conference several disappeared.

Jean Smith is an alias, her real name is Jean Malden and her background is quite a story. She was abducted when she was eleven and repeatedly raped by a group of six men. They left her for dead in an abandoned building outside Manchester but she managed to drag herself well over a mile to the nearest house. She was later able to identify four of the men, who were eventually convicted of kidnapping and rape.

'It was widely reported that Jean's mother campaigned for harsher penalties for paedophiles, arguing that the men should have been charged with attempted murder. She complained about failings in the investigation which meant that two further suspects were never charged, despite being locally identified. Her mother, a single parent, took the decision to relocate them to Brighton to escape the local gossip and changed their surname to Smith.

'The next part was not well known but Jean gave birth to a daughter named Hope, nine months after the rapes. Her mother was a religious woman and raised them as sisters.

Both girls attended an all-girls school and a retired teacher told us that their mother actively sought to minimise their contact with men.

'Hope was an extremely naïve child. As a teenager, she attracted the attention of a disturbed man that most of the locals avoided and in 2002 he murdered her. Jean and her mother were inconsolable. Jean even threatened to kill the suspect outside the police station and attacked a police officer who restrained her, receiving a police caution. The killer was convicted of rape and murder and was sentenced to life in prison. He was released a few months before the outbreak and his body was recovered as part of the clear-up operation and buried in one of the mass graves.

'Jean's mother is dead. She committed suicide twelve years ago and Jean inherited a sizable sum of money. There are old bank, employment and rental records for Jean Smith up until about eleven years ago but no records of a passport or driving licence and no photographs of her beyond the age of 8. The photographs we do have are grainy class photographs taken before the attack. There are no active bank accounts in her name, no bills, phone records or social media profiles, nothing to suggest she is still alive. She may be underground but if so she has hidden her tracks well.

'The women who disappeared after the conference resigned from their jobs, sold their properties, cleared out and closed banks accounts and shut down social media sites. A couple of them were reported missing by family members. We don't think any of them have travelled abroad.

We do know they were all victims of crime. Raped, victims of domestic violence, witnesses to the rape and murder of their children. Many of them actively campaigned about violence against women and children before they disappeared. Some wrote articles on the subject, others lobbied government or formed victim support groups. We haven't been able to trace any of them.'

The women looked at each other in quiet disbelief. Claire

spoke first 'How close do you think you are to finding Nicole Moreland?'

'We are still searching the Highlands. It's a big job and we don't have a big team. We have managed to narrow our search considerably but still have a long way to go. She may be aware we are looking for her, so we are monitoring all roads south.'

'Okay, let me know as soon as you have something. Is that all?'

'Yes. Thank you, Prime Minister.'

2025

October

My involvement in the outbreak has somehow been discovered.

At first, I am a little anxious but then I think about how well
Anne has concealed me in this identity and I relax. I am not
Jean anymore so they will never find me.

I consider telling the group what I have learnt but worry about
somehow exposing my role in the process. I imagine they will
move on from their hiding place soon and must trust in Anne
to see this coming.

2025

The Ten

The women huddled around the fire, meditating. They had been in the Highlands for months and that day was the coldest so far. The house was a remote second home, owned by a relative of one of the group. It was empty ten months a year and was the perfect place to hide. They had stockpiled two years of tinned and frozen food and had not ventured outside much at all. They spent most of the day meditating, usually under Nicole's guidance.

That day Nicole sat slightly apart from the rest of the group, hunched over a desk. She was writing an account of her actions in a journal. She didn't want to be misunderstood or hated and was troubled by the anger directed at her in the media. She struggled to remain calm, suffering terrible nightmares and panic attacks. She saw the faces of the dead everywhere and couldn't stop thinking about the men she'd known and the kindnesses she had forgotten. She imagined children crying for their fathers, mothers screaming as their sons choked to death on their own blood. It was torture. Her remorse was only tempered by her continued belief that the act itself was necessary.

She knew she was being hunted. Her face was everywhere. Anne had done her best to cover Nicole's tracks but there was only so much she could do. She was renowned in her field and had spoken in front of large audiences. Her face was familiar to her peers and she wasn't a chameleon like Jean. She couldn't have transformed herself into a different person or led a double life.

The sermons were Nicole's only contact with Jean now and the lack of one-on-one time was wounding, particularly when she was facing such public criticism. She thought about how unfair it was that the world blamed her for the outbreak, while Jean was safe. Still, when she really thought about it, she loved Jean and knew she should excuse the recent neglect. After all it took single-minded ambition to continue on this path and Jean had a lot to do. Perhaps it was selfish to expect personal attention at such an important time. Jean was so much stronger than Nicole and it took clarity of vision to continue on this path without doubt.

For now, she resolved to try and be strong for the group who thankfully were unswerving in their loyalty and devotion to Jean.

None of the women in the cabin would hear from Jean again. They were completely unaware that a significant police operation was underway and officers were silently getting into position around the property, waiting for their orders to enter.

2025

November

I slam my fist on the desk. I am distraught, this is not part of my plan. It was my responsibility to look after them and I should have been in a position to protect them. For goodness sake, I am a government minister! I shed a few tears, for Nicole in particular. They are all good people but I love Nicole and she has been through more than enough already. To be captured before there was time to appreciate the beauty of what we have done is a tragedy. There is little I can do to help Nicole now that she is in the system. She will likely spend the rest of her life in prison.

These women are my soldiers, now prisoners of war. They all agreed to do it, I didn't coerce or threaten them, they chose their path freely and with courage. They understood that words and campaigns were never going to be enough to substantially alter the psyche of half of the population. They experienced first-hand the consequences of societies failure to act. They were beaten by violent, chauvinistic men, controlled by husbands and fathers with a warped view of their place in the world, used and tossed aside by narcissistic individuals and raped by evil paedophiles who did not care about the lost innocence of their victims. When they met me, they were brought into the light. I gave them the first green shoots of hope. My virus is a healing force, a vehicle for change. I compare it to a forest fire that wipes out acres of woodland, viewed at first as a tragedy until you examine the renewed, fertilised soil underneath and its ability to create something stronger and better. The green shoots that those women saw when they met me will turn into a forest of my creation.

I tried very hard to protect them and chose Anne for her skills in that area. I fear that she has dropped the ball. I must speak to her to make sure that she is being more cautious with my safety. I can't afford to be discovered. All my hard work would have been for nothing. She must step up now that I am the only one left.

I feel vulnerable now that my group is under state control. Nicole in particular knows everything about me. Her capture could be a serious problem and I worry that she may be tortured into submission. I hope that she can resist their tactics because I can't stop them if they should decide to talk. I will talk to Anne about that as well. It is vital that I take the lead when society begins its transformation. The success of the plan comes above the safety of the group. They all know that.

I go home early, I am too angry to work and feel exhausted. It is not easy playing a role all the time and it is not easy seeing my plans crumble. I need to regain control.

2025

December. 'Anne Sanders'

Anne was grateful for her decision to remain apart from the others after the outbreak. Nicole risked far too much. They hid somewhere with a link to their past lives, they stayed together instead of dispersing. They made mistakes and mistakes catch up with you.

Anne didn't make mistakes. She remained behind closed doors, wiping CCTV records and changing passwords where she could. She did try to keep them safe but protecting Jean was always the priority.

Jean called to express her disappointment in Anne. It was hard for Anne to hear and she wanted to fight back but she knew it would make Jean angrier so she let her rant. Jean sometimes expected too much but now she was worried that they would talk, which made Anne worry about her own safety. She couldn't risk being locked up along with them, the mere thought sent her spiralling back to locked rooms and oppression. She didn't know how it had come to this, she'd given them clear instructions on how to hide themselves and she'd worked hard, night after night to cover their tracks.

She couldn't be complacent, she had orders. Jean was clear that there must be no loose ends but the ten women were a major problem. The longer they were in prison, the more likely it was that someone would talk. She had to get them out.

At about 3am that night she woke up with a start. She had

been having a nightmare. Nicole was in a cell, being tortured by a group of men in uniforms. She was talking. Anne was tied up in the room and couldn't stop her. The men in uniform turned towards her and changed into a group of angry women screaming 'you killed my children!' As they came towards her Anne had woken up with a start.

She got out of bed and went to the bathroom to get a glass of water. Her hands were shaking. If Nicole was going to give someone up under torture, it would be Anne, not Jean.

She turned on her desk lamp and began to work. Within a few clicks she was into the prison records for the ten women and the rota of prison officers guarding them. Maybe she could do something after all.

Social media was a goldmine for hackers like Anne. One of the prison officers was on Facebook, Twitter and Instagram. She created a fake Facebook account and sent her a message.

She must protect Jean. Jean gave her a home and a purpose. Jean loved her. She would forgive her this, after all the plan was more important than any of them.

2025

November

The public are baying for blood and I am struggling to sleep. The risk grows with every hour that the group are out of my control. Anne says she has a plan but I have yet to hear it. She tells me to relax but I can't. Every time I turn on the television their faces flash up on screen, taunting me. The world wants Nicole and the others to hang and it may be kinder to let that happen. Being locked away forever is no life.

The lack of sleep is causing headaches. Vicious stabbing, scratching pains that eat away my brain from the inside. I can't allow this to ruin what we have achieved.

2025

Houses of Parliament
Rt. Hon. Claire Flint MP

Claire walked out of Parliament with her bodyguard towards the underground tunnel between Parliament and No. 10. She was scared. The capture of the ten suspects had sparked mass protests, a petition calling for a return of the death penalty had received over 3 million signatures and social media was stoking the flames. The public wanted heads. Today, as the parliamentary debate reached its fifth hour, she felt railroaded into agreeing a review of the law but it felt wrong. Some of the country's worst laws originated from exceptional cases and though it was what the people wanted that didn't mean it was right. She was grateful for the tunnel today. As dark and damp as it was, it successfully blocked out the sound of the raging crowd outside.

2025

Prison guards

Laura paced the corridor at Whitemoor with her colleague, peering into the cells from time to time. Two of the inmates were suicidal and she was supposed to be on suicide watch but she couldn't give a shit if they succeeded and was all for giving them a rope.

The decision to hold 'The Ten' in an empty site away from the other female prisoners was foolish. There was no-one to distract the guards from the horror of what the ten had done. In the other women's prisons the prisoners were learning skills in farming or electronics but all these women did was meditate. Even retraining in policing would be better than this.

Before the virus she and the love of her life were happy. They had two fabulous kids, good jobs and a dream house. In January, it was snatched away from her. Her husband and her 14-year-old son died, followed closely by her brother and father. All because of these bitches. Her 9-year-old daughter desperately needed her but life was hard and she was probably going to lose her house. She lay awake at night worrying and crying in equal measure. She wasn't the only one, everyone was struggling.

To make things worse, someone had discovered that she was guarding the Ten. The anonymous messages were escalating. The first one was mild.

'We know you are guarding 'The Ten'. Why don't you release them

all, let us deal with them? We will make sure they don't hurt anyone else.'

She ignored it but the messages kept coming, getting more threatening by the day. Today's was the worst so far. When Laura read it her blood ran cold.

'If you don't let them out we will come after you. We want their blood but we will take your daughter instead if you don't let them go.'

When she looked through the cell doors at the bitches, most of whom were in some kind of meditative trance, she felt nothing but pure loathing. She wasn't about to lose her daughter because of them.

2025

I read the message from Anne and close my eyes. My heart is breaking. I may have said that there must be no loose ends but I didn't mean this. I am so angry with Anne.
I'm sorry, Nicole.

2025

Justice

The train doors opened at March station and determined women streamed from the carriages. Mobile phones were consulted and the crowd slowly made their way towards Elm Road, their number dwarfed by the crowd already snaking along the route. Across the market town the roads were unusually full of women, all heading north. Most of the women were in family groups. Sisters, mothers and daughters walked hand in hand, keeping close. As they passed through the town, front doors opened hesitantly. A woman peered out, saw the angry, eager faces of the women in the crowd and quickly closed the door. Others stepped out into the street and joined the throng. The atmosphere was frenzied, weapons were hidden in bags or brandished like swords, faces were twisted, teeth clenched.

The crowd surged up Elm Road as houses gave way to fields. Those from the town turned towards them, remembering husbands and sons who were buried there. The women picked up pace as the turning to Longhill Road came into view. A few women broke into a jog and others joined them. Finally, the prison loomed ahead. The women at the front of the crowd headed across the car park, opening bags to pull out bats, bricks and knives. They surged forwards.

The main gate swung open. 'The Ten' stood clustered together behind it, hands cuffed behind their backs. The four guards behind them shoved the women out of the gate and closed it behind them. The ten women looked around wildly seeking an escape route but the crowd was dense and unrelenting. They clustered together in front of the red brick building. Two of the women shook uncontrollably. One was crying, slow tears running down her cheeks. Urine soaked the trouser leg of another, pooling on the floor.

Nicole stood silently, eyes wide, scanning the faces of the crowd as they surged towards them, looking for compassion. There was none. She turned to the others. 'Just look at me, focus on me now. Don't look at them.' Those at the front of the crowd reached the ten women and encircled them, drawing silent.

Laura stood to one side of the crowd with the other prison guards she had persuaded to help. She scanned the crowd and the realisation of what she had done hit her. She turned to her colleague, terror in her eyes. 'Look at their faces. They are like animals, look at them.' As the angry crowd surged forward she closed her eyes and whispered 'Oh my god.' The women turned to the guards, shouting 'Is that them? IS IT THEM?'

Laura staggered backwards, shaking, her heart pounding. Her stomach lurched and she bent over and vomited onto the floor. Her colleague shouted at her over the noise of the crowd and tugged her sleeve.

'WE NEED TO GO, NOW! COME ON LAURA, WE NEED TO GO.' She dragged her towards the throng followed closely by the others. The crowd parted briefly to let them through and a woman patted Laura on the shoulder, muttering 'Well done'.

The crowd drew tighter around 'The Ten', the circle shrinking until there was just a few feet separating them from the cowering women. They stood, weapons raised, hesitating, waiting for someone else to strike the first blow and give them permission to attack. Nicole pushed the other women behind her. She was more terrified that she had ever been. She closed her eyes and thought of Jean but she could no longer see her vision, just the angry faces of the women in front of her. She opened her eyes and tried to hold herself still, wanting to speak. For a moment, the crowd paused to listen.

'For years my husband controlled me, beat me and raped me. All of us have suffered. What we did, it was necessary...'

A well-dressed woman in the crowd, stepped forward, angry tears rolling down her face. She screamed at Nicole.

'Necessary? You KILLED MY SON! He was twelve years old, he wasn't a rapist he was a good boy and now he is DEAD BECAUSE OF YOU, YOU FUCKING EVIL BITCH.'

With a roar, she launched a rock at Nicole. It missed its target, hitting Danielle, one of 'The Ten' who was cowering next to Nicole. A large wound opened in her leg and bled quickly, staining her prison scrubs and shoes. Danielle moaned and dropped to her knees.

Almost instantly the crowd erupted, surging forwards, launching missiles at the group. Nicole felt the first blow as a stone hit her arm and closed her eyes. She clenched her fists and screamed 'I'M SORRY! I...'

A missile hit the side of her head, silencing her. An old scar split wide open and blood spattered onto her shirt then poured down her face. She fell to the floor and the crowd surged forward. One by one the ten women fell, disappearing underneath a shower of blows. Bricks and knives hit flesh and bone, bruising, breaking, turning their bodies red.

The women at the front dragged themselves out from underneath the crowd, bloodied, bruised and breathless. They screamed 'WAIT! WAIT! STOP PUSHING...' but the mob behind them surged forward for their turn, kicking, punching, stabbing. Bodies turned to meat and flesh and bone. Blood ran down a nearby drain and still the crowds came.

2025

Rt. Hon Claire Flint MP

Claire was making notes on a report about the current economic climate when Jenny ran in. 'Claire, 'The Ten' have escaped and are surrounded by a crowd of women… it's all over YouTube, there are live streams…'

She handed Claire her phone. The live stream was coming from a vantage point in the car park opposite the prison. A large crowd was swarming around the gate and as they watched, women rained blows down on a mass of red on the floor. Red liquid splattered up and over the women closest to the centre. It fanned out in a mist over the crowd behind them.

'What is this? What am I seeing?'

'The bodies of 'The Ten' are on the floor. That's what they are beating.'

'Oh my god.' Claire looked closely at the screen. The picture was small, it was difficult to see what they were hitting and kicking. But the crowd was frenzied. 'Oh my god, Jenny. How did they get outside the gate? Where are the guards? Why aren't they stopping it?'

Jenny looked at her emotionlessly. 'They're dead, Claire. It's too late.'

Claire picked up her phone and called Elizabeth Vinn. She answered immediately. 'I'm seeing it Claire. It was organised on social media and we missed it. We received a phone call from someone who saw the crowds through the window. By the time officers arrived the crowd was too big. Cambridgeshire police have formed a cordon around the area and are trying to disperse them. Neighbouring forces are sending in reinforcements. An off-duty officer got to the front, Claire. The women are dead, they were dead before we arrived. We think the guards pushed them out of the front gate.'

'Get those crowds out of there as soon as you can. And stop them recording, it's barbaric.'

Claire put down the telephone and turned to Jenny. 'What are we becoming, Jenny? I know we have a long way to go and everyone is grieving but this? They look like animals. This isn't justice.'

As Jenny looked at her, a tear escaped from the corner of her eye and ran down her cheek. 'Isn't it, Claire? I wish I was there. Those women killed Mark and Jasper. My beautiful boy was fifteen and they murdered him.' Her voice cracked. 'I will never see him graduate, or get married, or meet his children. I'll never be able to hold him again. When Mark and Jasper were dying, I had to choose who to sit with. They made me choose between my husband and my son. Mark won't see Mia graduate. He won't give her away on her wedding day. Life will never be the same. Imagine how it felt to guard them? I don't know anyone who could have stopped themselves. They killed your brother. Ben will grow up without a father because of them, do you think you could have stopped yourself?'

Claire nodded miserably. 'I'm sorry Jenny. You are right, if I were in that square I probably would have done the same... but that is why we have a justice system. So that emotions can be balanced by rational judgement. Those women deserved to die, I believe that. But this? This will change us.'

'Claire, there isn't a jury in the country that could have tried that case. Everyone is a victim. They wouldn't have got a fair trial. This was just. Leave it alone.'

Jenny left the room, closing the door gently behind her. Claire sat down heavily on her office chair and put her head in her shaking hands. She felt utterly alone.

2025

December

My Private Secretary bursts into my office and tells me to turn on the TV.

As I watch the blood spray into the angry faces of the crowd my Private Secretary tells me what I am watching.

I feel every blow as if it were me on the floor. Those ten women are my family, my blood.

I collapse to my knees and cry, right in front of my Private Secretary. Mostly, I cry for Nicole. I loved her, she was my closest friend and she believed in me.

My Private Secretary is surprised and asks me why I am crying. I have to ask her to leave.

Anne did this. I knew she would do something.

I hate her. I think of my time with Nicole, all the late nights we spent together creating the virus.

This is an indescribable blow. The biggest and ugliest of all the sacrifices I made to get us here. A replay shows the lead up to the murders. Nicole is standing in front of the others, protecting them from the crowd. I can see that she spoke before she died and I wonder what she said. I fleetingly worry that she gave the crowd my name, then I relax. Nicole believed in what we are doing with every ounce of her being. She believed it so strongly that she gave her life for it. She put herself at risk for years because she knew we were on the right path. She would not betray me, she would want me to lead the country into the light. Her honour is intact.

I will remember them all as heroes.

It will be harder without her but I will carry on in Nicole's memory.

2026

January

Anne and I are the only ones left.

I am still angry with her but I still write to her often. I have asked her to release my letters to the world when I am gone. Everyone will hear what I have to say. Today I write;

'I look back on the past year with a mixture of sadness and hope. I have searched my conscience and questioned my choices. The world has changed and there are unexpected hardships in this new world. Men had roles to play, families to support and children to raise. They were loved as fathers, husbands, friends, or sons, they were cared for and they are mourned.

I grieve for the pain I caused. It was never my intention to hurt women-kind and I feel responsible for the losses you feel you have suffered. I tried to minimise your pain by immunising the children and in doing so I saved millions but I accept that for some that will not be nearly enough. In war, we sacrifice the innocent for the greater good. I mourn 'the Ten' as well but I know that they had to die for the country to truly forgive.

I speak to all women now. We have been fighting a war with men from the moment we were born. Our mothers and grand-mothers before us fought this war, women have been fighting it for generations. It is all you have ever known so you do not realise it is a war, or that there is a more beautiful alternative. Just think about the things you have had to battle for and compare it to the privileged position that men have taken for

granted.
You fought to be heard
You fought to prove yourself an equal
You fought to wear what you wanted
You fought to have sex on your own terms
You fought the glass ceiling at work
You fought stereotypes
You fought sexual violence.
You fought for equality
You fought for respect
Do you want your daughters to fight as you have? Do you want your young sons to grow up with male role models who shout, swear, rape, abuse, or dismiss women? Do you want to live in a world where men arrogantly assume that they will always be in charge?

Change has been slow and hard fought but we no longer have the luxury of time. Selfish and arrogant men are destroying the natural world. They pollute the earth and the sea, wage wars over territory, deny the impact of global warming and close their eyes and ears to atrocities in third world countries. They rule with arrogance and contempt for those below them, protecting the status quo. They deny women the chance to lead and show the world that things can be different.

They have failed. They have had their time. Now it is our time. We will show them the right way. They refused to stand aside, so I have moved them out of the way. Men were mentally weak, they were at the top for too long and became over-indulged and arrogant. They forgot that when you reach the top, the only way to go is down.

The mental strength of woman knows no bounds. We have untapped intellect, if something is physically demanding for us in this new world we will overcome it by inventing new solutions. There is nothing stopping us now, we are finally in control. Together we will create a new and beautiful world. Be strong, be proud.'

Deborah re-read what she had written and smiled, satisfied. She pressed send and then switched off the tablet and put it into her bag. She would forgive Anne because she needed her. She stood, turned off the lights in her office and walked out into her private office area. Mia was still there, working. She called out to her 'Goodnight Mia, don't work too late. It can wait until the morning.'

'Goodnight Deborah. I'll be finished in five minutes. I'm just getting ready for tomorrow's meeting on the breast cancer research funding.' Deborah smiled at Mia. She liked her, Mia was a bright girl who would go far under Deborah's tutelage. She resolved to bring the girl under her wing.

2026

Rt. Hon. Claire Flint MP (Diary Entry)

Ben is sound asleep. I watch him, feeling like a terrible mother. He gets snatched cuddles at the end of the day and I am only half present. I cannot pay him the attention he deserves and I rely on Mum far too much.

I no longer believe I am adding value to the recovery of the country. The lynching of the ten suspects in the square makes me doubt the strength of my leadership in shaping the country's future. I have lost any grip I had on the security and safety of the public. I misread the mood and I failed to provide those ten women with sufficient protection, leaving them isolated from the rest of the prison population away from the checks and balances that exist in a properly supervised facility.

I know that evidence against 'The Ten' was overwhelming but lynching has no role in a civilised country and it happened on my watch. I cannot forgive myself for that.

I feel I have no choice, I have let my country down. I intend to resign tomorrow. I feel anxious about it but some of my colleagues show great promise and I will be there to support whoever succeeds me. This is the hardest job I have ever had but it has been a great honour to serve my country in its hour of need and I will always be humbled at being given the opportunity to do so.

2026

Deborah

I write to Anne.
It is a snatched message because I have too much to do. I don't
have time to write in my usual eloquent way.
'She is stepping down. You know what to do.'

2026

Rt. Hon. Claire Flint MP (Diary Entry)

I feel such a sense of relief now that the decision is public. Jenny is angry with me for excluding her from my thinking but it felt like a very personal decision which only I could make.

As soon as my successor is appointed I plan to take Ben away for a few days, we may not be able to go abroad but at least we can go somewhere leafy and green. The city is still oppressive even without the traffic and the crowds.

I spoke to the Princess Regent this morning and we had a long discussion about my potential successor. I am not sure that the conversation was strictly permitted but she has a keen interest in who will pick up where I have left off.

My personal preference would be for Karen to take over but she doesn't want the job. She said she needs to focus on her girls. Their father is in prison awaiting trial and I think she worries about the media interest, which might start to become quite unpleasant if she were PM.

There are very few people prepared to throw their hat in the ring. Millicent doesn't have the support; Nancy's reputation was damaged by the lynching of 'The Ten' and is considering resigning as Justice Secretary. Katrina is great but lacks experience. Sarah is brilliant and ambitious and I think will almost certainly run. A lot of people in the party don't care for her but I have grown to like her a lot since working with her more closely. She is a hard nut to crack and may not get the support, which would be a shame.

Deborah would be excellent, she is a compelling public speaker and seems to have the right combination of ambition and public duty. Her changes in health since taking the role have been bold and I think she is brave enough to lead the country through this. I hope that she will consider it. She may be the only person we have left. I think I will call her tomorrow and try to persuade her to stand.

2026

News report, January

Claire Flint gave a farewell address to the House of Commons this afternoon, clearing the way for Deborah Walsh, who will become Britain's new Prime Minister tomorrow,

A relatively unknown junior minister until the outbreak, Walsh was quick to respond to the crisis and has become the face of the NHS during the recovery. With stories of her courage and compassion sweeping social media in recent weeks it was almost inevitable that she would be selected.

Ms Flint spoke warmly of her successor as a 'strong, courageous leader and remarkable orator who will unite the country and provide new energy, vision and leadership.' Following her address Ms Flint went directly to Buckingham Palace to formally offer her resignation to the Queen.

In a statement outside Parliament following her election as the party leader, Deborah Walsh praised her predecessor for her 'courage and determination as she brought the country back from the worst humanitarian crisis in living memory.'

News of the appointment was warmly received by European leaders and by the US President, who remarked that he would renew his previously rejected offer of assistance to the incoming Prime Minister, in the hope that 'Our two countries can work together to make Britain great again.'

After Claire Flint's shock resignation, just a three weeks ago, there will no doubt be relief across Whitehall today as the turmoil of the past few weeks comes to an end.

The new Prime Minister waved to the crowd outside No. 10 Downing Street as she entered for the first time this afternoon.

2026

Deborah, January 2026

I am finally Prime Minister. Now, to begin.

ABOUT THE AUTHOR

Caroline Cooper

Caroline Cooper is an English writer who lives in Hampshire. A mother of two, she has worked in central government, local government and policing during her twenty-year career.

'She' is her first novel.

Printed in Great Britain
by Amazon